MELTDOWN

Ben Elton

BLACK SWAN

TRANSWORLD PUBLISHERS
61–63 Uxbridge Road, London W5 5SA
A Random House Group Company
www.rbooks.co.uk

MELTDOWN
A BLACK SWAN BOOK: 9780552775106

First published in Great Britain
in 2009 by Bantam Press
an imprint of Transworld Publishers
Black Swan edition published 2010

A CIP catalogue record for this book
is available from the British Library.

Addresses for Random House Group Ltd companies outside the UK
can be found at: www.randomhouse.co.uk
The Random House Group Ltd Reg. No. 954009

The Random House Group Limited supports The Forest Stewardship
Council (FSC), the leading international forest certification organisation.
All our titles that are printed on Greenpeace approved FSC certified paper
carry the FSC logo. Our paper procurement policy can be found at
www.rbooks.co.uk/environment

Typeset in 11/16pt Giovanni Book by
Falcon Oast Graphic Art Ltd.
Printed in the UK by CPI Cox & Wyman, Reading, RG1 8EX.

2 4 6 8 10 9 7 5 3 1

Mixed Sources
Product group from well-managed
forests and other controlled sources
www.fsc.org Cert no. TT-COC-2139
© 1996 Forest Stewardship Council

MELTDOWN

Good and thick

Jimmy Corby graduated from Sussex in 1993. He celebrated with five friends: Rupert, David, Henry, Robbo and Lizzie.

These six were to remain friends throughout the nineties and for most of the noughties.

Mates. Proper mates.

Through good and bad.

Through thick and thin.

Except that there never really was any bad.

And there wasn't an awful lot of thin either.

Apart from Rupert's Amanda. And Henry's Jane. And David's Laura. They were all very thin. But by choice.

Good and thick. That's how the times had been.

Jimmy and his friends stuck together through good and thick.

Tired and broke

Jimmy scarcely noticed being tired any more; it had become as much a part of his life as eating or breathing. Of course he'd been tired sometimes in his old life. His fantasy life.

Seriously knackered, or so in his innocence he had believed. When shouting himself hoarse during an all-nighter with the Tokyo Exchange or pissed up at 5am in a pub with some of the guys, watching a live fight from Vegas. Or enjoying his second straight dawn, loved up on a beach in Ibiza with a bottle of Krug between his knees and a gap-year holiday-hippy chick on either side. Yes. He'd been tired. But not *really* tired. Tired to his core, tired in his *blood*. Tired to the point where he doubted his sanity. Tired until his mind dislocated itself from his body and just sort of floated a few feet above it as he went through the motions of being alive.

These days that was how tired Jimmy felt *all the time*. And there would be no respite, not for years.

He could hear the screaming long before he opened the front door. The screaming never seemed to stop. They could have recorded his life and used it as the soundtrack for a slasher movie. Both of the younger ones had clearly gone off at the same time and were competing to see who could drive their mother insane first. Jimmy knew exactly the sort of night that awaited him. Because it would be the same as last night. And the night before. The same as every night since that tearful moment when Jodie, the rock, the treasure, the person without whom they simply *could not do*, had left.

Jimmy thought about taking a last turn round the block. Of grabbing a few moments more of stumbling, agonized, half-conscious, semi-zombieficated peace before entering the maelstrom that was his home (or the bank's home since he had been forced to mortgage his entire equity in a failed effort to get on top of his mounting debts). But Jimmy was an honourable bloke. He loved Monica. He might have failed her utterly like the sad swine that he was, but he loved her and he knew she needed him, if only to give her three minutes' respite to pop to the loo.

One by one he unlocked the four beautifully tooled Chubb deadlocks set perfectly along the rich, shiny edge of the huge bright-red front door of which he had once been so proud. Despite its great weight the door swung open smoothly. Of course it did, it was so expertly hung. Hung on its *eight* big brass hinges. Such a full, heavy, clunkingly satisfying movement. A Romanian guy had done it; they still understood wood in Eastern Europe. Jimmy had admired the guy at the time but now he envied him. He envied him so much. To have a *trade*. To be able to actually *do* something. A real, palpable, physical skill that you could offer for hire. How good would that be? Particularly now that the market for aggressive, cocky wankers shouting themselves hoarse into a telephone had so comprehensively dried up.

The marble-clad hall was empty, of course. Empty and echoing as the red door shooshed and clunked shut behind him. No welcoming cocktail served by a lovely, eager, semi-posh girl with a degree in Fine Food and Catering, fresh-faced, chef-coated and anxious to explain the details of that evening's menu.

'Hi, Jimmy. Cool day? Wicked. Hope you're in the mood for Chinese duck? I've been marinating it since two and my black bean sauce is awesome.'

No. That was history. Jessica had gone the way of Jodie. Her fabulous catering and hospitality skills were now being wasted at a Garfunkel's while she searched for a new private chef's position, along with all the other drifting Jessicas for whom the supply of mega-rich employers was so rapidly shrinking.

She was gone and the big marble hall was empty and cold. The only thing in it besides Jimmy was screams. Blood-curdling, brain-mashing, life-sapping screams.

The volume ramped up massively as, head bowed with exhaustion, he made his way down into the basement. As he went, he noted that only one of the little lights that had once glowed so subtly beneath the thick frosted glass of the stairs was still working. How long had Monica agonized over the lighting? It had seemed so important at the time. She had had a pile of catalogues and magazines. A *pile*. All devoted exclusively to internal lighting.

Now there was just a single working bulb left. One by one the others had all gone out. Monica would probably see it as a metaphor for their vanished hopes and dreams. Or was it a simile? Jimmy wasn't sure; he wasn't bright that way, like Monica.

On the other hand, what had they been dreaming of in the first place, illuminating the steps of their basement staircase internally? It seemed rather a strange idea now, viewed from his new perspective. Now that his dreams involved feeding his children. But it really had seemed important at the time.

He would have liked to replace those bulbs. As a gesture of defiance, to prove to himself that he was still good for something. That he might be down but at least he could make the discreet interior lighting hidden in his basement stairs work. But he couldn't even do that. He didn't know if they had any spare bulbs. If they did have, he didn't know where they were kept, and anyway he wouldn't have known how to take the frosted glass off the stairs to get rid of the dead ones. Someone had always sorted that kind of stuff out for them.

Those were the days, when they had somebody to sort out their kids and somebody to sort out their light bulbs.

A nice little earner

The stairs had shone and twinkled like Piccadilly Circus a year earlier, looking as bright and jolly as Jimmy did himself as he perused the stock market on the gleaming new seventeen-inch MacBook that nestled on the breakfast bar among the cereal boxes.

'Wow,' he said. 'Whatever you're getting Rupert for Christmas, it isn't enough.'

Monica looked up from the couch on which she was languishing, her pyjama top pulled up over her huge tummy. She was rubbing coconut oil into it in a futile attempt to ward off stretch marks.

'Why? What's he done?'

'Only saved us about a hundred grand.'

'Jimmy, shh!' Monica admonished.

She didn't like him talking about money in front of their son Toby, or in front of Jodie the nanny for that matter. Particularly not such ridiculous sums. She said it just felt wrong somehow.

If Jodie had heard she certainly didn't let on. She and Toby were happily engaged in making an advent calendar for school. Constructing little cardboard doors that open requires concentration, even from a bright seven-year-old and a totally focused and almost insanely enthusiastic Australian girl with a degree in pre-school care and a Bondi Beach gold life-saving medal.

''Nother cup of fruit tea, Monica,' Jodie asked, laying aside the scissors and the Pritt Stick, 'before I get Toby in the car?'

'Go on then, let's go crazy,' Monica replied.

Jodie leaped to her feet, leaving Toby to his cutting and pasting.

'Strawberry Zinger? Lemon Pick-Me-Up?' she said, sifting through the various boxes.

'I don't know why you bother asking,' Jimmy said, still staring intently at his screen. 'None of them taste of anything at all.'

'Yes, it is weird,' Monica agreed, 'how anything that can smell so strong can taste of so little.'

'You might as well sniff a fruit pastille and drink a cup of hot water,' Jimmy suggested, trowelling butter on to his toast.

'Don't spoil her few pleasures, Jim,' Jodie said with a laugh. 'These things are about the only luxuries a preggers mum is still allowed.'

'They're only luxuries because they cost so much,' Jim said through a mouthful of toast. 'Work it out, it's 50p a shot for the smell of a raspberry. Insane. My dad would simply not believe it.'

'Five *pounds* fifty when I have one at the patisserie,' Monica admitted.

'Five pounds fifty for having a fruit tea in a patisserie in *Notting Hill*, dahhhling!' Jodie joked. 'Can't put a price on class, can ya?'

Having made Monica a Blackcurrant Booster, Jodie gathered up Toby's things, brushed his hair, sorted out his lunch money, assembled his sports kit, slipped a pack of Kleenex into his pocket because he had a sniffle and with her usual huge, cheery smile bundled him off to school.

'Come on, Tobes mate,' she said as they left. 'We'll play some more AC/DC in the car. This boy loves his full-on Aussie rock. He has to, I'm indoctrinating him.'

Toby spun round happily, sticking out his tongue and making the 'devil's horns' finger sign.

'For those about to rock,' the boy shouted, 'we salute you!'

'Right on!' Jimmy shouted back, punching the air. 'School is the new rock 'n' roll.'

'Do you want me to take Cressida as well?' Jodie asked Monica. 'She likes a bit of rock herself.'

Cressida, Jimmy and Monica's two-and-a-half-year-old, was currently exploring 'her' pan cupboard. The cupboard had been one of Jodie's many brilliant ideas.

'Leave 'em one cupboard they can open,' she had suggested, 'but don't tell them it's theirs. Fill it with plastic stuff and wooden spoons and let them find it themselves, then tell them they're very naughty when they do. Hopefully after that they'll never go looking for the knives and power drills.'

It had worked a treat.

'Aussie, Aussie, Aussie!' Jodie called across at Cressida.

'Oi, oi, oi!' Cressida responded dutifully, waving a plastic spatula.

'No, she's happy, let's leave her here,' Monica said. 'I'll watch her.'

'Okey-doke.' Jodie and Toby disappeared through the door.

'She's truly wonderful, isn't she?' Monica said after they'd gone.

'No better,' Jimmy agreed, eyeing with some suspicion the exquisite bowl of fruit salad that Jessica had prepared last thing the previous evening and left in the fridge. 'I suppose I ought to have some of this to make up for the toast and half a pack of butter. Want a flat tum for my new tatt.'

Jimmy had four tattoos: a Maori bracelet design round an ankle, a Gaelic cross on his right shoulder and the names of his two children in gothic script on each inner forearm. Having run out of arms, he had decided to locate the name of his third child beneath his navel in the manner of a number of premier league football players he admired.

'Yes, stretched tatt's not a good look,' Monica admitted, eyeing ruefully the cooing love doves she had had inked in above her right hip. 'Our wedding logo's starting to look like a couple of fat pigeons having a fight.'

'Looks good to me.' Jimmy smiled. 'I find preg birds sexy.'

17

'Hmm,' Monica replied. 'I seem to recall you don't find post-preg birds quite such a turn-on.'

'All I ever said,' Jimmy insisted, 'was that if you're going to spend five grand a year on gym membership you should use it occasionally, that's all.'

'Yeah. Right.'

'It was a financial observation, not an aesthetic one.'

'Oh absolutely,' Monica smiled, 'which is why you've decided to save the five grand by spending a quarter of a million sticking an entire flipping health club on the second floor of our house.'

'That's right.' Jimmy smiled disarmingly.

'Not very subtle, Jim.'

'I'm just saying if you want to use it, it's there. No pressure.'

'I'll think about it,' Monica said.

'And in the meantime Jodie can use it for her kick-boxing.'

'Speaking of whom, we'll have to give Jodie a raise when this one arrives, you know.' Monica patted her stomach.

'Do you think she'll be all right looking after three, or should we get another girl?'

'Don't even breathe it! Jodie would go mental. Can you imagine two girls trying to divide the childcare? How would it work? One and a half kids each? No. Jodie will want the lot and I don't even think she'd expect to be paid extra, but of course we would.'

'Oh for sure. Gotta be another third. Don't know what it is with these Aussie girls, they're just so positive.'

'It's because they know they're only doing it for a few years before they go and climb Everest for charity then marry a cricketer.'

'Well, she definitely gets a raise.'

'Amanda says we're insane what we pay. She says it isn't only workers that get exploited. It can happen to employers too. She says if you pay people too much it distorts the market and in the long run everybody suffers. Like the seventies car industry.'

'Amanda is a Nazi.'

Monica sipped her fruit tea. 'Yes, a nice Nazi but a Nazi nonetheless. We should certainly offer Jodie a raise. Everybody always seems to have an excuse for acting badly. It's like with recycling. Amanda says we're mad to bother because it's all a con and it gets shoved in landfills just the same. Or exported to China where *they* shove it in landfills. But how does she know that? It's a convenient theory because it means you never have to rinse out any bottles. But how does she *know*?'

Jimmy shook his head. 'We'll bloody double Jodie's cash and Amanda can stuff her distorted market up her cosmetically whitened rectum!'

Monica spluttered into her drink. '*God*, Jim, I didn't tell you about that, did I?'

'Yes you did and I wish you hadn't. The image lives with me still.'

'She swore me to secrecy. I must have been a bit pissed.'

'You were.'

'God, I'm *awful*. Poor Lillie.' Monica caressed her bump.

'Don't worry, you get drunk on a sniff of the cork at the moment, you're so hormonal.'

'I shouldn't have told you though.' Monica giggled. 'Mand said she was just getting Botoxed and they offered it up. I said God, Rupert doesn't bother you round *there*, does he? She said certainly not and that she did it for herself.'

'Let's not go there.' Jimmy grimaced.

'Speaking of Rupert, how did he save us so much money?'

Jimmy looked up from his fruit salad. He was doing his naughty grin. He put his finger to his lips and gave her a little wink. Jimmy could get away with winking. It never looked arch or smug with him, just *naughty*. He was blessed with a twinkle in his eye.

'What?' Monica insisted. 'Don't do your bloody little boy thing with me.'

'Which, incidentally, you love.'

'Which I do *not* love. I may have *said* I loved it, once, early on. But I do *not* love it. Now come on. What's Rupert done?'

'You don't want to know.'

'I *do* want to know.'

Jimmy grimaced as if he was about to confess to stealing the last biscuit.

'You know Gordon Brown's co-opted Rupert on to this Financial Services Advisory Board?'

'No, I didn't know actually,' Monica replied, 'or if I did I forgot somewhere between guzzling Gaviscon for my reflux and trying not to pee involuntarily on the sofa.'

'Well, he has, and consequently Rupert hears all sorts of stuff. He gave me the heads-up yesterday morning to say Caledonian Granite was going to hit the wall.'

'You mean the building society? It was all over Radio 4 this morning, I was listening in my bath. They wouldn't shut up about it and all I wanted to know was if Britney had been allowed access to her kids. It's collapsed or something, hasn't it?'

'Big time. First run on a Brit bank in centuries. Monumental balls-up, turns out they were giving mortgages away like loyalty points and now they're fucked. We owned fifty thousand shares.'

'Owned?' Monica asked with a tiny touch of suspicion.

'Part of a portfolio I put together a couple of years ago. Bought at 98p, yesterday morning they were at £2.02 and now . . .'

'They're worth one and a half pence, according to Radio 4.'

'Exactly. Bloody disaster for some.'

'But not us?'

'No. Thankfully. We got out.'

'So you sold up yesterday?'

'Well, it would have been pretty stupid not to, what with Rupert telling me they'd gone tits up. Nice of him to think of me really. I suppose he was feeling guilty because he'd suggested I buy in the first place.'

Jimmy returned to his fruit salad, searching about among the mango and star fruit for the last strawberry. He was avoiding Monica's eye.

'Jimmy . . .' She did not sound happy.

'Mmm?' Jimmy affected an innocent look. The same doe-eyed, open-hearted expression that prior to Monica's entry into his life had persuaded so many girls that when he said, 'You know, just for a last coffee,' he actually meant it.

'Don't look at me that way, Jim,' Monica said. 'Are you seriously telling me you acted on a tip-off? You *sold shares* on the basis of a tip-off?'

'Oh come on, Monica!' Jim smiled. 'What was I supposed to do? Sit there and watch us lose a hundred grand? That would be insane.'

'Rupert should never have told you.'

'But he did tell me. That's not my fault, is it? But once he *had* told me, I was stuck, wasn't I?'

Jimmy crossed over and took his wife's empty mug from her hand, fishing out the dead tea bag and flicking an expert slamdunk into the waste-disposal unit installed in the third of the three massive stainless-steel sinks.

'Jimmy, you *shouldn't* have done it.'

'Oh come on, why not?'

'Well, for a start it's hardly fair, is it?'

Jimmy frowned slightly and sprinkled grated chocolate on to his coffee while he thought for a moment.

'I don't really think *fair's* got anything to do with it,' he said finally. 'I mean money's a yo-yo, isn't it? Everybody's trying to guess the bounce.'

'Yes, but not everybody has access to government information, do they? Jimmy, I really think it's . . . it's . . .'

Monica glanced at the illuminated stairway as if wondering whether somebody might be at the top of it, listening to their conversation.

'Is the baby listener on?' she asked.

'Monica, it's not a walkie-talkie, it doesn't work both ways, besides which there's nobody upstairs.'

'Turn it off anyway.'

Jimmy sighed and did as he was told.

'There's no one but me, you and Cressie in the bloody house,' he assured her. 'What's on your mind?'

'I really think,' she said with a face that was suddenly very serious, 'that you selling those shares after Rupert told you what he told you could be construed as insider trading.'

Jimmy was quite taken aback, not least because it was

so unlike Monica to show an interest in that sort of thing. They always divided the Sunday paper with perfect equanimity. She took the review section and he took the business bit and they never swapped back.

'God, Mon,' Jimmy said, 'what do you know about insider trading?'

'I know that it's against the law.'

Jimmy tried to shrug in a nonchalant manner, but in truth he was slightly thrown.

'Well, I don't *think* it's insider trading,' he said finally. 'I mean, surely Rupert wouldn't have suggested it if . . . I mean, it's just like gossip, isn't it? A tip at the races or something like that. A bloke gets wind of something, he tells a mate. You take your luck where you find it.'

'That American friend of Lizzie's went to prison, didn't she? Martha Stewart. She just took a tip-off.'

'Gossip, Mon. Not a tip-off as such.'

'Jimmy, Rupert wasn't passing on gossip so much as *facts*. He's a government adviser. He's actually in the loop.'

'Well yes, but . . . I mean insider trading is like when you run a company and you know everything about it and then you make trades using information, privileged information that isn't available to the public. That's why it's illegal.'

'Exactly . . . and?'

'Well, Rupert doesn't own or run Caledonian Granite and nor do I. Neither of us has any association with it at all, so how can we be insiders? . . . It's fine. I *know* it's fine.'

'It does sort of *seem* like insider trading.'

'But inside what? I don't know anyone who works for Granite and nor, I imagine, does Roop.'

Monica didn't reply and Jimmy stared into his fruit salad for a moment. Insider trading? The thought had not even entered his head. Money just flowed towards him and he grabbed it, that was all. That was how it had always been for him. It wasn't as if he'd mugged anyone or put his hand in a till.

'Look,' he continued, 'I know it's a *leeetle* bit Dodgy Brothers, babes. I'll admit that, not saying it isn't. But that's the way things work. Knowledge, information. It's the petrol in the engine. Everybody does it. Sometimes you get lucky and pick up a tip, sometimes you don't. This morning we got lucky. Nobody died. The world's still turning. Yee-ha! That's Rock 'n' Roll. Don't knock it, dahhhhlin''.

He could always make her laugh and she laughed now, but he could see that she wasn't convinced.

'I think you should give the money to charity,' she said suddenly.

Jimmy stared at her.

'Give it to charity?' he repeated. 'A hundred grand?'

'Yes.'

'We give loads to charity.'

'Not that much, and anyway we should give more,'

Monica said. 'After all, that hundred K isn't really our money, is it?'

'What do you mean it's not our money? Of course it's our bloody money. Whose else is it?'

'If Rupert hadn't tipped you off you'd never have sold those shares and they'd now be worth as little as everyone else's. The money never would have existed.'

'But he *did* tip me off, Mon, and the money *does* exist.'

'Keep your initial investment then,' Monica said, 'and give away the profit. That's fair, surely.'

'Fair? Fair to who? We'd still be giving away over fifty grand.'

'I know,' Monica insisted, stroking her stomach, 'but we have another baby coming.'

'What, may I ask,' Jimmy said firmly, 'has that got to do with anything?'

'I just think it would be good karma. That's all.'

'Good karma!' Jimmy laughed. 'Giving away fifty grand! I can't do it.'

'Jimmy, I want you to do it.'

Jimmy could see that it was pointless to argue. Monica had her superstitious side and it was clear to him that after making the connection between a charitable act and her unborn baby she was going to stick to her guns.

'Give it away,' she said firmly, 'or I will.'

'Oh all-bloody-right,' Jimmy said. 'But I'm not going to just *give* it. That's too painful and boring. I've gotta make it interesting. You know, something fun.'

'O-*kaaay*.' Monica sounded suspicious. 'And how will you do that?'

Jimmy thought for a moment while spooning a glob of neat Nutella into his mouth.

'Tell you what, I'll stick it on a horse!'

'Tell you what back,' Monica said, '*no*!'

But now Jimmy was off on one, his imagination fired up with exactly the sort of idea that appealed to the eternal adolescent in him.

'I mean it,' he said. 'That's what we'll do. Some real long-shot bet. If it loses then nobody's any worse off, but if it wins . . . Now *that* will be a contribution worth making.'

'Fifty thousand pounds is a contribution worth making!' Monica exclaimed. 'I slave for months to raise that sort of money with my appeals.'

Monica worked very hard on her charity appeals. In fact people had no idea *how* hard she worked on them, something which Monica found just a little bit hurtful.

She always suspected that because she didn't actually have a proper *job*, her career-minded friends thought that she did nothing at all. They thought that she was a 'lady who lunched'. That really her 'charity work' was as much an excuse for social networking, meeting celebrities and having lovely meals in the restaurant at Harvey Nichols as it was for *making a difference*.

But Monica felt that she *did* make a difference. And

she knew what a difference fifty thousand pounds could make too. She was a fundraiser for Asylum Action, a charity that attempted to bring aid and support to the crowds of desperate refugees who, having fled the violence and misery of their war-ravaged homelands, found themselves caught up in the violence and misery of a massive transit camp on the French Channel coast. Those people needed medical care, legal advice and access to interpreters. Fifty grand could help a lot.

'You can't do it,' she insisted. 'You can't bet that amount. It's bloody stupid.'

'Why is it stupid? We got the money speculating.'

'You got the money cheating, Jim.'

'Don't be such a square, babe! Life is a speculation, let's speculate a bit more. It'll be fun. We'll make a party out of it. Next year's Grand National! Or maybe the Alabama Derby! I've always wanted to see that race and if we give the gang enough notice we could all go over together. I'll put the money in gilts with my bookie and when the book opens he can put it on the longest shot on the slate.'

'Jimmy!' Monica tried once more to protest but Jimmy headed her off.

'It's a *brilliant* idea!' He stuck his fist into a box of Toby's Frosties and drew out a handful. 'If we go in at, say, twenty to one we could be looking at over a million for Asylum Action. The committee will go crazy!'

'Or nineteen chances of nothing at all.'

'Can't accumulate if you don't speculate, babes. Gotta be in it to win it.' Jimmy punched up the cappuccino machine. 'It is after all well known,' he added, 'that charity is the new Rock 'n' Roll.'

But what do you actually do?

It wasn't as if Jimmy had ever expected to be insanely rich. He was the son of a bank manager. Provenance more solid and comfortable than a Sunday-night television drama serial. DNA-wise, Jimmy's kids should have been called Pipe and Slippers, not Toby and Cressida and the recently added Lillie.

Of *course* he hadn't expected it (the money, that is, not Lillie, who had been very much wanted), how could he have? As Jimmy was fond of saying about the size of his bonus, 'You couldn't make it up.' The sums would have seemed like pure fantasy to any previous generation working in the City.

When Jimmy was a kid, nobody except rock stars had made the sort of money he had ended up making. Then suddenly Jimmy *was* a rock star. Well, he'd certainly bought his London house *from* a rock star and he'd paid an extra million for the kudos. He didn't care what it cost. He wanted a big house in Notting Hill and he got one. 'A house is worth what you pay for it,' he used to say. Now he was discovering that in fact a house was worth what you could sell it for.

Of course, he hadn't planned to be as rich as he had become. That would have been like planning on winning the lottery or being plucked from the dance troupe to marry Madonna. It had been fate, that was all. Right place, right time. Jimmy had just got lucky. The same thing as being in on the beginning of a gold rush. Yee-ha! California, 1848. First wagon over the Rockies. 'There's GOLD in them thar hills!' You just grabbed a shovel and ran for it.

Nobody resented *them*. Nobody resented Klondike Pete and his best gal Sal the way people had suddenly come to resent Jimmy and his pals. Nobody called Klondike Pete a greedy, irresponsible bastard because he bent down and picked up lumps of gold when he found them lying around on the ground. As any fool would.

Despite what people might now claim.

No, Pete and Sal had been *pioneers*. Gritty chancers who created the wealth on which a great nation could be built. When their mines failed or the bottom dropped out of the price of gold, nobody said they deserved it. Nobody said, 'Oh, they should have been more prudent, those pioneers. They should have asked themselves how long they could all keep digging up gold before the price went down. They should have put down their picks for a moment and considered *self-regulation.'*

And hadn't Jimmy been a pioneer in his way? A gritty chancer? A wealth creator? And wasn't that a good thing? Gold wasn't anything in itself, was it? It was worth what people *believed* it was worth. Just like the pixelated numbers that had whirred across Jimmy's computer screens for fifteen years. As long as people believed they meant something, everything had been fine.

'Why are people being so mean now?' Monica had wailed after a particularly unpleasant encounter with a window cleaner. He had turned up to do his regular job and Monica had been forced to tell him that sadly, due to the downturn, his contract was being terminated. 'The man shouted at me,' she cried. 'He actually stood on the doorstep and *shouted* at me. He said that his trade was all buggered because of the likes of me. As if I'd created the bloody recession myself, deliberately, to spite him!'

Jimmy had got lucky, that was all. Unlike other men who had made many millions, he had not set out to do so. He had not been one of those guys who wrote little lists of goals while they were at university, saying things like 'Millionaire by 25. Prime Minister by 40.'

If Jimmy had written one of those lists he probably would have put down things like 'See Oasis live, date Kylie and try to avoid becoming an alcoholic.'

Jimmy didn't really *understand* how he had got to be so rich, not in any detail. He certainly wasn't very good at explaining it.

'But what do you actually *do*?' his parents were always asking.

It was a reasonable question and one which Jimmy had got used to dodging. He sort of got what he did when he was actually doing it, but when he *thought* about it, when he tried to put into words the abstract concept of spending one's working days in a marketplace that would not actually materialize for years (if ever), of trading in products that might never be made or grown, his imaginative and descriptive powers deserted him.

'Sounds like you're Alice and you live in Wonderland,' Jimmy's father would say. 'You've discovered a magic bottle that says "Drink me," except it's not you that's getting bigger but your bank account.'

'That sounds about right, Dad,' Jimmy agreed.

But then he'd never really got *Alice in Wonderland* either, not even the Disney version.

Jimmy's father was genuinely baffled by his son's enormous success and also, if truth were told, slightly irritated by it. Derek Corby had dealt in the business of money all his life, he understood it, and yet here was his son, who clearly *didn't* understand it, making sacks of the stuff every day.

'You're just jealous, Derek,' his wife always teased when Jimmy and his dad locked horns. 'I think you should be delighted. Imagine if he was still pinching money out of my purse like he used to when he was a student.'

There was some truth in what Nora said, but it wasn't just jealousy. Jimmy's wealth made his father uneasy. As a bank manager he knew about financial probity. It was the watchword on which his life had been built.

'The rules of banking are very clear, Jimmy,' Derek tried to explain when the Corbys were out together on one of their fishing Sundays, which Jimmy sometimes attended right up until the day he met Monica. 'The amount of money I am able to lend is dependent on the amount of capital I have in my—'

'Yeah, right, Dad, for sure,' Jimmy interrupted. 'Can we start the picnic yet, Mum?'

'Don't be ridiculous,' Nora replied. 'Not until we've caught at least one fish.'

'What is more,' Derek pressed on, 'and you need to hear this, Jim, the security on which I lend that money must be sufficient to cover the debt, should the borrower default.'

'Stop sniffing, Jimmy,' Nora scolded, handing her son a loo roll from the basket. 'You never stop sniffing these days. Are you looking after yourself? You seem to have a constant cold.'

'I'm fine, Mum,' Jimmy replied, rubbing his nose, a nose which his mother would have been shocked to hear was currently costing Jimmy almost as much a week to cater for as her husband earned at the bank.

'And I always, *always* remember,' Derek continued, so used to having his lectures ignored that he no longer seemed to notice, 'that the money I lend is not mine. It's not even the bank's. It belongs to the *savers*.'

'Got one!' Nora exclaimed, pulling a minnow from the water.

'Great!' Jimmy replied, digging into the hamper and going straight for the cherry Bakewells.

Derek sighed. There was no common ground between the financial world in which he operated and that of his son.

'I think the point is, Dad,' Jimmy suggested, his mouth full of cake, 'that money used to be a trade, and now it's an art.'

Derek Corby harrumphed. He didn't think money had any business being an art.

'You were always terrible at art,' Mr Corby senior pointed out testily. 'Your soldiers never had necks.'

The new occupant

Jimmy's position was pretty desperate but it could have been worse. People didn't cross the street to avoid him as he shuffled up the street. He didn't stink of piss and his hair wasn't horrendously knotted and matted with filth. He didn't have a beard that was alive with vermin or running sores all over his dirt-blackened skin. Not like the wretched wreck of a man who was shuffling up Webb Street, past all the houses that Jimmy had briefly believed he owned.

The man's name was Bob, not that it mattered. He didn't need a name because nobody spoke to him now. Sometimes he nearly forgot it himself. Except it was hanging round his neck on the ID that the people who ran the *Big Issue* had sorted out for him a year or two before. That had been during a brief period when some charity worker had tried to get him together; they tried occasionally, those charity workers, although Bob doubted that they ever would again. He was too far gone now, even for the freshest and most evangelical of do-gooders. He still wore the ID, even though it was at least a year since he'd been together enough to sell a magazine. It was useful when trying to get a bed for the night. The hostels always needed a name and ID. For their forms. But he didn't stay in hostels now either: they were too crowded, crowded with people better able to argue their way into a bed than he. A whole different breed from what he was used to. IT consultants and estate agents. Estate agents becoming homeless? That was funny.

Bob had seen them all. He was first-generation street.

A pioneer. A survivor from that time in the eighties when suddenly towns had become flooded by young people sitting in doorways. Some people didn't remember now, but if you were over forty-five or fifty you might recall that there had been a time when there were virtually no homeless people on the streets of Britain and begging was almost unknown.

Begging? Unknown in Britain? The thought actually made Bob laugh. But it was true, when he was a kid that was how it had been. It had all changed when Mrs Thatcher made it so young people could no longer claim housing benefit if they'd left home voluntarily. Overnight, it seemed, every abused kid in the country was on the street.

Getting abused.

Bob had been one of them and he'd been on the street ever since. He'd seen the doorway population change from almost exclusively young runaways in the eighties to the poverty-trapped underclass that emerged in the nineties through the boom years of the squeegie merchants to the shawled, shuffling Eastern European women of the early noughties with their drugged babies and sad little notes on bits of torn-up cardboard saying, 'Hungre. Plese help.'

Now it seemed to Bob that things were coming a weird full circle as the very yuppies who had tossed him coins when he first hit the streets more than twenty years before were joining him in the doorways. 'What was all that about?' he asked himself through a methylated, petrol-scented haze.

No, Bob didn't apply for hostels now. He was just too screwed up. Mentally and physically. His sores festered, his mind raged with whatever drug, drink or solvent he could push at it and nobody went within ten feet of him. He was literally dying as he walked. But it was taking a while. He marvelled at how his body kept on keeping on. And wondered why it bothered.

That night Bob found himself in Hackney. In Webb Street. A semi-derelict and entirely abandoned property development that had run out of cash. At one end of the street some of the properties had been nearly renovated. These desirable billets had been squatted by smart, savvy class-war warriors with dreadlocks and posh accents who changed locks and sorted out the leccy.

The other end of the street had not been touched, and the houses were almost as rotten and forlorn as Bob himself. It was into one of these that Bob managed to creep with his shot of meth and the remains of a hamburger that he'd found in a bin. The door had been boarded up but kids had long since kicked that in. He decided not to trust the stairs. His bones were brittle and thin and Bob knew that if he were to put his foot through a rotten floorboard he would probably leave it there. Turning into the first room he found, a room which had once been an elegant reception area and more recently home to a whole family of

Somalis, Bob lay down on the boards and went to sleep.

Bob was not quite the new occupant that Jimmy Corby, the nominal owner and developer of Webb Street, had had in mind when he began his development project. But then, as Bob often muttered to himself, it was a funny old world.

The price of love

Jimmy had never thought of his lovely Notting Hill home as a *big* house. And certainly not absurdly big, as he now knew it to be. Now that winter was pretty much upon them and he had to find a way to heat it while he tried to find a way to sell it.

How could he have not noticed how big it was? But the thought had never even occurred to him. It was just a decent-sized town house, that was all. In fact, it hadn't really been big *enough*. Not with a live-in nanny who expected her own kitchenette. Not with three day staff cluttering up the place. Not if you wanted to put in a gym and spa. A fully equipped Nautilus gym plus steam room, solarium and massive whirlpool plunger that you could almost swim in. The weight of the water had meant putting in new joists to support the floor. An entire health club at home! It seemed crazy now but it hadn't seemed that way a year before, when all he was thinking about was Monica getting her figure back. Then it had seemed . . . well, essential.

'We've got to have a gym,' he'd said. 'We're far too busy to get it together to visit the local sweaty jock strap.' And he'd sort of *believed* it.

Jimmy went down to the basement, a vast knock-through space encompassing a fabulous kitchen and family play area. Monica was there, of course. She was always there when one of the kids was going off because the beautiful polished slate floor afforded the most room in which to push a buggy in a figure of eight while trying to rock a child to sleep. Monica was doing just that with Cressida and trying to suckle Lillie on the hoof. She was wearing a nightie that Jimmy had put in her Christmas stocking the year before. It was pure silk and had cost three hundred pounds. A gorgeous little filler along with some sweet Cartier ear studs, some piccolos of Laurent Perrier and a brace of tickets for the Orient Express (while Jodie took the kids to Euro Disney). Now one strap of that lovely delicate silk was hanging down off her shoulder, exposing one breast, while the other side was dark and sodden with copious let-downs. The nightie was a short one, more of a slip really, designed to show a maximum amount of leg, legs that Monica had always been rather proud of but which were currently encased in varicose-vein-suppression stockings that had fallen down around her ankles.

'I was trying to go to the loo!' was the first thing she said. 'But Cressida was making such a row I thought she was dying. Take this one, I'm desperate!'

'Love you,' Jimmy said as he took hold of the buggy.

'Love you,' Monica replied as she hopped and shuffled towards the open toilet door with Lillie still at her breast.

Jimmy sighed a deep sigh. Ever since Jodie and the chef had left, Monica had been in a constant state of trying to get to the loo. Before that, neither of them had had any idea that fitting in one's own bodily functions with the needs of a baby and toddler would present such a never-ending series of challenges.

'The moment you want to go,' Monica observed, 'the toddler falls down the stairs and the baby's sick.' She was convinced that before they invented *Thomas the Tank Engine* to hypnotize children, mothers without nannies must have crapped on the carpet.

Jimmy picked Cressida up out of the buggy and the child began to calm down a little. Usually the buggy would have been enough to shut her up in the first place but tonight, probably sensing that Monica was alone and hence extra-vulnerable to persecution, Cressida had refused to be mollified.

A few moments later Monica re-emerged.

'Hi,' he said.

'Hi,' Monica replied. 'I have to get a clean nightie, this

one's soaked up half a boob's worth and now I feel guilty because Lillie won't get the milk. If you'd been here I could have expressed it. Cressida just wouldn't let me do a thing.'

'I had to go to Webb Street. I was meeting David.'

Tired though she was, Monica knew how difficult that must have been. David, like everyone involved in Jimmy's failed property development, had not been paid. And David was a mate.

'Oh, right,' she said. 'God, to have Jodie back. Just for a day.'

Jimmy carried on comforting Cressida. There was nothing to say on that score because there was no chance whatsoever of getting Jodie back, not unless she agreed to work for nothing and bring her own food.

For a moment they were silent, each holding a child, tiny bombs, either of which, if put down even for an instant, would immediately explode. Jimmy felt himself swaying slightly, fatigue enveloping him. For a moment he thought he was falling over, then he managed to blink himself back into focus.

'How's Toby?' he asked.

'Asleep. He misses Jodie.'

'Well, I suppose that's to be expected. She was with him all his life.'

Suddenly Monica's eyes filled with tears. 'I really do think . . .' she started, 'I mean, she might have found a way to . . . I thought she loved him. He feels so deserted.'

'Mon, of course she loved him. In a way. Like a nanny. But what do you expect her to do? We can't pay her.'

'I know, but . . .'

But there *were* no buts. Jodie was as much a victim of the downturn as they were. She had been lucky to be offered a job at half the money (and no board) at a Shepherds Bush backpacker pub and she'd grabbed it.

'If she hadn't taken that job,' Jimmy said, 'she'd have been as stuck as we are.'

'Perhaps not *quite* as stuck,' Monica said, and for a moment she couldn't help smiling.

Jimmy smiled too.

After all, Jodie might be poor and having to pull pints for pissed-up surfer dudes doing a year in London plus all the Aussie nannies who hadn't lost their jobs. But at least she had managed to avoid the added burden of an enormous property portfolio negatively mortgaged to the tune of whatever horror story the *Evening Standard* was publishing that day.

Jodie had done her best to soften the blow, ignoring the painful and sudden reduction in her own circumstances and trying to be kind and positive about Jimmy and Monica's. She had dropped back to see them twice in the first week of separation but it had all been too awkward. What was her position? Should she leap up and sort out the children's laundry as she had been doing for years? Should she sit on the rug and engage Toby in some brilliant game before settling down on a bean bag to read him something fun but improving while the adults ignored them both and sipped wine? Or should she sit on the couch and drink her coffee with Monica like some newly discovered friend, politely but firmly declining all Toby's demands to do all the stuff with him that she used to do? On her second visit Jodie had given in and done some painting with Toby, partly out of habit and partly out of sympathy. After half an hour she had realized that Monica had fallen back into old habits too and gone off to catch up on phone calls and emails. Jodie had had to disengage herself from a bewildered Toby and call to Monica that she needed to be getting back for her bar shift.

After that, Jodie didn't visit again. She and Jimmy and Monica all understood that the situation was mutually upsetting and unworkable. The only person who didn't understand was Toby, who simply found that some-body who'd always told him she loved him and who had seemed genuinely committed to his education in the finer points of Australian hard rock was now reject-ing him, leaving not so much as a Cold Chisel album in the glove compartment of the Discovery.

'How was it with David?' Monica asked.

'Pretty tense, as you'd expect,' Jimmy replied. 'His firm want paying, of course. Why wouldn't they? They blame David for the bad debt, which is understandable as it was him who brought in our commission. Poor old Dave's pretty stressed out in general now that his precious Rainbow Project has gone tits up too.'

'Yes, that's gone pretty sour, hasn't it?' Monica seemed to seize on the opportunity to talk about other people's troubles. 'It was even on the news. It looked so pathetic, two ridiculous-looking concrete spikes pointing at each other.'

'Yeah, it was in the *Standard* too. It's being used as a symbol of corporate excess. Hubris gone berserk. The headline was *Two Fingers to Caution*, which didn't really work because they don't look remotely like fingers. Of course, as originating architect David's name's all over it, so he's *seriously* shagged.'

Together they walked their two younger children around the kitchen for a while, Cressida back in the buggy, Lillie in Monica's arms.

'It's like some Greek tragedy, isn't it?' Monica said, breaking the silence.

'It's certainly some sort of bloody tragedy,' Jimmy replied, once more finding it in himself to smile.

'No, it's Greek,' Monica insisted, smiling too. 'Greek tragedies aren't just any tragedies. They need a fall.'

Monica had taken Theatre Studies as a subsidiary to her English degree and therefore knew her stuff. She had even been slated to play the king's mother in a third-year production of *Oedipus* until the student director had informed her that in his vision of the play she would be expected to allow the actor playing Oedipus to suckle her breasts.

'You mean *actually get my tits out*?' Monica had exclaimed in a voice that turned heads in the union canteen.

'Yes,' the earnest (and clearly very horny) young director had replied.

'And let a post-grad engineering student *suck them*?'

'He's mother-fixated. That's the point of the play.'

And that had been the end of Monica's acting career. Now she was playing a suckling mother for real.

'No, it really is a Greek tragedy,' Monica went on. 'All power, wealth and glory. Then the fall. You. David. You were both doing so *well*, weren't you?'

Over the Rainbow

Having had to study for a proper job, Jimmy's old uni mate David had taken rather longer than Jimmy, Rupert or Lizzie (and Robbo) to join London's financial elite. In fact until around '97 he had had even less money than Henry, which was astonishing because at the time Henry was a local Labour Party activist with a part-time job copy-editing other people's novels while he worked on his own, a 'literary' spy novel called *Security Blanket*.

David was the arty member of the gang. In the great

Brit Pop battle of '94 he had been the only firm Blur man. Jimmy, Rupert and Robbo had all been 100 per cent Oasis and Henry had sat on the fence.

'Just like a fucking politician,' Rupert had sneered.

Lizzie liked Enya and Clannad.

Right from the start David had walked the walk. He wore thick Jarvis Cocker glasses and desert boots, drank absinthe, briefly had an Italian girlfriend (an au pair) and had grabbed the attic room in the house that the five boys shared, where he slept on a mattress with a book about Jackson Pollock on the floor beside it. Nearby stood a number of big volumes full of black and white photographs which he got from his parents for Christmas and a stack of *Arena* magazines. However, he owned (as far as Jimmy could ascertain when he searched the room) no pornography at all. Which Jimmy found truly astonishing, particularly for someone who claimed to be a lover of beauty.

'What's the point of surrounding yourself with books of photographs if they're not of naked women?' Jimmy enquired and it was generally agreed that there was something in what he said.

During his first year, David had briefly had ambitions to be an artist and had even contributed an exhibit to a university art show, a used condom lying on a blow-up sex doll. The exhibit was picketed by both the Catholic Soc and the Fem Soc, the only occasion on which the two societies ever found common cause.

In the end, though, David switched his allegiance from Pollock to Corbusier and soon after qualifying as an architect had been taken on by a trendy practice. He had overtaken Henry in terms of annual income with his very first commission.

A decade after that, when Jimmy met him for beer and curry in order to approach him about taking on his Webb Street development, David was a wealthy man (and although Henry had by this time become an MP he still hadn't finished his spy novel). In fact, so successful was David by 2005 that, university mate or not, the prospect of heading up a street's worth of house conversions no longer tickled his fancy in the least.

'I'll recommend the job to my board as a favour, Jim,' David said patronizingly while stealing Jimmy's last poppadom, 'but there's no way I'll be able to take any interest in it myself. Things are looking a bit too exciting these days for me to worry about how to squeeze eleven en suites into a ten-bedroom house.'

'No problem, mate,' Jimmy assured him as he reached over and shattered the stolen poppadom with the flat of his hand. 'I don't need you ballsing things up with a load of pretentious asymmetrical cock wank anyway. Call me mad but I'm not into houses that look like a pile of glass cubes stacked up by an educationally challenged two-year-old. I need houses that look *posh*. Not hip. Which is why I want your firm's *name*, Dave. That I need, because that *is* posh. That's stylish, that adds zeros to the price. But as to your firm's mega-crappy signature style, which makes everything look like it was designed by half a dozen blokes working independently of each other in sealed rooms, you can stuff it.'

David rubbed his eyes behind his glasses. Glasses with the same thick, black, plastic frames he had worn at university, except of course that being Dolce and Gabbana instead of National Health Service they had cost four hundred pounds (which did not include the price of the light-sensitive lenses).

'You were a philistine arse at uni, Jim, and you're still a philistine arse,' David said, managing to capture the remains of the lamb massala on his nan bread with a single superbly executed sweep that left the little metal dish looking as if it had just been washed. 'And I'm afraid you always will be a philistine arse.'

'If preferring buildings where it's possible to work out which is the roof and which is the floor is being an arse then I'm guilty as charged. Anyway, bollocks to that, do you think your firm will take on Webb Street or not?'

David smiled and ordered two more pints of Kingfisher.

'Jim lad, they'll do anything I ask them to. Because I've got my NFM, mate. I is da MAN! You hear dat, bro? You is looking at da man innit, aiee!'

Jimmy flinched. He could be as naff as they came but David's recently adopted habit of falling into a sort of half-black 'yoof' accent that he'd clearly picked up off a comedy sketch show turned even Jimmy's stomach. Apart from anything else, he was so *bad* at it.

'Dave, please,' Jimmy said, 'you're thirty-three and you went to Winchester.'

'Das rye!' David replied, flicking his fingers to make them click but failing. 'I is da youngest geezah wiv an NFM *in da 'hood*!'

David had long ago explained to Jimmy what an NFM was. It was the holy grail of every architecture firm on the planet.

The Norman Foster Moment.

The architectural commission that would garner real-world attention and catapult its designers into the upper echelons of superstar architects. Those architects whose firms emerging democracies commissioned to design their new parliament buildings, and multi-nationals used when they wanted to build an art gallery to burn up a bucket of tax avoidance.

'You're not telling me they've actually commissioned your Rainbow?' Jim asked.

'Jim lad, they ate it up,' David purred.

'Fucking hell, that's incredible.'

'What do you mean? You always said it was a brilliant idea,' David protested.

'Yeah, I *said* that,' Jimmy replied, 'because you're a mate, but to be honest I thought it was just more Dave wank.'

Jimmy had heard the Rainbow pitch many times. David had rehearsed it at numerous gatherings and now, out of the blue, it seemed he had pitched it for real.

'Hooked 'em this afternoon as a matter of fact,' said David with a huge grin.

'Buildings in the shape of rainbows?' Jimmy asked. 'You seriously pitched it?'

'Of course!' David waved his nan about as he relived the moment. 'Vast arches with two sets of foundations! The skyscraper as a bridge! It's brilliant! I mean, that concept alone would probably have been enough; everybody knows that to be really successful a building needs a nickname and I had loads – Rainbow, Bridge, Arch, Speed Bump. The board loved them all. They would have commissioned me there and then but my pitch hadn't even *started*, mate.'

'There's more?' Jimmy feigned excitement. 'More than a bent building?'

'You're forgetting my coup de grâce. *Any* shitty old architect can offer up a building in a challenging and original shape!'

'Challenging and original?' Jimmy said. 'That's architect-speak for "stupid", is it?'

'No, it's architect-speak for "idiots like you wouldn't get it in a million years". But just being challenging and original won't get you the Shell headquarters in Nigeria, mate. And it won't get you the upper legislature of some pastel-coloured parliament in the outer reaches of the ex-Soviet Union either. No! You've got to have more than just a challenging and original shape.'

'The coup de grâce?'

'Exactly! The coup de grâce. I told them. The whole point about a rainbow is it has two ends. This is a building that can *cross national borders*!'

Jimmy took a swig of beer. Despite himself, he was impressed.

'Wow. I don't remember that bit of the idea.'

'That's because I only recently thought of it.'

'It's a big concept.'

'Damn right it's a big concept!'

'But . . . uhm. Why?'

'Why?' David gasped. '*Why?*'

'Yeah. Why cross borders?'

'Because it's *conceptually fabulous*, that's why! A building as a symbol of peace! A global handshake fashioned in glass and concrete! A multinational community in the sky! Quite literally a *bridge between nations*!'

'And your board loved it?'

'Crazy for it.'

'Well, that's brilliant, Dave. Seriously, congratu—'

'I haven't finished,' David said impatiently. 'I haven't told you my coup de grâce.'

'I thought that was the coup de grâce, building your Rainbow across national boundaries.'

'That's half of it.'

'What's the other half?'

'We build them across borders between countries with *unequal tax legislation*.'

A slow smile spread across Jimmy's face.

'I like it,' he said finally.

'What,' David asked, 'is not to like? You have one set of foundations in a major economy and the other across the border in a tax haven. France and Liechtenstein, for instance. That way your building not only symbolizes peace and international cooperation but also makes it possible to generate corporate profits and evade the tax on them *without leaving the office*.'

'Now that,' Jimmy conceded, 'is good. *That* is clever.'

'They went crazy for it, Jim, just crazy. They're going to float the concept at every major potential commission that comes up. I is on my way, geezer!' David said, waving his empty glass at the waiter. 'I is about *explain big time*. Ya nah wah ahm sayin', blood.'

'Yeah, well, bollocks to it anyway,' Jimmy replied. 'Are you going to recommend my housing-development project to your board or not?'

David agreed to do it for the price of the last onion bhaji and went on to describe his new concept for a building that worked like a Rubik's Cube.

'Never the same building two days in a row. The challenge will be finding your office in the morning,' he said.

'And that's a good thing?'

'If you have any sense of style it is,' said David.

A drink and a lifeline

Two years after that conversation had taken place, David was no longer 'da MAN' and David's firm would have been happy to take any commission that came their way, always assuming that it was a solvent one. Architectural practices were having a particularly hard time during the crunch, the assumption that the world could never have enough office space having proved to be an illusion. Jimmy and Monica were therefore faced with the fact that their old friend could no longer shield them from the debt they owed his bosses.

'I'm afraid David's Rainbow is screwed for the same reason Webb Street's screwed,' Jimmy said mournfully. 'Nobody can sell the property they have. They just don't need any more buildings, particularly bent ones that cross national borders. David ain't the golden boy any more. The truth is he doesn't know how long he can keep his boss from taking action against us.'

A flicker of fear passed across Monica's features.

'Taking action? What does that mean?'

'Well, suing us, I suppose.'

'*Suing us?* But . . . he's our friend, a founder member of the Radish Club. You were at Sussex together.'

'Yes, and I imagine Laura is saying exactly the same thing to him about us. We are their friends, I was at Sussex with him, we shoved the radish together on graduation night. And now I owe his firm a lot of money. Money they hold him responsible for.'

'They were happy to take the job at the time,' Monica snapped, tears welling up in her exhausted eyes, 'whatever David might have pretended about being too grand for it. Money's money after all and you were doing them a favour. You could have taken the work anywhere. They sent us round a magnum of Dom Perignon '89.'

'Yeah, Mon, I know. But they wouldn't have wanted the job if they'd known I wouldn't be able to pay for it, would they?'

Monica shrugged. There was nothing else to say. Perhaps it was the thought of Dom Perignon that led her mind to the bottles in the huge American fridge. Not Dom P of course, five-pound deal, three-for-two Pinot Grigs from Sainsbury's, but very tempting just the same. This was one habit that had not changed since disaster struck. Monica always loved to point out that being rich did not mean being stupid and that Sainsbury's cheapos were perfectly bloody OK if all you wanted was a good glug.

'How many did I have last night?' Monica asked.

54

Monica and Jimmy had always loved drink, much more than the obligatory cocaine and Es that they'd done in their early days together. Booze was their drug of choice and they appreciated it even more now that their lives had been torn to shreds. But with Monica breastfeeding they were trying, despite everything, to watch it.

'A large double G and T at six and a large single after your last evening feed.'

'So that's three units then.'

'Well . . . let's say three.'

According to the rules they had both drawn up, that was Monica's entire daily allowance.

'But we also had a large glass of wine each before we went to bed,' Jimmy reminded her. 'It was our little treat, remember? To prove we were still human beings.'

'So that's one more unit then?'

'Well . . . let's *say* one.'

'Which makes four, so a minus one to carry forward.'

The idea was that if Monica went over her limit, it represented a minus that had to be deducted from the following day's allowance.

Jimmy checked the list which was stuck to the fridge with a big plastic magnetic letter.

'Yes, but you were already minus three on the week so far, so now you're minus four.'

'But clean slate on Sunday? Fresh start?'

'Of course, we agreed.'

Monica took a bottle of wine from the fridge.

'I love these screw tops,' she said, holding the bottle in the hand of the arm that was supporting Lillie at her breast and unscrewing it with the other. 'I think they must have been designed by a nursing mother.'

She poured out two glasses. A unit each. Or three units each, depending on whether it was measured by her or by the government.

They both took a deep swig.

'Anyway –' Monica put down her glass with the air of somebody with something to say – 'I had hoped to avoid this, but if David is really going to be so mean . . .'

'He's not being mean, Mon. It's got nothing to do with him. He's just caught in the middle.'

'Well, it doesn't matter anyway because actually I think I might have some good news.'

Jimmy smiled a weary smile. He couldn't imagine how that could be. There was no prospect of good news ever again. Good news belonged to the era before it had emerged that American banks had been actively persuading penniless itinerants to take out huge mortgages on worthless properties.

'Great,' Jimmy said.

'Lizzie rang today and I ended up telling her how bad things were. I didn't think you'd mind.'

'Mon, she knows. Everybody knows about our cash-flow situation.'

That was how he liked to see their problem, how he

lived with it and managed it in his head. It wasn't utter financial ruin, a life-shattering car crash or a cosmic-scale fuck-up. It was just a cash-flow problem. A temporary thing. A money-management challenge to be ridden out. Once their assets regained their proper value, Jimmy would be able to service his debts and begin to rebuild his fortune. The fact that they were almost certain to be declared bankrupt long before that happened was something that Jimmy tried not to acknowledge even to himself.

'I know she knows,' Monica agreed. 'I rather think that was why she rang. She says she and Robson want to help. You know, just with the David thing and the Webb Street development. She hates the idea of all of us mates being in trouble with each other like this.'

'Mon, we don't need fancy sandwiches. I owe David's firm two hundred and fifty thousand in fees *already* and the same again if we ever complete.'

'She knows, Jim. Laura told her.'

'*Laura?* Fuck! You mean Dave's wife is trying to get Lizzie to lend us money so we can pay Dave? That is *fucked*!'

'Why is it fucked? We're all mates, aren't we? Lizzie and Laura were just chatting, that's all, and now Lizzie knows all about it she really wants to help. She says we can put up one of the houses in Webb Street as collateral and pay her back when the recession is over.'

Jimmy looked at Monica. For a moment he wondered

if he was hearing right. Whether the tiredness had finally made him unable to understand English.

'You mean she's offering to lend us the money? I mean, a hell of a lot of money?'

'Yes.'

'Unsecured?'

'I suppose so. Whatever that means. Like I say, she says we can put up one of the houses.'

'The houses are all negative equity. That's not a security. They're not properties, just a row of semi-detached debts.'

Monica shrugged. 'She says she'll wait. Till they go back up in value.'

'*Until the recession is over?*'

'That's what she said.'

Jimmy's initial anger at his old friends discussing his pathetic situation had lasted seconds. Not even that. *One* second. False pride had never been one of Jimmy's faults.

Now he was elated. Not just elated, ecstatic. He punched the air.

'Yee-ha!' he cried. 'Now *that* is Rock 'n' Roll!'

One of the symptoms of the extreme exhaustion and stress under which he now lived was that Jimmy found his emotions yo-yoing far more ferociously than they had ever done in his old life. And never so much as at this moment when suddenly he perceived a lifeline to drag him from his troubles. A wave of exhilaration coursed through his body.

'My God, Mon, that would be absolutely brilliant!'

Monica's smile was suddenly as broad as his. She was actually shaking. 'Wouldn't it?'

Jimmy scarcely dared to hope that the situation could be resolved so simply, but of course he knew that it could. Lizzie and her charming but basically useless husband Robson were still rich, very rich. Perhaps she really could help them out, just for a little while. A year.

And it wasn't like he'd be abusing a friendship. And in fact the loan would *not* be unsecured. He had the security. Of course he had the security. *Fuck yes*, he had the security. He owned a street. Him and the bank. The fact that the street was currently in negative equity was just a blip. That was all. A blip.

'I'm so glad you're going to let Lizzie and Robson help us, Jim. I'm so sick of this worry.'

'Of course we'll let them help,' Jimmy replied, emptying the rest of the bottle into their glasses before grabbing the phone. 'What's more, in the end we'll make a profit for them on it.'

'Oh Jim. You know Liz and Robbo don't care about money.'

'Yeah,' said Jimmy, 'they can afford not to.'

Lizzie was still rich. Her money was *real*. Concrete. It was secured by actual concrete *stuff*. She wasn't like Jimmy. She hadn't built her fortune on the shifting sands of the futures market but on foundations hewn from the solid, timeless rock of people's love of posh things, fabulous design and exquisite nibbles.

Lizzie had parlayed her charm, her good looks, her genuine love of food and her commitment to what she called the 'art of living' into a very substantial lifestyle business. A business that included cookery books, occasional TV appearances, three restaurants and an endless range of beautifully presented Lizzie Food treats. Fortunately for Lizzie and Robbo, despite the deepening financial crisis, there were still enough people left in the world prepared to pay three pounds for a single chilli-soaked olive presented in its own exquisite little box to keep the wolf from the door.

Useless old bugger

Lizzie answered the phone herself, of course. In the day she had a full-time PA as well as home helps and a staff of four in the office next door, but her rule was that after six was strictly private time. The staff went home and Lizzie and Robson cosied up and did for themselves. They'd never even had a live-in nanny, just a day girl. Lizzie was proud of the fact that despite a decade of feverish creativity she had never missed a single bedtime.

Of course the fact that Robson was basically a house husband helped. He was nominally a director of Lizzie Food, the company they jointly owned, but everybody knew that dear old Robbo just arsed about a bit and played with the children before shuffling off to the pub or the golf club, where he was an enormously popular figure with his unkempt curly hair, his slight paunch, his ability to make even the most expensively tailored garment look like a sack and his comical ambition to get his handicap down to under forty.

'Good old Robbo,' the members would say to each other as he struggled to find his car keys after a few lunchtime pints. 'Salt of the earth. Do anything for you. Lucky bastard too, catching that wife of his. Gives all of us crap blokes hope.'

Some of the members secretly wondered whether Lizzie might play for the other netball team, but nothing could have been further from the truth. Lizzie loved Robbo deeply and passionately. He was the perfect partner for such a fastidious and restlessly energetic woman, being quite possibly the easiest and most even-tempered man alive. On their famous drunken graduation night it was he who had volunteered to shove the first radish.

It was indeed considered curious that the thing Lizzie loved most in life was the *only* thing that was not perfectly presented and exquisitely designed. And as the years went by it almost seemed as if Robson was her portrait of

Dorian Gray. The more shambolic and shapeless he got, the more utterly perfect everything that Lizzie created seemed to become.

'It's just brilliant genetics,' Jimmy had observed about them on a curry night called to celebrate Lizzie and Robbo's third wedding anniversary, 'like that theory about ugly men marrying beautiful women in order to avoid producing a race of gargoyles.'

'That's not genetics,' Rupert had said, 'that's economics. Beautiful women don't marry *poor* ugly men.'

'I'm going to!' laughed Jane, an earnest young writer who had recently got engaged to Henry over an unpublished manuscript. Henry tried to smile but it was obvious he didn't find his new girlfriend's joke very funny. Henry was known to be extremely vain about his looks, particularly his splendid mop of blond hair.

'Watch out, Jane,' David observed. 'You don't really know him yet but you'll soon find out that vanity's name is not "woman" but "Henry". In our house in Sussex he spent twice as long in front of the bathroom mirror as any of us, including Lizzie.'

'We live in a shallow media age,' Henry said, trying to sound good-humoured. 'Appearance matters.'

'You're right about the bathroom though, Dave,' Jane said. 'He takes twice as long as me in there too!'

This comment provoked a 'woo-hoo' from the boys as nobody had been quite sure if Jane was yet officially sleeping with Henry. Jane reddened.

'I mean, you know . . . Occasionally,' she said, 'if I've stayed.'

'This is my very point, Jane,' Jimmy insisted, moving swiftly on to cover her embarrassment. 'Nature readjusts, opposites attract. It's Darwinian. If Lizzie and Robbo had married their *own* types, Lizzie's children would be sad burnouts with OCD and Robbo's children would be good-natured slobs scratching their balls and incapable of feeding themselves or changing the batteries on the TV remote.'

'Isn't that what Robbo is already?' David had asked.

'Guilty as charged!' Robbo volunteered. 'I am one lucky bastard and so I tell anyone who wants to know. The only plea I can offer in mitigation is that I never tried to force myself on her! Not that I wasn't interested, of course. As I recall, we all were. I'll never forget the day you came round, Lizzie, in answer to our ad about a spare room. *Ding-dong. Hello!* Bin-go! We couldn't believe it.'

'Yes, you did all look rather gob-smacked,' Lizzie said.

'What's this?' Monica asked. 'I thought you lot all moved in together.'

'Not quite,' Jimmy said. 'Us five boys had all been in hall in the first year and when we got a house together in the second year it had a sixth room. We wanted the extra rent so we stuck up an ad. That's when we met Lizzie.'

'God, do you remember?' Henry chipped in. 'First of

all we gave the room to that first-year bloke, the guy who didn't want to share the fridge.'

'That's *right*!' Jimmy said. 'Fuck me, I'd forgotten him. We had to chuck him straight out again, didn't we?'

'We certainly did after Lizzie turned up.' David laughed.

'I'd just split up with my boyfriend, you see,' Lizzie explained to the other girls. 'I mean I wasn't *looking* to move in with five blokes. I was just desperate.'

'*We* were bloody desperate!' Robbo exclaimed.

'That first-year chap had to go anyway,' Rupert said firmly. 'What was his name? Graeme?'

'That's right,' Jimmy said. 'Spelt e-m-e at the end, not h-a-m. I can still remember him spelling it out.'

'You see,' Rupert went on, 'that's suspect in itself. Silly bastard kept banging on about Gay Pride too. Like we cared. I told him, I said, listen, mate, gay sex is all very well but I don't want it shoved down my throat!'

'Boom *boom*!' Robbo shouted.

'So you were the same tolerant, caring, inclusive liberal then as you are today, eh, Rupert?' Monica enquired.

'Well, *I* thought it was funny anyway,' Rupert said.

'I just remember the bloke was tonto about the fridge,' Jimmy said. 'Bloody idiot wanted to get a ruler and divide it into six separate sections.'

'He did have to go,' David said. 'Lizzie was a bonus.'

'But *what* a bonus,' Robbo said, raising his glass. 'I was

64

absolutely knocked for six. But as I have already said, I did *not* pursue her.'

'No, you didn't,' Lizzie chided. 'I had to go after him.'

'Well, what kind of a twat would I have looked trying to get off with a uber-babe like you?' Robson protested. 'Utterly gorgeous, pursued by every rugger bugger on campus. *And* every bugger in the house. Come on, 'fess up! Rupert, Jimmy, David, Henry, you all had a punt at some point and got nowhere . . .'

'*I* never knew that,' said Laura, a law graduate who was in the middle of her pupillage and who had been going out with David for about six months.

'Ah, there are more things in heaven, earth and the Radish Club than are dreamt of in your philosophy, darling,' David assured her.

'I didn't get nowhere,' Rupert insisted, grinding out his cigar on an empty raita dish. 'I got a snog.'

'You got a New Year kiss,' Lizzie corrected him, 'and I was *very* drunk.'

'Well anyway, like I say,' Robbo went on, 'it never would have *occurred* to me that I stood a chance in hell with Lizzie and I certainly wasn't going to arse around making a fool of myself and getting my heart broken trying to pull totty whose shoes I was clearly not fit to lick. Quite frankly, I'd rather be in the pub getting pissed.'

'And that's where I pulled *him*,' Lizzie laughed.

'And I don't know about Lizzie,' Robbo shouted, raising his glass, 'but I personally have lived happily ever after! Garçon! More beer!'

'You can get the man out of the pub,' said Jimmy, clinking his glass against Robson's, 'but you will never get the pub out of the man.'

'And confusion on anybody who tries!' Robson shouted, accepting his pint, quaffing half of it and accidentally putting it down on a spoon so that it fell over and the rest of its contents spilt across the table.

'Come on, you, that's your lot,' Lizzie said, as she had said a hundred times before. 'Home time.'

'A *nasty lasty*, love, surely?' Robbo protested. 'I spilt most of that one.'

'Exactly,' said Liz, 'which might be God's way of telling you you've had enough. Any more and I won't let you drive, and you know how you hate me changing gear on Churchill.'

Churchill was Robbo's big and beloved old Wolseley, a vehicle as comfortable, as shambling, as worn-looking and as terminally unhip as he was, and driving it was (as Robbo was the first to admit) the *only* thing that Robbo did better than his beloved wife.

'Yes, can't have that.' Robbo got up. 'I shall have to drink your health at home.'

'Come on, Rob!' Jimmy protested. 'You can't go yet, we're celebrating your wedding anniversary.'

'And the *reason* there's an anniversary to celebrate,

mate,' Robbo replied, 'is that I have discovered the secret of a successful marriage. Do what your bloody wife tells you! The bill's on our account. Don't order any malts older than your last girlfriend, Rupert.'

'Lovely!' Rupert beamed. 'An eighteen-year-old Glenfiddich.'

Rupert had been a mature student and was already thirty-three.

'Honestly, Rupert,' David scolded. 'Have you ever dated a girl who's made it to her twenties?'

'Well, I certainly try not to.'

'But what do you find to talk about?' David enquired.

'Talk? We don't fucking *talk*.'

'Night, all,' Robbo said, leaning over to kiss the ladies goodbye. Inevitably his glasses and fountain pen slipped out of his top pocket and into a half-finished massala.

'Don't put them back in your pocket, Robbo!' Lizzie shrieked. 'Let me wipe them properly.'

But it was too late. Robbo had already scooped up his glasses and having given them a cursory wipe had put them back in his jacket, thus depositing bright-red curry sauce all over it.

'*God*, Robbo, you are *such* a klutz!' Lizzie said as if scolding a ten-year-old. 'Don't worry, I shall iron the grease out over brown paper.'

'Actually I wasn't worried,' Robbo said, turning and winking at the lads as Lizzie headed for the door, then adding, 'God! Look behind you, Henry! It's Neil Kinnock!'

Henry fell for it like a sack of spuds. Robbo had grabbed his pint of Kingfisher and sunk half of it before Henry realized he'd been had.

'Got to grab it while I can, Henry,' Robson said. 'When your lot get into power you'll probably ban beer.'

Lovely, lovely things

Lizzie was truly a pioneer of the *lovely, lovely thing*. Without Lizzie and a few others like her, the populations of Notting Hill, Kensington, Primrose Hill and many other not quite so salubrious but rapidly 'improving' areas of London in the late nineties would have had nothing to give each other for Christmas.

For what do you get for people who have everything they could possibly need or want, plus a shitload of stuff they *don't* need and often don't even want?

'You get them something *lovely*, of course,' said Lizzie.

It didn't really matter to Lizzie what that thing actually was, only that it should be *beautifully presented*. That was the real issue.

To previous generations of purveyors of luxury items

a biscuit had still been essentially a biscuit. That was the main item on the agenda. Of course it needed a nicely designed box, but what really mattered was what was inside the box.

'That,' Lizzie assured her young design team, 'is bollocks. What really and truly matters is the *box*.'

To her it was instinctive, a truth instilled in her by a good (and very pretty) fairy at her birth. Presentation was everything.

Lizzie *adored* a box.

She gloried in choosing the thick, creamy card from which it was constructed. Comparing the inks and dyes with which it would be coloured. Studying the weave on the ribbon with which its lid would be secured. Considering the dimensions of the cellophane window through which the scrummy cookies within could be glimpsed. All three of them.

Lizzie *loved* a box.

To her a box was a means of communication. She revelled in all the things a box could say, and in so many beautiful tones and typefaces.

Lizzie Loves Organic.
Only good things inside. Good but very naughty!
50% sustainably sourced cardboard! (Lizzie's promise!)
A little of what you fancy!
Cornish Clotted Creamery from VERY happy cows!
Responsibly traded cocoa beans taste better!

In the long run it didn't matter what was in the box at all. Everybody knew that a Malteser was actually nicer than Lizzie's raw ginger nuggets smothered in bitter chocolate, but who cared when the ginger nuggets were so beautifully presented?

You couldn't take a packet of crisps as a gift to a hostess, even though pretty much everybody likes crisps. But you *could* bring some of Lizzie's shaved turnip curls. Even though they tasted pretty grim.

They were just so beautifully presented.

Half a turnip diced and *lightly* fried (in sustainable, organic rapeseed oil) then vacuum packed in plastic before being placed in a bag of purest raw cotton which was then put in a little wicker basket designed to look like a miniature version of the sort of basket that a fantasy farm maiden might have used on Fairy Tale Farm to take her home-grown lightly fried turnip curls to market.

Lizzie designed and packaged *everything*. Her kitchen-accessories range with its great rounded plastic handles in bright Day-glo colours earned her a half-page in *Vogue*. Her salt and pepper shakers with their cute little feet and hands were the subject of a lawsuit when a major retailer pinched the idea and tried to flog a range at a tenth of the price.

Lizzie offered stationery boxes containing six sheets of writing paper and envelopes handmade from *rag cloth* to people who only ever sent emails.

She put gorgeous fountain pens with little bottles of green ink into the stockings of people who'd forgotten how to write by hand.

She sold individually wrapped shards of *genuine Louisiana peanut brittle* to people who threw up in the toilet if they ate a cornflake.

There was nothing, absolutely nothing, no matter how impractical, no matter how pointless, that Lizzie could not box up and make desirable.

Practicality wasn't the point.

The contents certainly were not the point.

The point was *loveliness*. Pure and simple.

And loveliness had made Lizzie and Robbo very, very comfortable indeed.

A loan secured

'Lizzie, it's Jimmy,' Jimmy said, trying not to sound desperate. Hoping to replicate the tone that he had used on the thousands of times he had said that same sentence when he had been happy and secure and not about to beg for money. 'Monica's told me all about your offer and I can't tell you how grateful I am and I never would have asked in a million

71

years, but since you've brought it up yourself . . .'

Jimmy knew that he *did* sound desperate, but suddenly he didn't care. All at once he decided to go for broke, throwing shame to the wind as he suddenly upped the ante, explaining to his old friend that simply finding the money to pay off David's firm's outstanding invoices would not actually solve anything either for him and Monica or for David and Laura.

There was a bigger picture which, unless addressed, would make small fixes a waste of money. The problem was that the Webb Street job was only half finished and the real fear was that, with property prices currently in free fall, the whole development would collapse under the weight of its negative equity before the upturn came.

'I'm going to be straight with you, Liz,' Jimmy said. 'If I can't service the interest on the mortgage, the bank will repossess and I'll be officially bankrupt, leaving all my creditors, including David and his firm, to divide up the value of my remaining assets, which are basically a bit of furniture and five flat-screen tellies. Which is of course ridiculous because I own a street. A fucking *street*! But if I can't keep the bank's hands off it for what I'm guessing will be at least a year it all goes to shit.'

There was a pause during which Jimmy could feel himself sweating. The answer came in that wonderful voice, warm and honeyed. The voice that listeners to Radio 4 knew for its mouth-watering ability to describe the *loveliest* and most *indulgent* puddings. Lizzie sounded exactly as if she were reading a bedtime story and in a way she was, because she was about to produce a happy ending.

'How much do you honestly think you need?' Lizzie purred.

'Honestly?' Jimmy asked.

'Honestly,' Lizzie replied. 'We've all been in denial about this for months. We've known you're in trouble and Rupert says it's big trouble, but until Monica phoned me today none of us had really sat down and *talked* about it. Tell me the truth.'

Jimmy gulped. 'Liz, if I could borrow a couple of million for a year . . .'

He could see Monica's jaw drop and her eyes widen in alarm, but he pressed on.

'I think that would just about keep the bank, David's firm and the other immediate creditors at bay. I mean this thing has to end, doesn't it? Of course it does. Capitalism is cyclical and Mon and I own a *street*. Look, I know you've said you'll take one of the houses as collateral, but how about this? How about I give you and Robbo *half* the entire future profit on the development? Only nine months ago that was projected at *twenty million quid*, Liz! I'll give you half. Lend me two now and post-crunch you'll be looking at ten, minimum.'

For a moment it seemed to Jimmy as if the figures were real again, like they had been before. Not fantasy figures as he had now got used to seeing them, but real hard money that really did exist. Or soon would. It was so easy to slip back into that familiar mindset and it felt good to do so.

Lizzie clearly sensed this and her voice, when she replied, seemed even warmer, even kinder, even more soothing than before and gently scolding in that wonderful, rather sexy way she had.

'Jim. Don't. This isn't a deal. You don't need to pitch me and you don't need to sell me. It's about *mates*, that's all. I know you'll pay me back when you can and that's all I need to know. Forget collateral. When it's all over you can get me a case of something yummy if you like. Some *really good* dessert wine would be lovely, or a nice *big bold red*, a Margaret River Cab Sav or something. But that's it.'

'So you'll . . . you really will?' Jimmy's voice was breathless with hope. 'Two million?'

'Are you sure that's enough?' Lizzie replied.

'Yes. That's enough, Liz.'

'Good, then we'll do it. And I don't want us to have to discuss this again. Mates help each other but it defeats the object if it affects the mateship. So we'll do this and then forget about it until you sort things out. I'll get Robbo to transfer you two million in the morning, it's pretty simple. We've got easily that in gilts. And I insist that you do not ring to thank me. I do *not* want to discuss it again. We'll get through this together. As mates.'

Jimmy could not believe it. After months of ever-increasing despair everything was suddenly turning around. Two million would definitely see him through for a year, eighteen months probably. Lizzie was just *amazing*. She always had been. Impulsive. Instinctive. *Organic*. Like her biscuits. She followed her heart and it never let her down. She'd married Robson, for God's sake! Only Lizzie could have guessed how good a marriage that would turn out to be. Everybody loved Robbo, of course, but surely no one in their right mind would *marry* him? But Lizzie had, thus ensuring herself a lifetime of domestic contentment to go along with her great business success.

'I'll set up a new account tomorrow,' Jimmy replied.

He did not need to explain further what he meant by that. Lizzie was easily a good enough businesswoman to understand that if Jimmy and Monica were borrowing from her then they must have exhausted all other forms of credit and that if Jim wasn't careful any new windfall would simply get sucked into his ravenous overdrafts.

'Just send Robbo the details,' Lizzie said. 'Now put Mon on. I want to hear how her nipples are bearing up.'

After Lizzie and Monica had discussed lactation for a while Monica hung up the phone. Then Jimmy put Cressida down and Monica put Lillie down and they allowed both toddler and baby to scream away to their hearts' content as they embraced, holding each other close as the full extent of the rescue package sank in. Jimmy almost cried with relief. Monica did cry, sobbing and sobbing with tiredness and happiness and surging emotions that she could scarcely contain.

'So we won't have to leave our house?' she said finally.

'No. We can stay,' Jimmy said.

'Oh Jimmy,' she said, her body shaking against his.

'I know,' Jimmy whispered, 'I know. Shh!' as her tears wetted his shoulders and her breast milk soaked his pen pocket.

They were saved.

Lucky Jimmy

Jimmy always thought it was very unfair of his father to be so disparaging about his profession and so suspicious of his wealth. It was pretty hypocritical too when Jimmy remembered how at first, after he had scraped a 2/2 in Politics and Modern History, Derek Corby had been delighted that his only son had ended up in the financial sector.

After all, Jimmy had been toying with the most horribly romantic notions. Like becoming a National Trust ranger or, worse, 'something at the BBC'. Faced with such airy-fairy ideas Mr and Mrs Corby were relieved indeed and much surprised when, out of the blue, Jimmy became what at the time they still called a stockbroker but the world would soon identify as a trader and would finally denounce as a stupid, reckless, greedy, irresponsible bastard.

Of course Mr and Mrs Corby weren't half as surprised as Jimmy was. He just didn't see it coming. Only a week before the day he stepped on to his first trading floor he had been trying his hand at independent documentary film-making. Videotaping homeless people on the South Bank in the hope of knocking together a ground-breaking social exposé edited on the TV in the flat where he was staying above a kebab shop in Pimlico.

'Rather amusing, don't you think?' his friend Rupert had drawled through the smoke of his unashamedly pretentious Gitanes cigarette. 'You making a documentary about homelessness when you are in fact homeless yourself. Why don't you give me the camera and you can be in your own film.'

Rupert had been the stock reactionary in the famous house in Sussex. The counterpoint to Henry's political and David's artistic pretentions. He cared neither for art nor for social justice. He cared about money.

He was very brainy and very arrogant, the former somewhat making up for the latter but not quite. He had got a First in Mathematics and it was no surprise to the other members of the Radish Club when he became the first of their little graduation group to move to London and get a flat of his own. A circumstance Jimmy had been delighted to exploit. Rupert didn't mind the situation either as they were both still in that happy, unattached, unencumbered stage of their young lives when it was possible to continue to live like students even though they weren't students any more.

'I'll pay the rent, you can do the booze runs and attract the totty,' Rupert said. 'Babes always love you and I can have your sloppy seconds. We'll get drunk and shagged three nights a week.'

They managed the drunk bit at least and for a month or two had been happy together. But the situation couldn't go on for ever and one day when Rupert returned from the bank to find Jimmy still under the Batman duvet on the couch where he had left him that morning, the conversation turned to what Jimmy actually intended to *do* with his life.

'Perhaps you should rob your father's bank,' Rupert suggested. 'Perfect crime if you ask me. After all, you have all the inside information that you need and yet would never be suspected. Victimless too, in any real sense. I mean the money's only notional anyway and the insurance companies are thieves who deserve to be fleeced.'

Rupert was so right-wing it was actually quite funny. That was his shtick, his conversational thing. He called himself a libertarian and liked to shock people by saying things like 'A crack whore and her pimp are the perfect business model. No, I'm serious, capitalism in its purest form. The free market operating as it should.

Supply and demand. Goods and services. Management and labour. I fail to see a moral dilemma. For fuck's sake, let them get on with it.'

Rupert had got his job at the Royal Lancashire Bank before he'd even graduated and everybody knew he was on the fast track to making millions both for himself and for his bank. There was just something about him, a sort of cheerfully ruthless amoral charm, that and a terrific command of figures, which meant you *knew* he would be rich. When Derek Corby had been introduced to Rupert at Jimmy's graduation, old Mr Corby had said, 'I hear you're going to be a banker like me,' to which Rupert had drawled, 'Not *quite* like you, Mr Corby.'

As the son of a commercial haulier he wasn't actually posh at all, but on the day he arrived at Sussex he started pretending to be posh, calling people 'old boy' and girls 'totty' and experimenting with a pipe. By the time he left he had clearly come to believe that he *was* posh, wearing brogues, tweedy jackets and sometimes even a cravat. Years later, after he had married the genuinely posh Amanda and was on his way to running a major bank, Amanda explained to him that brogues and tweed hadn't been posh since the fifties. Under her tutelage he would become rather trendy, favouring designer suits and hundred-pound haircuts. At twenty Rupert was trying to look like he was forty, and at forty he would be trying to look like he was twenty.

It was Rupert who suggested that Jimmy forget his

pathetic notions of a media career and try financial trading.

'Five years from now the BBC will employ only women, ethnics and poofs. What's more, the commercial media will be owned by proper professional Americans, as indeed it should be since they're the only people on Earth who have the first idea about entertainment. You wouldn't stand a chance in either, Jim lad. No, the only place left where a man can still be a man is in money. You're too thick and too badly educated to bank, so I suggest you trade.'

'Trade in what?' Jimmy enquired.

'Trade in wealth.'

'What do I know about money?'

'You know you *like* it, don't you?'

'Of course. Who doesn't?'

'Then that's all you need to know.'

It had been as simple as that. Rupert made a call to his friend Piers that very evening. Piers had attended the same minor private school as Rupert (who had been a scholarship boy) and hence could be prevailed upon to do a favour. He was at a firm called Mason Jervis who traded in a thing called 'futures' and who, like most of the city, were on a roll. They were looking for new traders, young, energetic guys to work the phones. No previous experience required, all you needed was a strong nerve, a free, creative spirit and balls of titanium. Rupert assured Piers that Jimmy had all these things.

'Piers mate,' he drawled into his fancy new mobile, 'Jimmy Corby's balls could handle a direct hit from a laser-guided smart bomb.'

Jimmy had never thought of himself as a kind of testicular Rambo. But his friend Rupert had gone to the same school as a bloke who had jobs on offer, so Jimmy was in.

After that he just went with the flow.

He told himself that he was doing it for a laugh. Secretly observing some weird post-yuppie world. He would do six months, earn enough to spend a winter snowboarding and then leave. Perhaps he would write a movie about it, working title *Thatcher's Children*. He'd read an article in *Time Out* about how the Brit movie industry was back in the game. Surely they'd lap it up. Lots of guys from his uni were now independent film producers and they couldn't all do movies about gay launderette owners or Empire nostalgia.

But inside his first month Jimmy knew that he wouldn't be writing any movies about traders. And he wouldn't be taking any time off to go snowboarding either. Who the hell would want to slide down some French Alp when you could be *surfing the future*?

'I'm a time traveller!' he shouted at his new mates as he ordered champagne and beer at the end of his first month on the floor, a month in which he had earned Mason Jervis thousands of pounds and gained an appreciative nod from Piers. 'I'm Michael J. Fox! I get in my time-machine DeLorean car, I go to the future and I *bring back money!*'

He told the same story to his old mates on the first curry night after he became a trader.

'It's just so fucking *exciting*,' Jimmy burbled. 'You take notional money, make a fantasy trade, hold on to your bollocks and out comes real money!'

'What? Out of your bollocks?' Henry asked.

'Might as well be. I am the man with golden bollocks.'

His new enthusiasm came as quite a surprise for some members of the old gang. Jimmy had never been a breadhead. He *liked* money but he had never been obsessed with it. He got it, he spent it. That was it with Jim, and when he didn't have it he lived off sliced bread and chocolate stolen from the Student Union shop.

But the truth was that it wasn't the money that obsessed Jimmy. It was the process of making it, the *trading*. The new, wonderful, high-octane guy-world in which he and a group of equally young, devil-may-care, fun-loving blokes *created money*. It felt so utterly exhilarating and also sort of hilarious. Here was the one thing everybody on earth wanted, dreamed about and worried about all the time and he and the guys were actually *making* the stuff out of thin air. If it wasn't so utterly beautiful it would be a crime.

He and his father immediately clashed. Jimmy would turn up waving a bottle of champagne and a sack of washing, suggesting that he take his parents to lunch in some country-house gastro hotel. His dad would point out that the sandwiches were already made for the fishing. Jimmy and his mum would hug and then he and his dad would argue. Derek Corby thought Jim's view of trading was baffling; worse, it was offensive.

'I'll tell you what stocks and shares are, my lad,' he told his grinning son. 'Stocks and shares represent part ownership in a company. If the company is successful then the stock price goes up. If the company is failing then the price goes down.'

Jimmy and his mother would exchange glances as if to say that Dad was off on one again, and Derek would continue to go off on it. 'The job of a responsible stockbroker is to study the performance of a company and determine whether the performance of that company is likely to go up or down. Having made his calculations, he then makes a prudent investment on behalf of his client. That's how it's done. End of story. And if you *don't* do it that way, Jimmy, it will end in tears. That I can promise you.'

'Dad, you're insane,' the newly confident and bullish Jimmy insisted. 'The value of a company doesn't have to have anything to do with what that company's actually worth!'

'I beg your pardon?' Derek Corby enquired. 'Something's value has nothing to do with its value?'

'Of course not. Not its *actual practical* value. Who cares about that? A trader doesn't hang around waiting for companies to post their yearly figures in order to find out what they're actually worth. How dull would that be?'

This was too much for a man who had begun his career at the National City Bank in 1968.

'Dull! DULL!' Derek Corby spluttered into his Scotch and lemonade. 'What has "dull" to do with the price of eggs! We're discussing *stockbroking*!'

Father and son were existing on different planets. Living in different ages. Never once in his entire life had Derek Corby imagined that the financial sector should be *interesting*. Quite the opposite. He believed that by its very nature it should be dull, very, very dull. That was why it was the financial sector. If you wanted your work to be interesting, find another profession. Become a soldier or an engineer or an entertainer in the halls. Derek Corby had sacrificed eight hours a day, five and a half days a week all his adult life to dull. It was what he was paid for. That was why he worked, not to be *stimulated* but to earn a decent living so that he could support his family and enjoy his leisure. What he did at *home* was interesting. Bridge nights, fishing trips and home brewing. *Holidays* were interesting, not work, two weeks rambling in the Lake District. That was why he worked, so that he might appreciate the rewards of his labour.

Jimmy always ended up drinking the whole bottle of champagne. His father declined to share it and his mother had only a thimbleful.

'The difference between you and me, Dad, is you *earn* money. I *make* it.'

'And as far as I'm aware,' Derek replied, '*making* money is inflationary. They *made* money in Germany in 1923 and the result was people needed a wheelbarrow full of Reichsmarks to buy a box of matches. The rules of economics don't change.'

'Oh yes they do, Dad. Cos you see we don't just make the money, we make the rules too.'

'Yes,' Derek replied, 'you used to make up your own rules at Monopoly, I seem to remember. I tried to explain to you at the time that it was called cheating.'

'Dad, come on,' Jimmy said, using his twinkling smile on the one person on whom it had no effect at all. 'It isn't cheating if you win.'

An essential hairdryer

Henry sat in his little office and despaired of the way things were. Here was the party flogging the nation's highest honours to the very people whose excesses Labour had been elected to curtail, and yet here *he* was struggling to make ends meet. Agonizing about whether he could put the cost of his wife Jane's hairdryer on his expenses chit.

He, Henry Baker, who struggled every day on behalf of the people's party and on behalf of his own constituents, was forced to live in a kind of genteel poverty. While Rupert Bennett and Jimmy Corby, *Jimmy Corby* of all people, were multimillionaires.

It was insane. He was spending his precious time trying to argue to himself that because he sometimes used his wife's hairdryer to dry his own hair, it was a legitimate professional expense. After all, he had long hair and clearly it was his duty as a Member of the Mother of Parliaments to appear at Prime Minister's Questions with it looking its best. That was obvious, surely?

What a waste of time. What a *criminal* waste of the time of an important parliamentarian to be forced to count every penny.

MPs' pay was a scandal. It was the press's fault, nasty, mealy-mouthed hypocrites. They acted as if MPs didn't deserve to be paid at all! Of course they *hadn't* been paid in the old days and the country had been run by mill owners and the aristocracy, the only people who could afford the luxury of a political career. Was that a good way of doing things? No!

If the people wanted to be governed *by* the people, then they should damn well expect to pay the people to do it.

Henry wrote a note to accompany the claim form that he would submit to the accounts committee:

Sir,

My hair is rather thick and luxuriant, a physical fact which causes me no small inconvenience. When I wash it, on warm days I am content to stick my head out of the window for a few minutes until my hair is dry. This affords me time to listen to the previous day's debates on my iPod (see separate claim). However, when it is raining I am forced to find another method by which I may appear before Parliament and my constituents in a hirsutely appropriate manner. My wife's hairdryer seems to me to be the most cost-effective method of achieving this. I estimate that my usage accounts for approximately 40 per cent of its operational time and I therefore enclose an invoice to cover 40 per cent of its cost (original receipt lost but Argos Catalogue number and price list attached).

Henry almost tore out his perfectly arranged hair with frustration. This was simply ridiculous.

He earned a fraction, a *tiny* fraction, of what he could command were he to go and work in the City. A fraction even of what he could get hiring out his skills to local government. Yet despite that, he had chosen to be a servant of the people. Why should he not be paid an appropriate amount, an amount that was comparable to professionals in other fields? Why should he be forced to such ridiculous lengths to get what in any nation with a media that had the remotest sense of proportion would be his by right?

It was immoral, that was what it was. He deserved better.

Henry turned to the issue of secretarial assistance. Jane often helped him with his letters. She was at home writing anyway and it gave her a break from working on her novel. Surely she should be paid for that? It was only fair.

Money is the new Rock 'n' Roll

It was astonishing. In quite a short time Jimmy had gone from being undeniably the poorest member of his little uni gang to being the richest. Richer even than Rupert. Which was, as Rupert himself pointed out, *seriously* insane.

David was still studying to be an architect. Lizzie (with Robson tagging along) was offering haircuts plus 'American-style' muffins from a stall on the Portobello Road, and Henry was going crazy reading unsolicited manuscripts for a publishing house while trying to get a local party to select him as a candidate at a forthcoming by-election.

And Jimmy, *Jimmy Corby*, the gang's good-natured Jack the lad who had scrounged bacon and eggs off every one of them back in Sussex, had lapped them all.

'Quite incredible,' they said to each other in amazement. 'Jimmy's rich.'

He didn't look very rich in those early years. He still slept among pizza boxes and empty beer cans. It was true that he now owned the pit in which he festered rather than passing out on other people's floors, but apart from that nobody would have known that by '95, after two years at Mason Jervis, at the age of twenty-three Jimmy was making a hundred and fifty K a year with half that again as a Christmas bonus.

His only real luxury was clothes. Not designer clothes, just new clothes. New clothes every single day. He was now working so hard at Mason Jervis that he had no time for laundry, no time even to make regular trips back to Sussex to get his mother to do it. Time spent worrying about your sweaty jocks was time spent away from the phones. Time spent away from all those hypnotic numbers on all those screens. Numbers that continued to climb and climb and he needed to *be there* to hitch a ride. While he was wasting real time doing a wash, a bundle of coffee beans years away in virtual time might have dipped and rallied. He needed to be there, otherwise how would he buy in the dip and sell in the rally? Fuck laundry. He needed to *trade*.

For a while, despite his wealth Jimmy had not been

averse to turning yesterday's pants inside out and calling them clean (even if he'd done the same trick the day before). Eventually, however, it was possible for Jimmy to do the sniff test at five metres and Piers took him gently aside and whispered a word or two about hygiene. After that Jim developed the habit of paying one of the girls to go out and grab him a new shirt, socks and underwear every day during her coffee break.

It became part of his morning routine, like his coffee and bar of chocolate. He would arrive at work in his previous day's clothes, do three hours' trading and then at about ten thirty pop into the toilet and bung on the new threads that the girl had brought him. He'd slip her a fiver for her trouble and bin the previous day's clothes on his way back to his desk.

A quick chew on a bit of toothpaste chewing gum and he was fresh and ready to spend another long day in the future.

It was obvious to his friends that Jimmy had become addicted to his work. Lizzie and Robson were particularly worried and tried to interest him in other things, like the theatre, which Jimmy thought was complete shit.

'Why go to the theatre when you can see a movie?'

'Because the theatre is offering the latest David Hare and the cinema is offering *Batman Forever*.'

'Exactly.'

But in fact Jimmy didn't even go to the movies any

more. Like many a gambler before him, he lived only to play the game. The difference between him and the traditional sad obsessive was that his was a game at which it was very difficult to lose and, unlike the poker players regularly testifying at the Canary Wharf branch of Gamblers Anonymous, Jimmy's illness was making him richer.

Richer. But no less screwed up.

It was obvious to anyone who cared to think about it that there was a downside awaiting Jimmy and his highly overexcited colleagues. Physical and mental exhaustion or, as the Americans put it more succinctly, burnout.

The human nervous system was not built to spend fourteen hours a day in a state of high tension and the other ten drunk, wired, having sex or unconscious. The vast majority of the guys on Jimmy's floor were destined to push it too far, lose their edge and be replaced by younger players.

Jimmy was heading that way faster than most.

'You'll be useless in five years and your firm will dump you,' Rupert assured him cheerfully when the old gang met at Khan's in Kensington for their regular curry and beer. 'But *what* a five years, Jim boy! People go their whole lives without having a single *day* on the sort of roll you're on. In the future people will look back and not be able to *believe* how much money you guys made.'

'That's right,' Jimmy, hollow-eyed and pasty-faced,

always agreed. 'You know my motto. Live fast, die young, leave a beautiful corpse, eh?'

Henry, who had spent all day searching for a decent typescript among the great mound of hopefuls that was his publishers' slush pile (while trying to summon up the courage to recommend his own under a different name), was having none of this. He earned less in a week than Jimmy was about to spend on a bottle of vintage champagne and he found Jimmy's attempts to pass off his sweaty-faced, coke-fuelled gluttony as boho chic deeply irritating.

'James,' he said sternly, flicking his blond locks aside, 'the phrase "Live fast, die young and leave a beautiful corpse" was coined to describe life in the *real* fast lane. Not the bloody City of London but down on the mean streets and out on the edge. It describes true originals who tested the boundaries of the culture and rewrote the rule book of youth. Jimi Hendrix, Sid Vicious, Kurt Cobain. Not always pretty but always original, guys who really did take it all the way, not by getting rich and drunk but by rejecting society's values in pursuit of the true punk ethic. Doing it, my pampered friend, for Rock 'n' Roll.'

'Henry,' Jimmy replied equally sternly but still with that disarming twinkle in his bloodshot eyes, 'Bowie just floated his back catalogue on the London Stock Exchange. Mick's in a tax haven. These days City traders *are* Rock 'n' Roll.'

In a way Jimmy was right. In some ways he was flying

the flag for the Rock 'n' Roll ideal. While an increasing number of musicians were turning vegan and going to the gym, while Sting was informing the world about the rainforests and tantric sex, Jimmy was *larging it*. In a different club every night, heading for self-destruction with the same relentless tunnel vision that had led the likes of Sid Vicious to their doom. Living on his nerves and his wits and feeding them only with booze, convenience food and endless columns of digits. When he added cocaine to the mix he was clearly setting himself up for a major car crash. A crash which, while it might not kill him, would certainly leave him with severe depression and therefore of no further use to Mason Jervis, a company that lived or died on reckless optimism, not drug-induced paranoid introspection.

This would almost certainly have been Jimmy's fate had he not met Monica.

Monica saved Jimmy because in her he finally found something more fascinating than gambling on the fantasy future of foreign agricultural products.

To Jimmy she was *that* beautiful. That much fun. That much more Rock 'n' Roll.

'Christ in a bucket,' Rupert observed when Jimmy explained this point to him, 'she must be one cracking bit of totty.'

'She is, Roop,' Jimmy replied, the love light glinting in his suddenly once more bright and shining eyes, 'she is one cracking bit of totty.'

Thank *God* for Monica

Monica and Jimmy got together over sandwiches. Literally. Their eyes met over the big tray of them that hung from her neck, lodged beneath her bosom which she later admitted she had been shamelessly using as a visual sales pitch. She was trying to sell Jimmy avocado, alfalfa and beetroot on walnut, a combination which, when she got to know him (later that day), she would realize was not his thing at all. Jimmy was very much a peanut butter sort of bloke, or Kraft cheese slices. And, above all, on white. Sliced white. That was how you made a sandwich. Pretty much all of the guys on the floor agreed.

Monica and her friend Tip had founded their own catering firm. It was called Sand Witches and they both wore pointy black hats. Their idea had been that all those thousands of unbelievably busy people in the City would not have time to go out for lunch and were working too hard to think about it anyway. Tip's brother was a trader and he'd told her that they all lived off Mars bars. The girls had therefore had the idea of bringing food, *seriously good food*, directly to the consumer. They were unbelievably excited about their idea, convinced it was a real winner.

Which it was. Unfortunately, three or four thousand other girls had had the same idea on pretty much the same day. In terms of female career options in the mid-nineties, catering companies were the new nursing and for a while it seemed as if every female graduate in Britain was setting one up. Unfortunately, this glut of bright sparky girls with their pesto and focaccia coincided with the arrival of Starbucks and Coffee Republic, who also sold sandwiches. It did not take long for almost all the sparky girls to go out of business and, apart from the two or three lucky ones who went on to cater for film premières and Gwyneth Paltrow's dinner parties or design food for Marks and Spencer, they all gave up.

Lizzie was one of those who prospered. She and Robson had ditched haircuts by that time and moved into food. Somehow, as with everything she touched, Lizzie had made it work and by the turn of the millennium Lizzie's Sarnies were being sold in Sainsbury's.

Monica and Tip, on the other hand, had lasted less than a week. They had not even got as far as buying their third batch of bread. The work had been hard and horribly unrewarding. None of the men in shirtsleeves glancing up from their phones had wanted their sandwiches, although plenty of them had wanted Monica and Tip.

Jimmy wasn't interested in Tip but he had wanted Monica right off the bat. He had elevated his gaze from her artfully exposed cleavage to encounter a fresh, open face with pale, porcelain skin, a splash of rosiness at the cheeks and large, almost startled-looking chestnut eyes. The fringe which hung above them and the long tresses which tumbled from beneath her witch's hat were of that deep, rich brunette in which hints of crimson lie hiding, waiting only for sunlight to make them sparkle.

Even as Jimmy asked Monica if she had any peanut butter and jelly ones, he knew that it was love at first sight.

'Jelly?' Monica asked. 'As in jelly-and-ice-cream jelly?'

'No,' Jimmy replied, 'jelly as in the American word for jam.'

'Oh,' said Monica, 'are you American then?'

'Uhm . . . no,' Jimmy replied, slightly thrown. He and his friends habitually used as many American words and expressions as they could, and nobody had ever thought it strange before. 'What I meant was peanut butter and jam.'

'Oh,' said Monica. 'Well no, I haven't.'

Then Jimmy asked her out and it was Monica's turn to be taken aback. It was, after all, very sudden, and not merely in the sense that he had hit on her within seconds of declining a radish, rocket and chickpea wrap.

They all did *that*.

'How about you let *me* do the catering, babes?' they'd drawl, with eyes flicking from her face to her cleavage. 'I finish at midnight but Annabel's does a serious all-night breakfast.'

Monica knew their game all right. They wanted *her* for breakfast and ta-ta in the morning. A line of coke and they'd be back to the future without a single thought for the immediate past and she'd be left doing the walk of shame with her dirty knickers stuffed in her handbag. Well, no thank you, there'd been enough horny boys at college and at least they had the decency to hang around in the morning in the hope of cadging a piece of toast and Marmite.

But Jimmy's offer was different. He wanted to take her out immediately. Right there and then. He was actually offering to leave his phone and buy her a coffee.

Even though she'd only been wandering the trading floors for three days, Monica knew that this was highly unusual behaviour. These guys were *obsessed*. They *never* left their phones while the trade was on. They wanted sex, of course, but sex, like everything else, had to be on their terms and Monica and Tip had soon realized that if these blokes could have shagged you while continuing to shout into their phones those would be the best terms of all.

And now one of them, a particularly cute one with his boyish face and lovely mop of sandy hair, his brand-new shirt clearly worn straight from the shop, the heavy folds of its packaged state firmly subdividing his chest, this nice-looking, eager, youthful chap had actually hung up both the phones he had been working and offered to take her for a coffee. *There and then.*

'Don't you have to keep working?' Monica asked. 'I thought that was the rule.'

Jimmy was aware that one or two of the other guys had already noted that he was engaged with a sandwich chick for more than the usual brief moment.

'Babes,' he said, flicking his cuff to reveal the gold Rolex beneath (actually a Hong Kong fake), 'the Jimster makes his own rules.'

The flicker of disappointment and distaste that passed across Monica's sweet features was for Jimmy that thing which his American colleagues had started to refer to as a 'wake-up call'. Something stirred deep in his memory, back before the nearly two years of phones and computer digits had numbed his personality, destroyed his good taste, ruined his sense of decorum and buried his self-awareness. He could remember what a complete wanker sounded like.

It sounded like him. Jimmy 'the Jimster' Corby.

'Did I say that?' he asked.

Monica nodded glumly. 'Yes. You called me "Babes" and you called yourself "The Jimster".'

'I didn't! It's a lie. You're a crazy woman. I should call Security.'

Monica couldn't help smiling at the speed with which he was recovering, but she stood firm.

'Also you thought I'd be impressed because you're wearing a Rolex.'

'It's a fake! I swear! Two hundred Hong Kong dollars! I may still have the receipt to prove it!'

Monica smiled again, but that did not mean she was letting him off the hook.

'That's even worse. Trying to impress a girl on the cheap. But it doesn't matter anyway because I have a rule that I never go for coffee with boys who refer to themselves in the third person. Or people who prefix their names with a definite article.'

'Pardon?' Jimmy said, his head swimming a bit. People did not normally bother with full sentences where he hung out.

'In plain English, babe. Bye bye, the Jimster.'

She turned and Jimmy cried out.

'Stop!' he said. Loudly and firmly.

He didn't know why he did it; he'd known her less than a minute. Heads turned. Piers, who still headed up Jimmy's group, looked up from his computer. Tip, who'd been working the derivatives desk next door, turned round too.

Jimmy didn't care. It was a scene from a movie. He'd called out in a crowded room to a girl whose name he didn't even know and now she was turning back towards him and giving him the cutest 'yeah, what?' expression he had ever seen.

'My name's Jimmy. I've been here for nearly two years,' he said, 'and I've never taken a break. I think I've earned one. Please, let me buy you a coffee.'

Jimmy didn't care about the laddish 'woohs' that followed him and Monica as they left the floor together. Nor did he mind that Piers would certainly want to know what the *fuck* was going on when he got back. What he cared about was the beautiful, funny girl whose name he would shortly discover was Monica.

Perhaps it was an instinct for self-preservation that led him to fall hopelessly in love that day. It certainly saved him. Saved him from career burnout and saved him from turning permanently into the appalling idiot he had been rapidly becoming. Saved him from becoming a man who called women he'd never met before 'babes' and who referred to himself as the Jimster.

Strangely enough, it also made him a much more useful operative for Mason Jervis. A potential group leader who would rapidly overtake Piers and be given charge of a national desk.

Loving Monica gave Jimmy a sense of perspective. Reminded him of outside interests. Reintroduced him to the importance of social communication. Brought to his attention the half-forgotten notion that you could do more interesting things with your earnings than count them. In another American term that had recently crossed the Atlantic, she 'grounded' him.

They were married just four months after they had first met. Lizzie catered the wedding, did the flowers and designed the invitations. David designed and supervised the erection of the marquees. Henry read the bit from

Shakespeare about 'the marriage of true minds'. Rupert sourced, ordered and paid for the wine ('so I'll be sure there's something decent to drink') and Robson was best man.

Effortlessly, easily and *so* satisfyingly, Monica was absorbed into Jimmy's little gang.

'Thank *God* for Mon,' Lizzie said. 'She saved Jimmy.' And they all agreed that she had.

The phone rings

Despite their elation over Lizzie's spectacularly generous offer of financial help, Jimmy and Monica still had the immediate problem of a screaming toddler and a screaming baby to deal with.

'You're rich, you're poor, you're rich again,' Monica laughed, 'but some things don't change, eh? Keeps things in perspective, doesn't it?'

'That's one way of putting it,' Jimmy replied.

She drained her glass. 'I'll take Lillie up to bed. You try and get Cressie to sleep down here.'

And so Jimmy began his long and weary perambulation of the basement of their Notting Hill house. Pushing the buggy round the huge glass coffee table, past the vast flat-screen towards the kitchen area, along the breakfast bar, around the polished granite water feature (no longer working), past the aquarium which was set in the wall to mirror the position of the equally indented flat-screen TV opposite, around the central fireplace with its stainless-steel hood and flue (as big as the roof of a shed) and back to the coffee table. It was a circuitous journey, particularly since Cressida's buggy was of the large, chunky-wheeled variety, built more for mountain walks than kitchen perambulations. Also the number of toys scattered about the floor further impeded a smooth passage. Jodie used to pick those up, she and the three day staff.

The walk was fraught with tension for Jimmy as he desperately wanted to keep Cressida quiet so that Monica could grab an hour of sleep before Lillie's first night feed. Just as he knew she would be upstairs willing Lillie to go down so that when Jimmy did finally get to bed he might manage a bit of rest and hence not be feeling dead when he faced his mountain of problems in the morning.

After a while Jimmy dispensed with the buggy, which wasn't doing the trick at all, and picked Cressida up. He knew that the only way to keep her quiet was to carry on walking, holding her to him so that her head lay on his shoulder. If he did that and sang 'Morningtown Ride' to her over and over and over again, then all would be well. Cressida would not scream and eventually she would fall asleep.

If Jimmy should deviate from those rules in any way whatsoever, the child would scream. Jimmy knew that as certainly as night follows day. He was not allowed to change arm. He was not allowed to stand still, scratch his arse or stop singing, and above all, *above all*, he was not allowed to sit down.

No matter how gently he tried to do it and no matter how meticulously he maintained Cressida's position relative to his chest, Cressie always knew when he was trying to sit down. Cressie knew if Jimmy was even thinking about sitting down. It was as if she had her own in-built altimeter that was programmed to go off if ever her distance from the floor fell below three feet.

Jimmy looked down at the little sleeping face. How beautiful she looked, that tiny person who exhausted him so. She was smiling now and reminding him so much of Monica (even though some people said Cressie looked like him, which Jimmy thought was just mad). He smiled back as he walked and whispered his song, now with a tiny spring in his step. One moment like that, one moment contemplating that perfect little face, was worth a thousand sleepless nights.

It helped of course that he could occasionally grab a swig of wine too, dipping in his stride as he passed the kitchen bench where he had opened another bottle, sweeping his glass up with the hand he used to steady Cressida's head and chugging a swig between verse and chorus. Unconditional love and undying devotion were all very well in keeping a man walking and singing through the still watches of the night, but a drink or two didn't do any harm either.

Jimmy would not be marking these extra units of booze on the list stuck to the fridge. It was his little secret, the only one he kept from his wife. She was breastfeeding, she had to watch her intake for fear of damaging Lillie's brain cells, but Jimmy wasn't. He could bash his liver for six and drink himself into a coma and Lillie's little brain would remain unaffected, and so, while maintaining the fiction of solidarity with his wife's enforced semi-discipline, he allowed himself many a sneaky swig when she wasn't looking.

Besides, he was celebrating. Drinking to the first glimmer of hope that had appeared on his horizon in a long time. True, it was not exactly a triumph to go two million pounds into debt to a couple of your oldest friends. Not something to be proud of or something he would ever have dreamed of considering even six months earlier. But these were unique times, capitalism's uncharted waters, and the rules were changing day by day. Jimmy knew, he absolutely *knew*, that if he could just get through this period without the whole thing imploding, his assets would regain their value and all would be well. Like millions of other guys across the world in early 2009, all he needed was a bridging loan, something which the banks were no longer prepared to offer. But Jimmy had friends, he had contacts. Why not use them? That was how it worked. It was how life had worked since the dawn of time. Family, friends, tribe, loyalty. That was what counted. A girl he knew from Sussex was going to help him out, that was all. He would have done the same for her, unquestionably.

Jimmy had always been generous with his cash. He had once given an entire day's personal profit to Comic Relief. A whole *day*. That was serious money.

Cressida was beginning to purr gently . . . Was she going down? Jimmy could scarcely dare to hope. It was only just past one. Gently he drew to a halt, and still Cressida remained unmoved. He had to try the ultimate test: could he sit down? Hovering over a chair, he slowly bent his knees. No good! He'd tried to rush it, she'd only been half gone, her altimeter was still taking readings. Instantly the bomb went off, but before she could ramp up the volume Jimmy was moving again. Slickly, smoothly, without a pause or a jolt, he straightened his back and was off again, moving, singing, patting and cooing.

She might not be asleep yet but he had at least prevented her from screaming blue murder and waking Monica. That was what mattered.

Then disaster struck. A huge, terrible, jarring noise ripped through the peace of the kitchen, so that the very fish in the wall looked up and took notice. Jimmy almost dropped Cressida as the high-pitched voice tore at his eardrums and ripped into his brain:

'London Bridge is falling down,
Falling down, falling down.
London Bridge is falling down,
My fair lady.'

It was that stuffed Pokémon toy. It had caught him many times in the past but not for several weeks. Now, however, consumed in thoughts about how best to distribute Lizzie and Robson's millions to avoid the money getting sucked into paying off non-essential debts, Jimmy had strayed from his path a fraction and fallen victim to one of the numerous electronic noise traps that littered their basement floor.

Since being forced to take a hand in the raising of his children Jimmy had learned that in the modern age no toy is silent, every single one emits endlessly repeated, mind-numbingly unforgettable, ball-crunchingly irritating tunes and jingles. And the big furry yellow Pokémon was the worst because its song was so loud, so high and so stupidly speeded up.

Cressida started crying instantly, and moments later Jimmy could hear her baby sister reciprocating upstairs. Monica and Lillie were two floors up, but when the Japanese created an irritating Pokémon toy they wanted the world to know. Inevitably, the next thing Jimmy heard was Monica. She had pushed the intercom button on their fiendishly complex internal phone system and her voice, metallic and desperate, emanated from the conference speaker.

'I had just half closed my eyes,' she said.

'Sorry,' Jimmy replied to the wall-mounted unit.

'I was dreaming that everything was going to be all right.'

'Everything *is* going to be all right.'

'Good. 'Night.'

''Night.'

Cressida finally fell asleep at 2.40am, after which (having sat with her for five minutes to make absolutely sure) Jimmy gently took her upstairs and began the infinitely slow process of lowering her into her cot. Fading out his song and gently disengaging first one hand and then the other before straightening up and slowly retreating as the last whispered chorus disappeared into silence. No *Danger UXB* technician in the Second World War ever approached an unexploded bomb with more care than Jimmy did the process of detaching himself from his sleeping daughter.

Lillie for once wasn't feeding but was sleeping peacefully in her Moses basket while Monica snored gently under the duvet. Toby was asleep next door. Incredibly, four out of five members of his family were asleep at the same moment. Jimmy wondered whether this could be the first time that had happened since Jodie. He almost felt like getting out the video camera.

The situation was so unusual that Jimmy thought about going through to the spare room to avoid any possibility of spoiling the peace. He often slept in the spare room, on those nights when Lillie simply would not give up the boob and Monica was half demented with exhaustion and he had to go to the site in the morning. But he didn't like doing it. It made the evidence too clear that they were no longer a man and woman in the true and proper sense of the words, just two jaded careworkers who happened to share shifts. When he had been rich he had never once gone to the spare room, even when Mon had been feeding Toby and Cressida. They had so much help both night and day that, tired though he was, he had always known he could sleep because Monica would in extremis express the milk and hand the baby over to the night nanny. For Lillie there were no such luxuries, which made Jimmy all the more determined to remain in his marital bed as often as possible. His disastrous career collapse had felt like castration enough without him giving up on sleeping in the same bed as his wife.

He decided to risk it and so undressed very slowly and in absolute silence, constantly vigilant for any electronic toys and beeping teddies that might be lurking underfoot. Approaching the bed, Jimmy gingerly lifted what was left of his side of the covers, debating in his mind whether Monica had left him enough to sleep under. Her habit of wrapping herself in 90 per cent of the duvet and then being extremely grumpy when Jimmy attempted to tug a little back was something that he had learned to live with. Of course Monica was convinced that she never had more than her fair share and if anything it was he who stole the duvet. It was an issue on which they could only agree to differ.

Determined not to disturb her, Jimmy decided that he could probably get by with what she had left him and so he lay down on the bed beside her and closed his eyes.

He had feared that it would be one of those nights on which he was too tired to sleep. When he would lie there, desperate, shivering under a half-covering of duvet, his eyelids twitching in a kind of hysterical half-wakefulness. In this dizzying state his mind tormented him with the urgent necessity of getting to sleep because of the mountain of shit that was waiting for him in the morning. Nights when he knew that if he didn't get to sleep he would be completely and terminally unfit to work the following day, and equally certain that it was only the knowledge that he needed to get to sleep that was keeping him awake.

On this night, however, Jimmy did not suffer this terrible condition. Perhaps it was because for the first night in so many awful nights he was hopeful. Hopeful of a solution to the maelstrom of circumstances that was sucking him and his family under. Perhaps it was because, all in all, he had drunk more than a bottle of wine plus a little Scotch. Perhaps it was because, despite all the hell that he was going through, he still had the love of his wife and children to sustain him and having all four of them sleeping peacefully so close by filled him with happiness. For whatever reason, on this particular night Jimmy slipped effortlessly into the arms of Morpheus before the clock radio on his bedside table had flicked from 2.59 to 3.00.

At 3.15 the phone rang.

A worm in the Big Apple

Maybe the five doormen noticed something was wrong. Maybe they didn't.

Of course no building really needs *five* doormen, but then the Castle Tower apartment building in New York City was never about utility, it was always about excess. The sort of people with apartments in the Castle liked to see a lot of staff about the place.

Maybe the half-dozen members of the concierge department spotted a new, more sombre mood in Lew Bronski as he emerged from the elevator and strode through the vast cathedral-like foyer, past the phalanx of uniformed lift boys towards the great glass revolving doors. Maybe the guys who saluted him as he stepped out of the building and into his armoured stretch limo waiting on Fifth Avenue noticed a change in Lew that day. A little tension in the jaw? A falter in the walk?

Maybe they didn't. A lifetime in high finance had taught Lew Bronski to keep a poker face at all times and he was maintaining one now at this supremely challenging moment in his life. This moment of complete and utter ruin.

Lew Bronski. Mr Wall Street. Genuine New York royalty. Chair of just about every high-end Jewish charity on the East Coast. Money guru to the stars. The guy who couldn't walk through his own country club without people throwing money at him to invest. King Midas himself. Lucky Lew the Lucky Jew was about to turn himself in to the New York City Police Department as a prelude to what he knew would be the rest of his life behind bars.

Late call

Before the second ring had finished crashing around the room and bouncing off the walls and the inside of Jimmy's skull, both babies were screaming and Monica had sprung up like a corpse popping out of the ground in *The Night of the Living Dead*. She yelped, she jerked, she looked wildly this way and that and then fell out of bed. There she scrabbled around on the floor, both awake and in a deep, deep sleep at the same time, attempting in her semi-conscious state to breastfeed Cressida's teddy bear, which immediately began to broadcast its pre-recorded version of 'The Teddy Bears' Picnic'.

Jimmy was in a marginally better state. He had been asleep for only a quarter of an hour so the telephone had not summoned him from quite such a faraway place as it had Monica. Nonetheless he had been fully immersed in the unconscious free fall of exhaustion and now he was twanging back like a man on the end of a bungee rope. One arm had gone to sleep and he flailed about with the other in an effort to find the phone and stop the terrible noise. All he did was knock the clock, his watch and his glass of water off the bedside table, in the process soaking the book he never got round to reading.

Through the ringing he heard Toby calling from the other room and, distracted though he was, it hurt him to the heart that in his sleepiness the boy was calling for Jodie. Jimmy hoped that Monica had not heard.

Finally he located the telephone, but at first he put the mouthpiece to his ear.

'Hello? Hello?' he blathered into the ear end of the phone.

'Yes, yes?' Monica was saying from the floor on the other side of the bed.

As if sensing the opportunity to make a bad situation worse, Cressida cranked up the volume a notch and began rattling the bars of her cot. She had a toddler's unerring ability to do and say the wrong things at the most brilliantly effective time. Her first words had been 'Poo poo' and she had said them loudly fourteen times during a rather solemn church service when Lizzie and Robson had restated their vows. Lizzie had been sweet about it but Monica could see she thought Monica should have taken Cressida out.

'Please, Cressida,' Jimmy pleaded, 'Daddy's trying to hear.'

'Jimmy?' a voice said on the other end of the line.

'What?' Jimmy replied.

'It's Lizzie.'

'Who?' Jimmy shouted back, hoping that he had misheard.

'Tell them to fuck off!' Monica called from the floor where she was on her knees between Cressida's cot and Lillie's Moses basket, trying to comfort them both at the same time.

'There there, Lillie! Mummy's here. Look, booby booby. Booby booby. Jimmy, you have to pick Cressie up!'

'I can't, I'm on the phone.'

'Who the hell is it? It's three fifteen in the morning! Just tell them to fuck off!'

'I can't hear who it is with Cressie and Lillie

screaming. Hang on,' he shouted into the phone, before throwing it down and staggering round the bed to gather up his other screaming daughter and begin an urgent chorus of 'Morningtown Ride'.

'Yes?' He grabbed the phone once more, in the hope of squeezing in a conversation between the verse about the driver at the engine and the verse about how maybe it would be raining. 'Sorry? Who's that?'

'Jimmy,' the rich, warm voice said. 'It's Lizzie.'

Jimmy felt himself go cold. Suddenly the screaming children seemed far away as he listened to Lizzie's lovely honeyed voice.

'Look, I'm sorry to ring you up at this stupid time,' she was saying, 'but I just had to speak you. You and Mon.'

It was like she was actually in the room and had punched him in the stomach. The wind was knocked out of him, the joy cruelly extinguished.

She and Robson were going to jack. Renege. Blow him out. Royally shaft him. That was it. Done deal. Done and dusted. Lifeline withdrawn. Why else would she phone at such an hour?

They wanted to get it over with. They'd talked and decided that lending money wasn't a good thing for 'mates' to do and they hadn't been able to sleep till they withdrew their offer. That was it. Had to be. Jimmy understood it all in a second. Once more he was buggered.

'Look, Liz,' he said, trying not to sound pathetic, 'it

doesn't matter about the time. I'd love to talk. Really. We need to talk. I'm going to take it downstairs.'

He put the phone down and turned to Monica, who was sitting cross-legged on the floor with Lillie on her breast.

'It's Liz,' he said. 'She must be having second thoughts. *Christ Almighty!*'

'But she promised . . .'

'Not in bloody writing. I should have gone round the minute she said it. This'll be about "friendship", about "mates", I know it will. Some bollocks about debt destroying it. *Fuck.*'

Jimmy was already out of the door, staggering slightly, still woozy from the booze. Monica stared at him like some undead creature who had risen from the lagoon.

'She's still on the line. I don't know, maybe I can talk her round,' Jimmy went on. 'I'll have to leave Cressida with you.'

He put Cressida down and she immediately started screaming again.

Still Monica did not reply, her eyes half rolled backwards in an agony of worry and sleeplessness. In the half-light of the room her pale skin was almost translucent and there were tears on her cheek. Jimmy longed to take her burdens from her but he had to get on to this. He had to turn Lizzie around. Otherwise the babies would still be screaming and they'd also be starving.

He would ask to talk to Robson. That was the way;

Robbo took a simple view of life. He wouldn't be worrying about the future of their fucking friendship. He would see that a friend was in trouble *now* and if that friend's friends did not help he wouldn't have a future in which to be friends.

This rather complex and rambling argument was forming in Jimmy's mind at break-neck speed as he rushed towards the stairs, and perhaps because of that distraction he did something he had not done for months. He forgot the stair gate.

He went over it head first, catching a foot between the bars of the collapsing barrier and falling with a terrible crash, ending up at full stretch down the first nine stairs with his feet still caught at the top and his head halfway to the bottom. Luckily he had taken the weight of the fall on his arms and by a miracle they had not shattered. It was a hell of a fall and a less fit, heavier man could easily have broken his back, but Jimmy was trim and in good shape so he ended up merely bruised and winded. Of course, being still half pissed helped to deaden the impact. A drunk man falls easy.

'Oh my God!' he heard Monica calling from above him. She had heard the crash and was now standing at the top of the stairs with Lillie in one arm and Cressida in the other. Toby was also there, his eyes filling with fear and sleepy bewilderment.

'Are you all right, Dad?'

'I'm fine! I'm OK,' Jimmy gasped back.

In considerable pain, Jimmy got up and staggered down the rest of the stairs to the ground floor and on down the stairs with the one remaining working bulb and across the basement room to the bench where the landline phone sat. Sinking to the floor, he reached up and pulled the phone cradle down by its wire.

'Hello, Lizzie. Are you still there?'

'Yes,' he heard his old friend's voice saying, 'I'm still here.'

'I'm really sorry about the delay,' Jimmy said, trying to calm down and prepare himself to make his pitch, a pitch more delicate and more crucial than any he had ever made during his days on the trading floor. 'Kids and all that. All three went off at once and then I fell down the stairs.'

'Oh God, I'm sorry. I shouldn't have rung.'

'No, please, Lizzie. Don't say that, I don't mind at all, we should talk. We need to talk.'

'Has Henry called? Did he tell you?' Lizzie's voice sounded almost relieved.

'Sorry? No, Henry hasn't called. Why – what's up?'

'Oh Jimmy.' Quite suddenly the beautiful silky voice broke with despair. 'Robbo's dead.'

The price of praise

Monica and Jimmy honeymooned in the States, doing the whole of Route 66 in a vintage Cadillac.

'Just let Henry try and tell me I'm not Rock 'n' Roll now,' Jimmy boasted, relishing the feel of the huge, shiny gas guzzler. Enjoying its lazy, soggy suspension, the satisfying roar of the big V8 under the hood. Stretching back on its padded bench seat which he and Monica re-christened whenever they passed a state line or a really exciting road sign covered with cool American destinations straight out of the song book of Rock, like Buffalo or Detroit.

They ended their trip in Las Vegas, where they reconfirmed their vows in the Elvis chapel and Monica bought Jimmy a skull ring to prove that although he was married he was still Rock 'n' Roll. Then, at the end of the most glorious month imaginable, they returned to Britain first class out of LAX to begin their married life together. But the honeymoon wasn't over by a long chalk. It was to stretch out in front of them for years ahead.

Jimmy's good fortune just wouldn't let up. Every year he made more money and every year he seemed to love Monica even more. Other men might torture themselves with thoughts of other women and some might even act upon those thoughts, but Jimmy never did. He was attracted to girls, of course, and on one occasion developed a horribly uncomfortable crush on one with variably coloured hair and nose rings who worked in the company PR department while waiting to become a rock star. He made the mistake one day of complimenting her on her amazing sense of style as they passed in the corridor.

'No shoes too high, no hair too big,' she said without breaking her stride and Jimmy had been smitten. He had gritted his teeth, however, and ridden it out.

Jim's mum was delighted with the change Monica seemed almost overnight to have brought about in her son. Suddenly he was clean and fit-looking. His hair was nicely cut and that awful constant sniffing appeared to have abated, which was a great relief.

Shortly before Monica's advent Nora had begun to worry seriously about Jimmy, who was sweating a lot and grinding his teeth. Nora wondered if he might be developing some terrible allergy.

'That's what it's all about these days. Allergies. It's because of the chemicals they're putting in the chickens. I mean whoever would have thought peanuts would need a health warning?'

Derek Corby read the Sunday papers and had a pretty good idea what Jimmy's symptoms were about, but he didn't want to worry Nora so he kept his own counsel.

And now all that had changed anyway.

'Whatever he had, she's cured him of it,' Nora said.

'It's like he was a little boy and now suddenly he's a man.'

Jimmy's dad agreed. Slaving away each day running his branch of the National City Bank for a salary that wouldn't have paid for even one of Jimmy and Monica's holidays that year, Derek conceded that in Monica, Jimmy had made the one truly clever decision of his life. 'And poor Monica made her silliest,' he would add grumpily, but his wife always assured Monica that he didn't really mean it.

It was Derek and Nora who helped the young couple to move into their first proper marital home, a small riverside cottage in Richmond. Monica's parents were old hippies who had sold up their pine-furniture business and gone off around the world in a boat, so they were pretty useless. Derek and Nora, on the other hand, were complete homebodies, thrilled and anxious to get involved. Fortunately, Monica loved them both.

'I always secretly longed to have straight parents,' Monica said as she unwrapped coffee mugs. 'When Mum used to pick me up at the school gates dressed entirely in purple with no bra and her bloody nipples showing, I used to die. Dad sometimes came in this terrible old minibus he used for work and which made more noise than all the other parents' cars put together. One time I had my bike with me and he opened the back to put it in and there was a mattress and duvet laid out for all to see, with empty wine bottles clanging around. It was mortifying. From that day on I was the girl whose parents had a shaggin' wagon. It was horrible.'

'Well, you can't get much straighter than my mum and dad,' Jimmy said, holding an Allen key and struggling to decipher the Swedish cartoons that were supposed to show him how to assemble his new shelf unit. 'They are the proverbial shortest distance between two points.'

At that moment Nora came down from upstairs, where she had been stocking the linen cupboard.

'Lovely fluffy white towels, Monica,' she said. 'Were they a wedding present?'

'Yes. Lizzie and Robbo. Lizzie designed them herself.'

'How do you *design* a white towel?' Nora enquired.

'Mum, it's 1996,' Jimmy said gently. 'I think you're going to find the twenty-first century very difficult.'

'I don't think I'll bother with it actually, dear,' Nora replied. 'I'll just carry on with this one and keep adding years to it.'

She went to help Monica with the crockery.

'I noticed there's a *super* little room right next to yours and Jimmy's, Monica,' she said archly. 'What could that *possibly* be for, I wonder?'

'Ah-ha!' Monica smiled. 'We shall see.'

'Well, never too soon to start, I say. You don't want to be an older mum, like all these women seem to want to be these days.'

'Mum!' Jimmy demanded. 'If you don't shut up I shall take Monica upstairs and impregnate her right now.'

'There, you see!' Nora said quite brusquely. 'There was me thinking you'd changed him, Monica, and it turns out he's the same awful boy he always was.'

But he wasn't. He really was different, and the board at Mason Jervis had noticed the change in him too. Jimmy had a promotion to announce.

'Actually this is a double celebration,' Jimmy said, clinking a glass as the four of them sat among the boxes over the picnic that Monica had assembled entirely from new ranges at Marks and Spencer. 'New house. New tier.'

'New tier?' Derek asked. 'Are you planning an extension? You'll never get planning permission in Richmond. Not in a million years.'

'New *management* tier, Dad. I'm not a drone any more. They've given me a desk to manage.'

'A *desk* to manage?' Derek sniffed. 'At the National City we let the furniture look after itself.'

'Don't pretend to be thick, Dad, please.' Jimmy smiled. 'You know bloody well what I mean. I'm going to be heading up my own group.'

But Derek Corby was relentlessly refusing to be impressed. 'As I recall, the last group you "headed up" was called the Electro Fanny Magnets and it was a crime against music.'

'We were just ahead of our time. Everybody's doing Goth Psycho Metal now.'

'He had a nipple pierced, Monica,' Nora said. 'Did he tell you?'

'Yes, he did, as a matter of fact. He said it was very erotic. Tried to hint at me giving it a try, didn't you, Jimmy?'

Jimmy shrugged as if to indicate that he couldn't really recall.

'Erotic? I don't think so,' Nora snorted. 'It went septic straight away. I was dabbing it with Dettol for a week and he ended up having to have it removed in Casualty.'

'Look!' Jimmy said in a firm voice, clearly fearful that more embarrassing episodes from his past were about to be revealed. 'Do you want to hear about this promotion or don't you?'

He had been given the news the previous Friday. The CEO had called him into his office, offered him a glass of Krug and explained that he was now looked upon as a coming man.

'The trading floor's fine for coked-up juvenile crazies,' the CEO had explained. 'Quite frankly you *need* an adolescent mentality in the bear pit, if only to put up with all the bloody shouting. But somebody has to manage all these overgrown teenagers and also manage the money they're making. You're a good trader, Jim, but you're an even better people person. You can communicate and you can motivate. You can build team spirit and *esprit de corps*. Those are much rarer skills than having the balls to take a chance on a basket of dodgy derivatives.'

'Thanks, Frank,' Jimmy had replied, trying to look and sound serious and discreetly placing his right hand over his left in order to disguise the skull ring Monica had bought him in Vegas.

'You're married, aren't you?' the CEO said, as if somehow locking into Jimmy's thoughts.

'Yes, Frank, I am. But if that's a problem, I can dump her. I have a watertight pre-nup and she'd get nothing . . . I'm kidding, of course. Love of my life and all that. I met her here, as a matter of fact, which is another reason for me to be grateful to the old firm.'

'She's a trader then?' the CEO asked with a slight frown. 'Not many women in our game.'

'No, not a trader. She was trying to flog me a bit of focaccia bread with what looked like half of Kew Gardens on top of it.'

'Excellent!' The CEO beamed. 'Not good to mix work and family. It can lead to all sorts of complications. Never comfortable to have breakfast every morning with someone you've just aced on a major deal. Or worse still, sacked. Anyway, well done. Marriage means stability, it means domestic roots and a commitment to the company pension plan. I believe you've just embarked on a personal property portfolio, haven't you?'

'Well . . . Monica and I have bought a house,' Jimmy

admitted, wondering if that was what the CEO meant.

'Good. A man with a personal property portfolio is far less likely to let himself get headhunted and be on the next plane to South East Asia with all the company contacts in his personal organizer than a man renting a hovel in Hackney. All in all, Jimmy, the board and I have decided you have management potential. What do you think of that?'

'Sounds great, Frank. Management is, after all, the new Rock 'n' Roll.'

That was how it had happened. Jimmy hadn't been trying to win a promotion, good fortune just followed him around.

'Good old Lucky Jimmy,' Robbo had remarked when his friend told him the story in the pub that evening. 'You marry a bit of top-class totty like Monica and then it gets you bloody promoted into the bargain. Talk about a win-win situation. Looks like we both married our meal tickets in a way.'

Derek Corby echoed Robbo's sentiment over the picnic lunch.

'This is all down to Monica, James,' he said. 'And I must say I'm delighted to hear that even ridiculous businesses like the one you work in still value domestic stability.'

'Only because it means I won't be trying to switch my pension fund or relocate to Frankfurt with a rival firm.'

'Which are perfectly legitimate economic reasons,' Derek said with approval. 'About the *only* economically legitimate thing I've ever heard about the business you work in.'

'Dad,' Jimmy said in a serious voice, 'how much would I have to pay you to say congratulations?'

'What?'

'I mean it.' Jimmy went on looking his father in the eye. 'You have a healthy respect for the value of money and they do say that every man has his price. I'm to be given a management position at Mason Jervis and it would mean a lot to me for you to say well done. So much so, in fact, that I'm actually prepared to *pay* you to do it. What do you say?'

There was a moment of embarrassed silence. Jimmy had such an easy-going spirit that even those who loved him most and knew him best were unused to a serious display of emotion like this one.

Derek Corby stared back at his son. Neither man seemed to blink.

'I'll do it for fifty pence,' Derek said.

'Bugger off,' Jimmy replied. 'It doesn't mean that much to me. I'll pay fifteen.'

'Twenty-five.'

'Done.'

Jimmy counted out the twenty-five pence and handed it over.

'Well done, Jimmy,' Derek said as he took the change

and his eyes were perhaps a little damp as he said it. 'I'm
very proud of you.'

Jimmy gave Derek a hug. Which Derek clearly found
slightly uncomfortable.

'What has happened to Marks and Spencers?' he said,
disengaging himself. 'A crisp used to be a crisp. Balsamic
vinegar? Cracked pepper? What was wrong with cheese
and onion? And what's "kettle-cooked" supposed to
mean? You can't cook crisps in a kettle, you couldn't get
them up the spout.'

There's always somebody worse off than yourself

'Dead?' Jimmy said.

It could not be true. He must have misheard. Jimmy
felt he must be either still dreaming or too drunk and
exhausted to understand English any more.

The sob that came over the receiver in reply made it
clear that he had not misheard. And Jimmy didn't need
to understand English either. That sob would have
meant the same in any language. Guttural, abrasive. Not
the sort of sound you would expect to hear from a
woman, even in deep distress. It was a shocking sound,

a kind of gagging belch rather than a sob. Harsh and abrupt and ugly, as if Lizzie was in the process of hacking up her whole insides.

'Lizzie, no,' Jimmy said. 'Not Robbo.'

Another great bark of pain. Like the hiccup of a very drunken man. Jimmy wondered if she was actually being sick.

'He crashed . . . his bloody . . . his bloody . . . He crashed his . . .' Lizzie was trying to speak, but for a moment her convulsions defeated her.

'Wolseley?' Jimmy heard himself saying. 'Churchill?'

'Ye-e-e-es,' Lizzie wailed, 'bloody Churchill.'

Her grief sounded more conventional now. More like the grief that an actress might conjure up, not burping and intestinal but a more recognizable, panting, tear-soaked misery.

'He crashed his bloody car.'

Churchill. Robbo's beloved Wolseley. The car he had always stuck with despite his ever-increasing wealth.

He couldn't have *died* in it.

'Are you sure he's . . . ?' Jimmy heard himself saying. 'I mean there's no chance that . . .'

It was stupid, of course. Lizzie wouldn't have been hiccuping and burping her agony into his phone at three fifteen in the morning if there had been any hope at all, but Jimmy was struggling to find a response.

How had it happened? How *could* it have happened? Robbo? *Fucking dead.*

In fact Jimmy already knew how it had happened, or at least he strongly suspected that he did.

Robbo had been driving pissed. He always drove pissed and they'd all been nodding indulgently over it for years. 'Not pissed but merely over the limit,' Robbo himself always insisted, believing himself, as all drink drivers do, to be perfectly capable of handling a car on the amount he had imbibed.

'It's not as if I'd ever drive shit-faced. I admit I *drink* drive but I strongly disapprove of *drunken* driving,' Robbo would say.

And it was true that he tended not to drive actually shit-faced. At least he hadn't since his university days, when on one memorable occasion he had parked his old Mini in the hedge outside the shared house. But like many people, he drove *a bit pissed*. If he'd had a few pints he'd still take his car. What was more, for twenty years he'd got away with it. He'd never even been stopped.

'The trick is to drive *normally*,' he'd say. 'It's the idiots who crawl along and indicate a mile ahead of time that get pulled.'

Yes, thought Jimmy, he'd always got away with it. Until now. If only he'd been caught and banned yesterday.

'The bloody fool must have gone out to get some fags,' Lizzie said, clearly making an effort to sound normal.

Jimmy could picture the scene perfectly. Lizzie had gone up, leaving Robbo to channel-surf and have a final Scotch and he'd run out of cigarettes. Of course he had run out of cigarettes, he *always* ran out of cigarettes, because unlike Jimmy he never stocked up on great boxes of duty-free when he travelled. Robbo would buy one packet at a time because he was always about to give up.

Now he never would give up.

'He must have swerved to miss something because he drove slap into a wall and wrote off the car. He died . . . he died instantly.'

'Oh my God,' Jimmy said, involuntarily picturing the scene and adding without really thinking, 'he must have been tanking it to write off Churchill. Those old Wolseleys are made of steel.'

'The police reckon on sixty-five,' Lizzie replied. 'I don't think . . .' She was struggling again. 'I don't think he wanted me to know he'd gone out. Thank God the street was empty. Nobody else was involved. The wall collapsed.'

'Oh Lizzie. Lizzie,' Jimmy said, his own eyes filling with tears. 'I'm so very sorry.'

'Yes. Yes. Thanks, Jimmy,' she replied. 'Anyway, I'll hang up now . . . I just wanted you to know. I have to think, you see. I really do have to think . . . You know, about what to tell the children.'

'Yes. Yes, of course . . .' Jimmy said. 'If there's anything . . .'

'I know, Jim. Absolutely,' Lizzie said and for a moment she seemed almost normal. 'Oh and Jimmy?'

'Yes, Liz?'

'Don't worry about that loan. Seriously. I'm still going to arrange it in the morning.'

'Lizzie! Please, don't even think about it,' Jimmy protested. 'Really. I mean, please.'

Had she read his mind?

Had she realized that in the midst of his absorbing the terrible, heartbreaking news of the death of one of his dearest, probably his *actual* dearest friend, the thought of the promised loan had crossed his mind?

Jimmy hated himself for it but it was true: one tiny part of him had listened to the tragic story and asked, what about us now? He had suppressed the thought instantly, of course. What was more, he had not deliberately summoned it, it had arisen despite him and he hated his subconscious for being so base.

Of course he never would have said it and now that Lizzie, either clairvoyant or just genuinely selfless, had brought it up, he tried to reassure her.

'Please, Lizzie. Don't. It doesn't matter. It simply doesn't matter at all.'

'No. No. It does and I will do it. It's important. Life goes on. You're in a spot. Robbo was your mate. Of course he'd want . . . he'd want . . .'

For a moment she could not continue.

'Lizzie, please. Don't, it's not important,' Jim protested gently.

'It is. I'll arrange it tomorrow or certainly this week.'

Lizzie hung up.

Jimmy agonized about whether to tell Monica that night. He didn't want to. He knew how devastated she would be, but what else could he do?

Unless she was asleep.

If she was, he'd leave her be, but if she was still awake she would certainly want to know why Lizzie had called. One thing was sure, Jimmy was confident that his darling Monica's distress would not be sullied by any secret thoughts about a lost loan. Her grief would be pure and it would be absolute.

He went upstairs.

For a moment relative peace had returned to the family bedroom, but not, it turned out, the peace of sleep, merely the peace of convenience. In order to calm the children (and shut them up) Monica had all three in bed with her. Lillie was on the breast despite the fact that her next 'controlled' feed was still an hour away, Cressida was having a cuddle and Toby was stretched out, legs and arms all over the place, slowly nodding off.

This was of course contrary to every firm boundary that Jimmy and Monica kept setting themselves and then breaking. They were officially control-feeding Lill, control-crying Cressie and getting Tobes used to sleeping in his own room. All these things had seemed so important an hour or two earlier.

'Sorry,' said Monica, and the exhaustion in her voice was painful to hear, 'I didn't know what else to do.'

'It's fine,' Jimmy whispered, sitting down on the end of the bed. 'It's OK.'

A flicker of confusion crossed Monica's face. Jimmy knew she was trying to remember what had happened and why he had left the bedroom. Sometimes Monica was so tired she forgot her own name.

'Mon,' he said, not knowing any better way to say it than to just say it, 'Robson's dead. He crashed his car on a bloody fag run and got himself killed.'

Jimmy hadn't expected that he'd be the one to break down first but suddenly he found himself weeping uncontrollably. Shedding more tears in a few moments than he had shed in the previous twenty years. He had not cried once during all their current troubles, even when Monica had been in bits. But he cried now. He cried and cried as he told Monica what he knew about the tragedy that had befallen their friends.

Strangely, astonishingly, Monica did not cry. Later, on reflection, Jimmy concluded that the revelation of a nightmare so close to them but so infinitely worse than the one they were living through themselves gave her strength. Perhaps it put things in perspective for her, perhaps it provided a kind of grim (and unsought) comfort in that it became blindingly clear

133

that in her own life things could be a whole lot worse.

For whatever reason, as Jimmy broke down Monica pulled herself together. She didn't even seem tired any more. Instead she rang Lizzie straight back and said she was coming over.

It was the right thing to do. Monica always understood that kind of thing. Lizzie needed help. She just hadn't wanted to ask.

Monica got up, went downstairs, put a coat on over her stained nightie, grabbed the keys to the Range Rover and was gone.

Half an hour later Jimmy found himself where he had found himself on so many desperate and zombified pre-dawns before – stretched out on a bean bag in the family room watching *Thomas the Tank Engine* with Lillie in his arms, Cressie on her little folding sofa and Toby asleep on another bean bag. Cressida loved *Thomas the Tank Engine* just as Toby had done before her (and secretly still did), although he was now too old to admit it. His favourite engine was James.

Jimmy, on the other hand, had come to loathe *Thomas the Tank Engine* because its repetitive style was driving him slowly insane. What was more, Ringo Starr's lugubrious delivery of the narrative, which at first Jimmy had thought rather charming, had long since lost its appeal. He never would have believed he could wish any Beatle to shut up, but after years of *Thomas the Tank Engine* Jimmy wished Ringo would.

And so, as Thomas and James went up the track (preparatory to coming back down the track), Jimmy lay on his bean bag and thought about Robbo and all the terrible changes that the previous nine months had brought into their lives. How had it happened? How had it all gone so wrong?

The Labour Party is the new Tory Party

Jimmy and Monica left Richmond and moved into the first of a series of Notting Hill homes in 1997, the year Labour was returned to power after eighteen years of Conservative government.

With the exception of Jane and Henry (who was a candidate), the whole gang spent election night together among Jimmy and Monica's packing boxes and, like so many other people in Britain that night, got well and truly caught up in the exuberant spirit of the moment. They had all voted Labour except for Rupert and Amanda, and even Rupert had conceded that he had only voted Tory out of duty and had secretly wanted 'our Tone' to win.

'We need a bit of fresh air,' he said as the results rolled

in and they celebrated each New Labour victory with vintage champagne and slices of Domino's pizza. 'And after Our Tone went and grovelled to Rupert Murdoch at his summer summit, I knew Labour were well and truly on side and the City was safe.'

For once Rupert spoke for them all.

'I'm happy to still call myself a sort of socialist,' said David between great mouthfuls of pepperoni, 'but *nobody* wants insane taxes, it's just counter-productive.'

'We just want a *fairer society*,' David's girlfriend Laura volunteered, opening box after box in search of something vegetarian. 'And I really believe New Labour can deliver. Jimmy, did you *only* order meat feast?'

'There's a couple of Hawaiians in there.'

'Which have ham in them.'

'Ham isn't really meat, Laura,' Jimmy said firmly, clearly feeling that it was important that new girlfriends understood that the Radish Club made its own rules.

'Be quiet!' David hushed. 'It's Michael Portillo's result! Thatcher's baby is about to get royally stuffed!'

The room cheered as another famous Tory scalp was taken. The general consensus (with Rupert and Amanda once more proving the exceptions) was with David's Laura, believing that they could all now look forward to a fairer and more caring society. And there was the added bonus that they would not personally be expected to pay for it.

'Something for nothing!' Jimmy shouted. '*Love* that!

No homeless. No getting mugged by the underclass, and all for a top tax rate of 40 per cent. Bargain, I call it.'

'Feel a bit deflated, Rupert?' Laura asked, having given up her search and begun picking bits of ham from a slice of Hawaiian.

'Yes, come on, Rupert,' Monica chipped in, 'you have to admit it. You can be as wry and arch as you like, but your lot are history.'

'A rose by any other name, Monica darling,' Rupert replied, his already somewhat chubby face illuminated by light from the vast booze fridge in which he was fossicking.

'By which you mean?' Laura asked in a voice that was clearly meant to say that she might be new around here but she was not going to be bullied by smug Tories.

'We're all "new" Labour now,' Rupert went on, 'because New Labour are basically slightly liberal Tories, and if you can't see that you're blind. The working class as we used to understand it is gone. The centre of the British economy has irrevocably moved from manufacturing to financial services. Thanks to St Margaret—'

'Boo! Confusion on her!' David shouted drunkenly.

'Oh, do stop pretending you're still a student!' Amanda admonished. 'If you listen to Rupert you might actually learn something.'

'Yes, David. Relax,' Rupert said. 'Whatever Henry and his Blairite chums might have banged on about at the hustings, there are no miners and industrial workers left for anyone to pretend to worry about any more. Your deeply compromised conscience is off the hook. *We* are the workers now.'

'That's true,' said Monica, spearing strawberries for a melted Mars bar fondue. 'Nobody can say that you boys don't work hard.'

'No, Mon,' Jimmy said, 'I don't work hard at all. I just turn up with my wheelbarrow every morning and shovel money into it. Of course I have to *be* there, but that's about it.'

'Oh, do shut up with your endless self-deprecation, Jim,' Rupert chided. 'You're worse than your sainted fucking Tony.'

'Can't really say I bust a gut myself,' Robbo conceded.

'Not that you haven't got plenty of gut to bust!' Jimmy shouted, hurling a bit of rolled-up garlic pizza at his old friend so that Robbo upset his beer and Lizzie nearly had apoplexy.

'Don't worry,' said Monica, 'we're tearing up this awful floor covering and sanding the floorboards. Can't imagine what the previous people were *thinking*.'

'Robbo does work hard, as a matter of fact,' Lizzie protested, mopping at the spilt beer with thick ribbons of kitchen towel. 'We run our business together. In fact we've just set him up with his own office. Haven't we, darling?'

'Robbo's had his own office for years.' Jimmy laughed. 'It's called the Frog and Firkin.'

'They do some very decent beers.' Robbo was grinning good-naturedly.

'When it comes to working hard,' said David, 'none of you know the half of it.'

'Sometimes I worry he'll burn out!' Laura chipped in.

David had finally qualified as an architect and emerged into a building boom of unprecedented proportions. Instantly he found himself working fourteen-hour days, trying to find new ways to make buildings look as if they were made entirely out of sheets of black glass.

'Just as long as you don't pave over any more of the Home Counties,' Amanda observed. 'Pretty soon there'll be nowhere left to hunt south of Birmingham.'

'And a good thing too,' Laura snapped. 'It's unspeakably cruel. That's a good enough reason to vote New Labour in itself. We had dinner with Henry and Jane the other night and he said he's absolutely passionate about banning it. In fact Jane's written a scene about it in her new novel. It sounds amazing, it's the kill seen from the fox's point of view.'

'How on earth would she know? Unless of course the fox is a middle-class townie novelist who thinks belonging to the National Trust gives her an understanding of the countryside,' Amanda snapped back.

'That is totally unfair, Amanda,' Laura retorted. 'Pain is pain and terror is terror.'

'And I doubt that Jane has ever truly experienced either,' Amanda said angrily.

'I don't really get that argument, Mand,' Monica said. 'I mean Tolkien had never been a hobbit or a dark rider, or an elf for that matter. But that doesn't mean he should have been banned from writing books about them, surely?'

'I wish he had been banned,' said Rupert. 'What a lot of childish *wank*!'

'Look, for fuck's sake let's not have the foxhunting debate,' Jimmy pleaded. 'I am so over it.'

'There's nothing to debate,' said Laura. 'The argument's been won. We live in a democracy and the vast majority of people think it's utterly cruel and obscene.'

'The vast majority also eat McDonald's and Kentucky Fried Chicken and if Colonel Sanders started deep-frying fox nuggets they'd eat them too.'

'Shhh!' Monica shouted. 'It's Henry!'

And together they all watched as their friend Henry, his new wife Jane beside him, achieved his dream of becoming a servant of the people.

They cheered and cheered and by the time the newly elected prime minister appeared on television to declare that Labour had won, everybody was completely drunk.

'We were elected as New Labour and we will govern as New Labour,' said Tony Blair.

'So that's all right then,' said Rupert.

And everyone agreed.

The grandpa project

Monica arrived, red-eyed, back at the house to find Jimmy and the children all stretched out asleep on the floor of the basement family room with the final frame of *Thomas the Tank Engine* still frozen on the big wall-mounted TV screen.

'Jimmy! Jimmy!' Monica cried out. 'Wake up! It's seven thirty!'

Jimmy was on his feet in an instant, exploding from the bean bag and becoming vertical in a single convulsion. As he did so, the TV remote fell from his chest and hit the ground, somehow managing to turn the DVD back on.

According to Ringo Starr, Thomas was still going up the track, preparatory to coming back down the track. Then he would meet James and say hello. For a moment Jimmy felt as if he were in a kind of parental Groundhog Day in which Thomas was always poised to go back up the track. Which of course he was.

'Right! OK! I'm hot to trot!' he blurted.

He was so on edge that he never really slept anyway, not any more. Jimmy believed that his sleep was more like the way a computer sleeps. It *looked* asleep, with its apparent inertia and gently throbbing electric heartbeat, but one tiny touch of its mouse and everything was back up and ready to go, every relevant document still open, sentences half completed, spell check still hanging on to misspelt words, ready to resume everything that it had been doing at the point of abandonment, without a pause. That was Jimmy, he never really slept. Or so he believed.

'Well, thank God you managed to get a bit of sleep at least. That's good,' Monica said.

Under normal circumstances this simple statement would have brought forth an instant denial from Jimmy, or at best a grudging half-agreement.

'Maybe half an hour,' he would have protested, 'and I wasn't *really* sleeping. Just dozing.'

He and Monica had been engaged in an unacknowledged sleep battle ever since Jodie had left. Each was absolutely certain that the other was getting more sleep than they were. Each constantly belittled the amount that they themselves had had while never failing to point out when they felt the other had been able to nod off. It was a pointless expenditure of what little emotional and intellectual energy remained to them both. But not this morning. This morning all pettiness was put aside. This morning Jimmy wished he *was* still asleep because this was the morning he woke up to a world with no Robbo in it.

'How was Lizzie?' he asked.

'She looks dead, Jim,' Monica said. 'That's the honest truth. She looks like she's died too.'

There was silence, except for the fittingly funereal

tones of Ringo Starr describing Thomas's progress up and down the track.

'Anyway, we'd better get moving,' Monica said finally. 'We're already pretty late.'

'I thought maybe you'd stay a bit longer with Lizzie, you know, with . . .' He could hardly frame the sentence as the realization flooded in on him once more that his friend of twenty years, good old Robbo, was dead.

'Jimmy, how could I? It's a school morning!' Monica said. 'Laura's with her. She still has a nanny.'

Was it his imagination or were those last words a veiled rebuke? Monica never, ever complained to him about their terrible reduction in circumstances. She was far too sweet and good for that. But the bald statement that Monica could no longer spare the time to comfort her widowed friend because Jimmy was now too poor to pay for a nanny hurt like hell.

'Come on, Jim,' Monica continued, 'we really have to get going.'

'But . . . but,' Jimmy protested, 'can't we just keep Toby home today? I mean . . . Robbo's *dead*.'

He hadn't even thought about getting his son ready for school. Who cared about school? The founding member and Lord Chief Radish had got pissed and smashed his car into a wall trying to buy fags.

'No, we can't,' Monica replied wearily. 'Toby's missed far too much already. Mr Lombard isn't happy and we're going to need all the good will we can get at that school if we have to delay . . .'

She was right and Jimmy knew it. They were hanging on by a shoestring at Abbey Hall as it was. Quite apart from the fact that they'd had to ask for a 'brief' delay in paying next year's fee, they were also now firmly bracketed with the 'problem' parents because Toby had been marked late or absent so many times. In fact they had recently received a very firm letter.

'God, I miss Jodie,' Monica said for the ten-thousandth time since her departure.

This was the real effect of losing all their money, and never more keenly felt than on school mornings. It wasn't the reduced material expectations, the holidays and the cars. Not really, not any more. They scarcely cared about those things now.

But God, they cared about losing Jodie.

It wasn't that they didn't want to bring up their own children, they wanted to desperately. It was just that they had had *no idea* what it really entailed. The shock had been terrible.

It had taken them both weeks to begin to understand the basic fact that every aspect of each of their three off-spring's lives now required at least one of them to be in attendance *all the time*. To prepare for it, supervise and police it, get them to it, get them back from it and clean up after it.

The readjustments that they had been forced to make to

their routines had been shocking and brutal. It was all the more painful because they realized how pampered and deluded they had previously been. It seemed incredible now, but both of them had actually believed that despite having a full-time nanny and various cleaners they were nonetheless bringing up their children themselves.

'I won't send Toby to boarding school,' Monica had often said. 'I cannot see the point of *having* children if you're not going to bring them up. I *like* my children, for heaven's sake. I enjoy their company. Why would I want to send them away?'

Monica still liked her children. She loved them absolutely. But at this stage in their lives she was discovering that she did not always enjoy their company. Their snotty, pooey, shrieking, fighting, weeping, never-endingly demanding company. Sometimes bored, often hysterical, commonly trying to kill themselves with household products and appliances and *always* in need of attention, they could in fact drive her insane.

'*Please*,' Monica now begged them on a daily basis, 'just give me one minute to myself! To *think*!'

With Jodie she'd had all the minutes she wanted. She had her whole life. She hadn't realized it at the time. She thought she was pretty busy with the kids. She had in fact described herself as 'a part-time charity worker and full-time mum'. But now she understood that she had been full-time on her own unbelievably privileged terms. She had always been able to escape, to have a moment to herself. To think. Now she didn't have a minute. Not one minute. Ever.

'And it's not just the bloody school who are on our case either,' Monica said as she started to grab slices of bread in order to make Toby's lunch. 'Mr Lombard says all school registers are scrutinized by the local council. If you have too many unauthorized absences they send round the truant officer.' Monica's eyes welled up. 'For Toby! *The truant officer.* Can you imagine?'

'Will I have to go to prison, Mummy?' Toby asked.

Jimmy looked down into the tired, anxious face of his little boy, a lad who had once been so jolly and un-complicated but who was now slowly becoming infected by the constant anxiety he could sense in his parents.

'No, of course not, darling!' Jimmy said, forcing a smile. 'Mummy and I were just having a laugh.'

Jimmy often found himself forcing smiles these days. It was something he had never done before. It just showed that sudden financial ruin could take the twinkle out of the most natural smile.

Monica continued slapping Kraft cheese slices between slabs of Sunblest while Jimmy began searching for clothes.

'Some of the boys laugh at my lunch,' Toby said, rub-bing his eyes. 'Gavin says cheese sarnies are for builders.'

Jimmy felt furious, suddenly dizzy with anger. He wanted to tell Toby to tell Gavin that he was a stupid little *bastard*. He wanted to go up to Gavin himself and tell him that if he bullied Toby he would punch him into next week and then wring his father's neck. But he couldn't, of course. He knew that if he gave in to such emotions it would lead to far greater disasters even than those currently enveloping him.

'Tell Gavin that Winston Churchill swore by cheese sarnies and that an empire was not built on chocolate Müller Corners.'

'Can't I go back to having school lunches?' Toby pleaded.

How could Jimmy tell him? How could he tell his son that he and Monica had decided the twenty pounds a week those lunches cost was an unnecessary expense? He, Jimmy, who only months before had regularly dropped that amount or more into the hands of beggars outside Soho House? But the truth was that he and Monica had only two cards left on which the credit was good. They were only weeks away from actual insolvency. Or, if they were careful, maybe a couple of months. Every penny counted.

Jimmy looked at the two empty wine bottles from the previous evening and felt a terrible pang of guilt. Of course Toby could go back to school lunches, he'd just give up wine. What had they been doing drinking *two* bottles last night anyway? It was ruinous.

Then he remembered the reason. They'd been celebrating, hadn't they? Celebrating Lizzie's promise.

147

A bridging loan to tide them over. He'd forgotten about that in all the subsequent shock and sadness.

And Lizzie had said that she would keep her promise, hadn't she? Despite everything, she was going to help him out. Once more Jimmy felt the surge of almost hysterical relief that he had experienced the previous evening. Not instead of his terrible sadness over Robbo, but alongside it. What was more, he felt no guilt for the emotion. Why should he? One thing was certain, Robbo would have called him a stupid *twat* if he had.

'By the way,' Monica said, washing an apple, 'Lizzie told me to tell you to be sure to send over the banking details for the loan. Can you believe it? She must be the kindest person on earth. I told her not to worry about it but she insisted. She said she won't need to handle it herself. Her PA can sort it out. It's amazing really, she's still thinking about other people.'

'It *is* amazing,' Jimmy replied, 'but not surprising. What's more, I'll do what she says. She and Robbo wanted to help us and we're going to bloody well let them. And Toby can go back to school lunches.'

'Yes!' said Toby, punching the air.

Monica glanced across at the various bits of paper stuck to the upper part of the huge fridge.

'Oh my God,' she said suddenly, genuine panic in her voice. 'Is it Tuesday?'

'Yes.'

'He needs his swim stuff!' she almost screamed. 'And

148

his gym kit and . . . Oh NO! We haven't done his grandpa project!'

'What?'

'His grandpa project. Shit!'

'Don't say shit, Mummy,' Toby said.

'I said *ship*, darling,' Monica replied, briefly on automatic pilot before returning to the real agenda of forgotten homework. 'He's supposed to have made up a little presentation about a grandparent either living or dead.'

'Oh my God!' Jimmy replied, feeling the panic rising. 'Not for today?'

'Yes to-bloody-day!'

What a terrible morning. Robson was dead and Toby hadn't done his grandpa project. The former might have been the greater tragedy, but the latter was real and immediate. They'd forgotten about yet another piece of homework and yet again their son would be in trouble at school.

Jodie had *never* forgotten homework. Not once.

Monica cursed herself. She had remembered it on Friday evening after Toby had brought it home, and she had decided to do it on Saturday. She had also remembered it on Saturday but had at that point decided to do it on Sunday. She had also remembered it on Sunday, when she had sworn to herself that she would help him with it on Monday. On Monday, she had forgotten it completely and now it was Tuesday and due in.

'Do it, Jimmy. Do it now. Make a grandpa project NOW, while I find him some clean pants and sports kit. We have to be in the car by eight fifteen at the latest.'

Jimmy knew there could be no argument. Toby's recent list of tardy and uncompleted homework was nearly as reprehensible as his attendance record. In the old days Jimmy had approved of homework. He had felt that if it was not too onerous and it concentrated on fun topics, homework probably helped to get children to understand that learning was a lifelong activity and not merely something to be endured between the hours of nine and three-thirty.

But that was before he had had to supervise the bloody stuff himself. Now he understood what homework *really* was.

A threat to family life.

An outrageous assault on the well-being of both child and (more importantly) parent or carer. Because what Jimmy had not understood during those happy times when he had watched his little lad busy with Jodie in the craft corner, scribbling away at his maths project or producing heartbreakingly sweet little poems, was that Jodie was actually *doing most of the work*! Or at the very least gently and patiently taking Toby through it until he understood it himself. And it was certainly Jodie who had done all the tricky bits, like creating a three-dimensional shape out of paper and glue and discovering the cubic capacity of a thing by immersing it in water. These days it seemed that parents (or carers) were *expected* to share in (i.e. do) the bloody homework. The forms actually instructed the parent (or carer) to get involved.

Now it was Jimmy and Monica who had to get involved and do all the stuff that Jodie had done. Except, of course, they didn't do it. They put it off, they rushed it, they cobbled it together at the last minute and during the process the whole family disintegrated into tears and recriminations.

'It's outrageous,' Jimmy muttered as he rushed upstairs to search out an old family album. 'We did *our* homework when we were at school and now we have to do our bloody kids' homework! One lifetime should not include two lots of bloody homework.'

'Don't say bloody,' said Toby.

'I'll say bloody whenever I bloody like!' Jimmy replied.

Before Jodie's departure Jimmy had never sworn in front of the children, never even said damn. Now they heard him say fuck.

'Has the government any idea of the amount of man hours lost to the country while parents try to do their kids' bloody homework?' Jimmy wailed from the next floor up. 'They could have avoided the whole damn recession! I could still be rich. Just stop telling busy working people to waste their time collecting empty egg boxes for Art when they could be turning the bloody economy around.'

'Just shut up and do it!' Monica shouted after him.

As he had passed Toby to rush up the stairs Jimmy had seen the fear and worry on his son's face and known that the little boy had scant faith in his father's ability to come up with something in twenty minutes that would rival the creations that all the other kids' nannies would have completed on the previous Saturday morning (or perhaps their mums had done it while the nannies did the laundry, got the breakfast and picked up and tidied).

Jimmy did the best he could and it wasn't a bad job considering that he had only minutes in which to do it. He found some photos of his father, a couple of old letters and a chequebook cover featuring the logo of the National City Bank, of which Derek was still a branch manager. This was the old logo, the one that clearly featured the letters NCB in a pleasant and undemanding font and that had been familiar to and trusted by millions. Not the new logo, the one that had cost almost a million pounds to develop and featured a splat shape that looked like pigeon droppings.

'See, Tobes,' Jimmy said, returning proudly to the family room, 'this is an old logo, you don't see it any more. That's historical, isn't it? Quite interesting, I'd have said.'

Toby rolled his eyes in despair while Jimmy began to stick his little collection to a big sheet of thick paper from the craft cupboard. Thank God Jodie had stocked it copiously only weeks before disaster struck and it still contained a Pritt Stick that had not had its top left off.

'I'm supposed to write an essay about Granddad as well,' Toby said.

'Well, why didn't you, Tobes?' Jimmy snapped. 'You're not disabled, are you?'

Tears welled up in the boy's eyes.

'You're supposed to remind me,' Toby replied miserably. 'You're supposed to help me.'

Jimmy felt terrible. He always felt terrible around Toby these days, simply because when Toby was born he had given him Jodie and now he had taken Jodie away from him.

'OK, not to worry,' Jimmy said, trying to sound light-hearted. 'You can do it in the car.'

But Toby didn't hear his father. He had already buried himself in his Nintendo machine. The Nintendo had been an issue in their old life too, with constant battles to restrict Toby to his two hours at weekends. Now, with everything in the house so miserable, Toby had taken to retreating into it every moment that he could. Sometimes it had to be physically wrenched from his hands, such was the boy's reluctance to connect with the real world. Jimmy understood. On that little screen Toby called the shots. Everywhere else he got bounced around as helplessly as if he was one of the pixelated figures in his games.

Monica had managed to find Toby's sports stuff and

a clean uniform. Now she tried to wrestle the boy into it while feeding him cornflakes, forcing the Nintendo from his hand and drying a pair of socks over the toaster. By this time, Cressida and Lillie were both lying on the floor screaming.

'Lillie needs changing,' Monica called out. 'She stinks.'

Jimmy laid aside the grandpa project, picked up the baby and carried her to the changing table.

Once more he remembered. *Robbo was dead.* But Lillie needed changing. He couldn't bring Robbo back to life, but he could stop his daughter getting nappy rash. Just because people died, babies didn't stop shitting themselves.

Luck or judgement?

In the year 2000 it was Henry and Jane's turn to move into a new home, a cause for yet another takeaway meal and champagne among the packing cases for the old gang.

'God, I can't believe we're actually in,' Jane said. 'It was *such* a worry, all the conveyancing took place over New Year and I thought we were going to get absolutely bollocksed by the Millennium Bug.'

'Might have worked out all right, actually,' Henry said, taking the cardboard lids off foil containers of Chinese food. 'Perhaps we could have bought at Edwardian prices.'

'What was the Millennium Bug?' Monica asked. 'I never really understood it and then it didn't happen anyway.'

'A millennium-sized load of old bollocks,' Jimmy said. 'I can't believe anybody took it seriously. Do you remember the scare stories? Oh my God! All the clocks will think it's 1907! Your washing machines will stop working! Your televisions will revert to black and white! Your bank account will disappear into the Bermuda Triangle and come back measured in farthings! Years from now people will be amazed anybody believed it at all.'

'Years from now people will have forgotten all about it,' Rupert said. 'Anybody with half a brain cell knew it was rubbish at the time.'

'Really, Rupert,' Amanda said sharply, 'that wasn't what you said all those nights you had to work late at the office last autumn getting the bank ready for it.'

Rupert, normally so smooth, so polished, looked momentarily thrown. It didn't last long, but it was long enough.

'I knew it was rubbish, darling,' he replied, poker-faced. 'It's just that the bank didn't.'

'Oh,' said Amanda coldly, 'I wonder if that *lovely* PA of

yours knew it was all rubbish too. Terribly depressing to give up one's evenings for such pointless activity.'

Of course all the boys knew that Rupert was a shagger. He always had been, or at least he had always tried to be. Now it seemed as if wealth and power were facilitating the process.

'Good flat this, Henry,' Jimmy said, changing the subject. 'Excellent choice. I mean, compact certainly, but really nice.'

'I don't make the sort of money you make, Jim,' Henry replied.

'It's only for when Henry's at the House of Commons,' Jane said. 'Of course our proper home's Berkshire.'

'No,' Henry said firmly, 'that's *not* the case, Jane. This is our primary residence, Berkshire's our second home.'

'Well, yes, I know we say that,' Jane replied brightly, 'but obviously that's to get the allowance.'

'If we say it, Jane,' Henry said, giving his wife a stern look, 'it must be true.'

'Oh right, yes, absolutely,' Jane agreed a little contritely.

'What's all this, Henry?' David enquired. 'Not indulging in a bit of creative accountancy, are we?'

'Certainly bloody not!' Henry replied. 'There's nothing remotely creative about it. It's bloody boring and stupid if you ask me. Basically, if you're not a central London MP you need two homes, one for

Parliament and one for your constituency. You get tax relief on the second one.'

'So you make the "second" one the more expensive one to maximize the relief.' Rupert nodded. 'Obviously. You're right, nothing creative about that, Henry. In my world we have to work a lot harder to pinch a perk.'

'It's not a bloody perk,' Henry protested.

'Don't let him wind you up,' Jimmy said. 'You know he loves doing it.'

'It is *not* a perk. It's a paltry and inadequate nod towards the fact that MPs are expected to run the country on what's barely a living wage. You bastards just make up your own salaries but Jane and I have to live in the real world.'

'Well, I suppose we're just lucky, mate,' Jimmy conceded, 'that's all. Very, very lucky.'

This was one of the reasons people found it impossible not to like Jimmy, no matter how obscene his bonus became. He never made the mistake of assuming that his immense good fortune was evidence of special genius. Almost uniquely among his stratospherically upwardly mobile peer group, he understood that he was not particularly brilliant or talented but simply one seriously lucky bastard.

It was the only real cause of contention between Jimmy and his old mate Rupert. Rupert was genuinely convinced that he was worth the extraordinary bonus that his bank had now got into the habit of paying him.

Which astonished Jimmy. Rupert was very clever, nobody could deny that, but Jimmy could never get over how *thick* Rupert was when it came to assessing how clever he was.

'Bollocks,' Rupert said through a mouthful of sweet and sour pork and Lanson Black Label. 'Luck has nothing to do with it, Henry, Jimmy's just trying to be nice. Basically you're a shitty little MP because that's all you're any good for and I earn what I earn because I am the best at what I do.'

'Which is shafting people,' Henry snapped back.

'I do my fair share of shafting, certainly,' Rupert conceded with a smile.

'Charming, isn't he?' Amanda said snidely, nibbling the end of a single bean sprout. 'Is that how you get such *lovely* PAs, darling? By shafting them?'

'Ah!' Rupert replied, poker-faced once more. 'If only.'

Jimmy and Monica exchanged glances. It was becoming something of a habit for Rupert and Amanda to take nasty little digs at each other in public and they agreed it was crap behaviour.

'*Nobody* is actually worth what you and I make, Rupert,' Jimmy said, once more trying to head off social embarrassment. 'How could we be?'

'I don't know so much,' said David, who had himself finally begun to make serious money.

'Well, I *do* know so much, Dave,' Jimmy insisted. 'The way I see it is this. If you didn't grab the money they shove at you you'd be stupid, but just because you do grab it does not make you clever.'

'I don't *grab* it, I earn it,' Rupert drawled, 'and so do you and all the other fellows. We earn what we earn as a direct result of the extraordinary profits we make for our companies. That's capitalism. We wouldn't be paid so much if we weren't worth it.'

'That is absolute rubbish, Rupert!' Henry shouted. 'You pay your bloody selves! That's the whole point. The culture of self-congratulation has developed so that you can all form a solid front and justify your own insane bonuses by banging on about the value of the blokes up the corridor at Wanker and Dickhead. *Bonus season!* What the fuck is that when it's at home? Nobody had heard of bonus season twenty years ago! The world still turned! People used to be *paid*. They didn't expect bonuses.'

'No doubt because in those crappy useless days when Britain was a basket case, they hadn't earned one,' Rupert replied. 'I'm telling you, mate, capitalism doesn't lie. The market is the one thing which *always* readjusts. You can rest assured that any service will find its true value according to the laws of supply and demand.'

'Not,' said Henry, 'if you control the economy and fix the prices. You bastards are a self-appointed elite. It's not a market any more, it's a personal fiefdom.'

Jimmy, who bored easily, particularly over issues of personal morality, had been discreetly rolling up a couple of pancakes intended for the crispy duck and now produced a beautifully spherical missile which he launched at Rupert, scoring a direct hit on the forehead so that he spilt his champagne.

'Stop that, Jimmy, now,' Lizzie shrieked, 'before it escalates! This is Jane and Henry's new home.'

'Remind me again, Henry,' Rupert asked. 'Is this your first or your second home? I'd love to know what my taxes are paying for.'

Lizzie bustled over with kitchen paper. She hated mess, particularly at dinner tables. (Hers were always exquisite. One Christmas she had sprinkled her deep-red and green cloth with shavings of real gold leaf.) Sadly for Lizzie, Robbo could not eat soup without it looking as if he'd sucked it up through the tablecloth and so her life was one of constant anguish about the state of the place settings. A bread fight in a small dining room littered with full glasses, far too much food and a lot of unpacked but not yet stowed china was her idea of hell.

'You *know* mess upsets me.'

'Rupert,' Jimmy said, tossing another missile. 'Face it, we're not that special. I bet if you took a bunch of kids from any comprehensive school in London and gave them the advantages we've had, you'd turn up a "genius" banker like you and an "essential" futures trader like me.'

'Bloody right,' said Henry, 'of course you would.'

'Possibly,' Rupert conceded, lazily inspecting a box of Henry's wine, 'if they were of Asian or Chinese stock.'

'*Stock!*' Laura protested.

'That's what I said.'

'Rupert, you can't say that sort of thing any more,' Monica squealed. 'It's *racist*.'

'Things like what?'

'Like *stock*. You sound like some awful Nazi geneticist.'

'Oh bollocks, Monica, everybody knows the bloody Indians and Chinese are good at maths,' Rupert snapped, 'just like black blokes make the best boxers.'

'Shut up, Rupert,' Laura said angrily. 'I mean it. It's not funny. It's bloody offensive.'

'Yes, it is!' Jane echoed. 'And quite honestly, Rupert, if you carry on like that you're going to have to go.'

'And as to you, Jimmy,' Rupert continued, ignoring Laura and Jane completely, 'and your ridiculous efforts to turn this into a class issue, the trading floors are full of comprehensive school kids.'

'Ah yes, the famous new breed of Cock-er-ney barrow boys,' Henry said snootily.

'Who almost exclusively remain at floor level,' said Jimmy. 'Don't see a lot of them in the boardroom, do we, Roop? And I doubt there's any challenging you on the ladder at the Royal Lancashire.'

'It's irrelevant anyway,' Rupert insisted, 'because that is not the point. The point is that those kids *haven't* had the advantages we've had and are therefore of no interest to a major private bank or brokerage. Personally, I would contend that "advantage" as you call it is merely another word for Darwinian natural selection—'

At this the whole room erupted into a chorus of liberal outrage.

'For Darwinian natural selection,' Rupert ploughed on loudly. 'The bank employs the people it feels will give it the most significant advantage in the workplace and pays them according to their market value. It's as simple as that. If there were hundreds of other people who could do those jobs their value would decline and they would be paid less. It's the rules of economics.'

'Look, Rupert,' Henry said, trying to sound measured and authoritative, 'I can see that you're being deliberately provocative but I think this is a serious enough issue for adult debate, don't you?'

'Blimey, Henry,' Jimmy said, smiling, 'you sound exactly like you used to when you were trying to stop me drinking your milk out of the fridge and nicking your chocolate.'

'And this is an issue of equal national importance,' Henry replied, smiling also. 'Rupert, you simply cannot claim that the preponderance of posh kids in the upper echelons of banking is due to some genetic advantage. I chair the parliamentary committee on social mobility and I know that your profession is a private members' club and you make your own rules.'

'Tell me, Henry,' Rupert enquired, dipping a spring

roll in the chilli sauce, 'how many MPs are there these days in the Parliamentary Labour Party who were born into the working class?'

For a moment Henry looked flustered and was of course rewarded with a chorus of good-natured catcalls.

'I think you'll find, Henry,' Rupert continued, 'that the Darwinian law of survival of the richest and best educated applies to all professions, including yours. It's simply that some of us aren't hypocrites about it.'

Henry was clearly thinking furiously and Amanda took the opportunity to press home Rupert's advantage. She might have issues with his working hours and choice of the most attractive PAs, but when it came to reactionary economic theory Rupert and Amanda were a team.

'Come on, Henry,' she said, "fess up. How many Labour MPs are there who aren't from the much-maligned middle class?'

'As it happens, Rupert,' said Henry, 'we search constantly to find new candidates from every under-represented group. Female candidates. Ethnic candidates . . .'

'I'm not talking about sex or race, Henry,' Rupert interrupted. 'I know you'll bend over backwards for a disabled black homosexual.'

'Woof woof!' Robbo shouted.

'Shut up, Robbo,' Lizzie scolded. 'That was so predictable.'

'I'm talking about *class* and *money*. Your entire party is more middle class now than it has ever been. You don't represent social mobility at all. You represent social *stagnation*.'

Henry was furious, that was clear, but he had no answer to Rupert and Amanda's point so he moved the goalposts.

'Well, to be honest, when I see how you and Jimmy live, Rupert, I realize I'm an absolute arse to care about politics or improving people's lives at all. What I should be doing is buying up successful banks, sacking all their staff and pocketing the savings.'

'Not jealous, are we, Henry?' Amanda enquired archly.

'Of course I'm bloody jealous,' Henry snapped back. 'It's bloody stupid. The money you earn makes everyone else look like a pauper! I'm an assistant chief whip, for God's sake. I'm tipped for the Cabinet, yet I doubt I make a tenth of what Jimmy bloody earns and he's an arse.'

'Never denied it.' Jimmy smiled but he didn't comment further. He wasn't sure what the difference was between his and Henry's income but he imagined that he might earn a bit more than ten times his friend.

'*Nobody* makes what you guys make,' Henry went on. 'Doctors, senior police officers, BBC execs, top council employees, politicians like me, all sorts of people who are responsible for the well-being of thousands earn a fraction of what a lucky little bastard like Jim earns. No offence of course, Jimmy.'

'None taken, Henry. If I were you I'd be jealous.'

'I'm not fucking jealous!' Henry shouted, contradicting himself. 'I'm outraged.'

'But actually I think you should be *grateful* about how much I earn, mate,' Jimmy said and, as so often with Jimmy, it was difficult to see how seriously he intended himself to be taken.

'So how does that work then?' David asked. 'I mean I don't mind earning more than Henry but I don't expect him to be grateful.'

'Well, think about it,' said Jimmy. 'OK, Henry doesn't make what I earn but he does all right, thank you very much. What is it now for an MP? About sixty grand a year? Plus all those expenses, this second home allowance thing. Got to bring it up to eighty at least, I'd say. Probably a hundred.'

'Oh please, Jim,' Monica said with some distaste, 'let's not start comparing incomes.'

'I'm not comparing anything. I'm just saying my guess is that in relative terms Henry makes at least twice what an MP would have made a generation or two ago. It's the same with all the other jobs you mentioned. Cops, councillors, doctors. BBC broadcasters. They all earn a much higher multiple of the average wage than they used to. In the fifties and sixties doctors weren't *seriously* richer than their patients, council bosses didn't think they should be paid *umpteen times* what the tenants they worked for made. BBC programmers didn't expect to be *massively* richer than the viewers. But they do now. They all expect much more money. Well, *we*'ve done that for you, mate. People like me and Rupert. Because whenever people say you make too much money, you say, "Look at those bastards in the City." It's the trickle-down. You look at our obscene bonuses and think that your merely very generous salaries pale in comparison, but remember that it's only *because* our bonuses are obscene that your salaries are so generous. Everyone's following our example. In the post-boom-and-bust world, if you take jealousy out of the equation everybody wins. Unless you're a member of the underclass, of course.'

There was a moment's silence. People weren't used to Jimmy doing anything but crack gags and chuck bread about. Perhaps he was joking now.

'Do you ever feel guilty about it, Jimmy?' Robbo asked suddenly. 'I mean about just how rich you are? I know Lizzie and I used to but . . . I don't any more . . . Why should we? I mean we've earned it, haven't we?'

'I find you get used to money,' Jimmy replied. 'Like when you have nothing you think you'd be happy with a tenner and that the bloke with a hundred is a total bastard. Then when you've got the tenner you start to think a hundred is fair but a thousand would be obscene. Then you get a thousand and suddenly that's all right too. Henry makes plenty compared with 90 per cent of the people he represents but he thinks that's OK, in fact he should get a bit more. It's us he thinks are taking the piss.'

'Yes I do, as it happens,' Henry replied.

'Look, Henry,' Robbo said, 'it's all very well for you to be snooty and pious. You don't have to deal with this sort of dilemma. You do an important job and you make a decent wage. That's great. Everybody's happy. I, on the other hand, married a genius who ended up inventing and running her own very successful business.'

'And that's a problem for you?' Jane asked.

'Well, in a way I suppose it is,' Robbo insisted. 'I mean I'm not like Rupert. I never expected to be this rich, nor did Jim. But when you *become* this rich, what do you do? Do you give it away? Would you?'

'Well, not all of it, I suppose,' Henry conceded.

'If not all, then how much?' Robbo pressed. 'Actually what happens is you end up just getting used to being that wealthy so you begin to think that that's the norm. That it's kind of logical and inevitable and *right* that you should have that much money.'

'Yeah,' Jimmy agreed. 'If I'd jumped from my first year's income to what I'm earning now I truly would have thought that the world had gone mad and that it was obscenely unfair, but because it just *grew* I don't find it that way at all.'

'Except of course it *is* obscene and deep down we know it,' said Robbo, 'and that's why I sort of envy you not having to worry about it, Henry.'

'My heart bleeds for you,' Henry replied drily.

'What I don't understand,' Monica said, 'is where all this money is coming from.'

Rupert rolled his eyes in a pantomime of indulgent frustration.

'Everybody asks that,' he said. 'Why? Why do they care as long as it's there? Why worry about where it's coming from?'

'Well, I'm certainly not complaining!' Monica hastened to add.

And with that, more wine was opened and Rupert went on to explain in some detail how the more he was paid, the better it was for the economies of emerging nations.

Nappy economics

'The wheels on the bus go round and round. Round and round. Round and round,' he sang, as he always did when changing Lillie. He reached into the enormous plastic Pampers sack, which for a panicky moment he thought was empty. It wasn't, there were three or four left in the bottom . . . A day's worth, for sure. But what then? Jimmy knew that they would have to buy more. He also knew that he would not be buying a bag of a hundred as he had done in the past, but a much smaller number.

Those two remaining credit cards had their limits and the day was fast approaching when those limits would be reached. It was a false economy to buy the small bags but Jimmy had by this time got used to the fact that the less money you had, the fewer options you had to spend it efficiently.

Nobody could understand how anybody living in a house like his could actually be at the point of counting pennies. Such a house could surely be mortgaged for millions. The problem was it had been mortgaged for millions already, to pay for Webb Street.

Jimmy had done it when he was rich.

He had done it in order to get richer. Exposing himself horribly in the process, under the impression that his salary and bonuses would always be there to pay the interest on the loan.

Jimmy's dad had warned him.

'Never use your house as collateral, son,' he had said. 'It's risking the seed corn.'

At the time Jimmy had thought that kind of thinking was exactly why his father's home was worth three hundred thousand while his was valued at seven million. Now of course he understood. His father still owned his house while he was calculating the cost of nappies. Of course with Lizzie riding to the rescue things were nothing like as bleak as he'd feared, but it was still going to be a very tough year.

'Lillie's fine. No poo,' Jimmy said, having pulled apart the Velcro.

And now he faced a dilemma. An appalling, shameful and ridiculous dilemma. There was no poo, it was true, but there was plenty of wee. Not so much that the nappy was a great bulging heavy sausage but certainly enough to activate whatever it was in the plastic which drew in the moisture and caused it to swell.

That was the dilemma. The nappy was not completely full; heavy, yes, but not so full as to be saturated. Should he change it? Should he spend eighteen pence immediately or rewrap it and wait until a change was absolutely essential? And it wasn't just eighteen pence, it was much more than that really because the next lot of nappies would be bought on his Visa or his MasterCard and he knew that this debt would not be paid off at the end of the month. The nappies that Lillie soiled with such frequency might be disposable but the debt they incurred would continue to grow at 13 per cent, possibly for as long as it would take the damn things to biodegrade. Jimmy had always considered himself a pretty green sort of guy, but these days he didn't give two fucks about any aspect of disposable nappies except what they cost.

He changed the nappy. Of course he changed the nappy. He was Jimmy Corby and he didn't care how much trouble he was in, his daughter could have a dry flipping bottom and a nice clean nappy. He owned a *street*, for God's sake, a street which with Lizzie and his dead friend's help he was now going to be in a position to hang on to.

Lillie immediately shat in the new nappy. That was her favourite trick, always had been. To wait until you'd cleaned her off, until you'd rubbed in the zinc cream, dusted on the powder and secured a new nappy, and then poo straight into it. The little baby girl gurgled happily as Jimmy changed her for a second time. It wasn't her fault, she could not possibly know that had she moved her bowels thirty seconds earlier (or had Jimmy waited for that time), he could have saved eighteen pence plus interest.

Jimmy put Lillie back on to her little padded mat with the dangly things above it and realized what it was that Monica had smelt when she thought Lillie needed changing.

'Cressida's done one on the floor,' he said.

'Oh *grosseramma*!' Toby said, looking up from his cereal.

'Well, what do you want me to do about it?' Monica replied, clingfilming a plain HobNob for Toby's mid-morning treat. Toby had given up asking if there were any Müller Corners, having finally come to understand

171

that there weren't. He told his friends he preferred HobNobs, particularly the plain ones as the chocolate ones were too sweet.

'You know the drill,' Monica continued, 'I read you the book. Put the poo in the potty and show it to her. You have to show her the poo in the potty and make appreciative noises. Then put her back on the potty.'

'I know the bloody theory,' Jimmy said, getting some toilet paper and picking up the turd, 'but it's not bloody working, is it?'

'It's not working because we're not consistent!' Monica replied angrily. 'That's the most important point of all. The book says you have to be consistent.'

'Bugger the book!'

'Don't say bugger, Daddy. It's swearing,' said Toby.

'I didn't, I said bother.'

'No you didn't, that doesn't even rhyme,' Toby insisted, drinking the milk from the bottom of the corn-flakes bowl.

'You know the theory,' said Monica.

'Yes, Mon! I know the theory.'

Both their tempers were rising now.

'Well, bloody well apply it then!' Monica said, suddenly snapping. 'Children need *routine*. You can't keep changing the rules. It says in *The Big Happy Baby Book* that—'

'You know what?' said Jimmy. 'Screw *The Big Happy Baby Book*. That book is fiction! It's written by a childless fantasist. I have shown Cressida a hundred turds! I've cooed over them, admired them, sung to them, pinned medals on them, placed them back in the potty on velvet cushions and stuck her on top of them and the little bitch *still* prefers to shit on the floor. All right?'

Monica began to weep.

'Shut up!' she cried. 'Shut up, Jimmy! I can't stand it. I really can't. We have to try. We can't just . . .'

She had been pulling a jumper down over Toby's head as she broke down and when his little face emerged he was crying too.

'Don't worry, baby. Mummy's just being silly,' Monica croaked. 'We need a brush, Jimmy. Look at his hair. Don't cry, baby, please don't cry.'

Cressida and Lillie were wailing too. Jimmy wasn't, but only on the outside. Inside he was crying as well and as he cried inside it occurred to him yet again that he had once more forgotten that Robbo was dead.

His best friend was dead and he couldn't find a hairbrush. Could life get any harder?

'Oh God,' Monica said through her tears as she inspected Toby's head, 'he's got *nits*.'

'Can't worry about that now,' Jimmy said, sticking a bit of toast between his teeth, shoving the makeshift grandpa project into Toby's fist and grabbing his sports kit.

'Try not to scratch your head, darling,' Monica called after them as they headed for the lift that connected the

173

family room with the garage beneath it. 'I'll put conditioner on it and comb them out tonight.'

A lift. A *lift*.

Jimmy was counting the cost of single nappies and yet he still owned and operated a private elevator. Jimmy had never been exactly sure what the word 'surreal' meant but he imagined that a jobless, penniless, debt-ridden loser taking a lift to his private underground car park might fit the bill.

Underfloor parking

When Jimmy and Monica had bought their last and finest Notting Hill house in 2003 it had had ample room to park three cars in a large area at the front. Indeed this had been one of the features about which the estate agent was most enthusiastic.

'Look,' the agent had said conspiratorially, 'don't say I said it but you could probably service the interest on your mortgage *renting out* one of your parking spaces. The parking problem in London is out of control. I mean they bang on and on about the homeless, but actually there are a lot less people with nowhere to sleep than people with nowhere to park, and they need help too.'

The first thing Jimmy and Monica did with the parking area was get rid of it.

It was Lizzie's idea. She took one look at the front of the house and very forcefully explained to Monica and Jimmy that it simply wouldn't do. Such an arrangement was ridiculous, insane even. Here they were, Lizzie insisted, the owners of one of the loveliest detached town houses in Notting Hill, a house which by some quirk of Georgian architectural caprice was set much further back from the road than the other houses in the street, and yet the previous owners had seen fit to squander this precious feature and use it as a place to *store their bloody cars*.

'Vandals!' Lizzie had pronounced. 'People who cannot appreciate beautiful things should be banned by law from owning them.'

She stood on the granite-paved surface between the big new family Range Rover and Monica's spunky little Mini convertible and spread her arms wide.

'I shall tell you what this is,' she said dramatically. 'This, Monica, is your front garden.'

'Oh my God,' Monica squealed with childlike excitement. Nobody had a front garden in Notting Hill. Not even Gwyneth.

Lizzie insisted that Monica summon Jodie the nanny from inside the house.

'She must bring sheets of Toby's thickest and most beautiful paper from the craft cupboard, and lots and lots of coloured crayons and pencils.'

Jodie rushed out with the required articles followed by a chuckling Toby, and to everyone's delight Lizzie set to work on the bonnet of the Mini, sketching out her entire garden concept right there and then.

Robbo smiled indulgently at his wife's enthusiasm and suggested to Jimmy that they mooch off to the pub. Which they did, leaving Lizzie scribbling away furiously while Monica brought strawberry tea and Toby and Jodie sat in the Range Rover and headbanged to 'Highway To Hell'.

Lizzie sketched palms, vines, great earthen pots with small trees in them, Japanese stones, soothing water features, pergolas with wind chimes attached and even a miniature English meadow. The end result was so lovely in itself that Monica had it framed and hung in her en suite.

And from that one beautiful vision plucked from the heady upper reaches of Lizzie's imagination had begun a feat of civil engineering more costly and more complex than had been the construction of the original five-storey house and those on either side of it put together. It was not, of course, the garden that was the problem. The problem now was where to put the cars.

'The answer's obvious,' Lizzie said as Monica and she toasted her creation with champagne. 'You put the cars *under* the garden.'

When Jimmy and Robbo got back from the pub (having had six pints in all, two for Jimmy and four for

Robbo), they found Lizzie and Monica giggling over their champagne and announcing that the deal was done and the whole design was complete down to the minutest detail. Not the actual engineering, of course, but where all the shrubs and herbs were going to go and what colour smoked glass to have in the lift.

'Of course it'll take years to get the planning permission,' Robbo said, searching for more beer in the huge steel fridge. 'God, Jimmy, why do you always buy American beer? It does not make you look cool and it's *too bloody sweet!*'

'Horrid little Nazis,' Lizzie said.

'Who? Americans?' Robbo asked.

'Town planners.'

'Ah. That I agree.'

'Don't they understand that a city is *alive*, a living, breathing entity, not some museum piece to be pickled in aspic.'

As it turned out, getting planning permission was a breeze because Lizzie had been able to show that when the house had been built in 1814 it had actually had a front garden. In fact, by a happy chance it was the paving over of this garden in the sixties in order to create the parking area that was now revealed as illegal. No planning permission had been granted.

Jimmy's luck held yet again. It turned out to be his *civic duty* to install a four-car garage under his home. The Historic Buildings Trust (of which Lizzie was a benefactor) had fervently taken up Jimmy and Monica's case and the council, mindful of their legal obligations towards a Grade 2-listed street, were positively anxious for the Corbys to proceed with the massive renovation. Indeed, at one point there was even talk of a council grant to part fund the work since it was perceived as being in the best cultural interests of the community. Jimmy and Monica were sent the paperwork and invited to apply but graciously declined the offer.

'Sure, it's silly to walk away from a co-funding initiative,' Jim said at the time, 'but have you seen the length of the form? You know what? Life's too short.'

The job was a colossal undertaking since the entire five-storey building had to be underpinned while the garage was excavated under the front garden and partly beneath the house itself. Understandably this had not endeared Jimmy and Monica to their new neighbours but, as David had said when he heard about the scheme at the next curry night, *fuck the neighbours*.

'I'm an architect, mate,' David said. 'Neighbours object to all building plans except their own. Believe me, the same bloke telling you your Kango hammer woke his baby is secretly plotting to add an extra floor plus patio that will directly overlook your sun deck.'

During the work many a historical artefact including a number of Roman coins had been unearthed. These Monica sent straight to the British Museum.

'I suppose they might have been worth quite a bit,'

she said, 'if we'd tried to sell them, but you know what? Life's too short.'

Eventually the work was completed, with 80 per cent of the parking space reclaimed as a splendid front garden (or local cat toilet as Jimmy and Monica soon discovered) and just 20 per cent reserved for the ramp which led up directly on to the pavement. This ramp was very steep but nothing that four-by-fours couldn't handle, so Jimmy got rid of Monica's Mini and bought her a brand-new Toyota Land Cruiser.

'Makes me laugh when Greenies claim there's no purpose for serious off-road vehicles in town,' Jimmy joked. 'They should see the angle on my exit ramp.'

What fun they all had as a family on the first few occasions they used it.

'Weeeeeeeeeeh,' Toby cried and they all agreed.

They held an opening party for the garden which a number of Kate Moss's circle attended (although not Kate herself) and during which cases of superb vintage wine were presented to mollify disgruntled neighbours. Everybody pronounced the garden a triumph and it was photographed for a number of magazines as an example of what could be achieved in London if people actually buckled down and made the effort. 'One Notting Hill home restored to its early-nineteenth-century glory,' the property section of the *Standard* read. And although it seemed unlikely that the 1814 garden had been based around Japanese plants and stones (real Japanese stones, specially imported), it was generally agreed that the over-all effect was *incredibly* soothing.

'No matter how terrible a day it's been,' Monica told her guests as she perched on the sixteenth-century Italian marble bird table, 'this place calms me. It never fails.'

Unfortunately it was not very long before the garden lost its calming effect, and not just because of the cat shit.

'People drop their litter in it,' Monica moaned. 'Can you believe it? Fast-food wrappers and the like. I feel awful seeing poor Juanita having to clean it up. It really isn't fair on her, but people never think of that, do they? Do you know what annoys me most? The little bags of dog shit. People go to the trouble of picking up their dog's muck in a bag, but then they seem to think that's public duty enough and leave it on my bird table.'

Off road, on road

Down in the sub-basement the pauper and his son got out of the lift and into the last remaining car. At least the car still felt good. It was a state-of-the-art 2008 top-of-the-topmost-range Range Rover with all the trimmings. Electric everything, a sound system that could have played Wembley Stadium, massive DVD screens in all the headrests, tinted glass and soft leather upholstery.

A huge tank of a car. An assault vehicle of a car.

Ton upon ton of shiny black steel that Jimmy was sure could knock a Humvee off the road without wobbling the suspension. It still felt good to drive it. Even now, after everything, perhaps not least because the tank was fully paid for, an as-yet-unliquefied asset. Jimmy still had it up his sleeve as a source of ready cash (if he could flog it without MasterCard, Visa, Amex or the bank finding out).

Jimmy tried to relax into the beautiful pale-cream upholstery. Or at least the upholstery which had been beautiful, pale and creamy for as long as Jimmy had employed a handyman and occasional driver to clean it. Sadly, now that the only person likely to valet the luxurious interior of his car was Jimmy himself, the soft leather had become a murky blend of soggy biscuit, McDonald's fries, baby puke, mud and chocolate.

'Why is the car always so dirty these days?' Toby asked.

'It's a survival tactic that I read about in an SAS book,' Jimmy replied, 'in case we are ever stranded on a mountain or in a hostile country. We could last for weeks just by sucking the seats.'

Toby laughed and Jimmy felt better. He was very

proud of the fact that, despite his troubles, most of the time he managed to stay positive in front of his children. Toby was a little boy and he had a right to start his day with a mind uncluttered by doubt and uncertainty. Unburdened by care. Even the dreadful news about Robbo had to take second place to that fact.

Jimmy flicked the remote, opened the automatic trap and powered the huge car up the ramp.

'Weeeeeehhhhh-hooo!' he said.

'Weeeeeehhhhh-hooo!' Toby echoed.

'Rock 'n' Roll!' they shouted together.

Jimmy glanced at Toby and felt a sudden surge of joy and even optimism. A joy quite separate from his cares and worries. Divorced from the misery of his bereavement and the pressure of his finances. A joy made out of love. He had three wonderful, healthy children. Tobes, Cressie and Lillie. They were his and he was theirs. In real terms, how wealthy could a man get?

'We're surrounded, Sergeant, and the men are starving,' Jimmy said, returning to his joke and putting on a British officer's voice. 'Put that baby seat in to soak and boil it up for a nourishing stale rusk soup. And get one of the chaps to go foraging for old crisps in the seat-belt-catch orifices.'

Toby chuckled, but he wasn't having it. 'That's stupid,' he said.

'Stupid!' Jimmy said in mock horror. 'I beg to differ,

Sergeant! Adequately providing for the well-being of his men is a commander's first duty.'

'Yes,' Toby insisted, 'but if the SAS were going to all the hassle of smearing food on the seats then they would probably just put some in a proper picnic basket and stick it in the boot. I mean seriously, Dad, why smear it on the seats when you could keep it fresher in a Tupperware?'

'Logical,' Jimmy conceded, 'although *slightly* dull. And the SAS do pride themselves on a certain eccentric flair. Not like those US Navy Seals who try to pretend they're robots. You see, you get your logic from your mother. She's the one with the steel-trap brain. I supplied your charm, your good looks and your ability to pick your nose while pretending to yawn. OK. Got a pen and paper? Let's write about Granddad.'

But even Jimmy could not stay happy and positive while on a school run. It simply was not possible.

Sad to say, the first word Toby took down for his essay about Granddad was 'Dickhead!' That was what Jimmy shouted at a motorbike dispatch rider who cut him up and almost got himself killed in the process as Jimmy tried to pull out into Notting Hill Gate.

In the old days PC, Pre-Crunch, neither Jimmy nor Monica had had the slightest idea of the daily nightmare that Jodie was going through on the school run. Many were the days when Monica had blithely watched Jodie take Toby into the garage elevator, both looking fresh and well breakfasted, smartly turned out, hair brushed and ready for the day. Monica did not know as she punched up the cappuccino machine and considered her nightmare day ahead that a *genuine* nightmare awaited Jodie and indeed every driver who ventured on to the streets of London between the hours of seven and nine-thirty in the morning, as the usual heavy traffic of one of the world's busiest cities was supplemented by an extra half-million or so cars (often HUGE cars) each containing one mum or nanny) and one small child.

Now that both Jimmy and Monica appreciated the full horror of the school run, Jimmy couldn't help wondering why they didn't walk it. It was only a mile and a half and it would probably be quicker on foot. He had in fact suggested this idea to Monica but she had refused even to consider it.

'The streets just aren't safe,' she insisted. 'What if Toby ran out into the road? He could be knocked down.'

'By a parent driving a child in a four-by-four?' Jimmy asked.

'Yes actually,' Monica replied angrily. 'Some of those mums drive like they're invading bloody Poland. It's incredible. I saw a cyclist go down last week. Horrible.'

'So we protect Toby from being knocked over by a frazzled, furious parent in a Range Rover by *being* that frazzled parent in a Range Rover?'

'Look, I don't care,' Monica said, the light of battle in her eyes. 'All I know is that if Toby's inside the Discovery he is totally safe and if he's outside it he isn't. You can't argue with that equation, Jimmy! I'm sorry, but end of story. We may be poor but we're not going to let poverty kill our kids. He goes to school in a car. You don't compromise on safety. Ever.'

Monica, like every other parent in the same situation, presented this point of view with an almost evangelical zeal, her eyes ablaze with moral certitude, as if merely by conjuring up the word 'safety' she had trumped any and all other arguments.

'Monica!' Jimmy protested. 'That's the argument the police use when they close an entire motorway because somebody's having a piss on the hard shoulder. You have to quantify the risk!'

But Monica was not prepared to quantify the risk and so Jimmy joined the school run along with every other parent and nanny in London.

They screamed at taxi drivers. Taxi drivers and bus drivers screamed back. Tattooed and dreadlocked anarcho-cyclists banged bonnets. Leather-clad motorcycle dispatch riders chased leaping pedestrians through tiny gaps in the acreage of steaming, fuming metal. The very air throbbed with frustration and fury as Londoners young and old began their working day in the worst possible mood to do good business.

Jimmy did his best to stay positive as he joined the fray, attempting to edge his tank towards the school while simultaneously dictating an essay about his father to Toby, who was trying to write it down.

'*My granddad has looked after people's money all his life*,' Jimmy said, then added, 'Are you trying to get yourself killed, you stupid bastard!'

A cyclist swerved. Jimmy slammed on the brakes. The cyclist screamed, 'Cunt!' Jimmy shouted, 'Arsehole!' and Toby jerked forward, breaking the lead in his pencil.

'Dad!' Toby protested. 'Don't brake like that! I can't write my essay now.'

'I had to, Tobes. I would have knocked him down.'

'He called you a cunt!'

'Don't say cunt.'

'I didn't. He did.'

'Then you did.'

'Only because he did.'

'Look, we have to do this essay, Tobes. *Granddad works in a bank and he—*'

'My pencil's broken!'

'There's pens all over the floor, mate. Grab one.'

'They're all broken and anyway it'll be a different colour. I can't write an essay in two different pens. Everybody will laugh and Mr Penfold will kill me. They're always laughing! I'm always getting killed. Because all my stuff's so crap!'

Jimmy glanced at his son, who was suddenly once more fighting back tears. Jimmy felt terrible guilt.

'Sorry, mate,' he said. 'Can we do it tonight? I promise. One day late won't matter, surely.'

Toby didn't answer. Instead, he angrily screwed up the paper he had been writing on and turned to stare out of the window. The school run had done its worst. The sunny mood had evaporated.

Toby was chewing his lip, clearly thinking of the embarrassments that lay ahead of him at school. It broke Jimmy's heart.

Toby reached into his school bag and pulled out his Nintendo.

Jimmy almost protested, but then didn't.

He had once been a dedicated gamer himself, but these days he hated that little box with a passion for the way it lured Toby away from real life. On the other hand, why shouldn't the boy escape? He had plenty to escape from.

Thanks to Jimmy.

Having it both ways

In 2005 the people of Britain were encouraged to 'make poverty history' by attending a free concert in Hyde Park (or sitting at home and watching it on television). The concert was called Live 8, a reference to the G8 world economic summit going on in Scotland at the same time and also to mark the twentieth anniversary of the Live Aid concert held at Wembley Stadium.

The tickets to Live 8 were free and distributed by lottery but, in order to avoid any accusation that the concert had cost money that might have been better used to provide food for starving Africans, there was a so-called 'Golden Circle' where those who wished to could register their objection to poverty by buying premium corporate seats at the front and enjoying luxury catered hospitality.

Jimmy, now on the board at Mason Jervis, was absolutely insistent that the company should purchase such golden tickets for senior clients and management.

'Forget golf weekends, paintballing and boring bloody Glyndebourne,' Jimmy said excitedly. 'Who cares about opera when you can Rock 'n' Roll! Besides which, this corporate perk saves lives. How cool is that?'

As well as encouraging his employers to take a more morally responsible attitude towards their tax-deductible freebies, Jimmy announced that he intended to do his bit personally, taking a table of his own as a private individual in order to treat his friends.

'There's a real movement going on here,' he argued, 'a new consciousness. People are beginning to realize that the kind of global inequality which we have always taken for granted is *not* a fact of life. It can be challenged. It can be changed. I want to be able to tell my kids that I was a part of that change.'

'Bollocks,' said Rupert, 'you just want to get pissed and watch U2.'

'Well, there's that too,' Jimmy said with a grin.

The idea behind Live 8 was not to raise money directly in the way Live Aid had done twenty years earlier. This time it was *consciousness* that was to be raised. Particularly the consciousness of the world leaders at the G8 summit. The organizers, led by Bono and Geldof, wanted those leaders to understand that ordinary people did not like the idea of babies dying in poverty. Particularly when those infant mortalities were the result of the actions of iniquitous Western politicians. The people had had enough of third world poverty and Live 8 was going to give that discontent a voice. The innovative idea was that on the day, the people would be encouraged to register their outrage at the heartless politicians who represented them by sending a text or by logging on to a website *insisting* that poverty be made history.

Predictably, not all of Jimmy's gang embraced the idea with the same enthusiasm.

'As a matter of fact,' Rupert said with his usual sardonic smile after he had stretched comfortably in his seat and studied the champagne list with the doubtful air of a man who does not expect to be impressed, 'people regularly get the opportunity to make their opinions known and also to make them count.'

'Oh yes, clever clogs,' said Monica, already on

the defensive, 'and how do you work that out?'

'They're called general elections,' Rupert replied.

'Oh . . .' said Monica, 'well, I mean apart from that.'

'What else could you want? Democracy is by definition an expression of the power of the people, and it can be achieved without the inconvenience of sitting on the ground for eight hours in a futile attempt to catch a glimpse of the top of Bono's head because a bunch of rich arses like us are sitting at the front obscuring the view.'

Jimmy and Monica exchanged glances. They had seriously considered not inviting Rupert, knowing he would be like this and try to spoil everything. But Amanda would have been so hurt if they'd been left out and so they felt they had no choice. Particularly since Rupert and Amanda's marriage seemed to be in particularly good shape at the moment. They had weathered the beautiful PA period and now looked pretty settled. They had even stopped sniping at each other in public, which was a deal-breaker as far as Jimmy was concerned.

But Rupert was still Rupert. The same smug, supercilious reactionary he had always been. It didn't matter whether he was in a student pub in Sussex or the Golden Circle at Live 8, he was out to wind people up and he never failed to do so.

Particularly Henry.

'Look, Rupert, you bastard,' Henry snapped, 'I'm one

of those iniquitous politicians who need to be getting the wake-up call and personally I'm quite happy to pick up that phone and smell the coffee. This generation is *talking* to us. We need to listen.'

'Which generation, Henry?' Rupert said. 'Bono's at least ten years older than you are. Paul McCartney's twenty.'

'Yeah, actually that's right,' David said. 'I think this whole event would have been much more relevant if they'd booked some hipper bands.'

'True,' Jimmy said with mock seriousness, 'that would really have made it work for the starving Africans.'

'I'm just saying if they want to connect with young people they need something off the wall and a bit alternative. Bit of Trance/Fusion maybe.'

'Your problem, David,' Amanda said, 'is you still think you *are* a young person. You really need to sort that out.'

'Anyway,' said Robbo, 'bollocks to *duff duff* dance trance wank. We want tunes. We want to rock!'

Henry, like any good politician, was not going to allow himself to be diverted from his political agenda.

'We all know that everything is a compromise,' he said, 'and it's perfectly possible to sneer – but at least it's happening, right? At least people are doing something.'

'Yes, they are doing something,' Rupert said, popping the first cork. 'And what they are doing is being a great big bunch of fucking hypocrites.'

'You mean us,' Henry asked, 'the politicians? Easy to shift the blame, isn't it, Roop?'

'I mean all of us. Every single person here.'

'Oh, give the bloody rich a break!' Jimmy chipped in. 'The whole Golden Circle thing has been gone over again and again. Somebody had to pay for the gig, why not the rich? And if they get a bottle of champagne and a decent seat for their trouble—'

'I don't mean just the Golden Circle, Jimmy,' Rupert said, 'and I don't mean just you politicians, Henry, although I know you think that you're the most important people on earth. I mean everyone in the whole park. They are *all* a great big bunch of fucking hypocrites. And the people watching it on the BBC. And the BBC, for that matter. Actually, *particularly* the BBC because they're not even screening the political appeals. It's just a free concert to them.'

Monica very rarely got angry and if she did she tended to bottle it up. She had been brought up always to be nice. This time, however, her cork popped along with the champagne and she let rip.

'How can you be such a nasty *bastard*, Rupert!' she said, her face going bright red. 'Every single person in this huge crowd *cares*. Apart from you, that is. Of course they care! How can you possibly doubt it? And they want things to change too. It's stupid and arrogant and utterly pathetic to be all cynical about it. In fact I wish you'd go, Rupert. I really wish you would. Sorry, Amanda, but it's just awful of him to be so negative and destructive. It isn't funny, you know, or clever. People are *starving* and it's just horrible.'

Such was Monica's passion that even Rupert's studied sangfroid seemed to take a momentary dent. The old gang weren't used to Monica getting up and having a go. She was famously a peacemaker.

Jimmy gave her a hug. He'd known she'd be extra-emotional that day. The concert had not begun yet but they had been playing documentary stuff on the enormous screens (the stuff the BBC wasn't showing). There was terribly moving footage of the devastating consequences of poverty in the developing world. Inevitably it was the children whose suffering featured most tellingly and Monica couldn't bear that, particularly since she was pregnant with their second child. The pictures of starving babies combined with Rupert's smug negativity had pushed her over the edge.

After she had said her piece she began to cry, which Jimmy knew she hated.

'Sorry,' she said. 'It's the baby. My brain's going to milk. It happened in Waitrose the other day, for no reason at all, while I was choosing a muesli. Don't look at me, I feel an idiot.'

'Come on, Mon,' Jimmy said. 'Rupert's just being the arse he always is. Trying to be clever. And this is supposed to be a party, isn't it? We're celebrating the human spirit, aren't we?'

'By getting pissed, gorging ourselves and watching top bands from the best seats,' said Rupert. 'Sorry, is that the wrong thing to say? Just me being an arse and trying to be clever.'

All eyes turned on Rupert again.

Henry and Jane looked particularly angry. As teenagers they had each individually attended the original Live Aid concert and had carried this coincidence as a kind of talisman for their mutual integrity ever since. Henry often said that Live Aid had been one of the reasons he had gone into politics in the first place. To try to make a difference.

Silently Henry opened one of the information packs that had been placed on the corporate tables and slid it across towards Rupert. It was the picture of a dead baby in its mother's arms, the mother, half mad with grief and hunger, still attempting to put her empty breast into its fly-blown mouth. Rupert glanced down at the picture and then shrugged.

'Make you think at all?' Henry asked. 'I imagine that even you care about that, don't you?'

Then Rupert smiled. You did not rise to become a senior director of an entire bank before your fortieth birthday as Rupert had done without being able to withstand a bit of emotional blackmail. Since taking over at the Royal Lancashire, Rupert had come to be known as Roop the Boot for the record number of redundancies he had instigated in the name of streamlining his bank's 'business model'. You couldn't shame Roop.

'Of course I care about it,' Rupert said easily, 'and I imagine that I probably *do* as much about it as you do, Henry. The only difference is that I don't insist on the right to congratulate myself on my moral integrity as well. I *know* that every step and every breath I take on this earth are selfish ones. I *know* that the only number in life that really matters is *numero uno.*'

Henry's lip tightened. He and Rupert had always been the least close members of the gang and had actually had a fist fight at university over the rights and wrongs of the first Iraq war. Of course after Monica had got so upset everyone had assumed that the discussion was over, and now they all clamoured to ask Henry and Rupert to drop it.

'Guys!' Jimmy said. 'Come on, this is supposed to be fun.'

'Let it go, Henry,' Jane said. 'You know you won't change Rupert.'

'Well, if we can't change the bastard at the Live 8 concert, when can we?' Henry snapped back. 'Come on, people, I've been in Parliament for eight years now. I know all about complacency and so-called compassion fatigue. Where I work, every day is a fucking compromise but that's no excuse for not trying. Things *can* change. Things *are* getting better.'

'We banned foxhunting,' said Jane.

'Exactly,' said Henry, 'and that's only the start. We're not just here to get pissed and watch U2.'

'Well, maybe not just to,' Jimmy put in, 'but it's a good basis from which to build a day.'

'No,' Henry insisted, 'this is supposed to be about raising consciousness. Let's start with our own. You just said that you do as much as I do. What do you mean by that, Rupert? What exactly *do* you do?'

'Amanda and I have a charity budget just as I imagine you and Jane do, Henry.'

'Yes, mate, we certainly do.'

'Oh *please*,' Jane protested, 'let's not have an argument about who gives the most money away. It's horrible.'

'So you give money to charity, Henry,' Rupert pressed on. 'So do Amanda and I, as it happens. Mainly school bursaries and my historic churches foundation but as Jane says, let's not quibble over causes and sums. What else do you do about the poverty that you want to make history? I don't mean as a politician, I mean as a private individual. What do you do that I don't?'

'Look!' Laura shouted. 'Come on, Dave, I think it's about to start. You'll have to put me on your shoulders later.'

'One one! Two two!' a man said on the stage into various microphones while another man hit the drums.

'Is that U2's drummer?' Monica asked, feigning excitement.

'How would you tell?' Amanda said. 'I mean could anyone recognize the other two members of U2?'

'Let's just forget it, hey, guys,' Jimmy said to Henry and

Rupert, pouring more champagne. 'This is a party and it isn't the time.'

'Well, I don't know about that, Jimbo,' David observed. 'I reckon if we are going to have a discussion like this then now clearly *is* the time.'

'Absolutely,' said Rupert, who still had Henry in his sights.

'So would your point be, Henry old pal,' he continued, 'that because I earn ten times more than you I am ten times more responsible for the death of the baby in that picture?'

'Rupert, this is not seemly,' Amanda snapped. She had appeared to be enjoying the earlier part of the conversation but now that numbers were involved she obviously felt it had gone too far.

'It's entirely seemly. Well, Henry?'

'Yes, actually,' Henry replied, 'in some ways I think I *am* saying that. Of course we all bear responsibility for world inequality but the inflation of corporate incomes is a symptom of the ever-increasing imbalance between—'

Rupert interrupted him. 'But this leaflet says that five pounds would have saved the baby's life. Clearly the mother didn't have a fiver, because the baby's dead. So by your logic of income comparison that makes you at least *twenty thousand fivers* more responsible for the child's death than the adults in its own community. Doesn't that make the difference between

197

your culpability and mine somewhat semantic?'

There was a moment's silence. It was clear that everybody knew Rupert was talking rubbish but for a moment they were not sure how to counter it.

'It's not that bloody simple, Rupert, and you know it,' Henry blustered. 'I earn a reasonable wage, you earn a ridiculous and obscene—'

'Let's stop this,' Lizzie said, 'please.'

'Yes, come on, guys!' Robbo chipped in, having finally got bored enough to protest. 'Do you think they do anything besides champagne? I'd love a beer.'

But Henry had no intention of allowing Rupert to have the last word.

'The people in this crowd are decent, caring, hardworking people, Rupert,' Henry shouted. 'They do not earn insane bonuses. They earn decent livings and they earn them doing proper jobs. Not bloody *banking*.'

'And every single one of them is in debt to a bank, Henry. As indeed are you. And like you, they want those debts to be cheap. Just like you wanted the mortgages on *both* your homes to be cheap.'

'Hang on, Rupert,' Jane began, angered at Rupert's implication. 'Don't start bringing in second homes! Henry's an MP, he has to work in two places. And what's more, we did both our homes up ourselves, working bloody hard every weekend for a whole summer.'

'Are you suggesting, Jane,' Amanda retorted, 'that because you did your own grouting your second home is somehow less unfair on the world's poor than mine?'

'You've got about *ten* second homes, Amanda!' Jane said, having to shout above the increasing noise of the sound check.

'At which point I refer you,' said Rupert, entirely relaxed once more, 'to the argument of the five-pound baby. The real difference between your wealth and mine is minute, it's tiny, it's *nothing*, compared to the distance between your wealth and this African mother's about whom you care so much. And all our wealth, the wealth of everyone in this crowd, all the cheap mortgages, ballooning property values, low taxes, cheap training shoes, all of it is created and maintained by the workings of the very system about which everyone here is claiming to be so angry.'

Rupert stood up and, turning his back on the stage, surveyed the vast crowd. So many happy, eager faces. Many girlfriends already on boyfriends' shoulders. Comedy hats in the shape of huge bananas, earnest banners, raised plastic bottles saluting the roadies on the stage.

'Look at that,' Rupert said. 'Just look at that, a sea of placards saying that those girls want to "make poverty history". Do you see any placards saying, "and I'm prepared to pay more for my Gap clothes and my Nike shoes in order to make it happen"? Is anyone pleading for higher interest rates so that their bank can invest more in the third world? More expensive petrol so that

Shell and BP won't screw the poor African quite as fucking viciously? No! They're bloody not. Because the people in that crowd want to make poverty history but *not* if they have to pay for it themselves. Not if it means sacrificing their cheap clothes, cheap food, cheap credit, cheap air travel and low taxes.'

Henry leaped to his feet, squaring off in front of Rupert. It looked as if Henry was going to hit him.

'Life involves compromises,' he shouted, 'so does principle. That is not an excuse for moral inertia!'

'Pardon?' Rupert curled his lip. 'Do I hear a politician making noise and saying nothing? How very rare.'

'Of course these people care about their own jobs and services, their homes and their well-being. But they still want some moral justice. How can you doubt it? I mean seriously, Rupert, how can you fucking doubt it? They are calling on us politicians to get off our arses and create a new mindset. To start working towards a fairer and more equitable . . .'

'They are fucking NOT,' Rupert replied, raising his own voice for the first time. 'They *say* they are but they don't mean it. Because if they did mean it, you'd do it. You're a politician, Henry, and you know that you and your cronies will do *whatever it takes* to get re-elected. If sending the entire contents of the Bank of England to Ethiopia would secure you another term, you'd do it in a second. But you know that it wouldn't because if people really wanted to make poverty history they'd vote Green or Socialist or Anarchist or some other pointless silly bollocks, but they *don't*. What people want is low taxes and cheap money, which is why they vote Tory or New Labour or Lib Dem. Why do you think the entire media is behind this event? Every newspaper proprietor? Because they know it will change *nothing*. It's a joke. A party. Just like Jimmy says. Yes, people would like to make poverty history, it would be very nice, but NOT if it means taking a cut themselves. Any more than Bono and U2 want to pay the tax they've been lucky to avoid these last twenty years just by being Irish. That's why we're all fucking hypocrites. You, me, Bono, Coldplay and every bloody overexcited shop assistant in the crowd. Why the fuck should *we*, having condemned half the planet to living in abject misery to support what we see as a basic lifestyle, then expect to be able to strut about in Hyde Park boasting about how caring and generous we are *at the same time.'*

On the stage the roadies seemed finally to have finished their counting and banging. At Jimmy's table there was an angry and depressed silence. Rupert had sat down but Henry was still standing, his fists clenched, his knuckles white.

'You're wrong, you *shit*,' he said, 'really you're wrong.' But as the noise of the crowd grew in expectation of the imminent arrival of rock superstars, he offered no further argument.

'Blimey, Rupert,' Jimmy said finally, 'you know how to piss on a parade.'

'Well, actually, on another subject entirely,' Rupert said, 'I have some rather fun news. I'm to be knighted by Blair for services to banking.'

'Yes, I'm to be *Lady* Bennett.' Amanda beamed. 'Of course I shan't insist that close friends use the title.'

There was a huge cheer. Familiar chords filled the air.

'Hello, Hyde Park!' said Bono.

A farewell piss-up

On the second evening after the night Robbo died, his many friends assembled in London. The funeral plans had not yet been put in place, but the death of such a hugely popular man had left many people struggling to cope and feeling the need to meet up immediately to share their loss. Therefore with the blessing of Lizzie (herself too upset to attend), Rupert had arranged a kind of pre-wake piss-up in the function room of his London club with a malt whisky tasting, several real ales on tap and a takeaway curry delivered.

Fittingly, in view of the character of the deceased, the

evening, though desperately sad, was good-natured and ribald. Rupert spoke first.

'Look,' he said, 'I loved the bastard dearly. We all loved him. He was the best and kindest bloke I ever knew. I think everybody here feels that and no doubt at the funeral we'll all get a chance to bang on about it. But this evening, since darling Lizzie ain't here, let's be honest, one of the things we loved about him most was that he was so utterly bloody useless!'

There was laughter, of course, and many comically stern cries of 'Shame!'

'Useless?' Jimmy shouted. 'Bollocks he was useless! He knew every British number one since charts began and he could burp the National Anthem!'

'That is very true,' Rupert conceded, 'and I bow to no man in my appreciation of those skills. But when it came to the practical side of life I don't think I have ever encountered such a cack-handed arse as Robbo, and were he here, he'd tell you so himself.'

There was a pause. The fact that Robbo was *not* there and never would be again was such a very recent and shocking development that it sounded strange to hear it referred to so bluntly. Even Rupert, a notoriously hard case and clearly determined to treat the gathering as a roast, had a tiny catch in his voice as he proceeded.

'You may or may not know this,' he went on, 'but Robbo's official position within his and Lizzie's firm was "business manager". He supposedly handled the investment, property and pension aspects of the family business. What a bloody joke!' Rupert shouted with mock outrage. 'As far as Robbo was concerned, business management meant sticking your cash in the bank and hoping for the bloody best! Can you imagine what it was like for a bloke like me having Robbo as a mate? It was torture! Absolute bloody torture, I tell you. As far as I'm concerned, making money out of money is a religion! A sacred duty! And here was this old arse sitting on shedloads of the stuff and doing absolutely nothing with it. Just eating curry, getting pissed and occasionally buying new fluffy dice for his ancient wreck of a car! No investment strategy. No tax avoidance. No offshore havens. This man *insulted my faith*!'

There was laughter, many cheers and much comical groaning at Rupert's speech. He delivered it well and made an effective point. It was certainly true that there could scarcely have been two more financially opposite personalities than the business manager of Lizzie Food and the celebrated CEO of the Royal Lancashire Bank, and it was rather touching that they should have been such old and firm friends.

Next, Jimmy got up to raise a glass.

Jimmy had probably been closest to Robbo of all the gang, but then Rupert, Henry and David also saw Robbo as their best friend. He was that kind of man. Jimmy knew that he must keep things fun. There would be time for solemnity later, but tonight required jollity and good-natured finger-pointing. That was unquestionably what Robbo would have wanted. Nonetheless, even on this deliberately raucous occasion Jimmy was determined to do Robbo justice. He himself was still struggling to deal with the fact that while grieving for his dead friend, he was also about to go deeply into that dead friend's debt. Robbo and Lizzie's loan would save Jimmy and his family from financial disaster and Jimmy wished with all his heart that he did not have the added complications of guilt and gratitude intruding on his grief. As he rose to his feet he struggled to put those thoughts from his mind and focus solely on celebrating the memory of the friend he loved.

'Let's be very clear about this.' Jimmy banged the table with one hand and held his slopping glass aloft in the other. 'Robbo was not remotely financially useless! In fact, Rupert, he had the only bloody decent economic strategy among us! And do you know what that strategy was, mate? To sit back and enjoy his bloody life, that's what! Fag Ash Rob knew what to *do* with money all right. He spent it on stuff he liked and ignored it the rest of the time. Brilliant! Inspired! A lesson for the whole bloody nation! In the truest sense of the word Robbo was a financial genius.'

This sentiment was greeted with huge cheers and much refilling of glasses. Jimmy was half drunk but he spoke with genuine passion, the passion of a man who had made the mistake of ignoring Robbo's example. A man who, instead of simply enjoying his good fortune and using it to enrich his life and increase the sum of his own happiness and that of those around him, had listened to siren voices (particularly Rupert's) and seen his money as merely a stepping stone to more money. He had tried to use money to buy more money and in so doing had lost the lot.

'Yes, Rupert!' Jimmy went on. 'Like you say, Robbo used his cash solely to eat, drink and be merry. Those were the things that mattered to him. He loved his food, his car, his booze, his mates, his wife and children. In that ascending order! That was what he cared about and you could stuff your *wealth management portfolios* up your arse!'

There was further huge cheering at this and much stamping of feet.

'Bravo! Well said!' David called out good-naturedly. 'Although I think you'd find he liked his booze more than his mates, or at least he preferred its company.'

'More than Rupert's anyway,' Henry shouted.

Jimmy took a swig of beer and surveyed the gathering with a boyish twinkle in his eye, that twinkle once so familiar to his friends but so often absent in the preceding months.

'Now I'm not saying Robbo didn't do his bit for Lizzie's business,' Jimmy went on. 'Never let it be said that our old mate didn't occasionally finish his beer, put down the crossword and make an effort. Some of you will, I'm sure, recall his famous plan to open a male waxing salon!'

Jimmy was on even more solidly popular ground here than he had been with his previous comments. It was well known among Robbo's friends that every now and then some residual store of latent energy had roused him to attempt a contribution to the family lifestyle empire. His efforts had been the cause of much hilarity over the years.

'You may remember,' Jimmy continued as the crowd settled back to enjoy what they knew would be a good story well told, 'that he decided to call it Back, Sack and Crack. It seemed like a good idea at the time. Well, it did to Rob when it came to him in the taproom of the Dog and Duck! Lizzie had just begun making hair products and Robbo was reading an article in the *Evening Standard*'s Friday magazine about male grooming. You may recall that this was at the time when David Beckham had been photographed wearing a dress! You remember that?'

There were cheers and nods at this.

'He called it a sarong but we knew it was a bloody dress. He's English, for God's sake! Anyway, the thrust of the article Robbo was reading was that heterosexual blokes who had previously been noted for their homophobia all suddenly wanted to look gay! So, armed with this brilliant bit of in-depth research and despite the fact that Robbo himself usually wore an old cricket jumper and never trimmed his bloody nose hair, he rented a shop and went on Morning TV, courtesy of Lizzie's celebrity, and made a complete arse of himself talking about metrosexuals! Do you remember?'

The answering cries told Jimmy that Robbo's friends did indeed remember.

'Pink is the new brown!' David shouted.

'That's right!' Jimmy called back. 'That's what he said, wasn't it. *Pink is the new brown!* Like Rob had ever given two seconds' thought to what colour his clothes were. I can see him now –' Jimmy began to crease up with laughter at the memory – 'that mad old arse sat on the Morning TV couch, his arms folded across his fat belly, his gut showing through the gaps between the buttons of his shirt, more hair growing out of his *ears* than most blokes have on their chests, actually trying to flog a male grooming business! I mean, for God's sake, you had to love the bastard!'

And they did love him. People cheered and toasts were proposed as Jimmy described how the salon had lasted a week before Robbo mooched back to the pub and picked up his crossword.

People cheered once more, cheering in a kind of hilarious sadness over the loss of a much-loved friend.

Henry got up to regale the gathering with Robbo's political philosophy.

'He said the problem with Parliament was that,

unlike everything else under New Labour, it didn't have a sell-by date,' he explained good-naturedly. 'His view was that there must surely come a point at which all the required laws had been made, when we should all simply pack up and go home. He felt that this point had been reached somewhere in the late nineteenth century and that after that it was all bollocks.'

With the speeches over, the curry arrived and people sat and drank and got more pissed. Jimmy found himself discreetly rolling half a nan into a missile, but then he remembered that Robbo was not there to throw it at. How could he be? It was his wake. What was the point of making a nan bomb with no Robbo in your sights? The other guys had always been secondary targets. Robbo had been his prey, just as he had been Robbo's.

Then he received a text from Monica. She had decided not to attend the evening, saying, 'It will be very boysey. I'd go if Lizzie was going.' When he heard the beeps, Jimmy assumed that there was some crisis with the children. That Lillie had lost her favourite Baa Baa perhaps.

But it wasn't about the children.

'Come home,' it said. *'Lizzie's here.'*

What an honour

Rupert might have been to a very minor private school and he might have only pretended to be posh at university, a pretension for which he had always been roundly ridiculed by Henry and the other lefties in the Student Union refectory. But years later he was to get the last laugh on his friend Henry and all those silly, parentally supported pinkos whom he despised. Because finally, after a dozen years of asset-stripping and exploiting venerable financial institutions, Rupert actually *became* posh. Or at least what passed for posh in the dog days of the Blair government. Which meant being rich enough and vain enough to pay for it.

They gave him his knighthood for 'services to banking', although he really got it for smarming around the Prime Minister and bunging half a million to the party at one of their gala dinners.

'For God's sake don't tell Dad,' he had told the excited soon-to-be Lady Bennett. '*Me* putting money into the Labour Party. He'll run me over with one of his trucks.'

Rupert's dad had been a committed Tory all his life, the sort of self-made small businessman for whom Mrs Thatcher was a goddess and unions the spawn of Satan.

'Silly old dinosaur,' the soon-to-be Lady Bennett replied. 'Doesn't he realize Labour are more Tory these days than the real thing?'

'Labour *are* the real bloody thing, darling,' Rupert replied.

'Except on banning bloody foxhunting,' Amanda moaned. Her father had been Master of the Hunt and she herself a fine country sportswoman.

'No, you're wrong there too,' Rupert said. 'All the townie Tories support the ban these days. Just like they support gay bloody marriage and calling everybody an institutionalized racist because they say Bombay instead of Mumbai. It's the strangest thing really, the Labour Party have taken on all the Conservative economic policies and the Tories have taken on all Labour's social policies. We're basically a single party state. It doesn't matter who gets in, it's still low taxes and don't offend the gays and ethnics.'

Rupert leaned over and kissed his wife. They were on their way to Buckingham Palace in the back of Rupert's Rolls-Royce, or more accurately the Royal Lancashire Bank's Rolls-Royce which Rupert habitually treated as his own, together with the driver that came with it. Amanda kissed him back. As far as she was aware, there was no gorgeous PA currently 'working late' at the office and within an hour or so she would officially be Lady Bennett. A girl could put up with a lot of miniskirted personal assistants for that.

As they drove through the gates of the palace, past the curious tourists and the soldiers in their splendid uniforms, Rupert put his hand on Amanda's pencil-thin thigh and let his fingers brush gently beneath the hem of her tiny dress. Briefly Amanda squeezed her thighs together to capture his hand. Amanda's inner thighs did not normally meet when she put her legs together but Rupert's hand filled the gap nicely. They giggled. Winning was *so* sexy.

Rupert took his place in the queue of the great and the good and when his name was called he made his way up the carpet to kneel before the Queen. Her Majesty appeared to be performing this tedious and familiar duty with her usual stoical commitment. As always, her face gave away nothing of what she was thinking. If she was reflecting on the changing nature of the shoulders upon which she was required by her first minister to lay her sword, no one would ever know. If the disappearance of the explorers, inventors, military heroes and time-serving civil servants whom she used to knight perplexed her, she didn't show it. If their replacement by political party donors, actors who'd made it in the States and on this occasion, just behind Rupert, a wrinkly rock star who had posed briefly as anti-establishment in 1964 and spent the following forty years in a jet-setting exercise to avoid British tax surprised her, of that she also gave no hint.

After the brief ceremony, the newly ennobled Sir Rupert left Buckingham Palace. Outside the gates, he paused for a moment with Lady Bennett to smile indulgently at the gaggle of photographers awaiting the emergence of the wrinkly rock star and habitual tax exile.

Turning on his phone again – he had been sternly instructed by a palace equerry to desist from sending emails in the honours queue – Rupert saw that among the many messages he'd received was one from the deputy chief fundraiser of the Labour Party.

'Congratulations,' the message read, *'a thoroughly deserved honour. What next for the boy wonder we are all asking ourselves!! If you PEER into the future LORD knows what you'll see. Lunch??'*

When he and Amanda were back in the bank's Roller, Rupert showed her the text.

'How do you fancy being married to a peer of the realm?' he said with a beaming smile.

'Darling, I would *love* it,' Amanda replied, leaning forward and whispering into his ear, 'although I do think it's unfair that the wife of a *lord* is still only called *Lady*, just the same as the wife of a knight.'

'Maybe I can get them to change that,' Rupert said. 'I find they'll consider fucking around with pretty much anything, even the rules of etiquette, if the price is right.'

Half a mile away in his Downing Street office, Andy Palmer, the fundraiser and press officer who had sent the text to Sir Rupert, put away his BlackBerry with a satisfied air.

'Money, money, money,' Palmer sang, half to himself

and half for the benefit of Henry, with whom he had been discussing seating arrangements for the next gala fundraising dinner. It was crucial to ensure that the biggest donors got to sit on tables with any celebrities that they had managed to cobble together with the promise of a nod from the PM.

Henry had by this time been an MP for seven and a half years and had risen to the rank of junior Cabinet minister. He was very much a coming man, having cleverly managed to maintain a foot in Tony Blair's camp while keeping very thick with his likely successor, Gordon Brown. He was seen as principled but pragmatic, the sort of politician New Britain needed and New Labour excelled in producing.

On this occasion, though, Henry was not happy.

'I cannot believe you got Tony to put Rupert bloody Bennett up for a knighthood!' he complained.

'Why not?' Palmer replied. 'I thought he was a mate of yours.'

'He is a mate of mine. Has been since uni, which is why I can tell you with authority that he is an absolute shit and an amoral arsehole and I can't believe he's going to be able to swank about the place insisting on being called sir.'

'Henry, be practical. He gave us half a mil.'

'So what you're saying is you're basically selling honours?' Henry stroked his beautiful blond hair in an effort to calm himself. He was as vain as he had ever

been. His hair was still thick and he kept it unfashion-
ably long. Henry also played guitar in a House of
Commons 'rock' band called Cross Party and this, combined with his hair, had earned him the nickname
Blondel, which he pretended to hate but secretly rather
liked.

'Of course we're selling honours,' Palmer admitted.
'Can't think of any better use for them, can you?'

'Yes I can!' Henry retorted. 'Recognizing public
service! People who actually make a contribution to
society rather than leeching off it! Hard-working
lollipop ladies, parents who look after disabled
children, limbless bomb victims.'

Palmer smiled a weary smile. 'That's what MBEs are
for. Those we can give away. Knighthoods we need to
sell.'

'This is *not* what New Labour should be about,' Henry
said. 'Rewarding bastards is not why I went into
politics!'

'Look, nobody particularly likes it,' Palmer said with a
shrug, 'but the whole bonus culture thing has put City
blokes at the centre of the universe. The party's broke,
mate, and we *need* them. What do you want me to do?
We've been in power too long and only bastards will
talk to us these days. Iraq's bollocksed us big time.'

Henry grimaced. That bloody word *Iraq*. Iraq. Iraq.
I-bloody-raq. God. They thought the war had made it
tough for those living in Baghdad. Well, it hadn't made

living in Westminster very pleasant either. Who would have thought in '97, when a whole new Labour generation had been swept to power on the promise of social justice, that the whole project would end up buried in the sands of Iraq? It was *so* unfair.

But what a cock-up it had been. Henry had voted for the war, they all had. How could they not? Those spooks had *sworn* the weapons of mass destruction were there! God, the US Secretary of State had waved his stick around on the floor of the UN pointing at supposed photographic proof like Kennedy and the Cuban missiles. But the WMD weren't there and now everybody was saying that Tony had started a war just so that George Bush would take his calls.

It was so depressing. Nobody had noticed the good they had done. They seemed to be getting no real credit for banning foxhunting, for instance.

'You need to understand,' Palmer went on, 'that people don't like us any more. We've screwed up and we need money to get us out of the shit. And money ain't free. If you want big players to bung you a crumb from their bonuses then you have to give them something in return. We don't have any credibility left. Face it, we squandered that sucking Dubya's dick. Oasis don't come to Downing Street parties any more like they did in the good old days of bloody Cool Britannia. All we have left to sell is snobbery. Fortunately for us, that's what the people with the dosh want.'

'How much gets you a peerage then?' Henry enquired bitterly.

'Oh I don't know, as little as twenty-five K if you bring something else to the party – you know, if you're ethnic or vaguely look like you deserve one. But it's a whole lot more if you're a tougher sell. We charge big time.'

'You do know that selling honours is against the law, don't you?'

'Look, mate,' Palmer snapped, 'the Tories have cosied up to money for centuries. Scratch the surface and you'll find they're rolling in it, they always have been. Our money's run out. The unions are fucked and the membership's falling. Is that fair? Is that good for democracy? We are the *people*'s party. Don't the people deserve a properly funded party? Besides which, why shouldn't we lick up a bit of the cream? *We*'ve created this fucking boom. It happened on our watch, not John fucking Major's or St Margaret's. It's our economy that's paying the bonuses these arseholes are buying their yachts with and we deserve a cut. As a matter of fact it's our *duty* to grab it. What will happen to all the important social legislation we've put in place if the Tories get back in? They'll probably bring back foxhunting.'

Henry's face showed that he could see the logic in this. Heaven forbid that the important gains they had made should be lost because the party couldn't afford a proper poster campaign to boast about them. Once more he stroked his hair to soothe himself. Yes, they

217

still had valuable work to do. People would get over Iraq. The New Labour project was working. People's lives were improving. Society was changing.

The next big thing was to get smoking banned and put some proper warning labels on alcohol.

Robbo's last bumble

Jimmy took a taxi home. These days he mainly used the bus – there was a pretty good service between Notting Hill and the West End – but on this occasion he was in a hurry.

If Lizzie was making good on her promise then he needed to be there. As his cab made its way along Oxford Street and across Marble Arch he was beset by an irrational fear that somehow Monica would try to complete the loan without him. That she would give Lizzie the wrong bank details so the entire million would disappear into the financial black hole that was his deficit at the Royal Lancashire and do him no good at all.

He tried to phone but for some reason, on this night of all nights, with a two-million-quid loan hanging on it, he couldn't get a signal along Notting Hill Gate.

Jimmy had recently switched to a cheaper network and he was now discovering why it was cheaper. The bloody signal kept drifting in and out. Tantalizingly he'd get a few bars on his display only to see them disappear again before he'd had a chance to dial.

Jimmy felt awful about his desperation. For worrying about money with Robbo dead. Lizzie was just incredible. An utterly amazing human being. To be bothering about his and Monica's problems at such a terrible time. It made Jimmy push away his anxiety and instead feel wretched and ashamed. He sat back in the taxi and found his eyes filling with tears once more. Lizzie and Robbo. The best of the best.

Eventually Jimmy arrived home and, having shoved a fiver and a tenner through the window for an eleven-pound ride, he clattered through the big door and down his unlit staircase.

Monica and Lizzie were there where he expected to find them, on the big couch in the family room with an empty bottle of wine between them.

'Jimmy,' Lizzie said, looking at him with red-ringed eyes, 'I'm broke.'

Whatever he had expected the first words between them to be, it was not these. He was struck dumb. What had she said? Broke? Or broken? Broken, surely. Of course she was broken, a broken woman. She'd lost the best man in the world. Why wouldn't she be broken?

But she hadn't said broken. He knew that. She'd said 'broke'.

'I'm so sorry,' Lizzie added.

That pulled Jimmy to his senses.

Lizzie was saying sorry to him? She'd just lost Robbo, the love of her life and the father of her children, and she was saying sorry to him. Whatever she was talking about, whatever had happened, it was Jimmy's job to reach out to her, not she to him. Despite all his failures, he was still man enough to understand that. He went over and sat on the floor beside her.

'Liz,' he said gently, taking her hand, 'what is this? What's happened?'

'The loan,' Lizzie whispered. 'I can't give it to you.'

'It doesn't matter, Liz!' Monica blurted, clearly repeating a sentiment she had already been pressing on her friend.

'Of course it doesn't matter,' Jimmy said. 'The only thing that matters is you and the kids.'

'They're OK. They're with Robbo's parents,' she said, her voice catching on the word Robbo.

Jimmy squeezed her hand in sympathy, but fear was gripping his innards even as he loathed himself for it.

'Tell me what's happened, Lizzie. Please,' he said.

'It's that man,' Lizzie explained, clearly trying to keep her voice steady, 'that cheat in America. You know, the one with the scheme . . . what was it called? The Ponzi scheme? Robbo fell for it . . .'

Jimmy could scarcely believe what he was hearing. It had been all over the papers. The biggest fraud in history.

'Do you mean Lew Bronski?'

'Yes. Lew Bronski,' Lizzie spat. 'That dreadful man.'

Now Jimmy understood everything. The press had been talking about Bronski's victims for days. It had sounded as if they were all American, but inevitably they weren't. Greed and stupidity were no respecter of national borders.

'Oh God,' Jimmy heard himself saying. 'How much did Robbo invest?'

'Everything. Absolutely everything. All our savings. The equity on Onslow Gardens. He even borrowed on our pension fund.'

'But . . . why?' was all Jimmy could find it in himself to say.

'We'd been hit by the crunch,' Lizzie said. 'Who hadn't? I was going to have to close the Knightsbridge gig, which was such a worry because the staff are all *mates*.'

Jimmy half smiled at that. Lizzie always called her employees 'mates', even though at her highest point there had been nearly fifty of them.

'Robbo knew I was worrying about having to make people redundant and I suppose he was trying to . . . help.'

Jimmy could see it all.

He knew that for all his solid English equanimity and immense good nature, Robbo had never entirely relished his position as the gang's hopeless arse. Even on their famous graduation night when Robbo had volunteered to insert the first and by far the largest radish, Jimmy had sensed a certain desperation in him, a desire to please. He had always taken with great good humour the endless ribbing about the cushy billet he had lucked on in marrying Lizzie. The fact that such a useless lump had scored this sexy and creative and ridiculously successful creature who seemed, against all logic, to love him unconditionally had been the subject of constant jokes.

And now Robbo, who had sat smiling so often under a rain of rolled-up nan bread, had gone out and fucked up in a spectacular manner. In an effort to save Lizzie's Asian Fusion restaurant and protect her from the agony of having to sack her mates, he had given all their money to a bloke who was running the biggest Ponzi scheme in history.

He had sneaked out while Lizzie was designing cup-cakes or trying to think of newer and ever more pointless table accessories (like her little silver plinths on which to rest your butter knife) and given their money to a shit. A man who leeched off fools. People who believed that he was some financial genius bring-ing them a 13 per cent return on their capital when the banks were offering only four.

'Robbo was so naïve,' Lizzie was sobbing. 'Even I know that when someone's offering nearly 10 per cent above the interest rate there must be *something* wrong. I mean you can't make money out of nothing, can you?'

But of course a lot of people had believed that you could. In fact Jimmy's entire adult life had been based on that same belief. Now he was broke and so was Lizzie. And she was a widow and her children had lost their beloved father.

And she would not be lending him two million quid either because his best friend had given it to a scammer. How desperate and sad Robbo must have been to have fucked up on such a colossal and embarrassing scale. Losing everything his wife had worked for.

God. He must have been desperate. Devastated.

And drunk, of course.

Then he had got in his car.

Funny. The one thing Robbo was pretty good at was driving. Never had a scratch or a dent, not one. But that night he had crashed and died.

A terrible thought flitted into Jimmy's mind.

A bankers' gathering

Henry, David, Robbo and Jimmy were sheltering from the baking sun beneath the cooling shade of a vast marquee striped in icing-sugar shades of pink and green.

'I must say Roop knows how to throw a party,' Jimmy shouted as he brought back four foaming tankards of fine local ale from the bar.

'Pamela Goddard knows how to throw a party, Jim,' Robbo corrected him.

'Oh yes,' Jimmy said, 'of course.'

It was perhaps a *slightly* touchy subject. In the past Rupert's parties had been designed and catered by Lizzie, but no longer. Rupert had been quite straight about it with his old friend.

'You're too fucking tasteful, Liz,' he said. 'I'm not throwing a party to attract BBC types, anglophile Yank pop singers and anorexic Oscar winners. I'm throwing a party for *money*. Big money, bankers on a spree. Americans and Russians. Particularly Russians. They want a bit of bling. They like a lot of pretty girls and what's more, they want nice girls with tits, not silly skinny poshos with diplomas in Fine Arts. They want pink marquees, limos from the helicopter pad and Rod Stewart at midnight. What's more, they don't want to have to scrape lemon grass and alfalfa sprouts off their roast beef canapés. They want *meat*, pure and simple.

You, Lizzie, are the patron saint of good taste and minimalism, I recognize and respect that, but when I pay a million quid for a party I want MAXimalism.'

As it happened, not only did Lizzie understand but she was mightily relieved. For her the vast parties that Rupert (or to be more precise, the Royal Lancashire Bank) had begun to throw in the mid-noughties had nothing to do with the appreciation of fine food and exquisite ambience which was her particular forte. They were simply a celebration of excess.

'It's like planning D-Day, darling,' she used to moan to Robson. 'Honestly, the *helicopters*. It was all about the helicopters. Russians in bloody helicopters. I'm a caterer, not an air-traffic controller. Much more fun not to have the responsibility of it all and just go along and get pissed with my *mates*.'

The purpose of these parties was supposedly to facilitate communication and business within the financial world, but Rupert and Amanda always invited their old friends.

'I think the corporate purse can stretch to me buying a drink or two for my chums,' Rupert would say. 'Considering how rich I've made the shareholders it's the least they can do.'

'Yes. You all *have* to come, it's going to be divine,' Amanda would add. 'We have Cirque de la Soubrette bouncing all over the place in the various catering tents and I'm longing to introduce you to Tony and Cherie.

He's promised to try and bring Bill Clinton, who's over here doing something for his foundation, but secretly I hope he doesn't because it means providing lunches for about three hundred secret service and it becomes all about *him*.'

So there they all were again, Jimmy and Monica, David and Laura, Henry and Jane and Lizzie and Robbo, enjoying a nice day of free food, wine and stellar entertainment at the expense of the Royal Lancashire Bank.

'Actually, I think Rupert was right to sack my Liz,' Robbo said, quaffing contentedly on his pint. 'I mean there's a place for class and this ain't it, is it? Don't tell the old girl, will you, but I prefer it this way. I mean you never got Thruttocks Old Ale when she had the gig, did you? If you could *find* a beer among all the bloody New World white wine, it was Japanese or "ice" beer, whatever that is.'

'No,' David agreed, 'and you never got to stare up the crotch of a Mongolian contortionist while you were drinking it either.'

The four friends glanced up and there was indeed a female trapeze artist in a tiny leotard suspended above them just as another descended from the roof of the marquee into the midst of the oyster-shucking bar on a skein of twisted and unfolding silk scarves.

'I saw Kylie talking to Simon Cowell,' Robbo said, plucking a mini New York roast beef bagel from a passing lovely. 'I mean that's great, isn't it? That's *proper* celebrity. You know, big-in-America celebrity.'

'Just as a matter of interest though, what do you think Kylie and Simon Cowell have got to do with banking?' Henry asked. 'I mean I don't want to be the moral party-pooper here, but this party is about a *bank*.'

'Yes it is,' Jimmy replied, 'and what Kylie and Cowell have to do with it is making everyone here who *is* a banker feel great about themselves.'

'And that's important, is it?'

'In terms of New Britain I think it is. If you don't believe in yourself you're not going to believe in your deal, are you? Besides which this kind of stellar social networking is sending out the message, isn't it?'

'What message?'

'The message of *who we are*. A couple of generations ago banking was boring and mundane. Today the people who work in money need to be creative, which is why it's important for a top player like Roop to introduce his people and his clients *to* creative people.'

'Simon Cowell?'

'Exactly. This is about cross-fertilization and it's also about letting the world know that money is at the heart of *everything that happens*. Without money, or more importantly *new* money, there'd be nothing. No property development. No rapidly expanding leisure market . . .'

'No *American Idol*,' Robbo put in.

'Well, you can laugh,' said Jimmy, 'but believe me,

Lizzie wouldn't be able to charge what she does for an olive if it wasn't for what's happening here. It's astonishing the way people have had to be re-educated about their attitude to the financial sector but they're finally getting it, I think.'

'Re-educated?' David enquired. 'Pardon my French, but what the *fuck* are you talking about?'

'It's obvious. Culture has changed and people need to catch up. Like these days we all know that an accountant is a *player*, right? If he's with a decent firm he's a hot sexy guy. He'll get the best girls and be dealing in vast sums and will be making life or death decisions every minute of the day.'

'Life or death?' Henry queried. 'I mean I'm not saying you're entirely wrong, Jim. We in government certainly recognize the importance of banks and the markets to the economy, but life and death?'

'Well, profit and loss certainly. If you have a good accountant you can save millions. The law is incredibly complex and it makes my head spin just to think about it, which is why I admire these guys so much. They are *cutting edge*. In terms of tax rationalization . . .'

'That would be tax avoidance,' Henry butted in. 'I mean just to be clear.'

'Which is entirely legal. These guys are artists. Every move they make is a *sexy, creative act*. But do you know, forty years ago people actually used to think accountants were boring. It's incredible. Can you believe it?'

'You've got a point,' said Henry, smiling. 'Here we all are, surrounded by glamour, money and bouncing circus acts, and we're here to celebrate the successful working of a *bank*. Nobody could deny there's been a cultural shift.'

Just then Jimmy's parents joined them. It had been rather mischievous of Jimmy to cadge an invitation for his parents but he had been unable to resist it. Derek Corby was now, after all, an employee of the RLB, as it had taken over the National City for which he had worked for thirty years.

'Hello, boys,' said Nora Corby. 'This is absolutely astonishing. Have you seen that there's a marquee which *only* dispenses champagne? They must have thirty or forty types. I didn't twig and asked for a gin and tonic. I felt such a silly!'

'I'll get you a G and T, Nora,' Robbo offered. 'This tent's got a normal bar.'

'Normal apart from the fact that there's a waterfall running down it and contortionists all over it,' Derek Corby observed drily.

'Would you, dear? But just a single, for goodness' sake!' Nora grinned. 'With this sun I shall have a hangover before I get tiddly. Haven't they been lucky with the weather?'

'I thought you knew Rupert, Mum,' Jimmy joked. 'Luck had nothing to do with it. He'll have had the Russian air force seed the clouds.'

'A pint for you, Derek?' Robson asked. 'It's bloody good ale and actually not too strong. Three point nine.'

Robson was an expert on the exact strength of alcoholic drinks. It was perhaps his greatest skill and a cracking party piece. People would call out the names of obscure Finnish vodkas and strange country beers and Robson would rattle back their exact percentage proof.

'Well, Dad?' Jimmy enquired as Robson headed for the bar. 'What do you make of it?'

'I like the little beef roll things,' Derek Corby replied.

'Oh come on, Dad. You have to admit it's fun.'

'Yes, it is fun,' Derek admitted. 'The circus people are clever and Nora thinks she saw Posh Spice. Personally I wasn't sure. All these skinny girls look the same to me. I just don't really understand why a *bank* would throw a party like this.'

'Oh God, don't get him started on that, Derek,' David pleaded. 'Jimmy thinks Rupert's a capitalist version of Chairman Mao running his own Cultural Revolution.'

'Also,' Derek continued, 'what business do two Cabinet ministers have being here?'

'What do you mean what business, Dad? It's a party. Why shouldn't they go to a party?'

'Because they are responsible in Cabinet for the laws and regulations that govern this bank's activities.'

'Actually I was wondering about that a bit myself,' Henry admitted. 'I mean I know I'm here, but only because Rupert's an old friend. The fact that there's people from the Treasury here could be spun to look dodgy.'

'Oh come on, guys, you're sounding like journalists,' said Jimmy. 'If you could buy Cabinet influence with a few drinks and a chance to see Rod Stewart in a private marquee then the financial sector would have a lot more influence than it has.'

'How much more influence could it have?' Derek Corby asked. 'It seems to me that it's already managed to arrange things so that it's virtually unregulated and free to go its own way.'

'Which is a *good* thing, Dad,' Jimmy said. 'That's why it's successful. Do you think politicians know how to make money? Of course they don't. If they did, they'd be doing it themselves instead of being politicians. If Britain's position in the world's money markets is to remain dominant, the last thing we need is government stepping back in like it used to and screwing things up.'

'So why *are* there politicians here then?' Derek asked. 'If they're irrelevant? Why did your lot give Rupert a knighthood, Henry?'

'He was knighted for services to banking, Derek,' Henry replied with a hint of embarrassment. 'Not saying I'd have done it myself but that's what Tony decided. Finance is Britain's most successful industry now, so I suppose honouring its major players is no different to honouring an industrialist a hundred years ago.'

Robson returned with the drinks.

'You won't believe it,' he said, 'there's a girl on the bar who's so bendy she can stick her head right through between her legs and rest her chin on the back of her bum. I mean fuck me! Sorry, Nora. But really, that is a *senior* talent.'

'That's all right,' Jimmy's mum said. 'I'm slowly getting used to the way people swear these days. Not that I don't think it's a shame. Language is losing its power. The F-word used to be a linguistic exclamation mark, now it's barely a comma. You'll all have to make up a new word for when you want to be extra rude.'

'I just can't help wondering,' Derek Corby said, almost to himself, as he glanced around the great tent. It was one of five great tents, each brimming with braying, shiny-faced men shouting at stick-thin women, all of whom made him and Nora look like the provincial branch manager and his wife that they were. 'I can't help wondering how many more years Brenda and Sean could have worked if Sir Rupert *hadn't* thrown this party but had spent the money on retaining their services instead.'

'What's that, Dad?' said Jimmy, leaning closer in order to hear his father above the growing din.

'Your father's been a bit upset recently, dear,' Nora confided. 'He's had to let quite a lot of staff go. Roop the Boot, you know.'

'First it was the school leavers,' Derek said. 'That was

bad enough, awful to have to deny young people with decent grades a start in life. I always used to love it each year when we took on a youngster or two. It brought eager faces and fresh smiles into the bank. I used to watch them grow up, taking their place in the community. Now we don't take on school leavers any more. I often wonder where they all go. They can't all be hoodies, can they?'

'Derek,' Henry said, 'it's hardly a bank's duty to promote eager faces and fresh smiles.'

'Isn't it, Henry? That's certainly the impression that they give in their adverts. In fact it seems to be *nothing but* eager faces and fresh smiles in the bank adverts, but none in my actual branch.'

'Internet banking.' Jimmy shrugged. 'It might seem sad but the truth is people are much happier going online at home than trudging down to the High Street for a fresh smile.'

'Are they? Are they really?' Derek asked. 'They might think they are, particularly now that they have no choice, but do you honestly think they're happier for it?'

'Yes, Dad, as a matter of fact I do,' Jimmy assured him. 'I love internet banking and so does Mon. And Jodie, our nanny, is always tinkering with Aussie dollars in the night. Everyone's a banker now.'

'Jodie is *such* a lovely girl,' Nora chipped in.

'It started with not taking on school leavers,' Derek continued, 'but now we've moved on to getting rid of who we've got. You remember Brenda, Jimmy? You met her sometimes when you were a teenager and Nora and I used to throw those open evenings for the staff. She bought you an Easter egg.'

'Yes, of course. Brenda,' Jimmy said, with no idea who his father was talking about.

'Yes, Brenda. She leaves next month after eighteen years. And Sean who came to us from school. He's thirty now and he'll be unemployed in a few weeks too.'

'Dad, please,' said Jimmy. 'Shit happens. They'll have all got their redundancy payments.'

'They wanted their jobs.'

'Well, I'm afraid they can't have their jobs, Derek,' Henry said firmly. 'I'm sorry but those jobs have gone, just like coal miners' jobs and the men who used to go around lighting the gas lamps. It's nobody's fault, but capitalism readjusts. New industries emerge. That's what this party is celebrating.'

'As far as I can see,' Derek replied testily, 'Brenda and Sean might still be *in* their jobs if their employer hadn't spent so much of their bank's money on this party.'

'You're being ridiculous, Dad. The two issues are totally separate. For a start, even if this party cost a million quid the money wouldn't keep more than twenty Brendas in their jobs.'

'Which actually would be very nice. Particularly if it was my Brenda. I don't think anyone would honestly miss this party, do you? I shall miss Brenda.'

'Well, the bar staff would miss it,' Henry pointed out, 'and the circus performers. And Rod Stewart. I mean, be honest, this party is also *generating* work.'

Derek Corby clearly wasn't convinced that the trickle-down advantages for the hospitality and entertainment industries were worth the human wastage at his branch of the Royal Lancashire, but he didn't comment further. Instead he confined himself to a moody swig of beer.

Later on, at dinner, sitting on an outlying table which he and his wife had been squeezed on to alongside guests from the growing financial services industries of Romania and Serbia, Derek Corby switched from moody swigs of beer to moody swigs of wine and then Scotch.

'Just because Jimmy's insisted on giving us a car and driver,' his wife whispered, 'it doesn't mean you have to get drunk.'

'I'm not drunk,' Jimmy's father replied, but he knocked a glass over while he said it. Not one glass but a whole set, since it would have taken a very sober man indeed to knock over only one glass on that table. Each place setting was supplied with a plethora of them: champagne flutes, a white-wine glass, an enormous red-wine glass, a water glass, a dessert-wine glass and a cognac bubble you could have kept a goldfish in. Derek dominoed the lot. Had he been playing ten-pin bowling it would have been a terrific effort.

Just then, far away on the top table, Rupert rose to

speak and so Nora Corby's embarrassment was partially covered by the general scraping back of chairs and last-minute refills.

After thanking the politicians and Rod Stewart and Penny Lancaster for attending, Rupert went on to cover a great deal of the same ground as his friends' conversation earlier. He extolled the virtues of the creative new banking sector and its massive contribution to the current pre-eminent position Britain held in the financial world. Indeed, anyone listening might have imagined that Rupert and his colleagues laboured principally in order to make Britain great again. The senior politician who had spoken earlier took much the same view and even went so far as to quote the Chancellor, Gordon Brown himself, when he spoke of the 'courage' that bankers and traders showed in their innovative and ground-breaking activities.

Rupert conceded that it was not merely the nation as a whole which was benefiting from the RLB's extraordinary success. His first duty as chief executive officer was of course to his shareholders, and in that stern task he had not been found wanting. Indeed, if anything the shareholders had done better than the nation as a whole, seeing their individual share price jump from £3.50 to £9 in just four years. Rupert hoped his audience would not think him conceited if he pointed out that when he had taken over as CEO the share price had been just £2.50. These figures were greeted with waves of applause, as well they might since there were many shareholders present and Sir Rupert had effectively trebled their wealth.

This, however, was not the end of the man's achievements. Sir Rupert also wanted his audience to be aware that he was proud to be at the helm of such an august and ancient institution as the Royal Lancashire Bank. It had been trading for over three hundred years, although never (he could not help but mention) as successfully as it was doing currently. Sir Rupert then chose to illustrate the longevity (and egalitarian nature) of the institution that he now had the honour to lead by pointing out that there was present at the dinner a local branch manager who had been with the bank all his life, having served with the RLB subsidiary the National City ever since leaving school.

It took Derek Corby a moment to realize that his son's old university friend was referring to him, and that a spotlight had swung over the heads of the important diners at the front and was illuminating him and half of Nora.

'Derek Corby,' Sir Rupert continued, 'is the father of one of my oldest friends. I've known him for fifteen years. I never imagined that I would ever be his boss, but after masterminding the takeover of the National City I find that I am. And I would like to thank you, Derek, for a lifetime of service to the industry we both love.'

Then a pretty young woman in a tiny black dress approached the table holding a magnum of champagne and an exciting-looking envelope.

There was applause. Derek Corby seemed somewhat frozen. Frozen like a shy bank manager in a spotlight. So much so that Nora had to reach forward and accept the gifts from the pretty girl.

The applause did not last long and was about to die altogether when Derek rose to his feet.

'Sir Rupert,' he said, blinking in the bright light and pausing for a moment to gather his thoughts, 'you are a vandal and a first-class bastard!'

Derek swayed slightly but he did not fall. Instead he took a swig of Scotch from the glass in his hand and continued.

'Let me tell you something,' he said, pointing a finger across the marquee. 'Your first duty is *not* to your share-holders. That is a modern idea which is trotted out whenever a job is cut or a service reduced. Business was not invented solely for the profit of shareholders. Your first duty and the duty of any employer is to your staff and to your customers, not to the bloody shareholders! Shareholders are sleeping partners. Their fortunes should rise and fall together with the fortunes of those who actually *make* the business in which the shareholders have chosen to invest. You and your like, Sir Rupert, have created a situation where shareholder profit is created at the *expense* of the staff and customers. They have become enemies. This is obscene! It's madness! It's completely barking! You have forsaken your duty, Sir Rupert, and I don't want your bloody champagne!'

It was a stirring speech.

A brave and noble effort.

Unfortunately nobody heard it. Derek did not have a microphone and people had begun talking to each other the moment Rupert sat down. Even Nora Corby caught only the odd word in the babble that arose after Sir Rupert had taken his seat.

Watching from a table much nearer the front, Jimmy beamed with pride and Monica got quite teary.

'Can you believe it?' Jimmy said. 'Dad getting honoured like that? Wish I could hear what he was saying, he looks really emotional.'

'Yes,' Monica replied, 'that *was* nice of Rupert, wasn't it?'

School leaver

Abbey Hall School was situated on Kensington High Street, along which Jimmy and Toby were crawling when Monica called.

'Are you on hands-free?'

'Yes,' Jimmy lied, struggling with the phone and watching out for cops.

'You must be on hands-free!'

'I am on hands-free! What is it?'

'Are you there yet?'

'I'm trying to get close enough so I can let him out.'

'You must be right by the gate and you MUST be actually on the kerb!' Monica shouted. 'He is NOT to cross traffic.'

'I know, I know. But I can't get to the kerb, can I?'

'Well, then you'll have to find a parking space. You might as well anyway because Mr Lombard's secretary just called. They want one of us to pop in.'

'Oh God,' said Jimmy.

'I know.'

This was the morning after Jimmy had learned that the Seventh Cavalry in the shape of a fat, unsecured loan from an old friend would not in fact come thundering over the horizon any time soon. If the head wanted to discuss the issue of Toby's outstanding school fees then Jimmy knew he did not have a lot of answers.

Jimmy had no choice but to manoeuvre his way back out of the scrum of unforgiving metal clustered around the little school gate and try to punch his way into the residential streets south of the high street. Living in Notting Hill, he had a Kensington and Chelsea residents' permit and was hoping to find a space. Inevitably there were none. There never were, and Jimmy was forced to swing his car into one of the numerous and much-resented diplomatic bays. He had no choice.

Hoping for the best, Jimmy took his son by the hand and walked back up to the school. It was past nine by the time they arrived and so both man and boy had to bear that horribly uncomfortable feeling of entering a school after classes have begun. Toby was clearly mortified and Jimmy did not feel much better, particularly after he noticed how dirty Toby's shoes were. Abbey Hall set great store by a neat appearance, believing it to be an essential part of school discipline; it was one of the things that attracted parents like Jimmy and Monica. Jimmy knew that all the other boys would have shiny shoes. As shiny as Toby's had been during the days when Jodie had done them for him. Jimmy himself had started to clean his own shoes at the age of seven but children just didn't do that sort of thing for themselves any more. Just like they didn't pick up after themselves either. The culture had changed. Kids had *everything* done for them and it wasn't Toby's fault that the support structure had suddenly disappeared from under him. The little boy was like the helpless survivor of a ship-wreck, cast adrift in a wild new world for which he was equipped with zero survival skills.

Toby joined his class, who were just heading off to assembly. He looked like he wished he was dead. Jimmy took his aching heart in search of the headmaster's office.

He had to wait in the secretary's outer office until assembly was over and then wait again while the great man bustled past him, hymnbook still under his arm, and closed the door behind him. Finally Jimmy was invited in, feeling almost as if it was his own head-master, not Toby's, to whose office he had been summoned. And like an errant schoolboy, Jimmy tried to get his excuses in first.

'Look, Mr Lombard,' he began quickly, 'I know that Toby's been marked absent a number of times and . . .'

Mr Lombard interrupted him. 'I'm afraid this is not about Toby's absences, nor does it concern his home-work. I'm afraid that what I need to discuss with you is non-payment of fees.'

'Ah,' said Jimmy.

He should have seen that coming. What else but unpaid fees would be on the mind of the head of a private school facing an impoverished parent? The establishment was, after all, first and foremost a business.

'I need to enquire, Mr Corby,' Mr Lombard continued, 'whether you see any possibility of settling the balance of your account with Abbey Hall in the immediate future. As you know, you are in arrears by more than a term now and Toby is not a scholarship boy.'

'No. Of course not. I understand that.'

'And yet for some months Abbey Hall has been effectively educating him for nothing.'

242

'Yes. That's right. I can see that,' Jimmy conceded, adding a rather pathetic 'sorry'.

'Were Toby to leave us now, Abbey Hall would not pursue you for the outstanding debt, but if he is to stay then we will expect your account to be settled in full. Not merely the arrears but also the advance payment which has now come due.'

The significance of this last point was not lost on Jimmy.

'*If* he is to stay?' Jimmy repeated. 'What do you mean, Mr Lombard? You're not saying . . . you're not going to *expel* him, are you?'

'Mr Corby, expulsion has nothing to do with it. Toby has done nothing wrong and of course won't be disciplined. Your taking him out of school would be cause for regret on both sides and it is of course your choice, not ours.'

'Choice?'

'Abbey Hall is a fee-paying school, Mr Corby. If you choose not to pay the fees then clearly you do not wish your son to be educated here.'

It was a neat way of putting it but not one that Jimmy felt minded to put up with.

'You mean you're chucking him out?' he asked.

'Mr Corby, are you in a position to settle your account with Abbey Hall and pay for next term?'

'Not if viewed within a specific short-term time frame.'

'Is that a yes or a no?'

'There are cash-flow issues still to be resolved.'

'Mr Corby, I must have a banker's order now.'

'And I have every expectation of being able to satisfy that demand within a structured temporal framework.'

'Does that mean now, Mr Corby?'

'Now as pertains to the upcoming financial year, I very much hope so.'

'But not now as in today?'

Jimmy had run out of vocabulary.

'No.'

'In that case I'm afraid that Toby can no longer keep his place at Abbey Hall.'

For a moment there was silence. It was all so sudden. Could this man really mean it? Toby was being thrown to the wolves.

'But . . . he's done so well here,' Jimmy said quietly.

'I don't like this any more than you do, Mr Corby,' the headmaster replied. 'If it's any comfort at all, I can assure you you're not the only family in this position. It's hard on us all.'

Jimmy looked the headmaster square in the eye.

'Last Christmas I donated five thousand pounds to the new gymnasium wheelchair facility,' he said.

'And we were extremely grateful.'

'Can't you take that and use it for Toby's fees?'

'I'm afraid not.'

'Why not?'

'Because it has already gone towards the gymnasium wheelchair facility.'

'But I don't care about that any more. Toby's not disabled. Let the disabled kid's parents pay for his bloody access to the gym.'

'I'm sorry, Mr Corby, but the two issues are entirely unrelated. Your generous donation was made almost a year ago and was spent soon afterwards. It has no bearing on the current situation. If you are unable to pay his fees, Toby must leave. I take no pleasure in this, in fact I deeply regret it, but although we have charitable status we are not a charity . . .'

'Except when you're asking for donations.'

'We are not a charity and the facts are as I have described them.'

Jimmy was horrified. Toby had been so happy at Abbey Hall, at least until he had started turning up with dirty shoes, untreated nits and a builder's lunch. He was getting a first-class education, a tried and tested route to Oxbridge and lifelong success among the nation's elite. The alternative was almost too horrible to contemplate.

'But what . . . what can we do?' Jimmy enquired.

'You must find a place for him in another school.'

'I can't afford one. That's the point. If I could afford one I'd be paying you, wouldn't I?'

Mr Lombard raised an eyebrow. He narrowed his gaze and he pursed his lips. He had something to say but he didn't want to say it, any more than Jimmy wanted to hear it.

They had arrived at the unthinkable.

'Mr Corby,' Mr Lombard said quietly, 'I did not mean a fee-paying school.'

'You mean . . . ?' Jimmy couldn't say it.

Mr Lombard was a busy man. It was clearly distasteful to him but somebody had to take the plunge.

'I mean that you must place Toby in the . . . state sector, Mr Corby.'

The headmaster said it as if he was pronouncing a death sentence. And of course in Mr Lombard's mind he was. He was the headmaster of a private school and he was casting out a boy that school had nurtured, condemning him to fall among the barbarians of the underclass, to be taken into the realms of the demoralized, terrorized, unionized leftist apparatchiks of the National Union of Teachers. To spend his days attempting to communicate with a peer group whose English was gutter Estuary, or worse, for whom it was a foreign language. To go to a place where knives, drugs and perhaps even guns were more common than books and where vast overweight mothers pushed chips and pies through the school fence into the faces of their pasty, angry children. Wasn't that a sort of death? Death of future. Death of prospects. Death of any remote chance of becoming a well-educated, rounded and cultured individual?

Death of the opportunity for this poor boy to join the

elite, to spend his adolescence and young adulthood forming the connections that would cushion him through his professional life.

State education. That absolute impossibility. The one thing that one *simply could not do*. The thing that Jimmy, Monica and everybody they knew had spent a decade decrying, insulting, despairing of and dismissing. The thing that had been ruined by its makers, deserted by its middle-class constituents and left to rot.

State education. The University of the Damned.

And here was this *private school headmaster* blithely condemning an Abbey House boy to this terrible fate. What of solidarity? What of *no man left behind*? What of all the principles of comradeship and loyalty on which Abbey Hall prided itself? What of the honour roll of the glorious dead from two world wars proudly displayed in the school hall? Had those men died for nothing?

Toby was an Abbey Hall boy. That was who he was. His name had gone down at birth. He had gone there immediately on graduating at four from the Jumping Beans Advanced Fun and Learning Module off Ladbroke Grove. Did it really mean nothing at all?

'But surely, Mr Lombard,' Jimmy stammered, 'surely there must be some way round this?'

'Can you suggest one, Mr Corby?'

'Well . . . I sort of hoped that . . . I don't know. I mean Toby belongs here, he's one of you. Doesn't that count for anything?'

'It's extremely distressing for all of us, Mr Corby.'

'Don't you have a system? I mean to help people through when . . .'

'We have waited a term, Mr Corby. We have let you build up considerable arrears.'

'Isn't there anything else?'

'We have scholarships, of course. We think it's important to put something back into the community in which we live.'

'Well then . . .'

'But they are all taken and massively oversubscribed far into the future. Besides which, although Toby is by no means without ability, were he to sit the exam I doubt he could compete with the standard of the non-fee-paying pupils to whom we offer an education. They are all of exceptional ability.'

Of course, Jimmy remembered, the scholars were all brain boxes, that was why they were there. It had nothing to do with putting anything back into the community. These kids were selected in order to push up the ranking of the whole school. Jimmy had appreciated that once. He had appreciated the fact that Abbey Hall outshone even its local rivals in the private sector in the exam league tables that he and Monica used to read with pride when they were published in the *Daily Telegraph*. Then it had felt good, good to know that through Jimmy's hard work they were able to send their firstborn to a school whose exam ratings were among the best in London. And of course very far above any level that the state could offer. It was stats like that which confirmed absolutely the necessity of *never* going anywhere near a state primary.

'Would you *like* to put Toby forward to sit the scholarship exam?' Mr Lombard enquired in a tone that seemed to suggest that Jimmy might as well put him forward to join the SAS because he had about as much chance of getting in there.

'No,' Jimmy said quietly, 'I don't think so.'

'Then I'm afraid, regretfully,' Mr Lombard said, 'that is that.'

Jimmy walked out of Abbey Hall as if in a dream. Mr Lombard had told him that Toby could stay for the last three weeks of the current term, but after that he must not return.

'That should give you time to apply to your local authority for a state place for Toby,' he had said, 'although I should warn you that the public system has different dates and shorter holidays than we do, so you need to get going if you're hoping to secure your first choice.'

Jimmy had resisted the urge to tell Mr Lombard to shove his last three weeks up his arse. His life was in crisis and the last thing he needed was Toby at home to look after while he tried to sort out the mess at Webb Street and find the best state school for him. Instead he thanked Mr Lombard with as much grace as he could muster and walked back, to find his car had been clamped and was being lifted up on to a low loader.

A quiet sleep

Jimmy watched his one remaining Range Rover Discovery disappear up the street on its way to the council car pound.

'Fuck!' he shouted. 'Fuck fuck fuck fuck *fuck*!'

He could not pursue the car to the pound immediately because he had a full morning scheduled at the Webb Street site, attempting to fob off builders, contractors and suppliers with promises of immediate payment (temporarily deferred).

He would have to let the car go and travel out to Pimlico later in the day to retrieve it. That inconvenience would be made considerably more unpleasant because Jimmy did not know for sure whether he had a credit card that could take the strain of the fine he knew he would have to pay.

In the meantime all he could do was make his way across London by tube to Hackney, a journey for which, thank God, he still had sufficient credit on his Oyster card. His Oyster card! Six months before he had scarcely heard of such a thing. It was something he had read about in the *Standard* but didn't really understand.

He owned one now though, a reduced-price travel card without which he could no longer visit the street he still technically owned. A street from which at one point he had expected to profit to the tune of many millions of pounds. Millions of pounds which at the time he had assured himself were not just enriching him but making a significant contribution to the economic well-being of the city. Millions which still existed, in a way, except in the topsy-turvy parallel universe of post-crunch Britain they had changed colour from black to red.

He fell asleep on the tube and nearly missed his stop. If it hadn't have been for the man with the accordion and the squirrel in his top pocket who loudly informed the occupants of Jimmy's carriage that he was there to cheer up their day and that any contributions would be gratefully received, Jimmy might have slept all the way to the suburbs.

Jimmy had found that exhaustion was like that; it came and went in oppressive waves. When his mind was engaged in some urgent activity like coming to terms with the fact that his son was about to join a crack-dealing course at the local hoodie hangout or processing the information that his best friend had killed himself, Jimmy was wide awake. Awake in a way that people who were not nearly dead with sleeplessness would never understand, a kind of electrified, other-worldish wakefulness which brought shape, colour and emotion into sharp focus. Jimmy was a big First World War buff and he imagined that this was the kind of wakefulness that the hollow-eyed veterans of the trenches had experienced after three straight nights of constant bombardment.

But when, as on the tube, some never-before-read advert for office air conditioning caught his attention or the legs of the girl sitting opposite drew his eye and momentarily took his mind from the living nightmare in which it struggled to function, Jimmy found that he drifted off instantly. On this occasion it had taken three choruses of 'My Old Man's A Dustman' belted out on the accordion to rouse him to consciousness.

By the time Jimmy got to Webb Street he knew that he simply could not operate any longer without sleep. He had scarcely had a wink the night before, after Lizzie had brought the dreadful news of Robbo's balls-up. He had tossed and turned all night, racked with conflicting emotions. On the one hand he cursed the fact that he was back in the shit, and on the other he cursed himself for worrying about that when Robbo was dead and Lizzie so utterly devastated.

Now, suddenly, he was too far gone to worry about anything. He simply *had* to sleep. But where?

There were still some increasingly angry men working on his site. Men who had not been paid. Men who were turning up each day only in the hope of being paid. Men who carried hammers, screwdrivers and nail guns. If he was once more to win them over with a dose of his ever more thinly stretched charm then he must have his wits about him. He made a plan. One end of the street was fully occupied. This was the end in which the re-development was quite advanced – whole houses had been gutted, and new walls and floors put in. Six gleaming new flats were emerging in each house, where previously there had been just a warren of squalid bed-sits. But at the other end of the street no work had yet been started and no builder currently trod.

Approaching the street from this still-squalid end, Jimmy slipped into the first doorway unnoticed. He had the keys to all the houses in his case, but he did not need them as a vandal had already pulled the padlocked barrier away. He crept into the house – and nearly let himself straight out again, the atmosphere was so horribly oppressive.

The smells of the past. The house's history.

Food, many different types of food. All the scents had lingered. People, babies, children, the elderly and infirm. Jimmy could smell them all. The nightmares of the recent past. Overcrowded toilets and inadequate plumbing. Unsealed skirtings and bulging wallpaper, beneath which Jimmy knew the bugs remained. The food and the people were gone but their smells and the bugs which had tormented them lived on.

The house was bare now, of course. The previous occupants' bits and pieces had been cleared out, leaving only the marks on the floor where their mats and strips of carpet had been and the nails, hooks and globs of Blu-Tack on the walls from which their decorations had hung. Jimmy thought that he would rather die than live in a place like this and yet right now he certainly meant to sleep in it.

He had intended to fold up his jacket for a pillow and lie straight down in the ground-floor front room. But to his surprise he found that the room was already occupied. A tramp was stretched out on the floor asleep. Looking at him, Jimmy realized that some of what he had smelt probably emanated from this sorry figure.

For a moment Jimmy thought he'd retreat back into the street and find another house. But he was reluctant to do that: if he went outside he might be spotted by one of the impatient builders or angry creditors and Jimmy did not want to meet any of them until he had had some rest.

He decided that it was a big house and he would simply have to share it, so he began to climb the stairs looking for the least oppressive room. The one with the least grease on the walls and stains on the floor. The one in which the ghosts of the previous occupants were least active.

Jimmy reached the third floor and selected the largest room. He rolled his jacket up into a pillow and lay down, his head already spinning in anticipation of rest. He fell asleep instantly. Asleep on the bare floorboards of his multi-million-pound nightmare. Had he not already been unconscious he might have considered the irony of the situation.

His phone woke him up, something which seemed to be happening a lot these days.

'Yeah. Hello. What?' he spluttered.

'Jimmy?'

'What, hello? Yeah?'

There was a momentary pause and then a voice of accusation.

'You've been *sleeping*! Where are you?'

Slowly consciousness was returning. He knew that voice. It was his wife. It was Monica. And she'd caught him having a nap.

'No!' he protested, still trying to get his brain and his mouth into synch.

'You have!' Monica said. 'I can tell by your voice. I woke you up! I know I did. Is that what you do when you go to *work*? Get secret sleeps? Have you been lying to me?'

Jimmy wondered whether she'd have been less outraged if she'd caught him sleeping with a girl instead of just sleeping.

'No, Monica. Seriously, I just nodded off for a moment. I'm working. I'm in one of the houses at Webb Street. I basically collapsed. I'm sorry.'

'Oh.' Monica's voice had lost its outrage. 'Well, I suppose it's good to get some use out of our street.'

'I'm not the only one. There's a tramp in the room downstairs.'

'Jimmy, you could be killed!'

'I don't think so, Mon. By the look of him he's half dead already. Oh, by the way, the car's been towed.'

'Oh *no*.'

'Yeah.'

'I was phoning to find out how it went with Toby's headmaster.'

'Not good, I'm afraid. But can we discuss it later? I have to find a way to say "next week" in Polish.'

'All right. Do we have a puncture-repair kit?'

'You want to go cycling?'

'No. My piles cushion's burst and now I can't sit down.'

'Oh. Try in my saddle bag.'

'I did. No good.'

'Sorry then.'

The conversation over, Jimmy staggered upright and steeled himself to face his obligations once more.

The price of everything

Rupert and Amanda were hosting a small dinner party at their Belgravia town house to celebrate Rupert's elevation to the peerage, and because it was Rupert and Amanda it was likely to be pretty posh.

Monica was in despair.

Every evening garment she owned was laid out on the bed in a huge pile. A great big glittering, shimmering, skinny-strapped, cheeky-hemmed, plunging-necklined, figure-hugging mountain of memories. Memories of carefree evenings, saucy, drunken nights, sheer tights, best, most expensive knickers and a smallish size 12 figure.

'None of them fit,' Monica wailed. 'I am the walrus.'

'Some of them fit,' Jimmy claimed. 'That jacket fits. You're just being paranoid.'

Jimmy studied his wife in the mirror while pretending to adjust his tie. Certainly she was a bit *rounder* than when she had last worn some of those dresses. Their second child, Cressie, was only just a year old and Monica had not been vigorous about getting her figure back in that time. She was possibly the teeniest tad less firm about the curves than of old. Her tum did bulge a little. But she wasn't a walrus. Not even a large seal.

Monica's image of herself was just paranoid self-delusion. It was all those other women, Amanda and

David's Laura and bloody Madonna with those ridiculous arms. Women who seemed to get skinnier as they grew older. Women who clearly spent every waking moment in the gym. Personally, Jimmy didn't go for the anorexic man-look in a woman. He would rather have a girl with a bit of a saggy tum and bingo wings than one with great big veins running up her forearms, and biceps like the thighs on a supermarket chicken.

'Your problem,' Jimmy said, 'is negative self-image. You look in the mirror and you see a Teletubby.'

'You think I look like a Teletubby!' Monica was on him like a Rottweiler.

'No, that's not what I said at all.'

'You think I've turned into Tinky Winky!'

'No!' Jimmy protested, struggling to find a way of making his point more clearly without digging himself in any deeper. 'I said that you are—'

'I have had *two bloody kids*!' Monica hissed through gritted teeth. 'Two entire human beings grew in here,' she said, slapping her stretch marks, 'and if you don't like what they've turned me into then you shouldn't have knocked me up, you bastard!'

'You haven't turned into anything,' Jimmy said firmly, refusing to rise to the bait. 'You were gorgeous before and you're gorgeous now.'

He meant it too, but Monica was only half mollified. There was a slight atmosphere in the cab which did not dissipate until they arrived at

Rupert and Amanda's and had been given a drink.

'Drinking my investments,' Rupert said, as Jimmy accepted a glass of wine from the pretty catering girl who met him and Monica at the door. Amanda never cooked, ever. She arranged menus.

'Which is actually an equal challenge,' she always insisted, 'if you take the trouble to do it *properly*.'

'Investment, Rupert?' Jimmy asked, beaming and taking a deep swig from his glass. He was still basking in the warm afterglow of the surprise pre-prandial tumble he and Monica had shared on top of her pile of dresses. It was so easy to get out of the habit of sex, he thought, particularly with kids in the house. You just had to make a bit of an effort, that was all. It was certainly worth it.

'Yes,' Rupert replied. 'I've moved into wine, so enjoy it, you bastards, because this stuff is the canine bollocks. Absolute gilt-edged security. Every single bottle, if stored properly of course. Personally I'd have kept it locked up.'

'Can you believe it?' Amanda said, sweeping down the stairs in a glimmering strapless gown which perfectly showed off the tight, knotted, perma-tanned little biceps which appeared to have been bolted on to her arms as extras. 'He actually thinks we should leave good wine in some cellar near Bristol.'

'Perfect storage facility,' said Rupert. 'Believe it or not, it's an old government fallout shelter from the Cold War. Goes on for miles. Lots of people keep their wine there. Ours is next to the Lloyd Webbers".

'Yes,' Amanda said, 'and Rupert wants to leave it there.'

'It was bought as an *investment*, darling,' Rupert insisted.

'It's *wine*,' Amanda replied equally firmly. 'Wine is a gift from God and it should be bloody well drunk.'

'As should we be!' David said, emerging from the reception room resplendent in his new electric-green Armani glasses. 'We should all be bloody well drunk because Rupert, our Rupert, the man who, to quote dear Oscar, knows the price of everything and the value of nothing, is a *fucking* lord of the realm!'

'You clearly don't understand the value of that wine you're glugging away at like cheap plonk, you pretentious arse,' Rupert said, smiling and refilling David's glass. 'And yes, Amanda, wine is indeed a gift from God, which is why it's so bloody valuable and, what's more, getting more valuable every day. It is in fact extremely generous of us to share such a fine vintage with our old friends, as I'm sure they are all pathetically and touchingly aware.'

This of course provoked a chorus of sarcastic exclamations.

'The funny thing is,' Rupert went on, 'if I'd waited a year or two I'd be *twice* as generous because by that time the wine would have been worth twice as much. I find that fact both exciting and curiously depressing.'

'But of course it would have tasted pretty much the same,' Henry said. 'Cheers.'

'What's taste got to do with anything?' Rupert asked. 'We're talking about *value*.'

'The value of a wine *is* in its taste,' Jane snapped.

'And how pissed it gets you,' Robbo added.

'Honestly, Rupert,' Jane went on, 'don't you realize how boring it is, the way you pretend nothing has any value except what you can sell it for?'

'Please,' Rupert insisted, scooping up a passing canapé and speaking through it as he munched, 'can you tell a hundred-pound bottle of wine from a thousand-pound bottle?'

'I don't know. I mi—'

'Of course you couldn't. Not in a million years. I'm the only person here who could, as a matter of fact. But then I might easily prefer the cheaper bottle, as might any of you. Therefore *taste* has no quantifiable value at all. It's subjective. A builder's mate's estimate is as valid as yours or mine, i.e., worthless. *Price* is the only true measure of value. Because the only real, quantifiable difference between a thousand-pound bottle and a hundred-pound bottle is nine hundred pounds. That's it. With wine as with all things, I know what I like. But if I want to know what it's worth I have to look at what it costs.'

'Nice nibbles, Amanda,' said Jimmy. 'Marks and Sparks?'

'How *dare* you!' Amanda replied.

'Wine is like modern art,' Rupert pressed on, never

one to pass up an opportunity to ruffle feathers. 'Both are now all about investment potential. Their aesthetic value is increasingly irrelevant. Particularly with modern art. At least with wine you can normally find something decent.'

Rupert had clearly expected to get a rise out of David and he wasn't disappointed.

'Ah ha,' David smiled, attempting to look like an indulgent liberal amused by a reactionary philistine but struggling to maintain his pose, 'are we to be treated to yet another rant about your one visit to Tate Modern which has enabled you to diss all post-nineteenth-century art ever since?'

'I'm with Roop on that,' Robbo said. 'Come on, Dave. You're among friends. Just admit it for once, privately. Modern art is all absolute bollocks, isn't it? Just one big pile of pretentious, pointless, self-indulgent wank. I mean really, you have to admit that surely?'

'I don't think I can face this discussion again,' David said. 'I personally find beauty in the intellectual and sensual challenge of the abstract. You, Robbo, find it in nice, figurative, story-telling pictures preferably featuring nude women floating winsomely in ponds.'

'That'll do for me too,' Jimmy said cheerfully.

'David, the reason you don't want to discuss it is because there's nothing to discuss,' Rupert said. 'Whether it's wank or not, which clearly it *is*, is a matter of personal opinion. My point was that the value of modern art is quantified by its price. That is self-evident. It has nothing to do with its aesthetic value . . .'

'I know that's what you said, Rupert,' David said, still trying to look easy and amused but struggling even harder to disguise his irritation, 'and you are wrong. Beauty may be in the eye of the beholder but it is beauty nonetheless. And the fact that a rich man is prepared to pay for it does not stop it being beautiful . . .'

'A rich *person*, darling,' Laura corrected him. 'I think you'll find women enjoy art too and gosh, do you know, some of them even *buy* it.'

'Yes, of course. Absolutely,' David said apologetically.

'And transgenders. Don't forget them,' Jimmy butted in teasingly. 'Chicks with dicks and men with muffs go to galleries too, you sexist, genderist, trannyphobic bastard!'

'Face facts, David,' Rupert said. 'A sheep pickled by Damien Hirst is worth millions, a rat marinated by an A-level art student is worth nothing. If Hirst had marinated the rat and the student had pickled the sheep the prices would be reversed. Modern art is about *investment*. It's that simple. So much more wealth is being created these days that places need to be found to put it. Therefore an important financial industry has been developed where the product of certain artists is agreed to be a gilt investment, just like gold ingots or government bonds. You cannot possibly believe that when Tracey whatsit exhibited her unmade bed there

263

weren't a thousand similar mouthy, ballsy-looking birds struggling away at art school producing similarly pointless and offputting mounds of old toss. Tracey got lucky, that's all. It could have been any old lesbian . . .'

'Actually, Rupert, she's not a lesbian,' Laura began, 'or at least I don't think she—'

'You are so offensive, Rupert, it's actually quite funny,' Jane added, but through gritted teeth and without the glimmer of a smile.

'We walked round the Tate together, David,' Rupert said. 'You insisted. Now come on. Honestly. Who knew which darkened tent containing a looped video of a pigeon breathing or the top of a bald head would become the looped video *de jour* and hence be worth a thousand times more than all the other looped videos in all the other little darkened tents? The financial market did that. Only the financial market can determine which bits of pretentious modern-art bollocks are of value and which aren't. And once it has determined which, it has to maintain that value. Art is a commodity, like property or football players – and wine is catching up fast, so sip it slowly, you lot, because with every second that passes each sip is worth more than the last.'

'Ignore him, everybody,' Amanda said firmly. 'Glug it. Swig it. Pour it into a plant pot. He's being a pompous bore, that's all, besides which we've got five thousand bottles underneath Bristol so I think we can drink a few without worrying about the market value.'

'I just wanted them to appreciate it, that's all,' Rupert said, slightly huffily.

'Oh I *am*, Rupert.' Henry sniffed deeply over his glass and proclaimed with heavy sarcasm, 'Such an elegant *nose* with a strong bouquet of . . . is it pounds? Yes, I think I'm smelling pounds . . . plus a certain euro-scented aftertaste with hints of yen at the finish.'

'The problem with you lefty types always sneering at profit,' Rupert said, 'is that you've got so much money yourselves you no longer appreciate the value of the bloody stuff.'

'We haven't got so much money,' Henry pointed out (as he always did), 'and it's extremely difficult to appreciate the value of things, Rupert, when the value keeps *appreciating*. I mean at what point does one stop to appreciate it? Surely you'd always be thinking, hang on, if I wait a minute the value will have appreciated and I can appreciate it even more.'

'Well, it's delicious anyway,' Lizzie said. 'Now can we please get off the subject?'

'Dinner's ready,' Amanda said, 'so come on through. We're starting with foie gras but I'm assured it's humanely produced, and they've done poached pear and vegan stilton for Laura and Jane.'

'Lovely,' said the vegetarians.

'Don't tell us what it *is*, Amanda,' Henry said. 'Tell us what it *cost*.'

'A fuck of a lot, Henry.'

'Well, that's all right then.'

Socks full of food

It took many hours to retrieve the Range Rover and it was pretty late when Jimmy got home, but Monica was still awake.

'I only just got Lillie down,' she said. 'I was about to clear up.'

'Sod that,' said Jimmy, heading for the fridge. 'I need a drink.'

The family room was something of a tip but Jimmy didn't care any more. If anyone had ever told him in his previous life that he would be virtually indifferent to treading on soggy rusk in his socks he would have laughed at them, but now he didn't even notice. Just as he didn't notice the crunch of toys and fallen fridge magnets under his feet either. And when he opened the fridge he didn't notice the vast array of bowls containing bits of half-eaten kiddie meals, diced carrots and mashed potatoes, all carefully preserved under clingfilm until the time when they would be deemed mouldy enough to be legitimately chucked away. Or the half-squeezed Frube Tubes and half-chewed, spit-soaked lollipops lying on saucers because Cressida insisted that such precious items be preserved at all costs.

He ignored all this, which in a previous life he would have deemed unacceptable to a civilized standard of living, and simply pulled the wine from where it nestled in the fridge door.

What Jimmy could not avoid noticing was the upturned plug-socket protector. Even a brain-dead dysfunctional like him could not ignore that when treading on it. He screamed in agony and staggered backwards, dropping a third-full bottle of wine in the process and going for six over a plastic fire engine.

'Are you OK, Jimmy?' Monica asked, fetching a mop and a dustpan and brush.

'I hate those plug protectors,' he gasped from the floor.

'We need them. Cressida's rushing about all over the place now.'

'I know, but I still hate them. And what's more, when you want to get one out of the socket, you can't.'

'Well, that's the point, isn't it? If we can't, then she can't.'

'Yes, but what about when you want to plug something in?'

'Like what? We have sockets for the toaster and the kettle.'

'I don't know. Something new? Like that breadmaker my mother gave us for Christmas.'

'Yes, you're right, Jimmy,' Monica said sarcastically, 'because bread is so difficult to find in London, it would be well worth risking our daughter's electrocution to bake some at home.'

There was silence for a while. Jimmy wasn't really interested in plug sockets; he was just putting off the awful moment when he would have to tell Monica about Toby being chucked out of Abbey Hall.

Then a tiny piece of emotional good fortune came his way. It turned out that Toby had made the decision for them.

'Jimmy,' Monica said, 'Toby's been talking to me and he wants to leave Abbey Hall.'

'Really? Why?'

'He's not stupid. He knows he doesn't belong there any more.'

'Is he being bullied?'

'I don't think so, not terribly. Teased, certainly, but he's tough enough for that, I think. No. He just knows that he's at a posh school but that his dad isn't rich any more. We've already pulled him out of the skiing trip and there was a note today about a trip to the theatre which will cost sixty pounds in all. He's worked out for himself that we can't afford that sort of thing any more.'

'That's pretty sad, isn't it? I mean if he's feeling guilty about how much he's costing us. Makes me feel a complete failure.'

'He isn't feeling guilty and this isn't about you, Jim.

It's about him. I think the penny's dropped for him in a way that it still hasn't for us. He doesn't feel like a rich kid any more. Maybe it's because we used to bang on so much about how lucky we were and how we should never take it for granted. I honestly think he took us at our word and never did. Take it for granted, I mean. And now he can see that everything's changed and he's accepted it.'

'Wow,' said Jimmy. 'He's a good kid, isn't he?'

'Yes.'

'As it happens, Mr Lombard was chucking him out anyway.'

'No! The bastard! I can't *believe* it. He's an Abbey Hall boy.'

'That's what I said.'

'Fuck him.'

'Yes, fuck him.'

'Toby's a good kid,' Monica said as Jimmy went back to the fridge.

'Better than us, I reckon,' Jimmy replied over his shoulder.

'Yes, but he's got our DNA. So we take some of the credit.'

'Oh certainly. We get the credit for nature and I suppose Jodie gets the credit for nurture. A lot of it anyway.'

'That's a bit sad, isn't it?'

'Yes. I suppose it is.'

'Funny it took us losing everything to work that out.'

Jimmy brought another bottle of wine and put it on the floor in front of them. Then he sat down beside Monica and for a while they just held each other.

Street Owning Man

Rupert's peerage celebration dinner was in full swing.

'How's Webb Street going then, Jimmy?' Robbo asked, his mouth full of chocolate soufflé and Sauternes. 'Have those bloody Poles worked out which way round we have the taps in England yet?'

'Don't talk about Webb Street, *please*,' Monica begged. 'I'm embarrassed.'

Webb Street had just become a massive part of Jimmy and Monica's lives and Monica in particular was still not quite sure how she felt about the whole thing. It was in Hackney, an unremarkable nineteenth-century thoroughfare which had escaped Hitler's bombs and been pretty much left to rot ever since. Such had been its dilapidation that even during the eighties, when almost everything else in Hackney had been gentrified, Webb Street had been left to the roaches and the crack dealers. But the noughties were not the eighties and in the heady joy of a new millennium Webb Street, untouched, unloved, owned by absentee landlords who were not allowed to raise their rents or evict sitting tenants, was, as Rupert had put it when he suggested the idea to Jimmy, 'a granny waiting to be mugged'.

'It's simple, mate,' Rupert had said. 'You work your way up the street, house by house, offering over-the-odds prices to landlords and fat inducements to tenants to bugger off. Then once you've bagged the lot you can develop a whole lifestyle community. The problem with lots of good houses in London is that they're next door to shitty ones full of shitty awful people. If you're developing a whole street that problem goes away.'

Jimmy had enquired at the time where Rupert supposed he was going to get the money for the over-the-odds prices and fat inducements with which he would gain control of all these homes.

'You're living in it, mate!' Rupert replied. 'One of the ten best houses in Notting Hill! Fully developed. Jacuzzi, gym, underground car park and ready to rock. You could raise five to seven million on that. We'd give it you tomorrow. You're sound as a pound. You earn easily enough to cover the interest payments. God knows, your bonus last year alone would have done more than that.'

And Rupert was right. Fired up by the enormity of the scheme, Jimmy had found it absurdly easy to borrow six million pounds from the Royal Lancashire using his home as collateral. That, plus some share options and two million borrowed against his elephantine pension pot, had been sufficient for him to purchase the twenty-four houses in Webb Street.

Quite suddenly and in a flurry of excitement, Jimmy and Monica had become major property speculators.

'I still can't quite believe that we actually own a street,' Jimmy said, digging into his foie gras and pulling a face that asked, should I feel a bit guilty about it, do you think?

Monica definitely did feel guilty. Or at least embarrassed. She admitted that she wasn't sure which it was herself.

'Don't put it like that, darling, please,' she said. 'We don't own all of it.'

'We do, babes,' Jimmy assured her, reaching for the wine with further expressions of mock tortured self-doubt. 'It's mad, I know. Bloody tonto.'

'We do *not* own all of it,' Monica protested. 'The end bit isn't ours. The bit behind the pub.'

'That's Webb Mews,' Jimmy said, 'and you're right, we don't own that. but we do own Webb Street. All of it.'

'And we're talking to Webb Mews,' David chipped in, 'because if we can get it plus the required planning permission then Webb Street will have its own private health club. Exclusive to one street, imagine that! God, Jimmy, I can remember you at university in your torn jeans, pinching food from the union shop. You were

272

virtually a bloody punk! Now look at you – from Street Fighting Man to Street Owning Man, eh? Let's face it, the Stones went the same way.'

'The Stones were *always* middle bloody class,' Robbo said. 'Or at least Mick and Keef were.'

'We *don't* own it,' Monica insisted once more. 'For a start, Rupert owns most of it, or at least his bank does.'

'Monica,' Henry said soothingly, 'don't beat yourself up about it. Really. What you and Jimmy are involved in is *wealth creation*, which is a very good thing. There is absolutely nothing to feel embarrassed about.'

'Hear, hear,' said Rupert. 'Well said, Henry!'

'My God!' Lizzie exclaimed. 'Rupert and Henry actually agree on something. Let's have a party!'

'We *are* having a party,' Amanda pointed out.

'More wine then!' Robbo announced. 'We must drink to Rupert and Henry seeing eye to eye for the first time since they agreed that they fancied you, Liz.'

'Shut up, Robbo!' Lizzie said, reddening. 'I mean it.'

'Joking aside, Monica,' Henry said, 'you and Jim should take pride in what you're doing. It's exactly the type of project that we in government have been trying to encourage.'

'What, me getting hugely richer?' Jimmy laughed. 'Blimey, was it in the manifesto?'

'I'm serious. A project like Webb Street is an engine of *growth and prosperity* in this city. As a Labour MP I'm thinking about what this kind of profit generation

273

means in terms of employment, consumer spending and a spur to further inward investment.'

'There, you see, Jimmy?' Rupert shouted, pouring more wine and thus recklessly reducing the value of his investment even further. 'Webb Street is a job-creation scheme! You and Monica are *philanthropists*. Bloody social workers.'

'Prosperity and equality are not mutually exclusive,' Henry said pompously. 'Tony has always made it clear that Labour is the party of business as well as the party of the people. After all, who is it that does business but people?'

After that, the evening degenerated into a discussion about the Congestion Charge, a subject on which everyone could agree.

They all loathed it.

What goes around

Detective Inspector Graeme Beaumont worked in Scotland Yard's Financial Fraud Division and he did so with an evangelical zeal. He liked chasing white-collar criminals. In his opinion, far too much press attention was paid to hoodies on street corners and not nearly enough to those who stole via columns of numbers on screens and mountains of paperwork spread across continents.

'You're mugging old ladies every bit as much if you pinch their pension fund,' he was fond of pointing out to the squad of bookish constables and civilian accountants who worked under him, 'as you are if you assault them at a bus shelter. Stealing is stealing and it doesn't matter if the crook flies first class and sits in the House of Lords. If he's a crook, he's a crook.'

Beaumont had been working hard at his desk all morning. And working, on this particular morning, with a growing sense of purpose. His was a tough and often thankless field of operations. Results were agonizingly slow to come by and months of meticulous work would often yield nothing. This morning, however, Beaumont felt he was getting somewhere.

Nonetheless, when the clock struck eleven he rose from his desk, crossed what was grandly called his operations room and inspected the contents of the small fridge that stood in the corner. Beaumont valued routine. He believed it disciplined and focused the mind. He felt that he was a better detective for strictly observing his eleven o'clock break.

Everything in the fridge was in order.

His milk had not been tampered with. His Twix lay unopened and the circular box of Laughing Cow Cheese Triangles with three remaining triangles in it was exactly how he had left it.

The constables and accountants who worked under Graeme Beaumont knew better than to tamper with Beaumont's section of the fridge. His milk was sacrosanct. His elevenses untouchable. Let them share a communal carton of milk for their tea if they wished. Let them organize an honesty tin in order to pay for tea and a packet of Penguin biscuits if that was their desire. But that way was not Beaumont's way. Beaumont knew a little too much about human nature to believe that such arrangements could ever lead to anything but tears.

It wasn't that Beaumont lacked generosity. If somebody had asked him for a splash of milk for their tea he would have given it. Gladly. It was simply that a lifetime of experience had led Beaumont to conclude that in communal fridges, as in most cooperative ventures, there would always be somebody who, through either sloth or greed, would ruin things for everyone.

Beaumont made himself a cup of tea, took a cheese triangle and one finger from his Twix and returned with them to his desk.

He was excited and anxious to get on but also somewhat vexed. The case on which he was working had given rise to a moral question. Should he declare a vested interest? The thought had been on his mind all morning. Sipping his tea and toying with the foil wrapping of the cheese triangle, he decided that it was all right. That there was in fact no conflict of interest and that he had no need to trouble his superiors with it.

The fact that he had in his sights two men with whom he had briefly shared a house some seventeen years before hardly represented a difficulty. Yes, it was true that those men had chucked him out of that house. Perfunctorily. That those two confident, well-established second-year students had rendered a vulnerable fresher homeless and distressed. That was undeniable. It was also true that he, Inspector Beaumont, had never forgotten the incident, feeling to this day that he had been appallingly treated.

But these things did not represent a conflict of interest. Beaumont's reputation was spotless, he had applied the law equally and fairly, without fear, favour or prejudice, throughout his career. The fact that he had a passing acquaintance with *Lord* Rupert Bennett and a certain Jimmy Corby was utterly irrelevant.

Beaumont had not sought out these men as objects of an investigation into insider trading. He had of course always been aware of them in a general sense. Of Bennett certainly. Bennett could not be avoided; his extraordinary success in banking meant that his name was known to anyone with even a vague interest in the financial world. And the almost equally enormous success of the other occupants of that extraordinarily lucky house of which he had briefly been a tenant was not unknown to Beaumont either. No single group of people could have done better in life. He had never been able to get away from the bastards.

The celebrated catering woman who had taken the room which Beaumont had thought was his.

The architect whose name sometimes came up when Prince Charles objected to a building.

Henry Baker, the flaxen-haired New Labour golden boy.

And Jimmy Corby. So rich. So successful. A man whose charmed life, although not in the public domain, was known to Beaumont via the old university grapevine.

Of course, Beaumont assured himself, he wasn't envious of these people. He did not *like* them, particularly Bennett and Corby, but he wasn't envious of them.

He had not, after all, done so badly in life himself and had no complaints on that score. He had a nice little house which he shared with his partner, a sergeant and another stalwart of the Gay Police Association. He had a number of citations to his credit. He was one of the most respected officers in the Financial Fraud Division.

And now he had a recently ennobled peer of the realm in his sights. A confidant of not one but two prime ministers. Quite a scalp to add to the growing collection of fraudsters, cheats and charlatans who imagined that the law was written for other people and did not apply to them. Until they met Detective Inspector Graeme Beaumont, that is. After which they thought differently.

Lord Rupert Bennett would soon be thinking differently.

Beaumont found his mind drifting back to that cold autumn night in 1991. He'd been a student at Sussex for only two months but he was already heartily sick of the hall of residence in which he'd been placed. The corridor on which he lived was full of hearty, noisy, sporty blokes who didn't wash up the communal dishes, didn't respect the fridge rules and from whom one's milk was not safe.

Therefore, when Beaumont had seen a room in a shared house advertised on the accommodation notice-board in the Student Union, he had gone round to the address immediately and to his delight had been invited to move straight in.

'We need the money big time,' the charming, kind-looking man who had introduced himself as Jimmy Corby had said. Also present at the interview was a pleasant curly-headed man in a shapeless jumper and Bennett in tweeds and brogues, smoking a pipe.

Beaumont had been hugely flattered that such sophisticated second-years would consider living with a nervous young newbie like himself. His personal confidence, which had been somewhat shaken by his experience with the rugger buggers in the hall of residence, grew accordingly.

Beaumont therefore gave notice at his hall. He applied for a half-term's refund, which was his due, and moved into his new room that week. He built shelves from planks and bricks for his books and hung his Gay Pride poster up on the wall. He put his clearly marked cereal boxes and rice jar in the kitchen and his toothpaste with his name on it in the bathroom. His loo roll he kept in his bedroom and took with him when he visited the lavatory.

Beaumont was very happy. He lived in that house for eight days and was unaware of any problems or tensions. It was true that he had faced strong resistance when he had suggested that he be allowed his own specific sixth of the fridge. But although that particular issue remained unresolved, nothing prepared him for the moment when he returned home from college one evening to be faced by Corby, Bennett, the architect and the bumbling one in the jumper to be told that it wasn't working out and he would have to leave.

They had of course assured him that he could stay until he found somewhere else (a day or two should be enough, he recalled Bennett suggesting very firmly), but pride and hurt had driven Beaumont from the house that very evening. An evening that was cold and stormy.

After wandering the streets in tears for an hour, he had spent a miserable, lonely night in a small hotel which he certainly could not afford. This was followed by a miserable, lonely entire first year in a grim bedsit, the only accommodation he could find. It cost him twice as much as the hall of residence, which he wished he had never left.

It hadn't been the worst experience that could befall a first-year student but it had been a painful one for Beaumont. Very painful. To be summarily rejected by such well-integrated students had shaken him badly. He had imagined himself a marked man. A pariah. He worried that word would spread that he was impossible to live with and people would avoid him throughout his three years. He thought people were staring at him in the corridors of the Union building.

Despite his fears, it did not work out quite that badly. Beaumont eventually found his feet and made one or two friends. But it took a long time for him to get his confidence back and he never forgot the loneliness of the night he'd spent crying in the little hotel and the year in that horrible bedsit.

And then quite recently Rupert Bennett had come back into his life.

Rupert Bennett, the man who had advised the Treasury on the Caledonian Granite rescue package. The man Inspector Beaumont had become convinced had made huge personal profits from trading on the information he had gained during that process.

Beaumont had been on Bennett's trail for months, but it was a labyrinthine trail left by a man who did not wish to be followed. Rupert Bennett had been very careful. He had made his share purchases from overseas accounts and he had laundered the profits through various third parties and tax havens. Try as he might, Detective Inspector Beaumont could not gather together enough concrete evidence to arrest his old housemate for insider trading. So he had instructed his team to look at the actions of his friends. To find out who was in his inner circle and see what, if anything, they had been up to in those heady days when the business of money had passed almost unnoticed beyond the law and into an unregulated, amoral free-for-all.

'After all,' Beaumont told his officers, 'the nature of insider trading is that it depends on the *passing and receiving* of information. It's just possible that we can get to Bennett via someone he knew. Somebody who was less careful than him. An old university friend, perhaps. A valued and trusted confidant.'

Beaumont sent his people to look for anyone who could be identified as a regular figure at the many social functions which Lord and Lady Bennett had organized. A list had been drawn up which featured a number of names that Beaumont recognized from his past. The team had then looked into the financial records of the people on the list to see if any of them had traded in Caledonian Granite shares at the same time as Bennett had himself. One name ticked all the boxes. Jimmy Corby.

It *has* to be private

On New Year's Eve 2007 the gang had all assembled at Jimmy and Monica's for dinner, cooked (as Monica was the first to admit) by the brilliant Jessica, without whom Monica would often tell you she *could not do*.

It was just as it had always been. The gang had fore-gathered as they had done so many times in the previous fifteen years, and before that in embryonic form at university. For curries, for movies, for birthdays and for weddings, to celebrate each other's professional elevation and the arrival of children. The cast had remained the same; only the quality of the food, the wine and the districts of London in which they met had changed.

Except this time something else had changed. The usual ten of them were not *quite* the usual ten, a development that had made those remaining rather uncomfortable. Particularly the women.

One of their number was no longer present. What was more, she had been replaced by a girl of twenty-two.

David and Laura were there as always. David was now a hugely successful architect, the twin prongs of his first Rainbow even now half constructed, poking up into the skies of Europe. His wife Laura was a barrister and mum and founder member of Kid Conscious, a charity which lobbied against smacking. Laura believed passionately that there were no circumstances under which it was ever justified to smack a child. In fact she had started the charity after being forced to sack a nanny for doing just that.

Henry and Jane were there, of course. Slightly grumpy old Henry and bright, intense Jane. Henry had by now won his first junior ministerial post and, having deftly leapt the loyalty divide between Tony Blair and Gordon Brown, was very much a rising star of the new Prime Minister's administration. He had finally given up on completing his novel.

'The thing I've come to understand,' he said, 'is that *Security Blanket* is a film, not a book at all, and I'm going to turn it into a screenplay. During the summer recess.'

Jane by this time had completed four novels and her big news was that she was about to be published.

'And it's not *chick lit* either,' Jane assured everyone. 'Not one of those books that are nothing but sex, shoes and shopping like you read, Monica. It's a historical love story set in two periods, the present and the First World War.'

'Sounds like chick lit to me,' Rupert remarked, 'and am I being dense or didn't they have sex, wear shoes and go shopping in the Great War?'

Lizzie and Robson were all present and correct too. The oldest relationship in the gang and the only one in which both members were original Radishers. Not that

Lizzie had actually *shoved* one, of course, on that famous graduation night; she had long since gone to bed. But she was still an original Radisher.

And Rupert was there. Lord Rupert now, of course, posh at last, courtesy of a Labour government.

But no Amanda.

Amanda of Rupert and Amanda was not present.

Instead, in her place sat Beatrice. Very bright, very pretty and doing her *very*, *very* best to chatter her way through a near-impossible situation.

'I can't *believe* Rupert's done this,' Laura whispered to Monica as they went downstairs together, ostensibly to see how the soup was coming on. 'It's such a dreary cliché.'

'I miss Amanda terribly,' Monica admitted. 'Not least because she occasionally put Rupert in his place. Of course I invited her for this evening *first* but she's decided to go to Scotland with the children, so I had to ask Rupert. But I've made it absolutely clear to Jimmy that Radish Club or no stupid Radish Club, Rupert comes second from now on, we're sticking with Amanda. Rupert buggered off, not her.'

'I know, and worse, he's landed us with fucking *Beatrice*.'

'We should try to be kind.'

'Why? The little bitch has run off with a married father with two young children. She knew what she was doing.'

'She's twenty-two, Laura. *Rupert* knew what he was doing. This situation is entirely Rupert's responsibility.'

'It's so stupid! Couldn't Rupert have just carried on shagging around a bit?'

'I know I'd rather Jimmy left me than did that.'

Laura gave Monica a quizzical look.

'Do you really think that, Mon? I'd say putting up with a couple of mid-life quickies is better than throwing everything away. And if he'd stuck to quickies then Amanda could have had a revenge shag and *we* wouldn't have been left with sodding Beatrice. One good thing though, Amanda will kill him in the courts. He'll lose half at least.'

'I suppose he'd rather have ten million and sleep with a girl of twenty-two than twenty million and sleep with one of forty. It's so sad.'

At the dinner table Rupert, of course, was riding out the situation with his usual bluff confidence, acting as if nothing had happened. He was almost forcing poor Beatrice into the conversation as if she had instantly become one of the gang and was having the time of her life, when in fact it was clear she would far rather have spent the evening hiding in the loo.

Despite the uncomfortable new dynamic, the conversation progressed along pretty much the same lines as it always did, turning, as so often in the past, from property prices to education. From education it would almost certainly move on to holiday locations (ski lodges – rent or buy?) before finally settling back on to property prices with the cheese. Property prices were the great and unifying subject, affecting them all with equal intensity despite the disparity in the values of their portfolios.

For the time being, however, the gang were stuck firmly on education. The conclusion was always the same. Private (or selective grammar) was the only option. It was a terrible, crying, awful shame, but the state system simply did not currently *offer a viable alternative*.

Only Rupert (and Amanda until recently) viewed this absolute certainty with complete approval. Rupert had nothing but contempt for even the principle of state education for any but the very poorest of the poor. He believed it was simply a fact of life that man was a selfish animal who sought for himself the best in everything, and therefore it was unreasonable to expect him to modify that outlook on a subject as important as the future of his children.

'And don't give me that bollocks about how the state should offer the best,' he thundered. 'How could it possibly? Is a council house as good as a mansion? Will welfare food stamps get you a table at the Ivy? No. Of course not. The state simply can't offer the best. It never has done and it never will. I can afford to send my kids to a school with three hundred acres of grounds, two computers a child, a fully equipped theatre and *three*

Latin teachers. Am I going to choose the local comprehensive instead? No, I'm fucking well not.'

None of the others felt that the situation was quite as clear-cut as that. Henry and Jane were the most anguished on the subject. As a Labour MP, Henry was theoretically a champion of state schools.

'I don't agree at all, Rupert, you Nazi bastard,' Henry said. 'There's a lot more to education than Latin and fully equipped theatres. It's also about being educated for *life*. For a world into which you must eventually *fit*. In the best of all worlds all children, rich and poor, would be educated in a superb comprehensive system. That's what we're working towards in government and that is what we'll achieve.'

'But you've been in power for more than ten years and you don't go for state education yourself,' David pointed out.

Henry was trying to look comfortable and relaxed.

'That is simply not so, David,' he replied. 'Jane and I use the state system and we're very happy with it.'

'Now come on, Henry,' David said. 'You know that's bollocks.'

'It's a state school,' Henry insisted.

'It's a grant-maintained grammar which you have no right to be in because it is two whole state schools away from where you live! You pulled strings and worked the system, Henry, and you should bloody well admit it.'

Henry was clearly fuming. His and Jane's decision to

seek out one of the few selective state schools left in London had made him very vulnerable to charges of hypocrisy. Particularly after he had laughably claimed that it was a choice made only because of the excellence of its choir.

'We are *not* being hypocritical,' Jane insisted, trying to come to Henry's aid but in fact making things worse. 'If the comprehensive system were as good as it ought to be, our kids would be in it like a shot.'

'And it will be,' Henry chipped in quickly. 'That's our pledge in government and we will make good on it.'

'Bloody hell.' Jimmy laughed. 'Like David said, you've been in for ten years, how long do you need?'

'They've been so busy banning foxhunting and starting wars,' Rupert sneered.

'I support the principle of comprehensive education for all,' Henry repeated pompously, 'and I am working to bring it about. The problem is that everybody's pulling out of it. More and more people can afford fees and we just don't have enough middle-class parents using the system, which of course means more of them leave.'

'Just like you and Jane,' Rupert said.

'I've told you, Rupert,' Jane snapped, 'St Bartholomew's Grammar is a *state school*.'

'It's grant-maintained and selective, Jane. Live with it.'

Lizzie and Robson definitely approved of state education and were anxious for it to be as top class as possible.

'I'd rather my taxes went on books, not bombs, any day,' Lizzie said.

She and Robbo doubted, however, that there would ever be circumstances in which they might put their own kids into a state school. They conceded that some kids might thrive at a comprehensive, but sadly not theirs. Tabitha and Jonah were extremely sensitive and intelligent children. They needed challenges and they needed boundaries. They needed *stimulus*. These things could no longer be found at the local schools and probably never would be again. Lizzie felt terribly angry about this.

'I'm sorry, Henry,' she said, 'but as far as I'm concerned the horrible irony of it all is that, after your endless meddling with traditional teaching methods, the Labour government have actually made it *impossible* to go state.'

'Oh, I suppose you think the curriculum should all be three Rs and the Battle of Britain?' Jane put in.

'I know I do,' Robbo commented. 'More Churchill and less bloody media studies, whatever they are.'

Jimmy agreed entirely with Lizzie and Robbo's position. He and Monica certainly felt that it would not be fair to subject a bright boy like Toby to the roughhouse of a state primary. In fact they were already beginning to see signs of sensitivity, brightness and creativity in baby Cressida.

Besides Henry and Jane, David and Laura were the

only members of the gang with any experience of the state system, having gone local with five-year-old Tilly. What's more, they were enthusiastic about the varied multicultural experience she was receiving. Tilly's best friend, they explained with some pride, was the most charming little Sudanese girl and the previous week the whole school had celebrated Eid together.

'It was fascinating,' Laura explained. 'I managed to get along for most of it and I must say I feel I know a little more about the Muslim world than I did. Which *has* to be a good thing, surely?'

'You see?' Henry crowed. 'That's the multicultural, inclusive and diverse state system in action!'

David and Laura conceded that they would be taking Tilly out when she was six, so that she could join her sister Saskia at St Hilda's Girls. Saskia was *loving* it.

Rupert (and previously Amanda) thought that Lizzie and Robson were pathetic liberals even to worry about it and that David and Laura were insane socialists to touch a state school even for a year. There was nothing, *nothing* good about the state system. It was simply a hugely expensive training programme for drug dealers and benefit cheats. Rupert (previously supported by Amanda) always claimed that anybody who could afford to go private and who even dreamed of putting their children through the state system was an abusive parent, sacrificing their innocent children at the altar of contemptible political posturing. They felt there was an argument for the authorities prosecuting these parents for neglect, just like they did with parents who let their five-year-olds eat their way to ten stone.

'With the exception of crazy champagne Reds like you, Henry, who hog the few good state schools,' Rupert said, 'everybody goes private if they can. No, Henry! I can assure you, *everybody*. So why do successive governments insist on acting as if state education was what people actually want? They'd do far better spending the money on enabling poorer kids to go private.'

'Which is what you're doing, isn't it, darling?' Rupert's girlfriend Beatrice chipped in proudly, seizing on a subject upon which she could comment. 'Roop has set up a bursary which supports two bright children through private education.'

There was a moment of uncomfortable silence. Everybody at the table knew about Rupert's bursary, which had been Amanda's initiative. It had been discussed many times at similar dinner parties, happier ones before Rupert had decided to drop a generation in his choice of partner. Beatrice's innocent interjection had brought the Amanda-shaped elephant at the dinner table into sharp focus.

Rupert rode it out with his usual panache.

'That's right, darling. We've had over a thousand applications already,' he said. 'What do you think of that? Eh? Even the bloody public don't want to go public.'

'Yes,' Jane said pointedly, 'Amanda must be very proud. She set it up, didn't she?'

'I pay for it, Jane,' Rupert snapped. 'I think you'll find that that is what they call the bottom line.'

At that point, with her usual impeccable, almost clairvoyant timing, Jodie put her head round the door.

'I'm off out now, Monica, if that's OK? Jimmy Barnes is playing at the Round House and I know the guy on the door.'

'Goodness, Jodie,' said Monica, 'I thought you'd have gone hours ago.'

'Toby was still sniffly so he had a couple of extra stories. I've given him Calpol.'

'Terrific. I'll look in on him in a bit.'

Jodie beamed a huge smile and left.

'That girl is *brilliant*,' Monica said as she always did. 'I could not do without her.'

Later that evening, after all their guests had left, Monica and Jimmy finished off the last bottle while she stacked up the plates ready for the cleaner to put them in the dishwasher in the morning and Jimmy dumped the bottles in the recycling bin.

'I hate recycling,' he said. 'It's a week-long reminder of how much we drink.'

'And apparently it doesn't do any good anyway,' Monica said. 'I read in the *Standard* that they just shove all the bottles in landfills.'

'Fantastic dinner, Mon,' Jimmy said, 'although a bit weird with the Beatrice thing.'

'She's all right, poor girl. I felt sorry for her really. I suppose we shall get used to her in the end.'

'If he keeps her.'

'Things have to change at some point, don't they?' she said wistfully. 'Nothing goes on for ever, does it?'

'Except us.'

'Ah, but we're just lucky.'

Loss adjustment at a funeral

Andrew Tanner carefully straightened his tie as he approached the church gate.

Such a very pretty church. Nice. But not easy to get to.

Network Rail seemed to be digging up half of Oxfordshire and it had taken Tanner two trains and a replacement bus service to make the trip from the City to the little village of Great Tew. It was worth it though, Tanner thought, because had he not made the trip he would always wonder if anything useful could have been gained from it. This way he would know and you could not put a price on peace of mind.

Peace of mind was probably the only thing on which Andrew Tanner could *not* put a price.

Putting a price on things was his job. He was an investigator and loss adjuster for the Wigan and Wigan Equitable Insurance Company and it was up to Andrew to determine what an item was worth and who was liable for that sum.

In this case the item was a life and its value was not in question. It was worth two million pounds. That was the sum which Wigan and Wigan would be required to pay out had the life ended as the result of an accident. The question was, had it?

Were Wigan and Wigan liable?

The interim coroner's report had been inconclusive. Not as to *how* the deceased had died. That was beyond doubt. He had died from massive injuries sustained when the car he was driving hit a brick wall at sixty-five miles per hour. The question was *why*.

Was the death an accident? Or had the driver *deliberately* jerked the steering wheel and accelerated towards that wall? The coroner would not say. He was waiting for further police and psychological reports.

An open verdict had been recorded and therefore Wigan and Wigan would not as yet make payment.

Andrew passed the two sombrely suited ushers at the church door, taking an order of service from one of them as he went. 'Excuse me,' Jimmy asked, 'but could you identify yourself, please?'

In light of Lizzie's public profile, there had been some press interest in her husband's funeral and one or two photographers were being held back by a constable at the church wall.

'Andrew Tanner,' Andrew replied. 'I am with Wigan and Wigan. The deceased's insurers.'

'Wow,' said Jimmy, 'that's amazing.'

'Amazing?' Andrew asked.

'Well, you know, you don't expect such old-fashioned business ethics, do you? Not in the modern world.'

'Business ethics?' Andrew asked.

'You coming to pay your respects to a valued client. I didn't think companies took that sort of trouble any more.'

'Uhm. No. Quite,' Andrew replied and moved on into the church.

'Isn't that something,' Jimmy whispered to Rupert. 'I'm with Wigan and Wigan myself and quite frankly I've been hating them because they're giving me such a hard time over the premiums on Webb Street, but something like this makes me see things a bit differently.'

'You idiot, Jim,' Rupert replied. 'It's obvious why the bastard's here, isn't it?'

'Is it?'

'Of course. *They don't think it was an accident!* I must say, I did wonder myself.'

Andrew Tanner turned and looked back at them. He had taken only a few steps with his slow, measured tread and was almost in earshot. Their heads were bent towards each other: clearly they had been whispering about him and now they were frozen, watching him as he watched them. Andrew inclined his head in acknowledgement and then went in search of a pew. Finding a place towards the back of the church, he glanced at the little booklet he had been given.

A service in remembrance of Robson 'Robbo' Cartwright. Husband. Father. Mate.

Andrew flicked through the pages. It contained the usual stuff, a couple of hymns, the Beatles' 'Let It Be' and that poem from *Four Weddings and a Funeral*. And speeches – 'Remembrances', 'Reflections', 'A Eulogy'. Every word no doubt serving to establish that Robson Cartwright was the best, the finest and most upright of men who had ever walked the earth.

But was he?

Or was he in fact a thief? For thief was the only word to describe somebody who arranged their death in order that his family might benefit from a policy which paid out only on illness and accident.

It happened all the time. Men and occasionally women at the end of their tether, broke, failed, shamed. Seeking to cash in on the one potential asset that remained to them. Their own life.

Andrew could see the two ushers standing in the church vestibule, glaring at him. They had been joined by a third, a trendily dressed man who wore conspicuously fashionable glasses. They were looking at him with such contempt. Such malice.

Andrew hated the way people treated insurance companies. They wanted full cover, of course. They wanted full cover and instant payment for when they fell asleep with a burning cigarette in their hand and scorched the couch, or wrapped their cars round lamp posts while trying to send texts. But they also wanted to pay minuscule premiums.

What's more, they wanted to make exaggerated and even false claims while still pretending to occupy the moral high ground! That was what really got Andrew Tanner's goat. The hypocrisy of it all! It would not be so bad if they were honest about it. If they admitted that they basically wanted a premium service for virtually nothing from a company that they expected to be allowed to cheat on with impunity. But no. Instead they reserved the right to paint the insurers as the villains, as cheating, money-grabbing and immoral, when in fact that was *them*! It was the clients, not the insurers, who were the cheats. It was they who made the fraudulent claims, expecting instant and full payment on losses that weren't even covered. Which, if paid, would force up the very premiums that these same hypocrites insisted should be kept to a minimum.

The widow and her children were entering the church now. There she was, Elizabeth Cartwright, celebrated lifestyle guru and in Andrew's opinion potential insurance fraudster. What else should he call the woman? Her lawyer had already been in touch with Wigan and Wigan to notify them of her husband's death. Of the *accident*. She was broke. The world knew that the dead man had lost the family fortune through greed, trying to grab ludicrous interest rates in what had turned out to be a vast Ponzi scheme. Now she wanted the shareholders of Wigan and Wigan to support her. She wanted to claim a two-million-pound life-insurance policy on the ludicrous assertion that her husband Robson, Robbo, that great guy, that great husband, father and mate, had died as the result of an *accident*.

Like hell, thought Andrew. A man learns he's lost everything and made his family destitute and that very night he drives off alone and smashes his car into a wall!

No witnesses. No one else involved.

An accident? Pull the other one.

The widow sat down among her family at the front and the service began.

Hymns were sung. Several of the ushers spoke their gushing eulogies. There were readings. An acoustic medley of Beatles songs and then, in a surprise change to the order of service, the widow rose to her feet.

The vicar had been on the point of bringing the service to a close and instructing the congregation to repair to the graveyard for the burial when Lizzie interrupted him.

'Excuse me,' she said, 'I have something to say.'

Andrew watched intently from the back of the church as she first arranged for a relative to take the children out and then turned to face the congregation.

He studied the bereaved woman with an expert eye. He'd seen a lot of widows in his time; it was part of the territory. Some were genuinely distraught. Some of them had mixed emotions. Some, of course, didn't give a damn. Glad the bastard was dead. You could see it in their eyes, a cold triumph hiding behind widow's weeds. Sometimes it was pretty clear to Andrew that the grieving widow had not been entirely unconnected with the circumstances of her husband's departure. And if the police couldn't see it he could.

But not one of them, not one widow in his entire experience, was so distraught that they were indifferent to what happened next. No matter how upset they might be, no matter how much they might protest that life was no longer worth living, they would still wonder how they were going to cope now they were on their own. That was Andrew Tanner's grim worldview. Every widow wanted her policy. They wanted their payout. They wanted their money from Wigan and Wigan.

And they could have it, yes they could. If it *was* their money. If the circumstances of the death fell within the remit of the contract.

And that remit *never* included suicide.

At the front of the church Lizzie raised her veil and looked about her, clearly gathering her thoughts.

'I had not intended to say anything today,' she began in a faltering voice that grew in strength as she progressed, 'and I don't intend to speak for long. Robbo would never forgive me if I kept you from the drinks! Besides, Henry, Rupert and Jimmy have already said quite enough on the subject of how wonderful a man Robbo was. What an incredible husband, father and friend. How every single person who ever knew him either liked or *loved* him. You all know it's true. Of course it's true, all of it. And I have only one further truth to add.'

Lizzie paused for a moment, once more surveying the congregation. Her eyes were dark-ringed with tiredness and bloodshot with grief, but she was not crying now and her exhaustion seemed to have left her. Sitting at the back, Andrew wondered whether it was his imagination or had she looked directly at him?

'I know what a lot of you have been thinking,' Lizzie said loudly and firmly. 'No, don't look down at your orders of service. Look at me! Look at Lizzie! Robbo's life partner, the one who knew him best. I know that since the news came through of poor Robbo's final failed investment everyone has *wondered*. Yes you have! Just a little. I know you have. Despite what you know of Robbo. Why did he die on that specific night, you've asked yourselves. The night of his lowest ebb. The night when he must have been desperate. *How* did he die? What was he thinking, all alone at that moment? Well, let me tell you the answer! He died in an accident and he was thinking about getting some cigarettes. He did *not* point his car at that wall in despair at ruining his family!'

Of all the silences that must have descended upon that ancient church in all the centuries in which it had contained the grieving of its flock, the silence that followed Lizzie's utterly unexpected raising of this dread topic might well have been the deepest.

'Robbo loved me!' Lizzie shouted suddenly. 'Robbo loved his children! Robbo loved his friends! He would never *ever* have deserted us!'

Lizzie's voice rang out in the beautiful acoustics of the church. People had jumped. Hymnbooks were dropped. As her distraught voice faded into the mellow stonework she went on, quieter now but no less intense.

'Robbo was many things,' she said, 'some of them funny, some of them a little pathetic even. I think perhaps a few of you thought he was a bit of a loser.'

'Never!' a voice rang out. It was Jimmy and his voice shook with passion. 'Bloody never!'

'No, Jimmy,' Lizzie said, and for a moment there was a tiny smile, 'not you. I know that. But some people did. But Robbo wasn't a loser!' Her voice was rising again now. 'And I'll tell you something else! He wasn't a coward either! He would have faced the consequences of what he had done like the man he was. He would have risen above it! He would have lifted *me* above it. *We* would have risen above it. As a family! So understand this, all of you. Put that terrible, unworthy thought from your minds. My husband, my friend, my children's beloved father, did *not* kill himself. All right! He died in the silliest of accidents on the stupidest of nights racing to get some cigarettes, wondering how he was going to explain to me that he'd been royally ripped off by some *bastard* on Wall Street! All right? Got it? Now let's bury the best man I ever knew and then go and get pissed!'

People cheered. People hugged. The widow herself collapsed into her pew and sobbed and sobbed.

At the back of the church Andrew Tanner rose quietly and left.

She believed it. Andrew was sure of that. But the fact that she believed it did not make it true.

Of course she believed it, who wouldn't? What wife would want to admit that a beloved husband would rather die than face the prospect of telling her the truth? What wife could ever accept that someone in whom they had invested so much, personally and socially, couldn't bring himself to stagger through the rest of his life in her company. Would rather accelerate his car into a wall than face her in the morning.

The very idea was a personal affront.

Of course she couldn't believe it. No widow ever could. Because what would it say about them? Deep down, Andrew thought, Freud was right, everything comes down to ego in the end, even grief.

Giving money away

Over breakfast on the day that he lost his job at Mason Jervis, Jimmy was feeling pretty chipper. He was used to beginning the day in a sunny and confident mood, he'd been doing it for his entire adult life, but it had to be said that in recent months that mood had started to evaporate.

A slight sense of foreboding had begun to hang over Jimmy's breakfast fruit salad (followed by a couple of chocolate croissants), as there had over the breakfasts of many previously confident and bullish businessmen in the grim autumn of 2008. The financial crisis which had engulfed the world so brutally and unexpectedly was deepening by the day and nobody could remember a time when share prices and lending rates had been the number-one story on the morning news for so long. The shocking collapse of a couple of major investment banks had shaken everyone. When well-known firms suddenly fold and you see guys very similar to yourself wandering out into Canary Wharf holding cardboard boxes with their staplers, family photos and the remains of last year's Christmas hampers in them, you know that an unfamiliarly chill wind has begun to blow.

Everyone at Mason Jervis knew someone who had lost their job and Jimmy knew several. Career mortality was definitely on the agenda and lately Jimmy had been scanning the morning news each day, anxiously wondering who was going to be next. On this particular morning, however, he had his old sense of sunny stability and comfortable well-being. In fact he was feeling pretty good about himself.

Virtuous, even.

The Bloomberg's Business Channel that was being broadcast on both the vast wall-mounted flat-screens in the family room (and backwards, reflected in the fish tank) was telling Jimmy that overnight he might, had he taken the opportunity, have become as much as *two hundred grand* richer. That was a sizeable piece of change even for a Street Owning Man like Jimmy. Yet he had let the chance pass.

On moral grounds, of all things.

Jimmy smiled to himself as he punched up his beautiful shiny cappuccino machine and listened to its satisfyingly throaty gurgle. Moral grounds, for God's sake. Things really were changing.

Once more Rupert was to have been the tooth fairy, slipping coins under Jimmy's pillow while he slept. He had tipped Jimmy off over lunch the day before. Just another of his nod-and-wink little heads-ups which he had occasionally gifted to Jimmy over the years.

'The fortunes of the corporate yo-yo that is Caledonian Granite are about to change again, old boy. And big time. That stock you dumped as it went down is about to bounce like a pair of rubber bollocks.'

Rupert explained that the stricken bank was about to receive its long-awaited visit from the Seventh Cavalry. After months of to-ing and fro-ing, and horror stories in the press about queues forming round blocks and grannies fearful for the future of the little bit they'd put by, the government had finally acted.

'Gordon's going to buy it out. Well, at least take a majority holding,' Rupert whispered over his salmon and Pinot Grigio. 'Can you believe it? New Labour bringing a bank under state control? Anyone would think they were socialists! Of course they had to do it. I told them so myself at the last Select Committee. You can't have banks collapsing. It scares the grey vote, which is the only vote that *does* vote these days. Upsets everyone, as a matter of fact. I've even had some arse from *Newsnight* trying to doorstep me about how the Royal Lancashire's dealing with its sub-prime. *None of your fucking beeswax, mate*, is the answer to that. Anyway, the point is the dear old Granite is about to get shifted from basket case to gilt-edged, Triple A status, government-owned safe haven, so I'm here to tell you, Jim lad, if you want to do yourself a favour, I'd grab your shares back and then some.'

Jimmy had almost done it too. Who wouldn't?

If a professional trainer were to tip you off about a runner in the National you'd take the tip. Of course you would. And it was the same with shares and members of financial Select Committees. Jimmy had actually called his broker from a Starbucks on his way back to the office and begun the deal while ordering a strawberry and cream Frappuccino. The Caledonian Granite price was not quite at the level of worthlessness to which it had sunk on the morning after Jimmy had sold his shares. At that point the institution had been within minutes of collapse and surely would have done so had the Chancellor not gone on morning TV and guaranteed people's savings. Since that grim day for British financial credibility, the price had risen but not by much. It was still deep in the doldrums.

'I want you to grab me fifty thousand shares in Caledonian Granite,' Jimmy said into his mobile as the gap-year euro student working behind the counter poured various sugary syrups into enormous paper cups.

'Fifty thousand?' his broker replied in some surprise. 'In *Caledonian Granite*? Do you know something I don't know, Jim?'

It was that question that turned Jimmy round.

Do you know something I don't know?

Of course he did.

Something he had no right to know.

Jimmy recalled the conversation he'd had with Monica those few months before, when he'd saved himself a bundle on the basis of another of Rupert's Caledonian tips. She'd said it was insider trading. She'd made him give the money away to charity and he'd bunged it on next year's Alabama Derby. She'd been right.

'You know what, mate?' Jimmy said. 'You're right. Stupid hunch, that was all. Been drinking. Forget it, will you?'

'Sure. OK,' the broker replied, a little surprised. 'If that's what you want.'

'Yeah. Sorry to have bothered you.'

'That's all right. Never trade pissed, eh?'

'Gotta be the rule,' Jimmy said and hung up before he could change his mind.

As he left the café with his drink he had felt rather strange about walking away from so much money. Slightly sick, in fact, although that may have had something to do with the sugary Frappuccino. The following morning, however, as he steeled himself to tuck into Jessica's fruit salad and watched the news of the government bailout send Caledonian sky high, he felt proud of himself.

Proud and a little cocky. He was the sort of guy who could walk away from a serious wad. *On moral grounds!*

Not only did he have the principles to do it. Much more importantly, he could *afford* to do it.

'I've just walked away from a couple of hundred grand,' Jimmy whispered in Monica's ear so as not to be overheard. Jodie was on a bean bag with Cressida, helping the child stick pasta to a collage. 'Rupert gave me a tip and I ignored it, babes. Did it for you.'

Jodie, ultra-brilliant as always, clearly sensed that Jimmy wanted privacy and got to her feet, scooping up Cressida as she did so.

'Come on, rock chick,' she said. 'Let's go and see if Hell Man Tobes has brushed his teeth yet.'

After she had gone Monica turned to Jimmy, looking suitably impressed.

'Wow. That is amazing.' She giggled. 'Well done.'

'Self-regulation, babes,' Jimmy crowed. 'It's what the City's all about.'

'Bloody Rupert always knows, doesn't he?'

'Well, he's virtually in the Cabinet these days so I *hope* he knows. Someone has to run the country for those arsehole politicians.'

They smiled at each other and he clinked his coffee cup against her peppermint tea, then, carefully avoiding her sore breasts, he gave her a big hug.

'Proud of me?' he asked.

'Well yes, of course,' Monica replied, but not perhaps with sufficient enthusiasm for Jimmy's puffed-up mood.

'You don't sound too sure,' he complained.

'Don't forget, Jim, you haven't actually done a *good* thing. You've just *not* done a *bad* thing.'

'I think you'll find,' Jimmy said, very slightly huffily, 'that these days, with everybody grabbing what they can, not doing a bad thing actually counts as doing a good thing.'

'Well,' Monica laughed, 'it's come to something when the decision not to insider trade represents the moral high ground. Wouldn't do for your dad, would it?'

Squeezed BlackBerry

Jimmy took the tube to work. This was not out of any premonition of imminent poverty. The blow when it fell came as a surprise. It was simply that the tube was how he always travelled to work, a fact that astonished his colleagues.

'It's not because of all that *green* bollocks, is it?' they would ask. 'You do know that global warming's a myth? In fact, apparently, using public transport creates more carbon than driving your own car.'

'Nothing to do with eco, mate,' Jimmy replied, 'just good old-fashioned common sense.'

It was at least three times quicker on public transport than using a driver, and besides Jimmy liked to read the paper on the tube, something which made him feel sick if he did it in a car. Leaving as early as he did, he usually got a seat and so arrived at work comparatively rested, well-informed and stress-free. Qualities which were often cited as evidence of Jimmy being a sane man in the nut house. A steady man, a grounded man. The sort of man the company needed.

But times were changing rapidly and as Jimmy descended into the underground network he was blissfully unaware that his easy-going charm was about to prove no defence against the boom-and-bust nature of unregulated capitalism.

The papers were full of the government bailout of Caledonian Granite. The Prime Minister was getting a lot of credit for it and many editorials went so far as to suggest that this might be the beginning of the end of the downturn. There were others, of course, who assured their readers that this was not even the end of the beginning and that a far greater financial crisis was looming. Jimmy wished they wouldn't write pieces like that. He and his colleagues all agreed that the more the papers talked about a crisis, the more likely one was to occur.

'Six months ago,' they'd tell each other, 'Joe Public wouldn't have known his sub-prime from his arsehole. Why does he need to know now?'

'He doesn't know now,' others would say. 'He's as ignorant as he ever was. The papers are scaring the public with language they don't understand. It's what Roosevelt said in '32, *we have nothing to fear but fear itself*.'

They all agreed that this was true, although sometimes Jimmy did point out that while Roosevelt said there was nothing to fear but fear itself, what actually happened had been nearly another half-decade of the greatest economic depression in history.

He shifted uneasily in his seat and tried to distract himself by turning to the football. It didn't help. The news was financial there too, with commentators speculating that the downturn might spell the end of the twenty-million-plus transfer fee.

Could the boom times really be coming to an end? It seemed so unlikely; after all, he'd had the opportunity to make two hundred grand only that morning. If a bloke could still make that kind of cash while he slept, how could the party be over? Except, of course, that the opportunity to make that money had arisen from a tip-off to cash in on the government bailout of a company which had collapsed because of the crisis. Just because some people can make a killing in a fire sale, it doesn't mean there wasn't a fire. Fuck.

Jimmy resolved to heed the signs, to start thinking about reducing his personal exposure. Webb Street was a very big project. Servicing the debts that he'd entered into so blithely consumed all of his income and a large part of his expected bonus. A bonus which he now had to accept would be much smaller than his previous one.

Perhaps he'd try to bring in a partner. He'd talk to Rupert. Maybe the Royal Lancashire itself would want to exchange some of its debt for equity.

But by the time Jimmy left his seat at Canary Wharf,

his naturally resilient and optimistic personality had reasserted itself and his doubts had faded. Jimmy's spirits always lifted as he emerged from the tube station. You simply could not ride those escalators and step out into the heart of Britain's financial capital without feeling the sheer pulsating energy of the place. It never ceased to give him a thrill; the buildings were just so *beautiful*. All black glass, mirrors and steel. Just like the cars.

Cathedrals to money. To success. To growth and expansion. This was the sort of thing that once upon a time they had only had in America. Now London had its own little Manhattan and we were finally taking on the Yanks at their own game.

It had all changed so much since Jimmy's first morning in the money pit back in the early nineties. Back then, most of the great skyscraping cathedrals had existed only in the dreams of visionary architects. Back then, the business of making money still retained its belligerent, hard-edged eighties feel. People modelled themselves on Gordon Gekko from *Wall Street* with all that 'lunch is for wimps' business.

Back then, brokers and traders felt under siege, the unrecognized prophets of a new and as yet unloved philosophy neither trusted nor understood by the public. The post-big-bang City strutted aggressively in its stripy shirts and braces, challenging the rest of the nation to come up to speed. Like the industrialists and mill owners of the nineteenth century, those guys knew that they were on the frontiers of new wealth creation and as such were inevitably resented and feared. To them the emerging futures and derivatives markets were like the Spinning Jenny weaving machine or James Watt's bouncing kettle lid, a new and unstoppable money-making innovation which the Luddites would of course attempt to smash.

It was all so peaceful now, thought Jimmy, as he strolled across the wide piazza that had been laid out in front of his building. Back then there had been tension in the air. The Poll Tax rioting of the late eighties was fresh in the memory; the disaffected still had teeth.

No wonder the Gekko clones had wanted to avoid lunch. For a start, there was nowhere to have it. There had been no splendid plazas and mall complexes nestling at the feet of the great glass towers then. No numerous coffee franchises and mouth-watering food outlets with their commitment to quality *and* protecting the environment *and* ensuring a fair deal for farmers in the third world.

No Starbucks. It seemed unimaginable now.

But the foot soldiers of the new economy had campaigned on booze, Snickers bars and cocaine. Those guys would not have dreamed of wasting fifteen minutes in a queue of PAs to get a bucket of vanilla-flavoured foam.

Society had sneered at them in those days, calling

them 'yuppies' and 'Thatcher's children'. Left-wing playwrights and smart-Alec comedians had dismissed Jimmy's predecessors as no better than robber barons. Back then Canary Wharf had felt like the forward base of an invading army, a New World outpost in which an elite force was massing to colonize and subdue the old.

But things had changed so quickly and now, with the new century already nearly a decade old, everything was different. There were no left-wing playwrights and comedians any more; there was no left-wing anybody. Britain was at ease with its prosperity. It was the world's fourth largest economy. Who could have predicted that? And yet it had happened on Jimmy's watch. That was pretty cool, he thought. The dirty, depressing, angry, violent, sullen and resentful little island into which he had graduated was already ancient history.

Money was no longer the preserve of nerds and Neocons. Cool people dug money.

No more 'lunch is for wimps'. Now there were chillout hubs in the corners of offices and it was possible to book a foot massage at your desk.

Greed was no longer merely good, as Gekko had said. Greed was actually *hip*.

The world had changed and it would take more than a poxy bit of toxic sub-prime to turn back the clocks.

Jimmy's office was in the Dildo. Obviously the Dildo was not the building's real name; its real name was the Banana. Designed by an internationally famous architectural firm to rival the Gherkin, it had for some time been the most talked-about building in Europe, although in the race to produce the most radically bent building David's rapidly rising Rainbow looked very much set to trump it.

The idea behind the Banana was that the vast tower should be curved. This would enable the top ten floors to each have the illusion of being the penthouse, as their glass-caged verandas (located on the convex side of the building) would have nothing above them.

The problem had arisen when the commissioning consortium had pointed out to the internationally famous architectural firm designing the building that a *real* banana was inherently badly designed as inspirational fruit for a landmark building. The problem was it tapered away so brutally at the end. The premium floors in a skyscraper are of course at the top. The internationally famous firm of architects had therefore been instructed to change the design to ensure that, instead of tapering away, it should swell out to provide more floor space at the top rather than less. This created a kind of 'head' on the banana.

Or in fact a Bell End. Hence the name by which the whole country came to know the Banana was the Dildo, or more commonly the GBC or Great Big Cock.

Of course the testosterone-driven occupants of the Great Big Cock didn't mind the nickname at all; it seemed very apt. Financial trading floors were the last exclusively male preserve, places where the vocabulary was numerate, not literate, and where nurturing and networking skills were of less value than aggression and adrenalin.

The three floors occupied by Mason Jervis were all prime property, situated in the middle of the Bell End of the GBC and each virtually the size of a football pitch.

Jimmy's pulse never failed to quicken as he emerged from the bank of lifts into the MJ reception area. This atrium stretched upwards through all three floors, the roof forming the floor of the business above. From where Jimmy stood, he could see not only MJ Floor 1 spread out before him but also, if he looked up, the balconies of MJ2 and MJ3, to get to which you needed to enter a separate internal lift. It was awe-inspiring. And all this hung sixty floors into the sky in a massive, bendy penis-shaped building that housed some twenty or thirty similar chapels to the financial sector.

What man could fail to be thrilled?

Jimmy headed up the Hungarian desk on MJ2. He was therefore in charge of all Mason Jervis's dealings with the burgeoning Hungarian futures market. Every day his guys placed thousands of multi-million-dollar bets on the next projected half-decade of the Hungarian economy.

A great cheer went up as Jimmy approached the forty desks that occupied his space. His corner of MJ2. His stake in the Great Big Cock.

Jimmy punched the air as he strode towards his guys. A bet had come good, some intricate packaging of as yet ungrown or unmade products had gone the way that the team were planning it should.

Probably a short.

Most likely the value of some small part of Hungary's future industrial or agricultural output had dropped in value, meaning that the package which Jimmy's guys had sold (in order to force the price down) could now be purchased back at a lower price, yielding a profit in the difference.

Brilliant.

Jimmy hadn't come up with the idea himself. Nobody knew who that anonymous genius was, but shorting had swept the financial world like a bushfire. It was so much easier and more exciting to bet on failure. Investing in the hope of appreciation was a long-term business requiring patience, foresight and a genuine understanding of the product you were speculating in.

Fuck that. Who had time?

Life was too short not to short.

There was very little Jimmy and his guys could do to force the value of a product *up*. But forcing it *down* just took guts and a cool nerve.

Jimmy smiled. It was good to hear a cheer and see the guys punching the air as of old and high-fiving each other. Things had been a little lean of late. The damn credit-crunch thing which had started in the trailer parks of the American Midwest had gone global and the weaker European economies, of which Hungary was one, were beginning to creak a bit.

'Dudes!' Jimmy called out as he approached the desks. 'Looking good! Wha'appen? Whassup?'

Smiling faces turned to him.

Jimmy was to ask himself afterwards if any of them had betrayed a flicker of nervousness. He thought that they probably had but he hadn't noticed it at the time.

'Good trade?' he asked.

'Big time, boss,' said a guy called Caleb. 'A sugar cane future, shorted and *sorted*!'

'Nice one, geezah!' Jimmy said, high-fiving his informant. 'But I guess you mean sugar *beet*.'

'Nah, *cane*, boss. Looks like it's finally emerging out of the shadow of corn syrup.'

'They don't grow sugar cane in Hungary, dude.' Jimmy smiled. 'They grow sugar beet.'

Now he did notice something. The blokes were all smiling as usual but there was something rather fixed, perhaps even a little forced, about their expressions.

'Yeah,' said Caleb, 'but Hungary's on hold.'

'Hungary's *on hold*?' said Jimmy, astonished.

'The desk,' Caleb hastened to reassure him, 'not the country.'

'How do you mean, the desk is on hold?'

'It just is. From this morning. The Man came down to tell us. We're not trading there any more.

We've been seconded to the Caribbean under Marcus.'

'Under *Marcus*?' Jimmy asked, finding it difficult to meet anybody's eye.

'Yeah,' Caleb replied without his usual good-natured smile, 'and the Man said he wanted to see you on MJ3.'

Jimmy smiled a confident 'I'm not bothered' smile.

'See you guys in a minute,' he said.

It took slightly longer than that, but it was over in less than five.

The Man tried to be kind, but it was clear that all he wanted was for the interview to be done with.

'We've pulled out of Eastern Europe altogether,' he said. 'If it's any consolation, all the guys are going. The heads like you today but I'm afraid most of the blokes will have to follow. The other desks just can't absorb them.'

It wasn't any consolation. Jimmy wasn't like that.

'The problem is all these damn countries were doing too well,' the Man explained. 'Their currencies were unsustainably high and they all started borrowing dollars on the strength of it. Now their currencies are returning to realistic levels and basically half a bloody continent is one big slab of negative equity. We just can't operate in their markets any more.'

Jimmy didn't attempt to argue the suddenness of the decision. Everything was happening suddenly in the second half of 2008. Banks were folding. Prices collapsing. Governments tottering.

'Head Office sent the news through at close of play in New York. I got it this morning,' Jimmy's boss said. 'The order was quite clear. Shut down immediately. Cut our losses and run. Your desk is closed.'

There was a moment's silence. Jimmy wondered if he was expected simply to get up and leave.

'Accounts will be in touch re your redundancy package,' the Man said. 'I'm sure it'll tide you over.'

'But . . .' Jimmy began. He was about to protest that his situation was a little more complex than most. That he had mortgaged his home and become a property speculator on the expectation of continued employment. That a poxy redundancy package would not begin to cover the interest payments on the debts he had recently and recklessly incurred.

But what would have been the point? Besides which, the Man did not want to listen.

'There are no buts, Jim,' he said. 'It's happened. To be honest, it should have happened six months ago. We've been carrying you in the hope that things would improve. In a sense, you've been lucky.'

Lucky? *Lucky!* Jimmy wanted to scream at the guy that had he been sacked six months before it would have been brilliant. Because he would not then have committed himself to a multi-million-pound property scheme that he could not afford. He would still have *owned his house*.

But he didn't say anything. He just sat there. Struck dumb.

Subtly the Man's attitude hardened a little.

'I'm sorry, Jimmy,' he said, 'but you don't work here any more. You have to go. I've had your desk boxed up for you. Goodbye . . . I'm sorry.'

Glancing behind him, Jimmy noticed two security guys hovering at the door. That was how it was done, he knew that. Once they'd dumped you they wanted you out immediately. Occasionally people turned un-pleasant. Occasionally people went back to their desks, drank half a bottle of Christmas whisky and then stormed in to try to punch the CEO.

Jimmy rose to his feet without another word.

Five minutes later, he was back on the plaza floor of the Dildo walking out through the security barriers.

Then he stopped.

This was all wrong. They couldn't just bundle him out of the building. He wasn't going to cause trouble or make a scene, but he'd known some of those people for years. He needed to say goodbye.

Jimmy turned and headed back to the turnstile. He swiped his card through the slot and then walked straight into the rotating bar, bruising his leg. The bar did not rotate for Jimmy any more. His swipe card no longer worked. It had already been deprogrammed.

He got out his BlackBerry. He would email Caleb and get him to come down and let him in. But Jimmy found he couldn't do that either. His Mason Jervis email server refused to serve him. Besides, Caleb's email address had disappeared from the screen, along with every other address stored in his business address book. Every professional contact of any sort, both within and without Mason Jervis, had gone.

Of course. Jimmy remembered now, this was another part of what they did. They didn't want you carrying away any secrets, taking valuable information and networking potential to a new employer. They'd closed him down. It was as if he had never ever had a life at Mason Jervis. And they had done it in the time it had taken him to descend from the Bell End to the bottom of the Great Big Cock.

An hour later Jimmy phoned Monica.

'Monica,' he said, his voice slightly slurred, 'I've lost my job. I'm in the pub and I feel *great*.'

First choose your school

For a little while Jimmy and Monica had dared to hope.

A quick Google of the various state schools in their area had thrown up a couple of really encouraging possibilities which were actually close by. Could it be, they wondered, that the socio-economic disaster which had befallen their son was not going to prove quite as terrible as they had first assumed?

The closest state school was a Church of England primary that sounded rather lovely. It had excellent SATS results and a stated commitment to a 'caring but disciplined educational environment'. Just like Abbey Hall really. The school also championed the concept of 'whole child' learning, which, when they skimmed the 'mission statements' section of the site, seemed to mean that they did a lot of art. Which was also very nice.

'Do you think we'd have to convince them that we're Christians?' Monica asked. 'I mean I'm happy to say I'm Buddhist if it'll get him in, but they might want some sort of proof.'

'Well, we are Christians . . . aren't we?' Jimmy said.

'Sort of . . . I suppose. Culturally, perhaps. But we never go to church, do we? Except for christenings, weddings and funerals and . . . we don't really believe in it. I mean, virgin birth, him rising again and all that. Not *really*.'

'But all that's allegorical, isn't it? They don't require you to believe in it. Not any more. Not *literally*. Just kind of . . .'

'Kind of what?'

'Oh, I don't know. In a "love is good" kind of way.'

'We can do that. We certainly believe love is good.'

'Of course we do. And all the kids were christened.'

'Only because it's such a lovely excuse for a party.'

'It doesn't matter, they're in. We have photos. And Abbey Hall was Christian, wasn't it? They had hymns and an end-of-term service and *they* accepted us,' Jimmy replied. 'Blimey, if we're good enough for posh Christians we've got to be good enough for state-funded ones, haven't we?'

'Yes, but we were paying the posh school. I imagine that makes a difference.'

Jimmy pondered this for a moment.

'Well, maybe we *should* start going to church. You know, just to show willing.'

'What? Out of the blue? It'd look a bit suss, wouldn't it? They must be used to that one. No, I think the best way is that when we apply we stress our "spiritual" side.'

'Blimey. Have I got a spiritual side?' Jimmy asked.

'Well, I certainly have.'

'OK, prove it.'

'What?'

'Come on, we're being interviewed. I'm the head of the school. Do you believe in God?'

'Yes, absolutely,' Monica replied firmly before adding, 'sort of.'

'Sort of, Mrs Corby? Sort of? This is a *church* school.'

Monica collected her thoughts.

'Well, I certainly believe in something bigger and more important than us . . .'

'Good,' Jimmy replied in his role of stern interrogator. 'Can you perhaps be more specific?'

Monica thought hard.

'A force. A *reason*, so to speak. I mean there has to be a reason, doesn't there? A greater purpose? Greater than us, certainly, and I'm very happy to call that God if you want. In fact, yes, I do call it God *and* I believe in it . . . and I was a Girl Guide.'

Jimmy looked at her for a moment and smiled.

'That was brilliant, Mon,' he said.

'You really think so?'

'Sold me. And if God is love, I truly believe that I love you even more now than when I first loved you. Which is fucking saying something, incidentally. Therefore, I experience God every moment of my life.'

'Wow, Jimmy,' Monica said, very touched. 'That's *lovely*.'

'Do you think I should say it?'

'Maybe. See if a moment comes up. But lose the swearing.'

Monica kissed him.

'That's got to be enough, hasn't it?' Jimmy said, printing out the application form. 'Enough for the Church of England? I mean we believe in something called God, we're English and we're big on love. That must cover all the bases.'

'I think so,' Monica said. 'I mean it would be different if we were pretending to be Catholic, those guys play serious hardball, but *anybody* can pretend to be C of E, I'm sure of it.'

Once more they studied the website and found themselves getting quite excited.

'It really does seem like a *very* nice school,' Monica said. 'Look, a stringent anti-bullying policy.'

'And free,' said Jimmy.

'A belief in bringing music teaching back into schools.'

'And free,' Jimmy said again.

'An emphasis on traditional subject matter but inclusively multicultural.'

'And absolutely fucking *free*,' Jimmy repeated. 'Amazing. We should have sent Tobes there in the first place.'

Monica thought the photos on the site of the previous year's nativity play looked very sweet and the school was also big on football, which would make Toby happy.

'It says they're always happy for parents to come along and help coach,' Monica said.

'I certainly have plenty of time,' Jimmy replied ruefully.

'Subject to stringent police checks,' Monica added.

'Ah. Well, I don't think I'm on the sex offenders list, but if they check my credit rating I'm off the squad.'

They both laughed. They had always laughed a lot together but not so much lately since their troubles began. It felt good.

The second-nearest school also had a good exam-result rating, and although not actually a church school it looked smart and well run. It was rumoured that a local rock star had sent his children there for a couple of years.

Neither school was quite Abbey Hall, of course, in that their classes were twice the size and their facilities considerably smaller. On the other hand, Jimmy doubted that they would turn Toby into a crack dealer before he had had time to get their fortunes on an even keel again.

'And they're co-educational,' Monica said, 'which frankly I prefer. For a start it means Cressie can start there next year and we won't have two separate school runs, which I was *dreading* when we were planning to send the girls to St Hilda's.'

They decided to apply for the C of E school as their first choice and the other one as their second, but felt confident that they would be happy with either. Unfortunately everybody in their area felt the same about these two schools and they were both massively oversubscribed.

Toby failed to get into either and was instead placed at Caterham Road, the large Victorian edifice on the very edge of the borough, from which, as far as Monica could see, the middle class had fled. It seemed to cater exclusively for tough estate kids and the children of newly arrived immigrants.

Monica cried for about three hours and then began writing letters and sending emails. She wrote to the head teachers of her preferred schools, she wrote to the boards of governors, she wrote to the council and she wrote to her MP. She went personally to the town hall on several occasions, demanding an interview with a representative of the local education authority.

Not surprisingly, every parent felt that their child had a right to go to the most desirable school. When Monica finally got to see someone from the authority, her one argument, that coming so suddenly from a posh school her son would be an obvious target for bullying, elicited very little sympathy.

'We have to find numerous places for children who have come straight from war zones,' she was told. 'I think your Toby will find readjustment easier than they do.'

Monica and Jimmy were eventually forced to face the fact that the only place the education authority was prepared to offer their precious, unique, more-special-than-the-rest son was at Caterham Road.

Monica was nearly hysterical at the prospect.

'We'll home-educate him!' she announced suddenly. 'You're not working, I'm not working. It'll be wonderful! We'll spend our days in the local library as a family. Have picnics together and visit museums and . . .'

Unusually for Jimmy, he put his foot down.

'No, Mon,' he said firmly.

'No? What do you mean, no?'

'A kid needs friends.'

'A *gang*, you mean. That's what he'll get. A gang. A knife gang. He'll get knifed.'

'Mon,' Jimmy said, 'I watch the local news every day. As far as I know, nobody has ever been knifed at Caterham Road.'

'Yes, but . . .'

'There are four hundred kids at that school—'

'Exactly.'

'They can't all be delinquents. They can't all take drugs. The majority have to be ordinary, OK kids. If those kids can make it at Caterham Road, then so can Toby.'

'But he's—'

'He's a nice, bright boy, Mon. That's all. Whose parents happen to be broke. Like lots of parents. That's the new reality. We have to face it. If it doesn't work out then OK, maybe we can look at other options, but we're not going to give in before we've started.'

'It's not about *giving in*,' Monica snapped, 'and it's not about you either, Jim. This is about Toby and—'

'Exactly, Mon! It's all about Toby and we *have* to give Toby the chance to make this work. If we start trying to cosset him now, trying to hide him from God knows what, wrapping him in cotton wool and locking the world out, he's going to look back and say that we didn't have any faith in him. That we didn't think he could cut it in the real world. That we didn't have enough respect for him to believe that he could survive stuff that most kids see as part and parcel of everyday life.'

'But . . . but he's so . . .' Monica didn't get any further. She was trying not to cry.

'Think about it, Mon. Seriously. What will he say when he's ten? Twelve? Fifteen? Sitting at home with a mad stir-crazy mum who's trying to simultaneously hothouse him for Cambridge and stop him ever meeting any other children? I don't know, maybe home education works for some people, geniuses or whatever. But Toby's not a genius. He's an ordinary kid. Like we were. I'd have *hated* home education. Wouldn't you? I'd rather have faced Caterham any day than be the weird kid with the weird mum. In fact I *did* face Caterham. You did too. We both went to state primaries and . . .'

'It was different then, and we started at the start, not in the middle, and it wasn't in London and—'

'I don't like it, Monica!' Jimmy said, more firm than gentle now. 'I wish it was different but it isn't. It's hard. It's going to be tough on all of us, mainly Tobes, but we have to face this together, as a family.'

Monica smiled.

'God. We've role-reversed, you bastard,' she said. 'I've gone all stupid and impetuous and you're pretending to be wise.'

'I used up all my stupid, gambling our entire lives on

331

a massive property development,' Jimmy said, taking her hand. 'I'm all stupided out right now.'

Together they went upstairs and looked in on their son.

'He's just so posh,' Monica whispered unhappily as they stared down at him. 'We've made him so posh. And now we're going to send him to *Caterham*.'

'We'll just have to help him with that, Mon,' Jimmy whispered back. 'We'll do it. I promise.'

And so in the remaining time that Toby had at Abbey Hall and in the brief school-holiday period that followed, Monica and Jimmy found themselves desperately trying to get Toby not to speak posh.

They began with the glottal stop.

'There are no Ts in *got to*, Tobes,' Jimmy would explain, 'not any more. It's a single word, *go-ah* to rhyme with *shocker*, as in *sorry, mate, I've go-ah go now*.'

It was a near-impossible task to undo five years of expensively acquired grammar and pronunciation in a matter of weeks. There was no accent posher than the accent of a pre-pubescent boy who has attended an expensive English prep school. Later on, those boys would deliberately acquire a kind of slurred Mockney which, although still posh, would at least be twenty-first-century posh. But at seven years old they all sounded like Victorian choirboys or Oliver Twist in the 1948 David Lean movie. It made Monica weep to hear it.

'They'll *kill* him,' she whispered desperately to Jimmy, but Jimmy persevered.

'Tobes, mate,' he said, 'it's *'orrible*, not *h-orrible*. The H is silent. All Hs are silent from now on, OK? Hs are the enemy. Repeat after me, *I 'appen to 'ave an 'orrible 'eadache.*'

Every man for himself

'Roop?'

The voice on the other end sounded buoyant enough but artificially so. Rupert trying to sound pleasant was never going to convince.

'Hello, Jimmy. What can I do for you?'

'I've tried five times this morning. You never pick up.'

'So I've picked up now. What's on your mind?'

'Mate, I need to ask a favour.'

'Well, you can ask, Jim.'

Jimmy tried to laugh. Laugh as if nothing had changed between him and his old friend. Laugh as they had laughed together just a few months before, when it had seemed that they owned London.

Jimmy did not own London any more, not any part of it. Certainly not his own house or the street he had bought against it. It had been only two months since his redundancy but already he had come to realize that the bits he had thought he owned actually owned him, holding him tight in a vicious coil of debt.

'OK, here goes,' Jimmy said. 'One of your guys from the RLB says there's a possibility that they might have to foreclose on Webb Street. I mean, that's got to be a joke, right? They're not going to do that.'

There was silence on the line.

'Roop?' said Jimmy. 'You still there?'

'Still here.'

'Well, what do you think?'

'Sorry. I didn't realize you'd finished.'

'Well, I have. They say they might want to foreclose.'

'They might. I mean if you can't service the interest on your debt.'

'Rupert, I have a cash-flow problem. I've lost my job. I won't be getting a bonus this year.'

'I know that, Jim. What do you want me to say?'

Suddenly Jimmy was angry. Rupert was being an arse.

'That you'll call off your people, Rupert! Obviously that's what I want you to say.'

'This is a branch issue, Jimmy. I'm the bloody CEO.'

'Exactly. You're the bloody boss.'

'It's a branch issue, Jim.'

'Rupert, you encouraged me to take out the mortgages. To go for the whole street! It was your idea. Now the street's worth less than the debt and falling. I'm fucked.'

'You're an adult, Jim. Are you saying that your decisions are my fault?'

'No, but . . .'

'But what, Jimmy? What are you saying?'

There was a pause.

'I'm saying that I'm currently fucked.'

'And what do you want me to do about it?'

'I want you to pick up the phone to your Hackney team and tell them to back off and give me some space.'

'And what excuse should I offer? That you're my mate?'

'Why do you need an excuse? You're the boss.'

'And how long do you think I'd stay the boss if it was known that I run the bank as a limit-free credit facility?'

'But that's exactly how you *did* fucking run it, Rupert!' Jimmy shouted. 'That's why I'm in this shit.'

'We don't give credit any more,' Rupert said. 'We've stopped lending and I'm afraid to say, Jim, that we want our money back. It's not personal and you have no right to make it so. A lot of people are in the same situation as you.'

There was nothing more to discuss.

'See you, Roop,' Jimmy said quietly.

'See you, Jim. Love to Mon.'

'Yeah. Love to Amanda.'

'Beatrice.'

'Oh yeah, that's right. Beatrice.'

Jimmy turned off his phone, cursing himself for

wasting money on such a pointless call. He knew Rupert. Why had he expected any result other than zero?

Sitting in his office at the Royal Lancashire Bank, Rupert hung up the phone too. The bank might want its money back but Rupert knew that it wasn't going to get it. Not from Jimmy or from any of its thousands of defaulting debtors. In fact, the truth was it had never had the money in the first place, not much of it anyway, and its capital had long since been swallowed up in the mountain of bad debt that Rupert had generated, lending all those excitingly vast sums of non-existent money.

The bank was broke. He knew it and shortly so would the world.

A negotiated settlement

Amanda had given up trying to be nice about her ex-husband in front of their children.

'Your father left us because he's a selfish, silly man who wanted to be with a girl half his age,' she would tell them, immune to the confusion and sadness this provoked in children who had been brought up to see their father as some sort of god.

'Why the hell should I lie?' Amanda said. 'I could tell them a lot worse. I simply refuse to bring them up in some fantasy that he still loves them really, so that he can waltz back into their lives when they're adults and blame it all on me. That's what happens, you know. The mum gets left with all the work and the hurt while the bloody shag rat becomes some jolly but remote figure who only has the fun bits and keeps dropping hints about mum never having been the easiest person to live with. They'll end up blaming me, I know they will, so fuck him. He's a bastard, a selfish bastard, and I will *not* lie to our children about it. If he had loved them as much as they thought he did, he would not have broken up their fucking home because he'd gone ga-ga over some bit of totty who no doubt never has a headache and sucks like a Hoover.'

Amanda had taken a firm and aggressive line from the start, but it got firmer and more aggressive with subsequent developments as the iron that Rupert had thrust into her soul hardened in its intensity.

First and to no one's surprise but Rupert's, it seemed, Beatrice managed to get herself pregnant. Monica and Lizzie had spotted that one coming a mile off. They'd whispered it to each other on the very first occasion that Rupert had introduced Beatrice to the gang.

'The girl's just besotted with Rupert,' Monica said, 'and she's terrified he'll eventually feel so guilty about his kids he'll go back to them.'

'If she knows Roop at all,' Lizzie replied, 'she'll know he doesn't do guilt.'

'Everyone does guilt in some way or other. It just depends what about,' Monica said. 'In the end, private stuff can get even the biggest bastard. Hitler did guilt. You know, over that niece who killed herself. Jimmy was watching a documentary about it on the History Channel.'

'They should call it the Third Reich Channel, that's all they ever seem to talk about. Robbo loves it.'

'Yes, well, Hitler had the SS put flowers on her grave every year.'

'Yes, Mon,' said Lizzie, 'but that was Hitler. We're talking about Rupert.'

Whether Monica or Lizzie was right about Rupert's capacity for human emotion and the likelihood of it leading him to return to his family, Beatrice had undoubtedly made the equation more complex by providing him with a second one.

'The bastard!' Amanda railed. 'A fucking *baby*. Our youngest is only five! I suppose he's imagining they're going to *play* together and that I'm going to pal up with fucking Beatrice for the good of the extended family! Well, fuck that! No. Seriously. *Fuck* that! I will never have the bitch or her brat *near* my kids.'

The news of the pregnancy had been hard enough for Amanda to take but when, in the light of the sudden and crippling credit crunch, Rupert attempted to re-negotiate the terms of their divorce she went apoplectic.

For here was an opportunity not only for outrage but, more importantly, for *revenge*.

The original divorce had been swift and businesslike. Rupert knew that whatever he did he was going to end up handing over half, so he might as well get on with it rather than rack up a million quid's worth of lawyers' fees pursuing a pointless exercise in avoidance. Amanda was not stupid and she knew her rights. They'd been married for thirteen years, they had two children and there was no way on earth she was going to let him fight her anywhere but London or LA, where the law was clear.

'I'm buggered for half so bring it on,' Rupert said to the lads over a boys' curry convened to discuss the issue.

'Quite right too, you bastard.' Henry grinned. 'Besides which, what difference does it make? Half of a squillion is still a squillion as far as I can see. You've still got more than you could ever possibly need.'

'I always need more, mate. That's why I get it.'

'Personally I think you should be screwed till the pips squeak,' David said.

'I am being, mate!' Rupert said with a wink and what he clearly believed was a rakish smile. 'Believe me, I am being.'

'Oh please!' Jimmy protested. 'You absolute wanker.'

'Did you ever think what this does to us?' David said.

'No, as a matter of fact I didn't. Not even slightly,' Rupert replied. 'What does it do to you?'

'Well, first and foremost it puts all our girls on the defensive. We have to defend *ourselves* for your shagging.'

'Not following,' Rupert said. 'What are you talking about?'

'I'm talking about months of "Don't you go doing it" and "If you do, bloody tell me so I can do it first."'

'He's right actually,' Henry said. 'The first thing Jane said to me when we heard was "Oh, I suppose you're jealous and now you want to run off with a twenty-year-old yourself." Amazing. I hadn't said a word. Not a bloody word, but she acted as if I'd been behind the whole thing.'

'The minute one bloke goes off with a younger girl,' David said, 'all the other girls get nervous and belligerent. That's what you've done to us.'

'Well, I'm sorry,' Rupert replied smugly, 'but I do not arrange my private affairs primarily to make your totty feel good about themselves.'

'We'd noticed,' David snapped.

'Anyway, it's all over now, thank God,' Rupert went on. 'Done and dusted, so everyone can forget about it. Amanda can have all the stuff, the houses, the cash, three of the cars and the art. I'll just keep the vintage Lamborghini, my golf clubs and the share options.'

'She'll see through that,' Henry sneered. 'RLB shares doubled in value last year and will again this year. By next year it'll be as if you'd never given anything away at all.'

'Property isn't doing so badly either,' Rupert replied.

'Not as well as the Royal Lancashire Bank, mate.'

'Nothing does as well as the RLB,' said Jimmy and Rupert conceded this point with a wry grin.

'Fortunately for me,' he said, 'Amanda loves the art. Let's face it, she chose it all. And besides, for some reason she has a sentimental attitude to the property.'

'For *some reason*?' Henry spluttered. 'You've brought up your children in it!'

'Yes,' Rupert agreed. 'That's probably it.'

And so the divorce had been finalized on a relatively equitable trade-off between Rupert and Amanda's considerable property portfolio, art investments and cash assets against their RLB and other banking stocks and shares.

'I know he's done better out of it,' Amanda told the girls, 'and I know he'll have found a way to hide some stock somewhere, but what can I do? If I know one thing about Rupert it's that he's good with money . . . Sometimes I wonder whether that's the only thing I *do* know about him. Anyway, as I see it I can accept a deal which gives me everything I love but let him rip me off. Or I can fight him, have him get belligerent, probably lose stuff I want – and do you know what? In the end he'll still find a way to rip me off.'

Amanda took the children to the country. She needed distance and besides, there were a number of prep schools she wished to visit. The eight-year-old had got quite out of hand since his father had left and she felt he needed discipline. She opened the envelope containing the decree nisi on the train and surprised herself by having a little cry.

Rupert didn't cry. He punched the air, flexed his muscles in the bedroom mirror and flew Beatrice to Paris for dinner. His life was about to reignite! He was still hugely rich, he was no longer encumbered by numerous properties or the constant presence of children and he had a *twenty-two-year-old* girlfriend. He was a student once more! A multi-multi-millionaire student. He was in a position to grab his young girlfriend and party for years to come.

It was over dinner in Paris that Beatrice dropped her monumental bucket of piss on Rupert's parade.

'No, I won't have any champagne, darling,' she said, a look of nervous exhilaration crossing her features. 'I don't think I should . . .'

'Should?'

I'm four weeks late, you see.'

Rupert stared at her over his oysters, his face also nervous but with no sign of exhilaration.

'Late?' he stammered. 'You mean late as in *late*?'

Beatrice's reply was to giggle coyly.

'But you're on the pill!' Rupert snapped. 'You *can't* be pregnant.'

'Yes, well, you see, I was counting up and actually I think I forgot one or two . . . You're always so *demanding* when it comes to bedtime I get in a spin.' Beatrice's look was no longer nervous. There was a touch of defiance now. 'You are pleased, aren't you, darling? After all, we do love each other. You did *say*.'

Rupert didn't reply. Yes, he'd said he loved her. And he did. He loved her for the wonderful, unencumbered, sexy girl she had been.

Now she was going to be . . . a mum.

His second student life had lasted less than a day.

Beatrice smiled a big, innocent smile and poured herself a mineral water.

'What's really great is that it will only be five years younger than your youngest,' she said. 'They can be proper siblings.'

They returned from Paris the next morning and Rupert spent the following week trying to decide what to do. Could he pay her off? She absolutely refused to get rid of it.

However, events took a hand and Rupert found himself with more to worry about than whether he'd still fancy Beatrice when she had piles, reflux and intermittent bladder control. Out of the blue the financial sector went into free fall. What had happened to Caledonian Granite the previous year was now happening to the entire British banking system. All the banks, but most particularly the Royal Lancashire, were suddenly exposed as shouldering enormous debts, debts far, far greater than any assets they could possibly have. They had been lending money and investing in expansion at an insane rate and there was no real money to cover these reckless transactions.

Overnight, as the world came to understand that the foundations of the great banking institutions in which they had placed their trust were shuddering, the share prices collapsed. RLB shares, which had been valued at £5, were suddenly valued at 50p and then 15p. The repercussions of this for the ordinary citizen and for the British economy were horrendous. They were also pretty bad for the chief executive officer of the bank, who had recently placed all his divorce settlement in one leaky basket. Suddenly Rupert was broke.

Which was how his ex-wife Amanda found herself with the opportunity for both outrage and revenge. Rupert had written to her in an effort to renegotiate the settlement. His argument was that it had been based on an assessment of his value that had now proved to be entirely false. He wanted to redivide the assets he had previously held with Amanda in order to get some of the property, art, cars and cash and to give her half of his millions of 15p shares.

'Fuck you. Sue me,' was Amanda's four-word text in reply to this suggestion, which Rupert had made 'in a spirit of fair play and hoping to avoid incurring further lawyers' costs'.

Rupert had therefore applied to a judge, who began by asking an obvious question.

'Tell me, Lord Bennett,' he said sternly, 'had the shares which you chose to keep in the original settlement continued to climb in the manner that you had expected them to, would you now be offering Lady Bennett a bonus "in a spirit of fair play"?'

Rupert claimed that he might well have done exactly that but the judge did not believe a word of it. He ruled in favour of Amanda, who did not attend the hearing but celebrated in a restaurant nearby.

Beatrice was in court, her tummy already beginning to show.

Into the abyss

The day had arrived for Toby to attend his new school.

Jimmy had talked a tough game to Monica about sending their son to Caterham Road, but in truth he was as miserable and scared as she had been at the prospect. He tried to overcome his fears, for his own sake as much as the boy's.

He told himself that the loathing and terror he felt as he approached the school with Toby on that first morning was all wrong. It was snobbery, it was prejudice and it was also probably a sort of racism. Jimmy was honest enough to recognize that the extraordinary and unfamiliar mix of ethnic groups that he saw milling about in front of the school scared him.

He just knew that this school was going to be hard as nails and that Toby would be lucky to learn anything amid the Babylonian babble of the twelve languages that were proudly listed on the much-sprayed and graffitied school sign.

Toby was clearly pretty scared too. He had slipped his hand from Jimmy's as they approached the gate, but up until that point he had been holding it tight. Starting a new school in the middle when everybody else has known each other for years is hard enough at the best of times, but when you're plummeting down the social scale as you do it you're bound to feel a bit intimidated.

'You'll be fine, Tobe,' Jimmy said. 'Just don't let on you went to a posh school. Remember, try and talk like they do on *EastEnders*.'

'I'm not going to say anything at all,' Toby replied.

'Any*fing*,' Jimmy corrected him.

As they approached the school and the pavement became more and more crowded with milling parents and scampering children, Jimmy's worst fears seemed to be confirmed. Every face looked to him to be hard and forbidding. He struggled to avoid catching anybody's eye. He was convinced that every adult and child assembling on the pavement had him and Toby marked down as interlopers.

Ponces.

Posh bastards.

The gates were still locked when they arrived and so they were forced to stand about with the rest of the parents, carers and kids waiting to be admitted. Some boys were kicking a stone around, their dirty, scuffed shoes getting more so by the minute. Jimmy glanced down and saw that Toby was discreetly trying to scuff his own. Jimmy had polished them that morning. How stupid! He regretted it now.

The boys kicking the stone looked so tough, their shouts and laughter so loud and harsh. Jimmy felt a bit scared of them himself so he could only imagine what Toby was feeling. Two boys who must have been Year Six looked particularly intimidating. One of them even had patterns razored into his close-cropped hair.

Then they both went for the stone in a close tackle and crashed into each other hard. They bashed heads and went down together, hitting the pavement in a noisy heap.

Then they burst into tears.

Jimmy looked around. A man who had been smoking a cigarette threw it aside and went to pick the boys up.

'Come on, lads,' he said, reaching down. 'Crying cos you've had a bump? Anyone would think you were Premier League players!'

The boys got the joke and at the same time realized that they had been making a fuss in front of the smaller

347

kids and quickly made an effort to pull themselves together.

The two little boys didn't look so much like thugs after that. They looked like little boys.

For a moment, Jimmy felt better.

Then he stole a look at some of the mothers. They really did look tough. Horribly so. There were mullet haircuts and quite a few tattoos and piercings. Bulging tracky pants and much flesh on display. Some were smoking and one or two were giving their kids crisps even though it was only eight thirty in the morning.

Jimmy tried to look away.

These surely were the ignorant, aggressive, self-assertive women so often described in the tabloid press. Stupid, self-righteous and strutting. Undermining class discipline by always taking the side of their delinquent children over the teacher, no matter what horror their kids might have committed.

One or two of them glanced Jimmy's way. He was a new face. Toby was a new face. Jimmy stared at the ground, desperate to avoid their curious glances. He was convinced that once these women had him in their sights they would mark him down as an enemy. They would band together in a knot of ignorant malice and mutter about who the fuck Jimmy and his little snob kid thought they were.

He began to catch snippets of their conversation. The accents were a mixed bunch, but the majority tone was the post-Cockney Estuary of the white London native.

'I couldn' do it eeva! Could you do it? I couldn',' one woman was complaining.

'I arsed Mr Hurley, 'e sez 'e sometimes doan unnerstan' it 'isself,' another replied.

'It ain't like it woz when we dun it.'

'An' I couldn' even do it ven!'

There was laughter at this.

'I 'ated maffs. Absolu'ly 'ated it. Nah I've go'ah do it orl over aggen.'

Suddenly Jimmy understood what they were talking about. It was the bloody new way of teaching maths! He knew all about that and he bloody hated it too. Some complete *twat* at the Department of Education had decided that the way maths had been taught for decades was wrong and long division was wrong and carrying numbers from left to right in subtraction was wrong and God knows what else was wrong besides.

This had occurred at about the same time that another ministerial arse had decreed that homework was a thing to be *shared* by parent and pupil. It was pure George Orwell! A faceless government suddenly required all mums and dads to do homework with their kids while simultaneously decreeing that it would be impossible to understand!

Why change the maths? Barnes Wallis had designed the Bouncing Bomb on old maths. Those two blokes who split the atom had done it using old maths. DNA had been discovered on old maths and the Spitfire designed with it. In fact an entire empire had been created and run on old maths! Now we had new maths and Britain was a basket case once more. Was there a connection? Jimmy felt that somehow there might be.

The parents at Abbey Hall had cursed this change in maths too. They had struggled with it and complained about it at the school gates just as these other mothers at the opposite end of the social spectrum were doing now. It seemed the National Curriculum (to which even private schools had to pay lip service) was a great leveller.

'They're goan' ta do an evenin', Mr 'urley sez. So's we can bleedin' learn ah ta do it. I'm def'n'ly goan'. Maybe I'll finally be able to add up me shoppin'! It neva comes aht right.'

'You should do it on your compu'ah. Get a spread-sheet off of Office.'

'I'm rubbish at the compu'ah.'

With each exchange these women were becoming a little less threatening. Less ferocious-looking. In fact they no longer looked ferocious at all.

Abbey Hall had arranged an evening to explain the new methods of teaching maths to the parents. Monica had tried to do her accounts on an Office spreadsheet. She had been rubbish at it too.

Just then a car pulled up and what appeared to be a huge bundle of white and pink layers got out of the passenger seat.

"Allo, June,' some of the mothers chorused.

'Morning all,' the bundle said. 'Twenty-six snowflake costumes. Took me three nights.'

'You love it, June,' a woman said.

'It keeps me busy,' the bundle replied, heading off towards the office entrance to the school.

Again Jimmy's mind went back to Abbey Hall.

They'd had a mum like June there. Daphne Phipps. She astonished everybody with the number of costumes she could produce. Prior to her advent, the school had hired costumes from a professional supplier for their joint productions with St Hilda's Girls. Daphne Phipps had set up a costume department and single-handedly clothed the entire cast of *Oliver*.

The thought of St Hilda's Girls School brought Cressida and Lillie to Jimmy's mind. Both their names had been put down at birth. Jimmy presumed that they were still there. He supposed he ought to write and tell the headmistress that the places would not be needed. It had been such a horrible fight to get on the list too. Every mum in Notting Hill seemed to favour St Hilda's Girls and Jimmy remembered Monica's panic when she heard a rumour that some mums were getting the sex of their babies scanned and putting down names *from the womb*.

'You can't put a foetus down on a school list,' she had wailed, terrified of getting gazumped by a belly. 'It isn't fair.'

Jimmy almost smiled at the memory. At least they would be spared all that agony and tension. Next year Cressida would be coming to Caterham Road.

Jimmy noticed some girls playing hopscotch on the paving stones. It would be nice for Toby to have girls in his class. Jimmy had been through the state system himself and, like Monica, had never really warmed to the idea of single-sex schools. He thought it was good for boys to have girls around. It was civilizing. He had never liked that aspect of Abbey Hall, but the question had never really been raised. It was a given. You simply *had* to go private, there was no other way. And in the vast majority of private schools, private meant single sex.

Jimmy was almost beginning to relax. Just a little. Toby too seemed to be calm. His lip had been quivering earlier but now it was still. He was looking about himself and perhaps feeling as Jimmy was, that, dress and accents aside, there was not much about this school gate that was unfamiliar.

Now there was a stirring among the crowd. Through the bars of the fence Jimmy could see a purposeful-looking woman striding across the playground holding a set of keys. The gates were about to be opened.

'Well, Tobes,' Jimmy said, 'I guess this is you.'

'Wotevah,' Toby replied.

Then Jimmy accidentally caught someone's eye. And in a single moment all his fear returned.

A man was staring at him.

He was a black man with scars on both cheeks and a look of ferocious intensity that Jimmy had never seen before in anyone. Tall and thin and dressed only in old jeans and a T-shirt, his muscular arms looked strong and wiry. They were scarred too.

The man started walking towards Jimmy. A tall boy followed him, a younger version of the man, equally intense and almost as intimidating.

Now the man was standing before Jimmy, his eyes staring into his. Jimmy tried to look back. He thought about saying something but could think of nothing.

The gate was open now. Kids were surging forward, the younger ones with a hug and a kiss, the older ones absolutely not with a hug and a kiss.

Jimmy wanted to move away but the man kept looking at him, holding him in his stare.

Jimmy felt his fists tighten. Enough was enough. It was time to stand up for himself. If he expected Toby to survive in this new and terrifying urban reality then he had to show some strength himself.

'Yeah?' said Jimmy. 'Wot?'

He could feel Toby's emotions even before he felt the boy's hand in his. Jimmy had never addressed anyone like that before. Jimmy was kind, he was considerate and, unless directly provoked, he was always polite. Yet here he was producing these two sullen, ugly syllables to address a complete stranger, a man who had as yet done nothing provocative beyond approach him and fail to speak.

Toby knew what that 'Yeah, wot?' meant. It meant 'Don't fuck with me, arsehole.' It meant 'I don't want trouble but if that's the way it's going then bring it on.'

It meant Jimmy was terrified. And Toby knew it.

'Hello,' Jimmy heard a voice saying. 'We are very lost.'

It wasn't the man who spoke but the skinny boy who stood behind him. The accent was strong, the emphasis quite disconcerting.

'HELLo. WE are VERy lost.'

The silent man held out a piece of paper.

Still he stared, but this time Jimmy noticed something else besides strength in his eyes. Something besides the intensity which Jimmy had taken for ferocity.

It was tears.

Jimmy knew what the piece of paper was that the man was holding out to him. Jimmy was holding one himself. Clearly the tall man had noticed this and that was why he had approached him. It was the registration document for placing a boy at the school. Now Jimmy understood. The skinny lad with the strong accent was new to the school too.

'My NAME is KORfa,' the boy said. 'This IS my FATHer.'

Jimmy was later to learn that Sharif, Korfa's father, had, like Jimmy, suffered a cruel and gruelling reduction in his fortunes over the previous year. But Jimmy was forced to admit that beyond that one fact any similarity in their situations ended, and the journey that had brought Korfa and his father to the school gate at Caterham Road on the same morning as Jimmy and Toby rather put Jimmy's troubles into perspective.

Sharif was a refugee asylum seeker from Somalia. He and his son had escaped a war zone where government and rebel forces were locked in a conflict of unimaginable savagery. Sharif would later explain to Jimmy in faltering English that his wife had been raped and then murdered before his and Korfa's eyes and that he and Korfa's elder brother had been taken away and forced to serve with the rebel forces.

Sharif had lost contact with the elder boy during fierce fighting and when he learned that his captors were planning to press eight-year-old Korfa into service too he had managed to escape. It had of course been a near-impossible wrench to leave the elder brother to his fate, but the chances were that he was already dead and for the sake of Korfa the father had resolved to flee.

Through a monumental effort involving courage and good fortune in equal measure, Sharif had managed to get himself and the boy out of Africa, across Europe and eventually to a transit camp in France. From there, with the help of dedicated relief workers, he was brought before a British immigration officer to whom he claimed refugee status.

Monica was later to discover that, by a strange co-incidence, the agency that had helped Korfa and Sharif was Asylum Action, the very charity for which she had previously been a fundraiser. On the day she worked this out she cried with joy.

Standing before the school gates as the children rushed in and the parents began to leave, Jimmy knew nothing of this terrible story. What he did know was that the tall man spoke little or no English and was worried and at a loss where to go and what to do with his form.

Jimmy held up his own form and smiled. The tall man smiled back. Glancing down, Jimmy could see that Korfa and Toby were smiling too. Neither was entirely alone any more.

'I WANT to learn ENGlish VERy fast,' said Korfa. 'Will YOU help ME?'

'Absolutely. Of course,' said Toby. 'I mean yeah, right, wotevah.'

Ten. Nine. None

Robbo's funeral was to prove the last full gathering of the old Sussex Radish Club and its female associates. Jimmy and Monica, David and Laura, Henry and Jane, Rupert and Amanda (who did not speak), and Lizzie with Robson in his coffin.

These ten who had met so often over so many years would never again all be together under the same roof. By the time they got to the wake in the local pub they were only nine, Robbo having been left in the church-yard. And in fact the remaining nine would not gather again either. The gang broke up that day. It wasn't announced, no collective decision was made, but had any of them thought about it they might have guessed that this would turn out to be the case. The previous six months had changed and divided them all for ever.

Lizzie was a widow. Rupert and Amanda were stand-ing at opposite ends of the pub. Jimmy and Monica were broke and in severe, friendship-ruining debt to David's company. David himself had seen his celebrated Rainbow project grind to a halt and then become a symbol of corporate excess.

Only Henry and Jane were in much the same position as they had been the year before. Jane was working on another novel (once more, definitely not chick lit) and Henry had continued to progress in both party and government. In fact he was emerging as one of the few beneficiaries of the economic gloom, in as much as he had become the public face of the Prime Minister's efforts to distance his administration from the financial free-for-all it had tolerated for so long. Henry's role was finally bringing the long-simmering animosity that had existed between him and Rupert since their student days right out into the open.

'How are things looking at the Royal Lancashire? Pretty roundly fucked, I imagine,' Henry said to Rupert after they had paid their respects to Lizzie and found some wine. 'Do you think you're going to have to come to us for a public bailout? That's certainly what they're saying at the Treasury.'

'Difficult to say at the moment,' Rupert replied rather huffily. 'We're trying to avoid it, of course. Not something we'd particularly enjoy, obviously. It depends on our next credit rating. If we lose our Triple A status I suppose we may need some sort of temporary bridging help.'

Rupert was trying to sound casual and unfazed but it was clear that he was badly shaken. He'd had a bruising few weeks. The almost overnight transformation of the once-mighty Royal Lancashire Bank from gilt-edged and venerable financial fortress to tottering basket case had shocked the nation. It had left Rupert and his board struggling to refinance their business and facing the prospect of virtual nationalization.

'Funny thing,' Henry said, smiling, 'that *you* may end up coming to *me* for money, eh? Who'd have thought it?'

'It's not your money, Henry,' Rupert snapped, 'it's the public's, and I shan't be coming to you either. *If* we end up needing government help, and I say *if*, I shall deal directly with the Chancellor of the Exchequer as I always do, and last time I looked, Henry, you hadn't climbed quite that high up the greasy pole.'

'All in good time, Rupert,' Henry replied, 'all in good time.'

But for Henry, the last of the old friends to remain untouched by the recession, the good times were running out too.

All perfectly legal

It was March 2009 and Henry and Rupert were facing each other across a table, quarrelling, just as they had done so many times before, two old friends who never seemed to agree on anything.

Except that this time the table was not laden with curries, nan bread and pints of beer. There was no Lizzie or Robbo to appeal for calm, no Jimmy to chuck a friendly bit of rolled-up bread and defuse the situation. This was the green baize table of a House of Commons Select Committee and the only things on it were a couple of jugs of water, some glasses and mountains of paper.

And Henry and Rupert were no longer friends.

The Royal Lancashire Bank had recently come within an ace of folding under the weight of its toxic debt. The government had had to bail it out and Rupert was forced to step down in ignominy as CEO. As a price for going, however, he had arranged a redundancy and pension package with the government's accountants which guaranteed him an income of a million pounds a year, to be paid from the now publicly owned bank's non-existent resources. It was to explain and justify this package that Rupert Bennett had been brought before the Select Committee, of which Henry was chair.

'Lord Bennett,' Henry thundered, 'you have destroyed not one but two banks, the National City and the Royal Lancashire. Both of them would without doubt have collapsed, had the taxpayer not taken on the responsibilities of your abject failure.'

Rupert shrugged.

'We've all been at the same party, we've all enjoyed the many good-time years. If my speculations at the RLB have failed it's not my fault, but the fault of the financial regulators who failed in their duty to properly police the expanding economy.'

Henry almost shouted his reply.

'Are you saying it's our fault, Lord Bennett? You ruin your own bank and you blame us for not stopping you!'

'You were there,' Rupert replied with effortless calm, 'all of you. You were with me every step. With me and a hundred like me. I was brought in to advise you when Caledonian Granite collapsed. You *knighted* me for services to British banking. You made me a Labour peer. How can you possibly pretend that you didn't know what I was doing and that you didn't support it 100 per cent? If it turned out I was wrong then you were wrong too. We were *all* wrong.'

Henry's face was red; he could feel his guts twisting. The bastard had him. Henry knew damn well why Rupert had been knighted *and* why he'd been made a fucking lord.

It had nothing whatsoever to do with service. Either to party or to country.

He'd *bought* the damn honours. No more, no less. But Henry couldn't say that. He couldn't stand up in a parliamentary committee room and scream, *don't pretend you got honoured for anything other than the fact that you were prepared to pay for it, you smug bastard.*

He couldn't say that because it was his party that had taken the man's tainted coin. The Labour Party, set up a century earlier because of the excesses of the likes of Lord fucking Bennett of Bel-fucking-Gravia, had ended up in their thrall and in their pay.

He couldn't say it because it was the one thing he and the rest of the party had been denying for the previous two years. Ever since the Cash for Honours scandal had broken, crippling what was left of Labour's moral credibility and ruining Blair's last months in office.

Ever since the police had come within an ace of knocking on the very door of Number 10.

If Henry so much as *breathed* the idea that Rupert had been anything other than a worthy recipient of a genuine honour, it would open up the whole appalling scandal again. And the last thing the government needed was another scandal. Public trust in Parliament was buggered enough without that.

Henry stared at his old friend in the dawning realization that the collapse of Rupert's career represented much more than just the collapse of a couple of banks. It was symptomatic of the collapse of something even greater, the collapse of the whole New Labour project. The collapse of that mission to improve society on which he and so many others had embarked, with what they fondly believed was passion and idealism, a decade and more before.

Suddenly the unholy alliance that Henry and his colleagues had made with the City of London was exposed for what it was. A tawdry, lazy, back-slapping exercise in greed. Greed for money and for power. Rupert and his ilk had bribed Henry and his, corrupting them before they had had a chance to make the world a better place.

Suddenly it all seemed so *obvious*.

With their glamorous parties, their invitations to stay on great big yachts and their party donations, the money men had created massive wealth for themselves and given back nothing to society but resentment and fear. They had destroyed faith in the City and respect for honour and rank, utterly compromising the Labour Party in the process.

And now, having brought down two banks, one of the

principal villains of the whole sorry episode was sitting before him, refusing to give up the million-pound-a-year pension settlement he had negotiated as the price for stepping aside so that Parliament could begin cleaning up the mess he had created.

Henry felt tired. What was the point?

'Are you going to give up your entirely unjustified pension, Lord Bennett,' Henry said wearily, 'or not?'

'Of course I'm not,' Rupert replied. 'It's perfectly legal.'

'Yes, but is it *moral*?' Henry replied. 'We shall have to let the public decide, won't we?'

At which point the committee steward called lunch.

During the recess Henry had an epiphany. It occurred while he was on his way back to his office to eat the sandwiches he had bought on the way into Parliament (and for which he *must* remember to submit a receipt).

Quite suddenly Henry made a decision.

He was going to bring the party back to its senses.

This was his chance. His great opportunity.

He had not been compromised himself by the various blows that had dented New Labour's credibility. The war. Cash for Honours. The current financial melt-down. He had been only a junior figure in any of it. He was therefore perfectly placed to be a new broom. Known but not tainted. Sweeping out so-called 'New' Labour and bringing back real Labour. *Old Labour*. A true party of the people.

He would start immediately. Straight after lunch.

He would return to the committee room and give 'Lord' Bennett such a roasting that it would make Henry's name. He would do this by ignoring the fact that Rupert's legal position was a secure one and concentrating exclusively on the moral issues.

Then he would call a press conference in which he would expose senior colleagues for having been in bed with the likes of 'Lord' Bennett for far too long.

After that he would stand for the leadership!

Brown was a lame duck. Blair was ancient history. What was needed was a new, dynamic, thrusting young figure to offer genuine, principled, moral leadership to the party and to the nation!

What was needed, Henry decided, was Henry.

The previous ten years had been a wasted opportunity. Henry would ensure that the party did not miss its chance again.

As he entered his office, Henry's secretary handed him his sandwiches and can of Orangina (£5.65 in total) and also a printout of an email she had just received.

Henry could see from her face that it was not good news.

'You'd better read this, Henry,' she said. 'I think something quite big is brewing.'

The letter was from the editor of a national newspaper. It informed Henry that they were in possession of a confidential document detailing MPs' expenses. They had noted with interest Henry's decision to charge part of the price of his wife's hairdryer to the taxpayer and intended to make it the centrepiece of the front-page story that they were publishing the following day. The headline was to be *Parliamentary Pigs with Snouts in Public Trough* and the story was intended to alert the public to the immoral way MPs topped up their salaries by claiming ludicrous expenses.

'They want to know if you've got anything to say,' Henry's secretary asked.

Henry was simply furious. He grabbed the phone. This kind of press harassment had to stop.

'Have I got anything to say?' he muttered as he dialled the number. 'Yes, I've got something to fucking *say*.'

When he was put straight through to the editor, Henry let rip. 'For God's sake, man, this is so trivial!' he shouted. 'We are trying to run the country, trying to make responsible decisions about people's jobs and services and you put this on us. A hairdryer! A few pounds for a bloody hairdryer! Is that the best you can do? Is it the silly season or something? Are you five years old? Laughing at me for using a hairdryer and claiming part of its cost! I am *supposed* to claim my expenses, didn't you know? That's the rule. Do you think I like it, wasting my time over bus tickets? You try it! Having to scrape together every bloody tab you spend because MPs are expected to be in two places at once the whole bloody time. *And* look respectable while they're doing it. And if we don't, if we look a mess, oh don't you let us know! This is just stupid. This is insane. This is petty and *poisonous* beyond belief. You will withdraw this ludicrous non-story immediately or I shall go to the Press Complaints Commission and I will win! I swear I will make things so hot for you you'll wish you'd tried to bully someone else! You have gone too far! Surely you can see that? This isn't journalism! This is gutless, brainless, principle-less bullying and it has to stop. A hairdryer, front-page news? For God's sake! Have you no shame? I claimed for a sandwich too this morning because alongside my regular constituency duties I am working a *fourteen-hour* day doing parliamentary committee work for which I receive no extra wages. Do you want to know what the filling was? What flavour crisps I ate? Perhaps you can laugh at them while you have a champagne lunch with your bloody publisher! You puerile, irresponsible, delinquent little hypocrite!'

There was a pause at the other end of the line before the editor replied. When he did, his voice was smooth and silky.

'It's not *just* a hairdryer, Henry,' he said. 'We thought the hairdryer would be a nice hook. You do have very distinctive hair, after all.'

Henry began to rack his brains. Not *just* a hairdryer? What else? What did they have on him?

'What do you mean?' he asked.

'Flipping, Henry,' the editor said quietly. 'Bit more serious than a sandwich, I think.'

'Flipping?' Henry replied, momentarily at a loss.

'The second-home allowance. We feel that you and many of your colleagues have been rather *creative* in deciding which of your homes should receive taxpayer support.'

The penny that had been spinning in Henry's mind began to drop. He got it. Oh fuck. All of a sudden, he got it.

'Our investigations seem to suggest,' the editor continued in the same quiet tone, 'that you all tend to think that your *bigger* and *better* home should be your second home, i.e., the one for which the public shares the cost. Now correct me if I'm wrong, Henry, but I thought that the idea of an allowance was to help out-of-town MPs like yourself fund a modest London residence to enable them to attend Parliament. Is that right, Henry? You would know, I presume. After all, you have been claiming it.'

Henry felt as if he was going to be sick. He hadn't seen it coming. He had *not* seen it coming.

Once more, in the absence of a reply, the editor went on.

'Which of your homes does the taxpayer support, Henry? Is it your rather grubby little flat in Battersea, or is it the beautiful six-bedroom house in four acres of grounds that you recently bought in your constituency? Because that's the one you've been claiming for, Henry. The beautiful house in which your wife Jane writes her novels, while incidentally finding time to do secretarial work for you, Henry, which the public *pays her for*. What is Jane, Henry? A novelist or a secretary? While she's working in that beautiful second home, bought, I might add, with the proceeds of the sale of your *previous* luxurious second home which the public paid to renovate before you flogged it?'

Henry was stunned.

Everybody flipped. It was common practice among MPs of all parties. They all changed the status of their homes to get the most advantageous public allowance. It was obvious. Common sense. It had never occurred to him that there was anything wrong. That the process might be viewed in the way in which the editor was now viewing it. It was just something they did.

'It's . . . it's perfectly legal,' he heard himself saying.

'Yes, Henry. But is it *moral*?' the editor replied. 'We shall have to let the public decide, won't we?'

Making a plan

'Above all,' Derek Corby said, 'you need to hang on to this place until we can work out a way for you to make a planned withdrawal. If they suddenly foreclose and you're forced out you could find yourself in very real difficulties.

It's astonishing how quickly people's lives can implode once the regular income goes. As a bank manager I've seen it a thousand times.'

Jimmy's parents had come to see their grandchildren, and Jimmy and Derek had stepped out into the famous front garden to discuss Jimmy's deteriorating situation away from the others. They warmed their hands on their coffee mugs and tried to avoid treading in cat shit.

'It all looks a bit hairy, doesn't it, Dad?' Jimmy said.

'The enemies now are panic and inertia,' Derek replied, as ever the authoritative father.

'Meaning?' Jimmy asked.

'We can't afford to do nothing, but nor can we afford to flail about doing just anything. We require a formal game plan to try to stave off repossession for long enough for us to develop an exit strategy that we can implement on our own terms.'

'Pardon?' said Jimmy and he almost laughed. His father still talked like a bank manager even though he no longer was one. He'd probably talked like a bank manager before he was a bank manager too. The baby Derek Corby had no doubt emerged from the womb at exactly the appointed time and demanded that his milk and rusks be properly itemized before he consented to accept them.

'Jim,' Derek said seriously, 'if the bank takes you by surprise and suddenly repossesses, you'll be forced to apply to the council for emergency accommodation.'

'I know,' said Jimmy quietly. 'Of course, because there's kids involved they'd have to find us *something*. They have a statutory obligation, but if there's no actual houses or flats available . . . they'll have to board us.'

Father and son looked at each other. They both knew that if Monica and Jimmy were turfed out of the Notting Hill house they would almost certainly be put into a so-called Bed and Breakfast.

Bed and Breakfast. B & B. Such a pleasant-sounding phrase.

Two things that everybody liked.

Bed. Lovely.

Breakfast. Just the job.

Together they were even better. Bed and Breakfast conjured up visions of family holidays by the sea, children frolicking in the surf. Ice creams. Fish and chips. A gentler, more innocent world. Jimmy had been on a number of such holidays as a child. Holidays which had of course been deeply out of fashion even then, but Derek and Nora Corby *were* out of fashion. And proud of it. And Derek genuinely did wonder why anyone would even think of going abroad when they could stand in the rain in West Wittering.

But the modern reality of Bed and Breakfast had nothing whatsoever to do with such rose-tinted memories.

The reality was terrible.

Jimmy knew it and Monica knew it. There were

families at the school gate whom the council were housing in B & Bs and it was clear to Jimmy that they lived in hell. Toby had become friends with the child of one such family. But the friend could never invite Toby for tea. He was too ashamed. His parents were too ashamed. Ashamed of the single room in which the boy, his siblings and his parents all lived, sharing a single bathroom with two other families in adjoining single rooms. Or maisonettes, as the landlord called them in the prospectus he had presented to the council when applying to become one of their designated emergency landlords.

Maisonettes.

Three families on a single floor. With three more families above and another three below. All in single rooms in which they were expected to eat, sleep and refrain from succumbing to utter despair.

That would be Jimmy and Monica, Toby, Cressida and Lillie if the bank evicted them from the Notting Hill house. All five of them in a Bed and Breakfast. Another family above them, a family below them. A family in front of them. A family behind them. A rabbit warren designed in hell.

'It's bloody insanity, of course,' Derek said bitterly. 'A system gone mad. The landlords are nothing more than criminals. They charge ruinous rates for slum rooms. Milking the system without heart or conscience. But then the system is so damned easy to milk. You can't just pass a law saying councils *have* to house families, you have to provide the bloody houses for them to do it with.'

Jimmy stared glumly at the cat shit.

'Anyway,' Derek went on, 'there's no sense moaning about it. We need to make a plan.'

'What plan, Dad?' Jimmy asked, and for a moment he sounded like he was eleven years old again. 'Our problem is the bank wants this house. It's a real asset, not some toxic waste of space that's pointless to repo because they wouldn't be able to sell it on if they did. This is a six-storey house in Notting Hill with a gym and underground private garage. If we lived in a shithole we'd probably be all right, but there are still plenty of people around who could and would pay top dollar for a house like this and the bank's getting impatient.'

'The first thing,' Derek said, 'is to try not to panic.'

'OK, Dad,' Jimmy replied. 'I'm trying not to panic. What's the second thing?'

'Well, initially you'll get a visit from their pre-litigation team.'

'*Pre*-litigation team?' Jimmy said. 'Shit. Closely followed, I assume, by their actual litigation team.'

'Well, that partly depends on you,' Derek said. 'Of course what they want is for you to go without a fight. So they're going to put a lot of emphasis on the *cost* for you of trying to stay. Believe it or not, the RLB actually charge you ninety pounds for the pre-litigation visit, which they add to your debt.'

'Jeez,' Jimmy whistled. 'Hardball.'

'Yes, and they're going to make it very clear to you that the cost of any court action that the bank might incur in getting you out will be added to your mortgage. That's their big stick.'

'So I'm buggered then? Might as well roll over.'

'Well, I'm not an expert on this although I've seen a lot of foreclosures from the other side, as a bank manager. If you want to get specific, detailed advice you'll need to contact a debtors' charity. There are a couple of really good ones, although they're all very stretched at the moment.'

Jimmy's face, which was already devoid of its usual cheerful expression, fell further. *Debtors' charity*. It sounded so Victorian! And he'd come to this.

In a matter of months.

Derek Corby clearly saw what his son was thinking.

'Jimmy, this is how it is. There's no way of avoiding it and certainly no time for false pride. What's happening to you is only what's happening to thousands and thousands of other people at the moment, and you need any help and advice you can get. It can actually be quite a lot of trouble to evict a family and my experience is that if you can demonstrate in *practical* terms that you're attempting to manage your responsibilities the banks and the courts will take a much more favourable line.'

'So how do I do that, Dad? What do they want to see?'

'Well, you have to show willingness to at least pay something. A lump sum plus a regular amount towards the interest that's accruing.'

'We've still got the Discovery. Our one remaining asset. I reckon I could get twenty grand cash on it in a quick sale. It's worth forty easy, but then it isn't actually worth that because nobody's buying cars any more.'

'Sell it,' said Derek, 'and hand the cash straight to the bank. Never mind your other debts.'

'I've managed to pay off most of the small traders and builders at Webb Street with stuff I've flogged from the house, pictures and gadgets and stuff. It's only the bank again, and David's architectural firm.'

'They'll have to wait. You need to secure your home.'

'We'll have no car, of course.'

'It doesn't matter. The most important thing is that the children have somewhere decent to live.'

'OK, Dad, I can do that. But as for trying to put down something regular towards the interest, I just don't see how we can. We have no income at all. We're living off extending our debt and my unemployment benefit.'

Derek glanced about himself and cleared his throat. It was as if he had something slightly dodgy and con-spiratorial to say and a spy might be lurking in the undergrowth rather than just the mob of incontinent cats.

'Your mother and I have been talk—' he said.

'No, Dad! Absolutely not,' Jimmy interrupted. 'Forget it.'

This was not the first time that his parents had offered to help and Jimmy simply wasn't having it. The basic fact was that they could not afford to. Derek's branch of the RLB had been closed as part of the emergency restructuring that followed Rupert's fall from grace and the government bailout. Derek had been forced into early retirement and with the markets so low it was the worst possible time to arrange an annuity and begin drawing his pension. Jimmy knew that his parents were facing a considerably poorer old age than they had expected and he had no intention of further reducing their circumstances.

'Jimmy,' Derek said, and to Jimmy's surprise this least tactile of men actually reached out and put a hand on his shoulder. 'Listen to me. This is a challenge for all of us, all right? Everything's changed and we're all trying to think differently. What *I'm* thinking is that my son and wonderful daughter-in-law need help. More importantly, my three grandchildren need help. We haven't seen as much of them over the last few years as we'd have liked, what with you always carting them off to Florida or skiing and all that. Now's our chance to be involved. To help. And we want to do it. We're going to sell the house—'

'No, Dad! It's the worst time to—'

'Which means it's also the best time to buy, son. That's an upside, of sorts. We'll downsize, as you used to say. Sell the house, get a nice flat and have a lump sum left over.'

'You don't *want* a lump sum, Dad. They've cut the bloody interest rates to zero. Your money'll just sit there depreciating.'

'It'll sit there servicing a standing order in your name of two hundred and fifty pounds a week towards the accruing interest you owe—'

'Dad—' Jimmy tried once more to protest.

'That and the twenty thousand for the car shows an awful lot of willing,' Derek said firmly. 'The RLB pre-litigation team will be forced to take a favourable view, for a while at least. I've looked into it and talked to a couple of chaps I know and it seems that if you can just get through six months you should be eligible for the government mortgage relief scheme. Of course you owe so much that the bank may lose patience anyway. But it's worth a shot. It's a *plan*, Jim, and we need a plan. So unless you can come up with a better one it's what we're going to do.'

Just then Monica and Nora came out with the children.

'I've made some sandwiches,' Nora said, 'and we're going to have a picnic in the park.'

'I made the chocolate biscuit ones,' Toby said proudly.

'Chocolate biscuit sandwiches?' Jimmy enquired.

'Yeah, Dad. It's a pretty basic concept. You get two bits of bread and butter and stick a chocolate biscuit between them.'

'I have to say that sounds brilliant,' Jimmy replied.

'*After* he's had his cheese and tomato ones and eaten his apple,' Monica said.

As they all made their way to the park, Nora dropped back a little in order to whisper to Monica.

'You know,' she said, 'I never mentioned it before, but lovely though Jodie was, I'm glad she's gone . . . No, really, I don't want to sound mean, because she really *was* lovely and I know that Toby loved her so much, and Cressie. It's just that I always felt a bit surplus to requirements. You know, when we visited. Jodie was just so good at everything and always there, playing with them, doing interesting things. I didn't feel I could get involved. I didn't want to get in her way, you see.'

'Yes,' said Monica, 'I can understand how that might have felt. I certainly never had a nanny when I was little. I didn't know anyone who did. It just sort of happened with us and then I felt I couldn't do without it.'

'Of course, I know that all this has been terribly hard on you,' Nora went on, 'since Jimmy lost his job and everything. But I did want to tell you that. I hope you don't mind. But at least now I feel *useful*.'

When they had all arrived at the park and Toby and Cressie were on the swings, Jimmy spoke to his father.

'Thanks, Dad,' he said.

'Absolutely no need to thank me, Jim,' Derek said. 'As I told you, your mother and I want to help. It's what we've always wanted.'

'I wasn't talking about the money,' Jimmy said. 'I'm thanking you for not saying "I told you so". All those years you've said it couldn't last and it turned out you were right, it didn't.'

'I take no pleasure in having been right on that score, Jimmy. Lots of people were at the party. Lots of people are suffering the hangover. It's a bloody shame, that's all.'

'Well, thanks anyway.'

Ending in tears

The MPs' expenses scandal when it broke shook the Mother of Parliaments to its foundations. It struck at the very core of the public's trust in their representatives and caused many to doubt that proper government could continue at all with its servants brought to such low repute. The scale and significance of the crisis were unprecedented and yet, as is often the case with public events of magnitude, the whole affair came to be identified with one or two specific images.

Just as a horrific terrorist attack can come to be remembered for a single photograph of a fireman emerging from the ashes with a bloodied baby in his arms, just so the great British parliamentary expenses scandal of 2009, for all its deep constitutional significance, eventually boiled down to such ridiculous and inconsequential things as a dirty moat and a chocolate teddy. And, of course, a hairdryer.

These were the 'expenses' that came to embody the public's sense of disappointment and outrage. Some idiot Tory had claimed to have the moat around his castle cleaned at public expense. A Liberal had put in a chit for sweets bought at the House of Commons shop. And Henry Baker, rising figure of New Labour (and founder member of the Radish Club), apparently thought that the public should pay for his wife's hairdryer because he sometimes used it.

BLONDEL'S BOMBSHELL

That was the headline that greeted Henry in the early hours of the morning that followed his parliamentary clash with Rupert over Rupert's RLB pension. Henry had waited up in terror and the early editions confirmed his worst fears.

Henry knew instantly that he would never, ever escape the ridicule of *Blondel's Bombshell*. That it would destroy his political career.

And he was right.

It is said that all political careers end in tears. Henry's ended in floods.

The fact that it was all so terribly, terribly unfair was of course beside the point. Henry was far from being the only MP who had made claims which in retrospect looked greedy and ridiculous. What was more, his hairdryer chit was not by any stretch of the imagination the most profligate of them. And there were many MPs guilty of the legal but morally dubious practice of 'flipping' their second homes, which was of course the real cause of the public's outrage. Many of those politicians had generated far greater profits in the process than Henry had done.

There was no particular reason why Henry should become one of the principal poster boys of the crisis. Except for the fact that making a claim upon the public purse for a percentage of the cost of your wife's hairdryer was just so *bloody funny*. And it didn't help either that he was identified with his luxuriant blond hair, hair about which he was clearly extremely vain.

Vanity is always an easy target. Particularly in a politician.

As the days of the scandal grew, Hairdryer Henry's position became more and more impossible. Every time anybody wrote about or spoke about the scandal they referred with mocking contempt to 'politicians who seem to think it's the public's job to pay to dry their wives' hair'. It wasn't long before the party moved to staunch the haemorrhage of credibility that Henry's claim had caused. He received a call from Andy Palmer in the Prime Minister's office, instructing him to fall on his sword.

The next day Henry resigned as an MP.

That same day, his wife Jane's publisher decided not to take up their option on her second novel. Her first, they explained, had not performed as well as they had hoped and the second did not seem to them to have quite the same emotional élan that had first attracted them to her.

Jane would always believe that the rejection was entirely down to the fact that she was no longer in their eyes (and in the eyes of her small public) a feisty female novelist, but instead the greedy, grasping hairdryer-claiming wife of yet another disgraced politician.

The curse of the Radish Club had claimed its final victims.

Downsizing

Despite all the pressures, Monica and Jimmy were not entirely downhearted. Something in the challenges they were facing had given them both a new spirit. They felt almost as if they had been children before and were now learning to be grown-ups.

Shopping and cooking on a tiny budget were hard work but also rewarding. What's more, the rewards were real and tangible. The family discovered that food tasted better if you really had to make the most of it. Monica constantly looked back in amazement at the amount of food she had thrown away in the past.

'I swear I used to scrape half a week's worth of food into that bin every night,' she'd say. 'God, I'd let Toby chuck an apple away if it had a blemish on it.'

Toby's diet had actually improved, as they were now spared the endless bargaining with him about eating a pea or two in exchange for a guarantee of chocolate.

'Sorry, mate, there *is* no chocolate,' Jimmy would explain. 'No crisps either. No freezer full of mini Magnums and fun-size Cornettos. No dozen Krispy Kreme donuts. No Frubes or other tubes. No "ordering something else" at Pizza Express, in fact no Pizza Express. We can't afford any of them.'

It was very liberating, in a strange way. All those battles over treats were in the past now. And when there was a treat, it really *was* a treat, made special by its rareness.

'You know, the truth is,' Monica said, 'that Tobes is actually getting treats for the first time in his life. He got so many before that nothing was a treat at all, just his due, the norm. Do you remember how Easter used to be? He couldn't fit his egg stash in a bloody bin liner. Now when he gets something at least he appreciates it.'

Toby had got used to it all quite quickly. Just as he had adjusted to Jimmy hocking his Nintendo DS for nappies. And that was another relief. Nintendo had been a cause of friction in the past. Monica hadn't wanted to buy him one but Jimmy said his son (with his room full of PlayStations and Wii) would be a freak at school if he didn't have one. Jimmy promised that he would be restricted to two hours at weekends. From that point on, they had fought a constant battle to enforce this rule, which had been draining for the whole family.

'He used to like books,' Monica had lamented at the time, 'but now all he wants to do is get his thumbs on that bloody little box.'

Now the box was gone and since the pawn shop didn't want books, they remained, and in the absence of both Nintendo and cable TV cartoon channels, Toby rediscovered them. They also discovered the local library, in which books could be borrowed for *free*.

'I had no idea they still did that sort of thing,' Jimmy said in amazement. 'It's just so nineteenth century.'

'Well, we might as well read books we don't own,' Monica observed. 'After all, we don't own anything else.'

Gradually life took on a semblance of normality. The month or two of hell that had followed Jodie's departure had slowly morphed into a new family-based lifestyle. The pressures were still great but they had each other, and the challenges they faced gave them something to think about besides Jimmy's so far fruitless efforts to get a job as a shelf-stacker.

The greatest relief of all was that Toby had settled in at school. State education had not turned out to be quite the nightmare they had assumed it to be. Certainly it was a bit rougher than Abbey Hall.

'Although not so much *rougher*,' Monica observed at the end of Toby's first fortnight, 'as more *rough and ready*.'

'And the kids aren't so bad either,' Jimmy agreed. 'Bit pathetic of us to be surprised really. I mean why wouldn't they be? Kids are kids, aren't they?'

It was true that by the end of his first day Toby had finally lost his beautiful accent and started to speak as if he was in a Guy Ritchie movie, but he had not so far been beaten up. In fact it turned out that, contrary to beliefs that Jimmy and Monica had held for most of their adult lives, the kids in state schools were not uniformly hard cases, made angry, aggressive and slothful by bad parenting, sugar and food additives, but were just the same mixed bag of individuals as the kids had been at Abbey Hall. A bully or two certainly, a few victims, and then a wide middle ground of kids just trying to muddle through their schooldays without getting into the shit with either the hard nuts or authority.

'Much like any school really,' Jimmy said.

There were problem parents, a few sullen, angry ones at the school gate, but they were the exception, not the rule. Of course there were a few of the dreaded dysfunctional families so often reported in the press, where assorted half-siblings dealt with itinerant step-fathers and then brought the emotional trauma to school. But again that was not so different from Abbey Hall.

'When you think about it,' Monica said, 'a good percentage of the parents there were divorced, weren't they? Plenty of absentee dads, as I recall, and what's a nanny if not a step-parent? I know I never used to think that at the time, but now that I know what's actually involved in bringing up kids I realize that Jodie was more their bloody mum than I was. Certainly in terms of how hard it is.'

One other great and unexpected relief about ending up in the state system and in one of the less desirable schools was that they were finally free of the pressure of trying to get their kids into somewhere better. When they had been rich this had been one of the great woes of family life, particularly for Toby himself. He'd had the endless stress of going for interviews with head-masters in intimidating oak-lined studies and spending weekends with tutors, cramming for some archaic entrance exam that simply had to be passed or his whole future would be blown at the age of seven.

All that was over for Toby now. He was in a bog-standard local primary school and it was his absolute *right* to be there. No more pressure, no more selection. He just had to make of it what he could and when he was finished he would go to a local comprehensive. Again with no interviews, no entrance exams. It was his right.

Some of the teachers were brilliant too. And some weren't. Just like at Abbey Hall.

Toby found he actually *liked* his school. The fact that he wasn't the only new boy helped a lot. He and Korfa had stuck together from day one. Both refugees from another culture. Each with something to offer the other. Toby had the best vocabulary and the clearest speaking voice in the class and Korfa had fearlessness and a cheerfulness born of having seen things that made every breath he drew and every bite he ate a cause for celebration.

Not that fearlessness was particularly required in Toby's class. They were a good enough bunch in general, ruled over by a popular teacher. But Korfa's cheerful nature was a tonic for Toby from the first moment they met. Korfa laughed often and long in a pitch that was high even for an eight-year-old, particularly such a tall one. And whenever Korfa appreciated anything he made a point of saying so.

'OH this IS very NICE,' he would declare when presented with a blank sheet of paper on which to draw a picture, or a free school meal courtesy of the council. 'I like THIS very MUCH. Thank YOU so MUCH.'

Korfa made enthusiasm cool.

That was a new concept for Toby, who even at eight

had begun to take on the attitude beloved of boys in any school, posh or state, that the cool thing to do was not to give a stuff about anything.

Korfa gave a stuff about *everything* and by his example invigorated the whole class.

And it wasn't just Toby's attitudes that were changing. Monica and Jimmy also found their eyes being opened and long-held prejudices challenged.

'You know, sometimes I used to listen to Rupert,' Monica said, 'going on and on about how state handouts were actually holding people back and creating a dependency culture and I used to kind of *agree* with him. But the truth is that handouts are the only thing that's keeping us *up*.'

'That's true,' Jimmy admitted.

'I mean without them,' Monica said, her eyes a little teary, 'we'd be on the streets. Our children would probably be taken away.'

'I know,' Jimmy agreed. 'Rupert always was an arsehole.'

'I think we all were.'

A major beneficiary of the parliamentary crisis

Rupert Bennett emerged from the glass and marble headquarters of the Royal Lancashire Bank for the last time.

It was quiet. Deathly quiet.

For the first time in months, no cameras popped and no flashes flashed. Nor was he obliged to fight his way to his car, flanked by security men and lawyers, while journalists shouted impertinent questions at him from behind police barriers.

They were all gone. He had the steps to himself as he descended them one final time. Those steps which for so long he had bestrode like a colossus. For once he was not being called upon to explain how a man who had wreaked havoc on two banks and brought the Treasury to its knees could justify feathering his own pension nest with funds intended to shore up the tottering financial edifice that he had virtually destroyed.

Henry had saved him.

His old friend/enemy. How ironic was that? His old sparring partner had rescued Rupert from the storm.

Because Henry was the story now. The chair of the very parliamentary Select Committee that only the day before had been calling upon Rupert to hand back his pension in a spirit of contrition was now himself engulfed in such a tidal wave of moral criticism that Rupert was suddenly yesterday's news.

Blondel's Bombshell had saved him.

The nation had swapped its outrage over the cynical and deliberate asset-stripping of the institutions on which its prosperity depended for an absolutely brilliant story about a politician who'd claimed his wife's hairdryer on expenses, another who'd had his moat cleaned for free and a third who had a fancy for chocolate teddy bears.

Perhaps, it occurred to Rupert as he bounded down the steps of what was no longer his bank, the run of bad luck which he had recently endured might finally be ending.

But it was not to be.

'Lord Bennett?' a voice said.

Rupert turned and realized that he was not actually alone on the steps. A small, insignificant-looking man had clearly been waiting for him.

'Yes?' Rupert replied with suspicion.

'I was wondering if I could have a few moments of your time. I'd like to ask you a few questions relating to your business transactions.'

So there was one left.

One little oik for whom the penny hadn't dropped that the story had moved on.

'If you wish to discuss business transactions,' Rupert said pompously, 'I suggest you go and see Members of

Parliament like Henry Baker. A hypocrite who, while calling upon me to pay back an entirely legal pension negotiated in good faith after many years of service, sought at the same time to offload the cost of his and his wife's personal grooming on to the taxpayer. Put that in your damn paper and leave me alone.'

'I'm not a journalist, sir, and I'm not interested in your pension plan or in MPs' expenses. I'm a police officer. Detective Inspector Beaumont.' The man brought out a card. 'I deal in financial fraud.'

Rupert had been about to get into his car, but now he stopped and turned.

'Well?' he asked warily.

'I also knew you briefly at university,' Beaumont said.

'I'm afraid I don't recall,' Rupert replied.

'No. I didn't think you would.'

'Is that why you've come to see me?'

'No.'

'Then kindly tell me why you have come, Inspector.'

'I'd like to talk to you about your share trading in Caledonian Granite, Lord Bennett. About transactions you made while working as a financial adviser to the Prime Minister and hence with access to privileged information. It's called insider trading, Lord Bennett.'

Control-crying

'Tonight, Jimmy,' Monica said, her jaw firmly set, 'we're going to control-cry Lillie to sleep.'

The threat of bankruptcy had continued to bring Jimmy and Monica closer together. Closer to each other and closer to the children. Many marriages might have buckled under the strain of so many seismic jolts, but Jimmy and Monica's seemed to gain strength from them. And something in the new-found family solidarity gave Monica the courage she needed to tackle a challenge that they had been putting off ever since Jodie had left.

'Oh God, really?' Jimmy said, unable to disguise the fear in his voice. 'Do we have to? I've got an interview with the bakery at Brent Cross Tesco tomorrow and I really don't need the extra stress.'

'It's time. We have to get Lillie to put herself down. Otherwise we'll be sitting outside her hotel room on her wedding night singing "Morningtown Ride" till she goes to sleep.'

They both knew the theory: babies would never settle down to sleep alone as long as they knew that by crying they could draw their parents back to lull them to sleep with endless hours of soothing stories and songs. Thus ensuring that the parent had no life. The only way to break this crushingly debilitating and time-consuming cycle was to leave the baby to cry.

That was the theory. Wait outside, no matter how long it took, no matter how heartbreaking the screams. Just tough the little bastards out.

Jodie, the nanny without whom one could not do, had done the dreadful deed with Toby, and on the night it was done Monica had had to leave the house.

'He's dying, Jodie!' she had shouted as Toby did his brilliant impression of a baby choking himself to death with tears and snot. 'We have to go to him.'

'He's not dying,' Jodie had replied in a voice as calm and steady as Toby's was glass-shatteringly alarming. 'He's crying because he thinks we'll come, and when he finds out we won't, he'll stop.'

'He'll stop because he's *dead*!'

'Then I guess I go to prison for neglect. It's a risk I'm prepared to take. Now why don't you just go and join Jim at the pub with Robbo. Give me two hours and when you come back we'll have broken the little swine!'

That had been seven years before.

A few years after that, Jodie had done Cressida as well. But now Jimmy and Monica had only each other to look to for help. It was up to them and them alone to gain control of their younger daughter and regain control of their lives.

'We have to do this,' Monica said firmly. 'It says so in *The Big Happy Baby Book*.'

'The only way that book is ever going to get Lillie to

go to sleep on her own is if we whack her over the head with it.'

'Jim, we can't just give up! Otherwise we'll never get to sleep or have sex again.'

'Yes. You're right. I know you're right,' Jimmy admitted, already numb at the idea of the hours of horror ahead, before adding, '*Are* we ever going to have sex again?'

The idea had taken him by surprise. After all, it had been quite a long time. It wasn't that they hadn't had *any* since the day he had been chucked out of the Bell End of the Dildo with a squeezed BlackBerry, but it had been rare. A combination of the never-ending demands of a breast-feeding baby, a curious toddler and a life that was imploding into a black hole of catastrophe had somewhat taken the lead out of Jimmy's pencil and the bite out of his mustard.

'Well . . . aren't we?' Monica asked in a small voice. 'Or are my stretch marks too hideous?'

'Mon, please! You know it's not that. It's . . . well, blimey, darling, you know what it is. We've lost everything.'

'Poor people have sex too, you know,' Monica said. 'In fact from the scrum of kids at Toby's school gate, I think some of them have rather a lot of sex.'

'Right,' Jimmy replied with renewed resolve, 'control-crying. Let's get at it.'

'Yes, let's,' Monica said. 'And we're going to get her

off the final night feed at the same time. The bar's closed.'

'But . . .' Jimmy struggled for an excuse to avoid the all-night misery that awaited them. 'Have you thought about the expense of weaning her? As long as she's on the breast she eats for free!'

'The government won't let us die. We'll apply for emergency formula.'

Monica dug into the pocket of her dressing gown and drew out two sets of earplugs.

Jimmy knew that further protest was pointless. He put his arms around her and hugged her long and hard, as if he were a soldier preparing to go to war, which was pretty much how he felt.

First they put Toby to bed in his little room, warning him to expect a lot of crying, then they put Cressida and Lillie down in theirs, read a couple of stories to them, sang a few rounds of 'Morningtown Ride' – after which Cressie was asleep – and left them.

One second later the screaming began.

It went on for ten minutes. Then twenty, then an hour. During this time both Jimmy and Monica suffered agonies. They loved their children, they loved them at least as much as they loved each other and certainly more than they loved themselves, and they could not bear to hear one of them in such distress. Screaming with longing and fear, choking with the terror of loneliness and separation. Drowning, it seemed, in tears and snot.

But they did not break. Jimmy probably would have done but Monica would not let him.

'We have to get our lives back,' she said, with tears in her eyes, 'for their sake as much as ours.'

And so the long evening wore on. Another hour passed and then ten minutes more . . . and then, long, long after they'd both given up hope, Lillie stopped crying. She was simply too exhausted to continue.

For a moment the silence was too oppressive for them to speak.

'She may be dead,' said Jimmy. 'We need to check.'

'No!' Monica insisted. 'We might wake her up.'

She ran to the baby listener and turned it on. It had not been on before; the last thing they had wanted to do was amplify the nightmare, but now they needed to listen. She had placed the other radio unit on a shelf between Lillie's cot and Cressida's bed. She turned it up to full volume.

Sure enough, they could hear them, breathing, gurgling. *Sleeping*. They were both asleep. Lillie had fallen asleep in the absence of her parents.

And it had taken only two hours and ten minutes.

Jimmy and Monica embraced. The embrace turned into a passionate kiss and before they knew it they were making love.

Later that night the whole family slept through. Lillie, utterly exhausted by crying herself to sleep, did not wake up for her usual night feed. She closed the bar voluntarily.

All in all, it was a very good night.

Too sad to care

It was when Lizzie put her coffee mug down that Jimmy truly realized how fragile she'd become. Because she put it down directly on the polished surface of her beautiful dining table *without a coaster*. Jimmy had never, ever seen her do that in all the nearly twenty years he'd known her.

Lizzie hated rings.

She could spot potential mug or glass marks from across a crowded room. She could sense them. Her ears would prick up, her eyes widen in alarm and she would dash from one room to another, holding out an exquisite Chinese lacquered coaster in her hand, arriving miraculously at exactly the point when some thoughtless guest was about to place the wet bottom of their wine glass on to the gorgeous inlaid wooden lid of her eighteenth-century harpsichord. It was like a superpower. Like one of the X-Men. Lizzie was Coaster Girl, and there was no potential ring on furniture that she could not prevent.

Of course, Robbo himself had been the worst ring-maker of all. For a while Lizzie had called him Bilbo Baggins because wherever he went, a ring would be found. She used to follow him round at parties with a cloth and a stack of amusing little laminated squares depicting bloated British holidaymakers on Spanish beaches (from Lizzie's Coaster Brava range) or lovely plastic discs with the face of a rock star on them (from her Rock 'n' Roller Coaster range).

But that had been when Robbo was alive. Now he was dead and Lizzie, beautiful, full-lipped, full-figured, raven-haired goddess of all things lovely, was thin and drawn and grey-streaked and putting her mug down without a coaster.

Jimmy knew that if she didn't care about leaving a ring any more, she didn't care about anything any more.

'Sometimes I'm just not sure I can face the day,' she told him. 'Honestly, I wish I'd been sitting beside him in the car when he . . . when he . . .'

Killed himself?

Was that what had happened? Lizzie had made it clear at the funeral that she did not believe it and would never believe it. Jimmy didn't believe it either, although at the back of his mind he recognized that it was a possibility.

'Wigan and Wigan are contesting my life-insurance claim,' Lizzie said, as if reading Jimmy's thoughts. 'That awful man Andrew Tanner has written saying they're withholding payment and are prepared to test the claim in court.'

Jimmy could believe it. He used Wigan and Wigan himself, having done so on Robbo and Lizzie's recommendation. He was now behind on all his premiums and the firm had proved one of his more vociferous Webb Street creditors.

'They don't stand a chance, Liz,' Jimmy said. 'They'll have to pay in the end and we'll nail them for the interest too.'

But Jimmy was not entirely sure.

The police had established that although Robbo was certainly over the limit when he crashed he had not been spectacularly drunk, and the CCTV footage of the incident offered no clue as to why the car had swerved so violently. As far as it was possible to establish, it appeared that up until moments before the crash Robbo had been driving normally.

The coroner's verdict remained open.

'But Lizzie,' Jim went on gently, 'currently you're broke, really, really broke, and you have a great many liabilities.' He had come round to help Lizzie with her accounting. 'We need to make a plan for you,' he continued, knowing that it was his father's wisdom he was imparting, not his own.

'I don't need a plan,' Lizzie said in a voice as leaden as it had once been golden. 'The kids are going to be OK. Amanda has managed to squeeze them on to her school bursaries programme, and that's all that matters. It's so kind of her because I know how oversubscribed it is.'

'OK, Lizzie, so the kids have schools to go to. We have to start thinking about you.'

'I don't want to think about me,' Lizzie said, her voice beginning to crack. 'I don't care about me. I deserve this.'

'Why? Why?' Jimmy asked. 'Why do you deserve this?'

Now the tears came in earnest. She looked so washed out, Jimmy wondered where she was still finding them.

'Oh Jimmy, supposing he *did* mean to do it? I mean just for a moment, for one insane, distraught moment, and then it was too late? Supposing I didn't love him well enough for him to know that I wouldn't have minded about him losing all the money. If in all those years I hadn't shown him that he could trust me to support him through anything . . .'

'No, Lizzie. That's madness. Don't go there,' Jimmy said. 'He was going to get some fags. He lost concentration.'

'What if he left me, Jim?' Lizzie said, openly weeping. 'What if the insurance man is right and Robbo left me? If he cared more about his shame and his failure than he did about me? About living *for me*! Because if that were true then I don't care enough about me either! I don't care enough to bother about anything at all.'

'Liz,' Jim protested, 'it was an accident and it's time to pull yourself together. You're not like me, busted flat

399

with nothing to offer. You're Lizzie of Lizzie Food, your name's still good. You can get out there and make money. Just think of something beautiful and sell it.'

'I don't think I will find anything beautiful ever again,' said Lizzie.

Art imitating life

In a blinding moment of inspiration, the solution to Jimmy and Monica's mounting fiscal problems dawned upon them both.

They would become novelists.

The precedents were extremely encouraging.

'Look at Jeffrey Archer,' Jimmy said. 'He was broke, wasn't he? So he wrote *Kane and Abel*. Brilliant. Simple as that, he had a problem, he fixed it.'

'And J. K. Rowling,' Monica said.

'Exactly. Another classic case. Broke. Single mum. Eking out coffees in an Edinburgh café. Writes *Harry Potter*. Problem solved. Bloody obvious when you think about it. That's what we need to do.'

'Of course it is. We'll start tonight.'

And so after they'd put the children to bed they made

a pot of coffee, allowed themselves a small plate of digestive biscuits and sat down to think.

Within an hour the ideas were taking shape.

Monica decided to write a children's book that adults would enjoy. She wanted it to contain lots of adventure and magic and dragons and dark forces. But (and this was terribly important) it would be very different from *Harry Potter*. That was essential.

She planned to set her story in a pre-human world which was populated by trolls (although in her mind they looked more like pixies than trolls). It would be a sort of medieval society, but with trolls instead of people. The story would take place at the court of the great Troll King. Here, a lowly but feisty troll girl working in the scullery would suddenly discover that she had magic powers! She would be the unwitting inheritor of dark secrets and ancient sorcery.

'There'll be a wonderful scene when she first works it out,' Monica explained. 'She'll spill all the food on the floor and be heading for a terrible beating when all of a sudden she'll make it right again! Just by wishing it! The spilt jugs full, the ruined pies back in their dishes. She doesn't know how it happens but it does happen. Anyway, the great Troll Wizard hears about it and, recognizing that the girl is special, takes her on as one of his apprentices, but the evil Wraith Goddess from the Dark Side also hears about the girl and vows to steal her power. What do you think?' said Monica with great excitement.

'It's Harry Potter,' said Jimmy.

'*What!* Don't be ridiculous!' Monica snapped. 'It's about trolls and the hero's a girl.'

'Yes. It's about a troll girl Harry Potter who goes to magic school.'

'She doesn't go to magic school, she's apprenticed to a wizard.'

'Having previously been put upon and bullied.'

'Of course.'

'Will she make friends with some of the other apprentices?'

'Well, obviously.'

'A bookish one and a geek?'

'No! Absolutely not,' Monica replied angrily. 'You're being totally negative. I don't think the two stories are remotely similar.'

'They aren't remotely similar, Mon,' Jimmy said, smiling, 'they're very, very similar.'

'But my story is about *trolls*.'

Jimmy shrugged and returned to his laptop. He had been typing furiously when Monica interrupted him with her troll idea.

'All right then,' Monica said huffily, 'what have you got?'

'Do you want to hear?' Jimmy sounded rather smug.

'Of course I want to hear.'

'It's going to blow you away.'

'Don't be so sure.'

'Us,' Jimmy said happily.

'What do you mean, "us"?'

'I'm going to write a story about us,' he said. 'At least about us up to a point when it gets a bit dark.'

Monica looked suspicious.

'How do you mean it gets dark?' she said. 'How dark? It's not going to be all sex scenes, is it? Because that I would *not* be happy with.'

'No. No sex . . . Well, actually I don't know yet. But possibly a murder, certainly a suspicious death. It's about this guy who does exactly what I did, right? Screws up, buys a street five minutes before the recession hits and ends up in the same shit as us, right?'

'So far I think people would rather read about magical trolls,' said Monica. 'Is there anything else?'

'Yeah, of course. That's where the plot kicks in. This bloke decides the way out of all his troubles is to do a canoe thing!'

'A canoe thing?'

'You know, that bloke who went off in a canoe and faked his death for the insurance. People are always doing it. There was an MP, John Stonehouse, he left his clothes on a beach and then turned up years later in Australia. That's what my man decides to do. Fake his own death.'

'Maybe he should just try to write a novel like us.'

'No, no. Honestly, Mon, this is great. I've got it all worked out. You remember Bob?'

'Bob?'

'The tramp at Webb Street who sleeps in one of the houses sometimes. He's a total wreck. I told you about him, right? Every time I go there I expect to find him dead.'

'Oh yes, I remember.'

'Well, get this. My man, in my story, has the same thing, a tramp hanging around his development site. And one day this bloke *does* find him dead.'

'The tramp?'

'Yeah, that's right. My hero turns up and goes in one of the houses and finds the tramp dead . . . or,' Jimmy's eyes filled with gleeful enthusiasm, 'perhaps my bloke kills him?'

'Why would he want to kill a tramp? Is he a nutter who kills homeless people like in that horrible *American Psycho* book?'

'No,' said Jimmy, 'he's very sane. Very together. He has a plan and he needs a corpse.'

'I thought he needed a canoe.'

'I'm not *doing* the canoe story, Mon!' Jimmy was becoming ever so slightly frustrated and suspicious that Monica was being deliberately obstructive because he'd poured cold water on her troll wizard idea. 'That's just an example of a famous insurance scam. My story's totally different.'

'Oh. Well, you didn't say.'

'I'm *trying* to say. This tramp's got ID, see,' Jimmy went

on, 'just like my bloke at Webb Street. It's hanging round his neck, an old *Big Issue* seller's badge and accreditation. Now it's already occurred to the man in my story that with the way things are going in his life, what with the spiralling debt and fear of bankruptcy and all that, a false ID might not be such a bad thing to own.'

'Is that what *you*'ve been thinking, Jimmy?' Monica asked in sudden alarm, 'or did you just make it up for your story?'

'We-ell,' Jimmy admitted, 'it did sort of occur to me before, you know, just as a kind of fantasy thought. But the point is my man has been planning to go through with it.'

'Stealing the tramp's ID?'

'Exactly. At first that's all he has in mind. Pinch his badge while he's unconscious from sniffing petrol and use it to open a bank account. That way if my guy ever gets his hands on a bit of money it won't have to go straight to his creditors.'

'Jimmy!' Monica said angrily. 'You *have* been thinking about doing this! Don't tell me you've just come up with all this now?'

'I've said it had occurred to me, Mon,' Jimmy admitted, 'but just as an idea. I wasn't going to *do* it. It's a story!'

'Well, it had better be. Identity theft is a serious crime, Jim, whoever you steal from.'

'Believe me, Mon, this guy would not miss it. I doubt he even knows the ID is still round his neck. I doubt if he even knows his name any more. You wouldn't so much be stealing an identity as reincarnating it.'

'Jimmy!'

'All right, all right,' Jimmy said, smiling. 'I've told you, I'm just using the idea for my story. Anyway, like I say, that's the bloke's plan, pinch the ID while the tramp's asleep. But then of course a better idea occurs to him. Because on the day he's going to do it, he turns up at the street and finds the tramp dead.'

'Of natural causes?' Monica asked.

'If you can call sniffing petrol and drinking meths a natural cause, yes. But *maybe*, to make the story darker, my man actually kills him.'

'Just to get his ID? I thought you said he could lift it off him when he's unconscious.'

Jimmy grinned.

'Ah! But now he's had a better idea. A canoe idea. You see, he's in so much trouble with the debts that it occurs to my man that the best thing of all would be to . . . disappear.'

'Disappear?'

'Well, not so much disappear actually. But die.'

'The man, you mean? Not the tramp?'

'Yes, the man. You see, if he dies all his problems die with him, all his debts, any other shit I put on him. Maybe he's being done for fraud, I don't know. But whatever, his life is ruined. He needs a fresh start. A clean sheet. If he could "die" he could get all that. What's more, if he can make it look like an accident his wife gets the insurance. A spare corpse gives him the chance he needs.'

'How?'

'Well, it's obvious. The tramp's about his height, right? What my man needs to do is to turn that tramp's corpse into *his* corpse and then burn it, OK? All he needs to do is to plant a few personal things alongside Bob's body. You know, his watch, his wedding ring, maybe he's got some distinctive dental work which he gets removed and puts in Bob's dead mouth. Of course all Bob's teeth have long since rotted—'

'This is revolting, Jim,' Monica protested.

'It's not a chick book, I'll admit that,' said Jimmy. 'Anyway, my man then torches his own building. A real white-hot conflagration which totally consumes the body. The next day the fire brigade find a few charred human remains, that's all. Remains which, because of the molten watch or the teeth or whatever, are soon identified with the debt-ridden owner of the property – who is now clean away with a brand-new identity and all his troubles behind him. What do you think?'

Jimmy sat back with a big smile and stole the last digestive.

'Well, it's not bad, I suppose,' Monica admitted, 'if you can make the characters interesting.'

'Of course I can. It's *us*, isn't it. Aren't we interesting?'

'Well, we are to us. I don't know about to anybody else.'

'Of course we are. Anyway, I've got a murder. That's always interesting. My man will definitely have to kill the tramp rather than just stumble on his corpse.'

'I suppose so. Proactive is always good in a story,' Monica agreed. 'But personally I still think my troll girl magician is a better idea.'

Coping

Jimmy and Monica's new life was coming to seem more and more normal – as far as it's possible to be normal when you're living from hand to mouth, huddled together in a six-storey house with the largest whirlpool spa in London slowly stagnating above you and a four-car private garage just a lift ride below.

There was certainly a normality which most Londoners would have recognized to their daily budgetary struggles. Struggles in which every penny was carefully counted and apportioned in order to cover the basic essentials for the family.

There was also a kind of normality (although a far

less common one) in Jimmy and Monica's efforts to deal with the increasingly disastrous fallout from their previous existence. They still discussed vast sums of money around the tea table just as they had always done. Twenty grand here, a hundred grand there. This property, that property. Share portfolios. Pension schemes. The only difference was that now the sums they discussed were debts, not assets. When they talked about the price of a work of art they liked, a gorgeous gown or a shiny chrome ten-slot toaster it was with a view to selling it, not buying it.

They divided these two worlds, day-to-day survival and past and future debt, between them, one taking charge of each. Monica looked after what they called 'reality'. It was up to her to make ends meet on the meagre state benefits and emergency hardship payments that she negotiated with Social Security. Jimmy, on the other hand, was in charge of the insanity portfolio, which meant he had to attempt to make sense of the legal and financial issues surrounding their enormous debts.

Two budgets. One tea table.

'If we do potatoes and cheese tonight and tomorrow,' Monica said, pen in hand, making small piles of coins in front of her, 'we will have two pounds fifty left for Sunday lunch so I think we can run to a chop each for you, me and Toby. There's a fantastic two-for-one promotion at Asda, but I'm holding off to see what Lidl offer.'

'Sounds good,' Jimmy replied, punching up spread-sheets on his laptop. 'The Royal Lancashire have foreclosed on Webb Street so it's off our hands now. That means they've taken on the debts on the work done, so David's company are finally off our backs too.'

'Great.'

'Yeah, but this house is all debt. We still owe seven million on it.'

'Oh well,' Monica said with a confused shrug, returning to her own lists. 'Toby's going to need new shoes soon. There's some quite good trainers at TK Maxx for six pounds.'

'Sounds reasonable.'

'Yes, I think it is. But we don't actually have six pounds. Not this week.'

'Oh.'

'Do you think you could get the RLB to add it to what we owe them? Seven million and six wouldn't make much difference to them, would it?'

'I don't suppose it would, but sadly things don't work like that. When you owe a bank seven million they don't lend you any more.'

'No. I suppose not. Well, Toby's going to need new shoes.'

'We could try the BBS.'

'I don't think we'll be lucky.'

The BBS was the Bank of the Back of the Sofa, a blanket term for strip-searching the house. For some time they had been able to supplement their meagre resources by wandering through the *Marie Celeste*-like rooms of the now-unused upper floors of their house. Digging behind cushions, delving into jars and between cracks in the beautifully sanded and varnished floorboards. They had had some remarkable windfalls that way. Scrunched fivers had been found in old trousers. Dresser tops had revealed treasure troves of foreign coins that could be exchanged at a place on the Portobello Road (at ruinous rates). Toby's desk drawer had contained a bank book started by his granddad at the City Bank which Jimmy had quietly snaffled, leaving behind an IOU. Each trawl, however, yielded less and less and after a few months of trying the same trick Monica clearly thought there was little chance of them lucking upon enough change from their old life to buy a pair of kids' trainers.

Jimmy glanced down at his wrist.

'I could probably get fifty quid for this, you know.'

His fake Rolex. He'd worn it for more than fifteen years. Through all the good times he'd never replaced it. Why bother? The thing worked perfectly well and still looked great as far as Jimmy was concerned. What was more, once he'd got rich nobody ever dreamed it was a fake, which he thought was rather amusing. And of course it had sentimental value. It had been the very first thing that he and Monica had talked about, just seconds after they'd met and he'd tried to pull her and she'd ticked him off for thinking she'd be impressed with a Rolex. Monica had often joked since that if it had been the real thing she might never have gone for that coffee with him at all, because it was one thing to be a cocky little sod who thought ostentatious displays of wealth looked cool, but it was quite another to pay two thousand pounds to be one.

Jimmy smiled at the memory. He saw that Monica was smiling too.

'Hey,' she said, 'you can't flog the fake Rolex. It was the thing that first attracted me to you. That and the fact that you called yourself the Jimster.'

They both laughed.

'Besides,' Monica went on, 'you need a watch, so you'd only have to buy another one. We'll get the shoes. I'll speak to the people at the Social tomorrow. They might make some kind of emergency payment. Otherwise you and me can skip the chops on Sunday and we'll just do one for Toby. That will free up a pound. You can often get a good pair for that from the Oxfam shop.'

'Excellent thinking.'

'And there's the unclaimed lost property at the school. Sharif gets all his stuff from there. He doesn't mind at all.'

'Loving Korfa's dad. Amazing bloke.'

'And Korfa.'

'Absolutely. That friendship's been a godsend, hasn't

it? Him and Toby have really looked out for each other.'

'Weird, isn't it?' Monica said. 'That was the thing we worried about most, even more than the knives. I mean if we're honest. All those kids who were trying to learn English as well as keep up with the national curriculum. Classes stuffed with confused immigrants making it impossible for anybody to learn. We were dreading it.'

'I suppose we were.'

'And now a confused immigrant with minimal English has turned out to be Toby's best mate.'

'His English isn't minimal any more either. Thanks partly to Tobes. I'm pretty proud of that actually.'

'Good old Tobes.'

'Yeah,' said Jimmy. 'Nice to know there's at least one alpha male in the family.'

'Jimmy,' Monica said, '*stop it.*'

Slippery customer

Inspector Beaumont sat opposite Rupert Bennett, trying to decide at what point to show his hand.

It would have to be played so carefully.

The card he held was no ace. A jack at best, or even a ten. He knew he did not have enough evidence to convict

Bennett directly. He and his team of police and Inland Revenue accountants were almost there, but not quite. There was easily enough circumstantial evidence to embarrass Lord Bennett severely but there just wasn't enough to secure a conviction.

And of course Rupert was a man who could handle embarrassment.

It was a doubly irritating situation for Beaumont because his target was turning out to be just as smug and supercilious as he remembered from their brief acquaintance in Sussex. Beaumont did not normally take a personal view of anybody in his line of duty, but Rupert really got on his nerves. The man seemed to think himself untouchable. He positively gloated over Beaumont's inability to nail him cold. It was as if it made up a little bit for all the other reverses Bennett had suffered at the RLB.

Beaumont was also forced to admit privately that it was painful to him that Bennett showed absolutely no sign of remembering that they had once briefly shared a house. The incident had left such a deep impression on Beaumont, but had clearly made no impact at all on his sneering adversary.

'You'll find nothing, my friend. Absolutely nothing.' Rupert beamed. 'Principally, of course, because I've done nothing wrong. But if I had done something wrong, which I haven't, but if I *had*, I think I'm rather too clever a chap to let myself get cornered by PC Plod.

You've searched and you've searched and you've come up with zilch.'

'Not quite zilch,' Beaumont pointed out, accepting an elegant glass cup filled with the creamiest caffè latte from a lovely young PA. 'If I had zilch I can assure you I wouldn't be here.'

'Perhaps you just prefer my coffee to the swill I imagine they give you at Scotland Yard.'

They were meeting in the splendid premises of Lord Bennett's aggressive new company. Maximalism offered investment advice to those gutsy traders who were making themselves ready to profit from the much-predicted bounce when it came.

'Zilch in terms of anything that would interest a judge or a jury,' Rupert replied, 'and quite frankly if you continue to waste my time with your silly questions and deeply hurtful insinuations, I may be forced to get my lawyers to make a claim against you for police harassment.'

'I don't deny that I am currently stumped, Lord Bennett,' Beaumont admitted. 'You've been extremely careful in your dealings. You set an excellent example to fraudsters everywhere.'

'Mind your language, Inspector,' Rupert said. 'You are being recorded.'

'Oh, I don't doubt that, my lord,' Beaumont went on, 'but I also don't think there's any chance of you trying to sue me. We both know what you did, and while I don't have enough to get a criminal conviction I think you know that I've got enough circumstantial to defend myself should you bring a libel action. It's me that wants to meet you in court, not you that wants to meet me. So I will say what I want. And what I want to say is that you, Lord Bennett, are a liar and a crook and I'm going to get you.'

Rupert pretended to yawn and took a cigarette from what looked like a solid silver box.

'You could arrest me for this, I suppose.' He waved the cigarette about. 'Apparently a man's no longer allowed to smoke in his own office in case his PA gets cancer. What bollocks, eh?'

Rupert lit his cigarette and drew deeply on it.

'No smoking in the workplace,' he said. 'Smoke-free building etc. Are you going to nick me?'

'No,' said Beaumont, 'not for smoking.'

'Then I think we're done, Inspector.' Rupert smiled. 'I am a very busy man.'

'Of course you are,' Beaumont agreed. 'You've a new business to run. And a fat pension to spend and no doubt many a hidden offshore portfolio to manage. The ill-gotten fruits of the as yet unproven insider trading, eh?'

'Look, Inspector, do forgive my French, but why don't you just fuck off and bother someone else?'

Beaumont got up.

But did not leave. It was time to play his jack.

416

A good card, but not a great one. It would still require bluff.

'You know what I've found, Lord Bennett?' Beaumont said after a pause.

'You've found nothing, Inspector. We've already established that. And I think I told you to fuck off.'

'I've found,' Beaumont continued, 'that the one thing which invariably brings down even the cleverest of criminals . . . is vanity.'

'Really?"

'Yes, really.'

Beaumont was speaking in the most easy and conversational of tones. As if he was exchanging opinions with a friend rather than fixing his prey with a steely eye. 'And the funny thing is that the cleverer the criminal, the more vain he usually becomes.'

'*Please*, Inspector. Is this really going anywhere?'

'You're a clever man, Lord Bennett. And obviously a vain one. Beautiful clothes, lovely PAs, a gorgeous young girlfriend, I believe.'

'You really do have to fuck off now or I *will* bring a harassment action against you.'

Still Beaumont did not move.

'So there you are, a vain, pompous man, with all this incredible insider information that you get from your privileged position as a government crony. A position you got for being so *clever*. Insider information which you are only able to use because you are so clever.

417

And it's frustrating, isn't it? Because the cleverer you are, the less anybody can know about it. It all has to be so *secret*. Isn't that frustrating? It must be. Even the money you make has to be hidden. Hidden genius producing hidden profit. Where's the fun in that?'

Bennett did not answer. Nor did he continue to threaten Beaumont. So far Beaumont had played his hand well.

'So, like many clever men before you,' the policeman went on, 'you occasionally gab a bit. Just so people will know who *da man* is. You'll be amazed how often it happens. A man goes to every possible length to cover every single clue to his crime and then he boasts about it to his mates or to some girl down at the pub.'

Rupert was not smiling quite so confidently now.

Clearly something in what Beaumont was saying was ringing tiny bells. It had been a long punt but Beaumont could see in Rupert's eyes that it had made an impression. Beaumont pressed his point home.

'Like anybody, you want your *mates* to look up to you. You want them to think you're one hell of a bloke. So maybe you let slip a bit of information, do them a good turn, just for the swank of it. To let them know that you are a clever, clever bloke who can turn knowledge into money.'

Beaumont's tone was becoming less conversational word by word, more confrontational, more like a man who might be on the right track.

'Did you ever do that, Lord Bennett?' he said. 'Did you ever let some pal in on the info over a pint or a glass of wine? Just assuming that that pal would know that it was sensitive stuff? Just assuming he'd be as careful as you were about how he used it? Maybe you didn't even think it through that far. Maybe money was coming so easily to you that you came to believe it was your right. Your right and the right of any favoured associate.'

'I thought we were talking about a clever man, Inspector,' Rupert replied. 'Only fools gab to fools.'

Rupert had had time to pull himself together now and to any but the most astute observer he would have looked like a man without a care in world.

But of course Inspector Beaumont *was* the most astute observer, and somewhere deep down behind Rupert's impeccable sangfroid and arrogant self-assurance Beaumont sensed fear.

'Not in my experience,' Beaumont said.

'Well, Inspector? Your experience doesn't seem to be getting you anywhere. I suppose if you refuse to get out of my office I shall have to leave you to it as I have a meeting. Help yourself to cigarettes, won't you, and there's one or two fine single malts in the cabinet. I used to get given them all the time when I ran the RLB.'

'When you ruined the RLB.'

Rupert smiled and got up from behind his desk but Beaumont blocked his way, only five foot six to Rupert's six feet but an intimidating figure nonetheless.

'All I have to do,' Beaumont said, staring Rupert directly in the eye, 'is find one fool. One easy-going guy who never really *got it* in the first place. The original template for the phrase "more money than sense". Now if I could find a man like that, a man who was a friend of yours, a man with less brains but far, far more charm than you, Rupert. A man everybody liked, including you. Someone you just *wanted to impress*. Someone you couldn't resist showing off in front of. Now if ever you tipped off a man like that I'll bet he wasn't careful what he did with the tip. Which means I'll be able to find him. In fact . . . he wasn't. And I have.'

'Have what?'

'I *have* found him, Lord Bennett.'

Beaumont paused for a moment to let this sink in.

'Really?' Rupert replied and still it took a sharp eye indeed to see that he was rattled.

'Yes, really. Do you want to know who it is?'

Rupert stayed silent now.

'He's an old university friend of yours,' Beaumont continued. 'You shared a house with him in Sussex. And in answer to your question, yes, I have finished. For now.'

Teacher training

Jimmy and Monica were beginning, in a tentative sort of way, to make new friendships. They often bumped into Korfa and his dad in the park and Monica had started going into the school each morning to help slow readers in the younger classes. Of course she had to take Cressie and Lillie with her, but the school was so desperate for help that they were happy for her to do so. The class sizes were thirty-plus (as opposed to fifteen to twenty at Abbey Hall), and what with the language difficulties and the presence of some children with behavioural problems, the staff were terribly stretched. Monica had been welcomed with open arms and soon found herself doing four mornings a week as an unpaid teaching assistant. She didn't mind. Some of the kids were nightmares, but most of them were great, and even the nightmares sometimes revealed themselves not to be nightmares at all, just a bit different.

Monica was pleased to be able to keep an eye on Toby's progress and, having done so, to stop worrying about him. He was blessed with his father's good nature and had adjusted well. He'd loved his old school, but not at the end. Being a poor boy in a rich kids' school had been hard. At Caterham Road a lot of families were poor and no family was rich.

Of course, Monica and Jimmy knew that no kid from

Caterham Road Primary had ever made the leap to Oxbridge. There was no hot-housing there and the next step for Toby would be one of the three local comprehensives, one of which was generally considered to be bloody awful. Having said that, they all had sixth forms and lots of kids seemed to get decent qualifications. Many went on to university and Toby's teacher assured Jimmy that those who did fared very well.

They had, after all, learned to get by early on.

'If every inner-city state school kid joined the so-called underclass,' the teacher said, 'you'd have wall-to-wall hoodies from here to the home counties.'

'I used to think that was exactly what we did have,' Monica admitted.

It wasn't that she and Jimmy enjoyed being poor.

In the majority of ways it was sheer hell. To lie awake at night worrying about the few pounds Toby was required to find for a school museum trip. Or worse, the money needed simply for food.

Jimmy had sometimes thought in his old life that wealth was not all it was cracked up to be. He had occasionally argued, when particularly stressed about a deal, that a vast income brought its own pressures. He now understood that, however hard they might have seemed at the time, those pressures were as a molehill to a mountain compared to the pressure of raising a family on Income Support.

Nonetheless the challenges their new life created

continued to bring out unexpected strengths in all of them. They were pulling together as a family as never before. Even Cressida, who at three years old could scarcely have been expected to understand what had happened, seemed to throw less of her diced carrot on the floor these days, perhaps sensing from her mother's anxious face that each plateful of food was now precious.

'I really think she understands that we need her to do her bit,' Monica observed.

'Bollocks,' Jimmy replied. 'I think it's just that now we don't bribe her to eat it with biscuits and sweets she's actually hungry.'

Of necessity they all spent much more time together. There was no money for babysitters and nowhere they could afford to go anyway. There were no more meetings to attend except down at the Social or at the school. No business lunches or dinners. In fact, very little social life left at all.

It wasn't that the old Sussex gang had completely rejected each other. Not consciously anyway. Perhaps it was just that having met so regularly and for so long as a golden generation, it was simply too painful to come together with most of them in such straitened circumstances.

Jimmy and Monica still saw Lizzie, primarily in an effort to prevent her from breaking down completely, but even those visits were becoming less frequent as

Lizzie withdrew further and further within herself. Amanda spent most of her time in the country. Henry and Jane were lying low after the Blondel affair, and they had not seen David and Laura since the Webb Street debacle.

Around this time, however, Jimmy did bump into David again. At the school gate, of all places.

Jimmy was waiting to pick up Toby. He still sometimes felt a little uncomfortable and out of place, although less so than he had at first.

Around him were numerous other parents and carers, older siblings and pre-school tots. Most were poorly dressed, in cheap trainers, tracksuits, leggings and anoraks. Jimmy's clothes, all bought before his redundancy, were of superb quality but he was always careful not to appear too smart. Toby, like any kid, hated his parents to stand out and Jimmy had no wish to stand out either. One thing he had no need to be embarrassed about was his fake Rolex. Compared to some of the shiny yellow bling that many of the dads wore, it was positively dowdy.

Jimmy looked discreetly about him at the other parents, wondering if he was in fact the poorest person in the whole crowd. All of them were probably in debt, all of them at the limits of whatever credit they had once been afforded. But not in debt to the tune of millions and millions of pounds. Not at the limit of a credit that had once seemed limitless. Jimmy's debts dwarfed theirs by a thousandfold. Did that make him poorer than them? Jimmy decided that it didn't, not really. Debt was debt and if you were in it you were screwed.

'Jimmy?'

He looked up and was surprised to see David standing before him. David with one or two new sartorial touches. White glasses today, a tiny goatee beard, long sideburns and a rakish-looking shoulder bag.

'David!'

They shared the moment of embarrassment that people who should have been in contact with each other but haven't been feel when they accidentally meet.

'I'd been meaning to call . . .' said Jimmy.

'Me too,' David replied.

'Blimey,' Jimmy added, 'what are you doing here then?'

'What do you mean, what am I doing here? What are you doing here?'

'This is our school. Toby goes here.'

'No! Wow. This is my gig.'

'Gig?'

'I'm going to be working here. Well, work experience actually, although I think they might find it's an experience for them too.'

'Working? In a school?'

'Yeah, I'm retraining. As a teacher,' David said with a smile. 'The government's set up this fast-track six-month thing for professional people. Reckons schools need people like us and let me tell you, from what I've seen, they're bloody right. Lots of architects and bankers are having a crack at it.'

'That's amazing. Well done, Dave. I'm trying to get a job shelf-stacking.'

'Why don't you try teaching?'

'I reckon my skills are a bit specific for that, Dave. Don't think kids need lessons in how to be an arsehole.'

They both laughed. For a moment it was like old times. A moment which morphed almost immediately into a mutual but unspoken realization that it was not like old times and never would be again.

'So Toby goes here then?'

'Yeah. What about yours? Did Tilly join Saskia at St Hilda's as planned?' Jimmy asked.

'Yeah. We can still afford that,' David said. 'Laura's got loads of work actually. The more foreclosures there are, the more lawyers they seem to need.'

'Right. I think I'm part of that equation myself. Not that I can afford a lawyer, but my bank certainly can.'

There was a moment's pause. This reminder of the reversal in Jimmy's fortunes made them both feel uncomfortable.

'So,' said Jimmy, 'if Laura's still bringing home enough moolah, what are you doing this for?'

'I can't sit around all day. It kills you. And I've always quite fancied the idea of teaching.'

'Yeah? Lots of people seem to be saying that these days.'

'I have to tell you that the real teachers, the ones entering the profession the proper way, absolutely hate us. You know, the ones who've done the whole three-year teacher training thing. They think we fucked up our own professions and now we want to fuck up theirs. But what can you do? In a recession it's every man for himself.'

'That's right, I suppose,' Jimmy said, although his expression suggested that he wasn't entirely sure. 'So I'll be seeing you around for a while then?'

'Just a couple of weeks. It's part of the course,' David replied. 'I doubt I'd actually end up teaching here. Not enough facilities.'

There was a pause.

'Well, see you around then. I'll call,' David said.

'Yeah. Absolutely,' Jimmy replied, knowing that he wouldn't.

Taking back what's theirs

Jimmy could scarcely believe that he was facing the prospect of being forced to file for bankruptcy, a situation that only a year before he would have thought of as a kind of death.

Bankruptcy.

He could remember the word from his youth, when his father would mention it as if it was the plague. He'd pull a dreadful, gloomy face and tell his wife about the awful fate awaiting bank customers who had over-stretched themselves and how hard he himself had tried to help them stave it off.

'When you're bankrupt,' Derek Corby had told Jimmy as a boy, 'you've lost all control. Your life is taken out of your hands and it can take years to get it back. Sometimes you never do get it back.'

The funny thing was, Jimmy didn't really care any more. He'd lost control anyway.

The real problem wasn't bankruptcy. Bankruptcy he could face.

The real problem was eviction. That was the terror that continued to haunt him and Monica.

The bank could force them from the two floors of their house that they had made home and the council would then place them in a dreaded Bed and Breakfast. This was the appalling prospect which Jimmy's parents were trying so hard to help them avoid with their monthly standing order, a standing order which, as Derek said, 'showed willing', but which did not even scratch the surface of the interest on the *interest* on his debt.

The threat of eviction haunted them. And then one evening, Jimmy hit upon the solution.

'It's not going to happen, Mon,' he said. 'I won't let it. We are *never* going into emergency accommodation.'

'What will you do?' Monica asked, putting baby bottles into soapy water to soak.

'I'll tell you what I'll do,' Jimmy replied, as he mashed up boiled carrot and apple and spooned the resulting mush into the compartments of an ice-cube tray ready to be frozen and made to last all week. 'I'm going to do what I used to do. What I always did do, even before I was rich. I'm going to dodge, I'm going to weave, I'm going to improvise and take my chance.'

'Yes, but what are you *actually* going to do?' Monica said, smiling at this reminder of just what a Jack the lad Jimmy could be.

'I'm going to move us into a house in Webb Street. That's what I'm going to fucking do.'

'Don't swear, Daddy,' came a sleepy voice from the top of the unlit stairs.

'Daddy said fudging, darling,' Monica called out.

'No he fudging didn't,' came the reply.

'Yes he did, now go to sleep.' Monica turned back to Jimmy and spoke in a lower voice. 'Don't you remember, darling? We don't own Webb Street any more.'

'No,' said Jimmy, 'and nor do any of the other people who are living there rent-free. They're squatters. And that's what we'll be. We're going to squat the street we used to own. How's that for irony?'

Crusty Nimbys

Despite the radical nature of their lifestyle choice, the squatters of Webb Street were beginning to develop some distinctly bourgeois attitudes.

None of them would ever have imagined themselves as Not In My Back Yarders, the kind of people who are all for development and change as long as it doesn't affect them. After all, as squatters they themselves were usually the targets of Nimbys, folk who could see the logic in the homeless occupying empty properties but didn't want squatters moving in next door or, worse still, taking up residence in their holiday homes. The problem was that when you came down to it *everyone* had a back yard, even squatters, and in this case it was the other end of Webb Street.

The undeveloped bit. The rotting, neglected, rat- and bug-infested, boarded-up and broken-windowed bit that Jimmy had not got to before the recession hit. But it wasn't the rotting properties that the efficient and highly organized 'top end' squatters objected to, it was Bob the tramp.

He just *so* brought down the tone of the street. Of course the various activists, eco warriors, cycle dispatch riders and trapeze artists who had squatted the top-end houses would not have put it that way themselves. They didn't hold with snobbery or elitism in any shape or form. The world and all the houses on it were, as far as they were concerned, common property.

It was just that Bob was so utterly revolting.

Stinking as he did, and caked in blood from whatever it was he was coughing up, he hung around, shambling up and down the street, begging at their doors. This was not what proper squatting was about. Proper squatting wasn't about screwed-up substance abusers. That was what small-minded fascists *thought* squatting was about.

Proper squatting was organized, politicized. It was a legitimate and responsible lifestyle choice taken by legitimate and responsible people. Bob was giving the wrong impression altogether. When journalists came down to write about their new and radical initiative in sustainable urban management taking place in Webb Street, those responsible for the initiative wanted their efforts to be reported in the righteous and glowing manner that they believed to be appropriate.

And they didn't want a pustulous petrol head screwing up the photo opportunity.

These squatters thought of themselves as custodians

of a precious human resource. Better tenants in every way than any absentee landlord. Caring for the houses they occupied, improving them, bringing them to life. *Property for People, not Profits* was their mantra. They were not scroungers, they were not freeloaders, they were not ne'er-do-wells. They were in fact the future. And it worked.

Bob didn't fit into that mould at all. Bob was just a plain old-fashioned tramp and his presence was a constant reminder to the happy house occupiers of the fact that they themselves were only one eviction from the street. That much as they liked to see themselves as legitimate custodians of urban resources, to the rest of society they were just Bob with a college education and rings through their lips. Bob's presence connected them with everything that the public feared most about the radicalized homeless, all the clichés that they fought so hard to dispel with their careful property management and their commitment to supporting the council's recycling policies.

And besides, on a purely hygienic and aesthetic level, the squatters of Webb Street did not much like living next door to a festering, stinking, disease-ridden tramp who was beginning to attract more of his ilk.

They wished he would just fuck off.

Unfortunately he didn't seem to have any intention of doing so. Instead he continued to live in several of the houses at the bottom end of the street, the end to which Jimmy was forced to go in his search for an empty property.

It was not a little frustrating for Jimmy to walk down Webb Street from the top end, past all the nearly completed and beautifully renovated houses. Had he thought of it sooner he might have squatted one himself, but he hadn't and now every single decent property had long since been grabbed.

There were slogans and posters in most of the windows:

> *Power to the People*
> *Government is crime*
> *Property is theft*

Property might be theft, Jimmy thought to himself, but that hadn't stopped the new tenants from fixing locks on all the doors and windows in order to secure their occupation. But he was not one to waste time in pointless regret. He would simply have to find the least worst property at the other end of the street and get on with it.

Once Jimmy had made a decision he was usually pretty energetic about following it through and the idea of making a family squat in Webb Street was no exception. The morning after he had had his idea and for many days afterwards he made the long trip to Webb Street by bicycle and worked hard at making one of the houses he used to own habitable.

'All the good houses have already gone,' he told Monica. 'The whole street's crammed with super-cool, beardy, dreadlocky anarchist types with bald, pierced, tattooed girlfriends who work in circuses or sell falafel at markets. But up at the other end, where we never even got round to starting the conversions, hardly anybody's bothered at all. That old tramp I told you about still hangs around. He's going to be our neighbour if he doesn't die first.'

'Lovely,' Monica replied without enthusiasm.

'Anything is better than a council Bed and Breakfast, Mon.'

'But how will we get Toby back to Notting Hill for school each morning? He's really settled in, we can't make him move again.'

'We've still got our bikes. We'll cycle like I've been doing. It takes about an hour.'

'An hour's cycle ride to school,' Monica protested, 'then an hour back? He'll be shattered.'

Jimmy could see from Monica's face that she was about to list the incredible danger that such a mammoth daily journey would involve. She was no doubt picturing her first-born wrapped round the bull bars of some speeding Humvee driven by a mad nanny who was late for her Pilates class.

'Mon,' Jim said firmly, 'kids used to walk miles to school, it was the *norm*. One of the reasons they're all getting so fat is that they don't do that any more. What's wrong with an hour's bike ride? It's a good thing, surely. We used to spend nearly that long in the Discovery some mornings and there's cycle lanes almost all the way. Anyway, don't you see? There's nothing else we can do. Your parents live on a boat. Mine are in a one-bedroom flat in Reading. It's up to us to find somewhere to live and Webb Street is perfect. We have a head start there. We know all the service providers. There's any amount of cement and tiles and paint and all sorts of stuff still locked up in the houses from when the building work stopped and, most important of all, there's a whole squatting community already set up. We can join it. We won't be alone. They know all the legal stuff. They even have lawyers. My dad said the most important thing in a crisis was to have a plan, right? Well, either we wait until we get thrown out and are at the mercy of the council or we take control like thousands of other Londoners have done and prepare a squat.'

Monica did not look completely convinced, but she didn't protest further. Slowly they were all learning to put their previous attitudes behind them.

Jimmy selected his house. First he discreetly replaced the broken locks on the front door with two of the four Chubbs that had been fitted so beautifully to his Notting Hill front door by the talented Romanian carpenter. Then he began work in earnest.

Astonishingly the water was still on and the gas only needed reconnecting. There was no electricity for the time being but Jimmy had a good set of cordless power tools that he was able to charge at home and take with him to work. One of the super-cool squatters had explained to Jimmy that once he moved his family in they could easily get the leccy reconnected as the various power companies did not care who owned the houses they supplied as long as the bills were paid.

Jim worked every single day. Preparing the surfaces was a massive task as the premises were so dilapidated. He found, however, that by asset-stripping the floors he didn't intend to occupy he could forage enough sound timber and plasterboard to service the ones that he did.

He balked at nothing: no cockroach, no bug infestation, no nightmare mystery stains worried him in the slightest. He worked with a light heart for he had once again found a sense of purpose to his day, a purpose which was far more satisfying than any work he had done in his past life. He was coming to see that being rich and working simply to get richer could be in many ways a soul-destroying business. Particularly if the work you were doing had long since become routine. But being poor and working to survive, working to keep your wife and children from sinking into an abyss of poverty, *that* was a thrill. Jimmy was painting and decorating for his family, for his kids. He was working to put a roof over their heads. No goal could have lent more vigour to every blow of his hammer and every stroke of his brush.

The process wasn't costing him anything either, in fact he was spoilt for choice when it came to fitting out the kitchen and bathroom. After all, he had five en suites gathering dust above his head in Notting Hill, all beautifully equipped with the most splendid baths, bidets, basins and shower units.

In the end, however, he took all his stuff from the en suite in the attic nanny flat, Jodie's being the only bathroom furniture that would fit into the stripped-out room he had prepared at Number 23 Webb Street. In fact Jimmy thought he could probably have fitted that room into the massive free-standing cast-iron tugboat of a bath that he and Monica had once shared. Jodie's bath and basin also had the advantage of being the only ones in the whole Notting Hill house featuring taps that were not so smoothly designed that you couldn't turn them off with a wet hand.

Next Jimmy stripped out Jodie's kitchenette. He removed the work surface, the fitted cooker, fridge and microwave and the lovely chrome power points, planning to reassemble it all carefully in Webb Street. He was able to shift the whole lot with the help of an anarchist with a van, who did the job for a pink bidet from Monica's old bathroom and a still-boxed-up juicer that Derek and Nora Corby had given them one Christmas.

Jimmy made tremendous progress and after six weeks of fourteen-hour days he had his chosen floors cleaned and sanded, all the walls prepared for decoration, half the wiring done and he'd made a start on the plumbing. In fact he reckoned that he was no more than a month away from being able to move the family in if the bank suddenly snapped the thread on the sword of Damocles they had hanging over him and chucked them out of Notting Hill.

'We'll be camping for a year and washing in a bucket. But we could do it.'

Then, one afternoon, just when Jimmy thought his year of bad luck was coming to an end, it got worse again.

A different sword of Damocles, one forged at Scotland Yard and of which Jimmy had been blissfully unaware, landed bang on top of his head.

He was working at Webb Street when he heard a knock at the door. Outside was a small, very neat-looking man of about Jimmy's age.

'James Corby?' the man said.

'Probably,' said Jimmy with a smile, 'it depends who you are.'

'Your wife told me I might find you here.'

'Oh . . .' Something stirred in Jimmy's memory, a strange familiarity. 'Do I know you?' he asked.

'Slightly,' Beaumont replied. 'We once briefly shared a house in Sussex. When we were students.'

'God! That's right. It's you! How are you, mate? Not come looking for your milk, have you? I think it will have gone off.'

Beaumont was pleased. Pleased that Jimmy had remembered him even if he clearly had no idea of the pain he had caused.

'I'm afraid not, Mr Corby,' Beaumont said. 'I'm a policeman now. Detective Inspector Graeme Beaumont. And I'd like to speak to you about your share specu-lations. In particular the trade you made in Caledonian Granite in the autumn of 2007. You may recall that you disposed of your stock hours before the price collapsed.'

A matter of pride

Jimmy returned home quite late that evening, after Monica had finally got all the children down. The last half-hour or so had been spent dealing with Cressida's current nightly ritual of re-emerging from her bedroom fifteen times in order to say that she couldn't sleep and being told to go back to bed again.

'Well?' Monica whispered after shushing Jimmy to alert him to the fact that his elder daughter had only just gone down. 'What was it all about? Why did a policeman want to see you?'

'You were right,' Jimmy said, 'about those Caledonian Granite shares. It was against the law.'

Monica was silent for a moment as the scale of this new disaster sank in.

'Have they charged you?'

'Not yet. They showed me evidence of the trade I made the day before Caledonian collapsed. I said I'd made lots of trades in those days. That I couldn't remember them all. That I must have just got lucky.'

Through all of his previous travails Jimmy's sunny manner had never quite deserted him. Now, despite his efforts at bravado, the twinkle had finally dulled in his eye.

Monica crossed the room and hugged him. Then she went and put the kettle on.

Jimmy made an effort to pull himself together.

'Did Rupert call?' he asked.

'Yes,' Monica replied, rather surprised. 'How did you know that?'

'Did you tell him I was with the police?'

'Of course not, it's none of his business who you're with. But he sounded very anxious. Said he needed to see you.'

'I'm not surprised.'

'Oh my God!' said Monica. 'You mean they're on to him too? He must be worrying that he'll be next.'

'No, Mon, not next. First. He's first. That's the whole point. It's him this cop is after. He told me that they'd go easy on me if I was prepared to say where I'd got the information about the Granite shares. That they might not press charges at all.'

'What did you tell them?'

'I told them that I couldn't remember making the deal. That it must just have been a lucky guess.'

Monica made the tea. It was clear she was thinking hard about what to say next, wanting to phrase it right.

'Jimmy . . .' she said finally, 'perhaps you should just tell them the truth.'

He looked at her, genuinely surprised.

'Monica, I could *never* do that.'

The angry frustration that spread across her face showed that she had known what he'd say.

'Why not, Jim?'

'Well, for a start I'd be admitting to having made an insider trade . . .'

'Which you did. Which they know about anyway. That's the whole point!'

'I think maybe he's bluffing. If he really had me then he could have nicked me and offered to drop the charges, but he didn't.'

'What difference does it make? He'll certainly leave you alone if you tell him about Rupert, so just do it. Rupert got us into this mess.'

'*I* got us into this mess, Mon. Nobody forced me to

try to make an extra fifty grand by picking up the phone.'

'Rupert must have known when he gave you the information that it was illegal.'

'I should have known it myself. You did. You pointed it out, remember?'

'Yes! And you didn't keep the money! You did the right thing, you shouldn't have to suffer for this.'

'That's not how the law sees it.'

'Jimmy, you've got kids. We're broke. You can't ruin us to protect Rupert. He's a shit. Look what he said about Henry in the papers, saying Jane's hairdryer was far worse than him milking the public for his pension fund. *And* he tried to cheat Amanda on her settlement. You should turn him in.'

'Mon,' Jimmy said firmly, 'you have to understand I would *never* do that. Rupert's been my friend for nearly twenty years.'

'But he isn't your friend any more, is he!' Monica shouted, all her pent-up emotion suddenly finding form in anger. 'And actually I don't know why he ever was! I really don't. All those dinners, all those holidays. He was *always* a complete shit. A reactionary, super-cilious shit. Why did we put up with him? Sharif's worth a hundred fucking Ruperts *and* he didn't walk out on his kids.'

'Mon, we liked Rupert. Don't pretend we didn't. Maybe you don't like him any more but that's because everything's changed. We're poor and we've screwed up

442

and he represents the problem. But when we were rich like him, we liked him.'

'Well, I don't like him any more! It was his bloody idea to invest in Webb Street, which is what ruined everything in the first place. You'd never gone into debt like that before. Everything was paid off, then that bastard persuades you to—'

Jimmy banged his hand down on the table. He'd never done that before. Monica's jaw dropped in surprise.

'Monica, listen,' Jimmy said quietly. 'That inspector left me in an interview room, alone, to sweat for three hours. He was hoping that I'd come out having decided to play ball. But that wasn't what I ended up thinking.'

'No?' Monica asked angrily.

'No. What I ended up thinking was that me, sitting there in that police station, was a *consequence*. A consequence of something that I had done. Something that *we* had done. We invested in Webb Street because we wanted to make millions of pounds in profit. That's all. That is the end of the story. Rupert may have suggested the scheme but I did it and I did it because I wanted to be richer. The same reason I took Rupert's tip on Caledonian Granite. I wanted to get richer. I didn't need any more money, but I wanted to get richer. I have to face that fact. It's *my responsibility*.'

'Your responsibility is your family, your children!'

'Mon, calm down,' said Jimmy, 'you'll wake them up.'

'Good! Perhaps they should hear that their dad

443

would rather leave them and go to prison than tell the truth to the police about some complete arsehole who's royally done him over, just because he used to be at university with him and you both shoved radishes up your bums on graduation night!'

Jimmy couldn't help but smile at this, but Monica wasn't smiling. He tried to hug her, but she wasn't having that either.

'Mon,' Jimmy said gently, 'this isn't about Rupert. It's about me. Don't you see that? About everything I've done and where it's brought me to. For the first time in my life I'm coming to understand that actions have consequences. In fact it seems to me that this whole bloody crisis is based on people thinking they could get rich without there being any consequences. That the rules didn't apply to them. That personal responsibility was something for other people. That what *really* mattered was what you could get away with. And that was all that mattered. If you could get away with it, it was OK. Nobody followed their conscience, they just followed the profit. It's time I did follow my conscience. If I can get out of this I promise you I will, but not by trying to pretend that it's somebody else's fault other than my own.'

Monica tried to reply, but stopped. Then she tried again, but once more could not frame an adequate response. He'd flummoxed her.

'God,' she said eventually, 'you sound like your bloody dad.'

Jimmy smiled.

'Is that a good or a bad thing?'

'Good . . . probably,' she replied, suddenly resigned and quiet, 'as long as you don't buy a cardigan and start collecting trains.'

'I have to *learn* something from all this,' Jimmy said, 'otherwise what's the point? And what I've learned is that if I turn Rupert in to avoid facing the consequences of what I did then I'm a bigger shit than he ever was. I can't help it, Monica, but that's the way I am. There isn't much left that I have to be proud of, but at least I can take responsibility for my own actions. Like I say, I do still have some pride. That's probably all I have got.'

'You've got us,' Monica said almost in a whisper.

'Yes. And I can still look you in the eye. If I had to stand up in court and turn evidence against Rupert to save my own skin, I couldn't even do that.'

Monica shrugged.

'Well, I think you're wrong. Rupert deserves to go down for everything he's done. They should have put him away for destroying your dad's bank. You don't deserve prison. You're just a bloody idiot.'

'Even an idiot can learn a lesson.'

There was silence. For perhaps the first time in their whole marriage a distance had developed between them. Once more Jimmy crossed the room and tried to hug her. This time she tried to hug him back, but her heart wasn't in it.

'It'll be all right, Mon,' Jimmy whispered, 'just you wait.'

'How? How will it be all right?' Monica asked.

'I'll make it all right. Just you see if I don't.'

'Yes. Because you're so good at that, aren't you, Jim.'

She said it with some bitterness, but again Jimmy smiled. She had a point.

'I'm going to bed,' Monica said.

But then she remembered that she hadn't yet checked for notes in Toby's school bag.

'Oh God,' she said.

Sure enough, there it was. What's more, it was a note that somehow she had managed to miss for two days and which related to the following morning.

Dear Parent or Guardian

As you know, our topic this term is the Great Age of Exploration. Could you please send your child into school on Wednesday dressed as an Elizabethan.

Monica wanted to scream. She was exhausted, penniless, about to be made homeless, her husband was being done for insider trading and now she was going to have to construct an Elizabethan ruff out of Sellotape and kitchen paper.

Life went on.

'Oh God,' she repeated, starting to look for a pair of scissors. 'You go to bed.'

446

'Can I help? Make him a sword or something?'

'I think you've done enough for today.'

The makeshift costume took her an hour.

After which, while once more on her way to bed, Monica remembered that she hadn't washed Toby's sports kit either.

Two phone calls

The following morning Jimmy left for Webb Street before the children had woken up. It was now more urgent than ever to get the renovations done as quickly as possible.

'I've got to get you sorted out,' he told Monica. 'The sooner we start living there, the sooner we can claim squatters' rights. I swear I am not going to leave you and the children in a Bed and Breakfast . . . if I have to go away.'

Then he mounted his bike, slung his bag of tools over the handlebars and headed off. His low point of the previous evening seemed to have passed.

'It'll be all right. I promise you I'll make it all right,' he shouted over his shoulder and was gone.

Shortly after he'd left, Rupert phoned.

'Where's Jimmy, Monica?' he asked with scarcely a word of greeting.

'He's on his way to Webb Street,' she replied coldly. 'You remember Webb Street? You told us it was going to make us millions and now your old bank's got it and we're about to be evicted from our home because we mortgaged it chasing your stupid scheme.'

Rupert ignored the challenge. He was clearly in no mood to deal with embittered ex-friends.

'Can you give me his mobile number?' he asked.

'No. I'm the only one who has it and we only use it for emergencies. We're counting the pennies, Rupert, don't you remember? We only have state benefits to live on, not a state-funded mega pension like you.'

'This is an emergency,' Rupert snapped. 'Give me the number.'

'No. If you want to talk to him, go to Webb Street. He's at Number 23.'

'What did he tell the police, Monica?'

'He didn't tell them anything, Rupert,' Monica said angrily before adding, 'yet'.

'What do you fucking mean, "yet"?'

'I mean that he's being his usual pig-headed decent self but I'm going to nag him till he sees sense, that's what. I've told him to turn you in. The police have offered to keep him out of jail if he tells them who tipped him off about the Caledonian Granite shares. At the moment he's not talking, but if I have my way he's going to get his memory back very soon.'

'Is that so?' Rupert's voice was hard and cold.

'Yes, it is.'

'Goodbye, Monica,' Rupert said and hung up.

Monica put down the phone. She had plenty of shit to handle without bothering to think about another load.

Life, as John Lennon said, is what happens when you're making other plans.

It was a school morning and Toby couldn't find any socks.

Where *were* all the socks? She hated socks. Passionately. And she had to make him sandwiches because he hated the school dinner that day, which was a shame because they got free school dinners.

She found two dirty socks in the laundry basket which passed the sniff test, gave them to Toby and started to dress Cressie and Lillie. Meanwhile she was also trying to help Toby with his maths homework while he ate his cornflakes, except there was only dust left in the box so she had to make him toast. Then she remembered about it being gym day so she packed the sports kit which she had washed late the previous night and hung over a cold radiator but which was nearly dry, except that there were no plimsolls because Toby had left them at school. Monica did not relish the thought of rummaging through the school's pile of left-behind gym kit looking for his runners but she knew that it would have to be faced. She looked at herself in the mirror and wondered if she could really go out without washing her hair and decided that she could, but she'd have to wear a hat.

Toby tried on the paper ruff that Monica had made and said that he'd rather poo a red-hot cannon ball than wear it and Monica said that was fine by her because it had only taken her an hour in the middle of the bloody night to make.

'Can I just wear my Kaiser Chiefs T-shirt?' Toby asked.

'No.'

'Why not?'

'Because it's not Elizabethan.'

'Yes it is,' Toby said triumphantly. 'What do you think the Queen's name is?'

Monica had to stop and think for a second on that one, but when she got it she couldn't help but admire her son's logic.

'It's Elizabeth-the-Secondian,' said Toby triumphantly.

'All right,' Monica conceded. 'If you think you can get away with it, wear it.'

'Yes!' said Toby, punching the air and looking just like Jimmy.

Eventually they all set off for school, where Monica found Toby's gym shoes and then did some reading with the younger ones. Or at least she read with some of the younger ones and others she merely minded while they bounced from wall to wall, but at least it gave the teacher a chance to teach those kids who weren't hovering three feet from the floor on sugar highs. It was generally agreed among the parents and teachers that this year's Receptions and Year Ones were buggers.

Then, around mid-morning, the school secretary stuck her head round the door and said that there was an important phone call for Monica on hold in the school office. That it was the police.

It turned out to be the policeman who had come to interview Jimmy the day before. He wanted to know if Jimmy owned a Rolex watch.

'I think I saw one on his wrist, Mrs Corby, but I need confirmation.'

'Well,' Monica said, perplexed, 'it was actually a fake, but a pretty good one.'

'I see. Did he also own a ring with a skull motif?'

'Yes he did. It was his wedding ring. Can you tell me why you need to know, please?'

There was a silence over the phone. A silence which sent a chill to Monica's very core.

'Is Jimmy in any more trouble?' she asked, trying to stop her voice from shaking. 'Has anything happened?'

'I would rather not say at present, Mrs Corby,' Beaumont answered. 'I will be in touch shortly.'

The line went dead and Monica replaced the receiver with a trembling hand. Suddenly the very last words Jimmy had said to her as he cycled off that morning came into her head.

'It'll be all right,' he had said. 'I promise you I'll make it all right.'

What had he done? What had he *done*?

Sifting through the embers

It was one of the top-end squatters who had seen the flames first. She'd been practising her juggling in the street and smelt smoke. But even though the alarm was raised very quickly, it still hadn't been quick enough. Number 23 was gutted.

As the chief assistant fire officer later concluded in his incident report, 'The fire took hold with extraordinary speed and ferocity. Every floor was ablaze before our engines arrived and there was no possibility of getting anywhere near the building, let alone entering it.'

It had been very distressing for the firemen and women on the scene. The juggler told them that on most days a man called Jimmy was in the house all day painting and decorating and that it was definitely his bike that could be seen chained to the step railing and slowly succumbing to the flames.

Time and time again the brave fire officers had tried to penetrate the dense smoke and heat, and time and time again they failed. Soon it became apparent to even the most tenacious and determined among them that any sacrifice would be pointless, as by now anyone inside that inferno would long since have been consumed by it.

Eventually the fire brigade managed to put the fire out. After cooling the wreckage a little with their hoses, they were able to make a preliminary foray into what was left of the house. Very quickly they located what they had prayed they would not find. Charred human remains. A body, burnt to a crisp, scarcely anything left of it but the half-incinerated skeleton. Not a shred of clothing, of course. But on the corpse's wrist could be seen the half-melted remains of what had clearly been a Rolex watch, and on its wedding finger a gold ring with a silver skull on it.

It was shortly after this discovery that Inspector Beaumont arrived on the scene. He was looking for Jimmy to try once more to persuade him to cooperate with the crown in pursuing Rupert.

Having learned from the chief fire officer of the discovery of the corpse and the jewellery found on it and having spoken to Monica to confirm the ownership of that jewellery, Beaumont was forced to the depressing conclusion that Jimmy Corby was beyond cooperating with anyone.

'Suicide,' a voice at Beaumont's shoulder said. 'Suicide, pure and simple.'

Beaumont turned round and found himself shaking the hand of a man who introduced himself as Andrew Tanner.

'Of Wigan and Wigan Insurance,' Tanner explained. 'We insure these buildings.'

'You've moved quickly, Mr Tanner,' Beaumont said.

'We have excellent connections in the Fire Service, Inspector, and as chief loss adjuster I attempt to personally attend any potential claim that I deem potentially suspicious. And to do so as soon as possible.'

'Suspicious?'

'This house was part of a failed property development, Inspector, a misguided financial speculation. However, when the property was insured the market was booming and the valuation was much higher than it would be today. This house is therefore worth considerably more burnt to the ground that it was when it was standing.'

'You suspect arson?'

'When negative equity which is heavily over-insured goes up in flames, Inspector, I *always* suspect arson. However, having arrived to find that there was a body in the building and having discovered that the former owner had been working on it, I've changed my theory.'

'You suspect suicide.'

'The man was desperate. If he simply burns down the building, the bank, as current owner, takes the insurance. If he burns it down *with himself in it* then his wife and family pick up the life insurance, which, incidentally, is another of our policies. *If*, that is, the fire is deemed to be an accident. I intend to make sure that it is not deemed so.'

Beaumont stared at the blackened remains of the house. He watched as the charred corpse was removed by police Forensics officers and taken away for further examination. As he did so, he considered what Andrew Tanner had said.

'I don't think it was suicide, Mr Tanner,' Beaumont said eventually.

'Please, Inspector, I know this game,' Tanner replied. 'Corby was a fit man. A strong man. His body was found on the ground floor. Are you seriously telling me that once that fire took hold he couldn't have made it to the front door or a window? Of course he could. He just didn't want to, did he?'

'If I was going to kill myself I don't think I'd choose to *burn* myself to death. I mean how agonizing would it be? Anything would be better, surely? Why not just dive head first out of the top window? That'd do it. Or drink a bottle of Scotch and open a vein. Anything but burning.'

'Because he had to make it look like an accident,' Tanner said with a touch of impatience.

'Only a coward would desert his wife and children like that,' Beaumont replied. 'I knew Corby slightly. I don't think he was a coward.'

'Of course he wasn't a coward, Inspector,' Tanner said. 'How brave would you have to be to pull off a stunt like this? A lot braver than most men, that's for sure. He wanted to provide for his family and the last asset he had left on earth was his own miserable failed life and the insurance attached to it. Alive, he'd let his wife down totally. Dead, he could leave her comparatively rich and his kids provided for. Life insurance, Inspector. That's what this is about. It's what it's *always* about.'

It certainly sounded plausible.

But Inspector Beaumont wasn't happy. He simply did not believe that Jimmy Corby had planned to kill himself.

On the other hand, if it was an accident it was one hell of a coincidence, happening just when all Jimmy's troubles were collapsing in on him at once. And, as Andrew Tanner had pointed out, Jimmy was very fit and still relatively young. Surely he could have got out in time?

But Beaumont knew something that Andrew Tanner did not. There was another possibility altogether.

Not suicide. Not an accident.

But murder.

Jimmy's wife was not the only person who would profit from his death.

Someone else had a very real interest in silencing Jimmy Corby.

Grilling the lord

Early that evening Beaumont was once more questioning Lord Bennett.

'Mrs Corby tells me you called her this morning trying to get hold of Jimmy Corby. She says she told you he was at 23 Webb Street. Is that correct?'

'Yes it is, and I went to see him there this morning.'

'You went to talk to him about Caledonian Granite?'

'I went to see how he was.'

This time Beaumont was not meeting Rupert at the sumptuous new Maximalism office and they were not sipping creamy lattes served by a gorgeous PA either. Beaumont had had Rupert brought in to Scotland Yard.

'I don't think that's true,' Beaumont said. 'I think you went to see Corby because you wanted to ensure that he would not talk, and when you decided that you could *not* be sure you took matters into your own hands.'

Rupert had of course brought his lawyer with him. The man began immediately to object to Beaumont's leading statement in the strongest possible terms. But Rupert stopped him, angrily saying he wanted to speak for himself.

'You're crazy, Inspector!' Rupert blurted. 'I'm not a murderer, for God's sake. I went to talk to him . . .'

'About keeping quiet.'

'As a mate. I went to *thank* him because I knew you'd

pulled him in because you were trying to get to me. I was sorry to cause him any more bother than he was in already. We were friends. He was pleased to see me. We've been a bit distant lately but we made up. I knew he was broke so I took along a bottle of whisky and some beers. We had a nip or two and a chat, that's all.'

'In the middle of the morning?'

'Jim Corby and I have had a drink or two on every single occasion we've met for nearly twenty years. The credit crunch ain't gonna change that.'

Beaumont leaned forward over the desk so that his face came within a foot or so of Rupert's.

'You didn't go to Webb Street to drink *or* to chat. You went there to get a guarantee out of your old friend that he would not talk to us about the Caledonian Granite share tips.'

'Inspector, I protest at your—' the lawyer began, but once again Rupert silenced him.

'Inspector,' he said, calmly, smoothly almost, 'as I think we've discussed many times before, I have nothing to hide regarding Caledonian Granite and you have not shown me a single bit of concrete evidence to suggest that I do.'

'My bit of *concrete evidence*, Lord Bennett, has been reduced to a pile of ashes and a half-melted Rolex!'

'Inspector, you are talking about my oldest friend!' Rupert snapped.

'A friend who is very conveniently dead.'

'A circumstance which I would appreciate being given time to mourn!'

Beaumont got up from his chair and paced the room for a moment.

'So why did you go to Webb Street if not to discuss Caledonian Granite?' he asked. 'God knows you've had opportunity enough to buy him a drink without the trouble of going all the way to Hackney in the middle of the morning.'

Rupert's poker face deserted him for a moment. Unless he was a very good actor, something in Beaumont's question seemed to make him want to unveil a little truth.

'I . . . I wanted to help him,' Rupert said slowly and only after some thought. 'Truly. I mean it. Jim and I were friends, real friends, not like with the others.' There was a faraway look in Rupert's eyes as he spoke, almost as if he was speaking to himself. 'I never gave a toss about that fool Henry, of course, with his ridiculous quasi-socialist posturing. David was all right if a bit pretentious, and of course we all loved Robbo.'

Beaumont knew all of the people Rupert was talking about, but they did not concern him. He let Rupert go on, hoping that as he unburdened himself he might let something slip. Something that would give a clue as to what exactly had happened at Number 23 Webb Street.

'Jim was my friend,' Rupert went on. 'You have to understand that, Inspector. I *am* capable of friendship,

459

you know. We'd roomed together. Laughed together. We'd had a hell of a nineties and an incredible noughties. We were the boys and I just couldn't stand the idea of old Lucky Jim Corby scarcely even being able to afford a bloody drink. I went back because I'd decided to help him out, if you really want to know.'

Rupert actually looked embarrassed as he said this. As if it was a sign of weakness, contrary to every principle of warped Darwinian elitism that he had always held so dear.

'I'd decided that for the first time in my life I was going to do something unselfish. The world knows I still have some money, it's no secret. Maybe I've got more than the world thinks. Not that *you*'ll ever find it, Inspector. So I'd decided to offer to set Jim up again. Not here in Britain of course, even I couldn't cover his bloody debts. A man would very soon go broke himself pouring money into that particular pit. No, my idea was to get him to do a bunk, grab Monica and the kids and shoot through. I'd set him up somewhere nice and he could start trading again. Britain's fucked anyway. Everybody knows that. Basket case. Ugly people, ugly country. They deserve their bloody awful grubby politicians.'

'Do you think they deserved you, Lord Bennett?' Beaumont asked. 'The people who put their savings in your bank?'

Rupert looked at Beaumont and sneered.

'Screw 'em. Who cares?' he said.

Beaumont sneered back.

'I do,' he said.

'Well, bully for you, Mr Plod,' Rupert replied.

Beaumont realized that this wasn't getting him any-where with his investigation.

'So you went to Webb Street to offer Jimmy Corby a new life abroad?'

'Yes. But he wouldn't take it. Said the time for running was over and he needed to face things head on. All he'd take was some cigarettes and a box of matches.' Rupert's eyes seemed for a moment to fill. 'I never should have given him the matches.'

'You gave him the matches?'

'We used to love smoking together. Stood on fifty pavements after the ban. But he gave up after he lost all his money. Realized for the first time how expensive they were, I suppose. We had a couple of smokes together with our drinks. He loved it, took down half a fag in a single drag. Used an old paint tin for an ashtray. Never crossed my mind there was any danger in it.'

Beaumont looked at Rupert long and hard. Lord Bennett was a ruthless man, there was no doubt about that. For his entire adult life he'd been creating disasters and then escaping the consequences. Had he done it again? Clearly he had gone to Webb Street on a mission to stop Corby speaking out about the illegal share tips.

But how had he intended to do it?

Was he merely going to try to buy Corby off with the

offer of a new life abroad as he was half admitting? Or did Lord Bennett hope to silence Jimmy more permanently?

Truth less strange than fiction

Monica knew it wasn't suicide.

Nor had it been an accident.

And it wasn't bloody murder either.

Because Jimmy wasn't dead.

'It's his *story*,' she wailed. 'He made up a whole story about a fake-death canoe scam and now he's gone and bloody done it!'

It was late evening, the children were in bed and Monica was sitting in the family room of the Notting Hill house with Inspector Beaumont.

'What story?' Beaumont asked.

Desperately trying to remain calm, Monica told him. The story about the dead tramp. The one about a bankrupt house owner using another body to fake his own death.

'Are you seriously suggesting, Mrs Corby,' Beaumont asked, 'that your husband would murder an unconscious tramp in order to claim life insurance?'

'That was just for the *story*! The tramp must have been

dead already,' Monica said, trying not to cry. 'Jim's been waiting for him to die for ages. Obviously the silly fool found the corpse and grabbed his chance. Why didn't I work it out? He told me himself that he was going to dodge and weave and that he would make everything all right. I might have guessed he'd try to find a way out of all this shit . . . but not this! I should have let him sell that bloody fake Rolex. Why didn't I let him sell it?'

Inspector Beaumont was concerned.

'Understandably you're very upset, Mrs Corby, but you have to face the possibility that there's a much simpler explanation. We'll have the forensic report first thing in the morning, then we will at least be clear whether the corpse found at the house was—'

'I'm telling you *it's not Jimmy*,' Monica half shouted, fearful of waking the children but scarcely able to contain herself. 'It all *fits*. It's his story! Exactly the way he described it. We have to find him. We've got to stop him before he makes it any worse. He's in enough trouble already. He's hiding somewhere, I know he is. His mobile's been off since the fire. He's hiding out. I have to think!'

Beaumont tried to think too. Seldom in his career had he been completely thrown, but this was one such occasion. He had come round to tell Monica personally the circumstances of what he had been quite convinced was her husband's death, and the moment he had done so she had flown into this near-hysterical anguish claiming that Corby was still alive.

'What about the tramp's ID?' he said eventually. 'In Jimmy's story that was crucial. If you're right about what he's done he'll be using that.'

'Of course!' Monica said in a moment of hope.

'Do you know the tramp's name?' Beaumont asked.

'Yes! Yes I do,' Monica blurted. 'Bob. His name was Bob.'

'We'd need a surname,' Beaumont replied gently. 'We can't go looking for new bank accounts and passport applications for just Bob.'

'Oh . . . yes, of course,' Monica said. 'I'm afraid I don't know his surname.'

For a moment there was silence as both Monica and Beaumont wondered what they should do next.

Then they heard a key turn in the front-door lock.

Moments later Jimmy walked down the unlit stairs.

'Hello, Mon,' he said. 'Hello, Inspector. Blimey, what's the matter? You look like you've seen a ghost.'

Scrap metal

After Rupert had left Jimmy at Number 23 on the morning of the fire, Jimmy had gone for a walk. He was pretty pissed and he needed to think.

Rupert's offer of a getaway, of a new start overseas in exchange for a silence that Jimmy had intended to keep anyway, was tempting to say the least.

Exciting. Intriguing. A second chance. A clean slate. Wow.

Jimmy reeled out of the house sucking on his cigarette and staggered down the steps, nearly falling over his bike as he did so. He thought he'd slammed the door behind him, but of course he hadn't. Whisky, beer and fags on an empty stomach at eleven in the morning had made him careless.

That was when old Bob the tramp had grabbed his chance. He'd smelt the solvents Jimmy had been using on his gloss brushes and he was after them. Instead he found the whisky and the cigarettes . . . and the matches.

Jimmy wandered up and down Hackney High Street for an hour or so, breathing deeply and sobering up, and by the time he headed back to Webb Street he had decided that he would not, under any circumstances, accept Rupert's offer of an escape route for exactly the same reason that he had decided not to turn Rupert in.

The reason he had explained to Monica the night before.

It was time to take responsibility for his own actions.

Things had consequences and they had to be faced.

Jimmy was therefore returning to Number 23 with the intention of getting back to work on renovating the house for his family to squat in, but by the time he got there the Fire Brigade were already in attendance and it was all too late.

Standing unnoticed at the back of the little crowd that was gathering, Jimmy realized that once again his old good luck had turned relentlessly bad.

'I didn't know anyone was in the burning house,' he explained to Monica and Inspector Beaumont. 'I just thought either me or Rupert had left a fag burning and that all my months of work were going up in smoke. I thought that yet again I'd blown it. That I couldn't even squat a building properly. So I just wandered off. I knew you weren't expecting me home till late, Monica. I've been doing fourteen-hour days anyway.

'I needed time to think. Time to get up the courage to tell you that our new home was ruined. So I went walking. My mobile had been in the house but I wouldn't have called anyway. I walked pretty much clean across London before starting for home. Just feeling stupid. Feeling that I'd messed up yet again. Of course now I understand what a truly horrible bloody palaver I've caused by wandering off like that. But I didn't know anyone was in the house, did I? And honestly, Mon, I *never* would have thought you'd think I'd do what you thought I did!'

'But Jimmy,' Monica protested, 'your story . . .'

'And your watch and wedding ring,' Inspector Beaumont said sternly. 'They were found on the corpse.

They were actually on its wrist and finger. How did they get there?'

'I take them off to paint,' said Jimmy. 'I always do. Of course I do. Let me tell you, Mon, you couldn't clean paint off that watch, it'd take the gold colour straight off with it. Same with my Vegas ring. Paint solvents and cheap jewellery don't mix. Each morning I'd take them off and leave them on the mantelpiece, same place I left the whisky bottle today. I suppose Bob must have found them and grabbed them. Probably thought they'd be worth a shot or two of meths. He put them on. Poured himself a drink. Lit a cigarette surrounded by paint and solvents, threw away the match and . . . Poor sod. Poor bloody sod!'

CCTV footage from the streets of Hackney confirmed that Jimmy had indeed been wandering across London, deep in thought, at the time the fire started. It had been an accident after all.

The Radish Club

The graduation party had crawled round many pubs and clubs and had visited not one but two curry houses, one early and one late. Now it had finally returned to the place where it had started, the rented house which they had all shared for two years. Lizzie had long since staggered off to bed and the one or two other girls who had started the night with them had also pulled the pin and called a cab.

Only the lads were left. The gang. The boys. Jimmy, Rupert, Henry, David and Robbo. The core gang, minus Lizzie of course, whom Robbo had recently stunned everyone by pulling.

They were all *so pissed*.

Reeling, belching, dribbling drunk. The suits that they had worn earlier in the day for their degree ceremony were crumpled and stained. Henry, as a committed radical, had not worn a suit but had instead had on a T-shirt which objected in no uncertain terms to the first Gulf War. That, however, was as crumpled and stained as the rest of their attire.

It was the last night of their student days and nobody wanted to go to bed.

'This is it, boys,' Jimmy said, struggling to get his finger under the ring pull of another can of beer. 'Playtime's over! The real world is about to begin! We must mark this occasion!'

'I thought we were fucking marking it,' Rupert observed. 'If eleven pints and two curries plus tequila shots isn't marking it, what is?'

'We must make a pact!' Jimmy said. 'We must always be the best of friends. Or in the case of Roop and Henry, best of enemies. Friendship like ours cannot be allowed to wither on the vine of mundane existence.' Jimmy raised his still-unopened can in a gesture of flamboyant solemnity. 'We must carry it with us through life!'

'Oh, do fuck off, Jimmy, you absolute wanker!' David slurred.

'Guilty as charged!' Jimmy shouted. 'I *am* an absolute wanker both spiritually and in very practical terms. However, I speak the truth! Our friendship must endure! Wherever we go and whatever we become!'

'But where will we go! What will we become?' Henry enquired through a mouthful of cold chips salvaged from a previous day's takeaway.

'Well, I don't know about you, but I'm going to the toilet,' Robbo said, rising unsteadily.

'No, wait, Robs, this is serious,' Jimmy insisted with the sudden intensity of the very drunk person who has seen the truth and needs to share it. 'We should think about this. Where will we all be in ten, fifteen, twenty years? Come on. Let's look into the future. Robbo, you need a piss so you go first.'

'In ten, fifteen and twenty years,' Robbo replied, 'I hope to be *exactly* as I am now. Unchanged! That is, drunk! Very, very drunk.'

'Good answer!' Jimmy shouted. 'The *right* answer.'

'Can I go to the toilet now?'

'Yes, you may. David, where will you be? What will you become?'

David chewed on a cold chip for a moment before answering.

'I shall have designed and built the most famous building on the planet and will also be shagging Madonna,' he said finally.

'You do realize she'll be pushing fifty by then?' Jim pointed out.

'I do realize that, Jim,' David answered, 'because I am not a moron. And she will no doubt be a fat, sagging, great big wobbling jelly of cellulite by then also, but I shall still love her and I shall still shag her. What's more, I shall shag her in the penthouse of my fabulous building.'

'Good answer! The *right* answer,' Jimmy shouted, finally managing to open his can and in the process spraying himself with beer. 'Henry?'

'Minimum Cabinet minister. Maximum Prime Minister,' Henry replied promptly, 'in a second-term Labour government.'

'Bad answer!' Jimmy shouted. '*Wrong* answer. Boring answer.'

'Nonetheless the true answer,' Henry insisted. 'You wait.'

Rupert threw an almost empty can at him.

'Haven't you got it yet, Henry, you arse?' he said. 'Hasn't the penny dropped? There is never going to be another Labour government *ever again.*'

'We shall see, you Nazi bastard,' Henry replied. 'We shall see.'

'Yes we will, you commie moron.'

'Come on,' Jimmy pressed. 'Your turn, Rupert.'

'I shall be rich, of course. Incredibly rich. What other ambition is there?'

'Good answer!' Jimmy shouted. 'The *right* answer!'

'Stupid arrogant answer!' Henry shouted back.

'So what about you, Jim?' David asked. 'What's going to happen to you?'

'I shall be broke, of course! Stony broke as I always am and no doubt in deep shit as I also always am. And that is why I'm insisting that we all promise to stick together, so I can come round and borrow money off all of you.'

'Good answer!' Rupert said.

'The *right* answer!' the others chorused.

Then Robbo returned from the toilet (having neglected to fasten his trousers).

'Well, if we're going to have a pact,' he said, swaying badly, 'we need a gesture! A symbol! A solemn ceremony of commitment!'

'That's right! We do!' Jimmy shouted, knocking over his beer. 'But what gesture? What symbol? What ceremony could possibly be solemn enough for such a monumental occasion as this?'

'I know just the thing!' Robbo replied triumphantly.

Lucky punt

Inspector Beaumont never pressed charges against Jimmy. His evidence was inconclusive, besides which his department were eventually able to build a case against Rupert without Jimmy's testimony. The case, however, was tried in Lord Bennett's absence because he had by that time absconded overseas.

Beatrice and his youngest child he left behind, penniless, but in a gesture of great generosity Amanda took responsibility for them, settling a small income on them both to be used until the child turned eighteen.

'Don't want my kids coming to me in ten years and saying that I let their sweet little half-brother starve. Life's too fucking short,' Amanda said.

Despite his protestations that teaching was a vocation, David got out of it the moment the property market began to move again and returned to architecture. But he would never again find himself in a position to pitch projects of the dizzying scale of his beloved Rainbow.

Lizzie found the strength to fight Tanner and eventually beat him, gaining her life insurance. More importantly, she established for herself and her children that Robbo had not deserted them.

Henry made a small media career out of his agonizing notoriety, writing jokey columns in the Sunday papers and appearing as a guest on satirical panel shows, where he was mercilessly bullied by smart Alec comedians who forced him to suffer endless jokes about receipts and hairdryers. He remains convinced to this day that he did absolutely nothing wrong.

Jimmy and Monica's position remained very dodgy indeed. He wasn't in prison, but apart from that everything was still very bleak. Bankruptcy and eviction continued to threaten.

Then their luck began once more to change.

First of all, their horse came in. Literally.

Jimmy was watching the news when the penny dropped. The Alabama Derby had just been run and in the process had produced two rare sporting curiosities. The first was that there was more money riding on the race than ever before. This was because the previous year's race had been cancelled after a twister ravaged the state and various bets had been rolled over. The second curiosity was that for the first time in its history the least favoured horse had triumphed.

As Jimmy watched the footage of the unlikely horse passing the finishing line, every hair on his body seemed to stand up and pay attention.

He had a bet of fifty thousand pounds in gilts riding on that horse.

The bet had been scheduled to be placed on the longest shot at the next Alabama Derby. That derby had only just been run. A year late.

In the horrors of the previous year Jimmy had not noticed that the race had been cancelled. Later, when he did think about it, he had assumed that it *had* been run and that his horse, the longest shot, had not surprisingly failed to win.

Now he knew different.

As these thoughts were passing through his head, the phone rang. It was his bookmaker. They had not spoken for nearly two years but the man had good news.

When Jimmy had finished talking to him he called Monica into the kitchen and told her that a twenty-to-one outsider had won the Alabama Derby and that they were richer to the tune of approximately one million pounds.

'My God! That's brilliant news!' Monica said.

'It certainly is! We're saved, Monica!' Jimmy was almost stammering with excitement. 'We can pay the interest on this house for ever now and property's already recovering! In a year or two we can sell up and buy somewhere smaller and have a huge lump sum left over that we can—'

Monica stopped him.

'What are you talking about, Jim?' she asked.

'What do you mean what am I talking about?'

'I mean what are you talking about?'

'I'm talking about the derby win, of course. Like you said, it's brilliant news.'

'Yes. It is. But not for us.'

'Excuse me?'

'That money isn't ours.'

'Pardon?'

'You placed that bet for charity. We discussed it in this very kitchen. I remember. The money wasn't ours then either, you'd got it from Rupert's dodgy tip. That's why we decided to donate it to charity. Don't you remember?'

'Well, yes . . . I *remember* but . . .'

'Jimmy, there aren't any buts. It isn't ours. We decided. I thought that's what we'd learned. About accepting the consequences of what we do? Good or bad. That's what you said when you refused to turn in Rupert. That the whole recession happened because nobody acted according to their conscience any more but only to try to make a profit.'

Jimmy began to stammer a reply, but for the moment could find none.

'So are you?' Monica asked.

'Am I what?' Jimmy croaked.

'Are you going to act on your conscience? The money isn't ours, Jim. It really isn't. Legally or morally.'

'Yes, but *practically* . . .'

'Legally or morally, Jim. And just think of the good it could do. A million could change so many lives. Lives that are far worse than ours are, even now.'

Jimmy could scarcely believe it, to have the cup of happiness so cruelly dashed from his lips.

'You really mean it, don't you?' Jimmy said.

'Yes I do.'

'You're really not joking?'

'No.'

Jimmy eyed her narrowly. A thought had occurred to him.

'This is about Lillie, isn't it?' he said finally.

'I don't know what you're talking about,' Monica replied, but there was a second's hesitation before she did so.

'Yes you do,' Jimmy said. 'It's your bloody superstitious nature! Of course it is! I remember you sitting where I'm sitting now, rubbing gunk into your tum and making the bloody connection in your mind between me doing a good deed and your bloody bump!'

'Well,' Monica said defiantly, 'karma doesn't go away, Jim. Luck doesn't only last a day! For all the shit we're going through, all our kids are healthy, thank God. That puts us so many trillion miles ahead of anyone whose kids aren't and I'm not bloody messing with it, OK! We made a deal and Lillie turned out fine. We're sticking to it. Besides which, as I keep saying, that money *isn't ours* and it's you that's been banging on about conscience and consequences every time the financial news comes on. Well, face it, Jim, for once you acted on your conscience and here's the consequence. We are giving a million quid to Asylum Action. All right?'

Jimmy's mind was racing. Desperately looking for a way out. A compromise.

'How about I can keep our initial investment? The price of the shares when I bought them in the first place, fifty thousand at ninety-eight pence? That would give us nearly fifty grand, which would be pretty—'

'You did that, Jim! Don't you remember? When we had this conversation the first time around. You took off your fifty K and only invested the profit. You can't do it twice.'

Jimmy bit his lip. He ground his teeth.

She had him.

'Fuck,' he said.

Monica held Lillie to her and simply would not budge. So Jimmy Corby, jobless and debt-ridden, donated one million pounds to charity.

As Jimmy said at the time, fuck.

However, as it turned out, the lucky streak that began with the derby long shot had not finished.

The survival plan that Derek Corby had put into action worked. The willingness they had shown to the bank with the lump sum raised on the sale of the Discovery, plus the small standing order that Jimmy's parents set up, held off the RLB repossession team until six months had elapsed and Jimmy was able to claim a small amount of mortgage relief. Shortly thereafter property prices finally began to revive as the newspapers started to run headlines about the recession being over.

Jimmy knew that it wasn't over, of course, but he was very happy that each day of false optimism reduced the level of his negative equity. Until eventually the value of the Notting Hill house rose once more to exceed the level of the debt Jimmy owed on it. The Corbys were solvent again, able to refund the mortgage relief and put the house on the market. The threat of bankruptcy finally lifted.

And it was just as they were preparing to move house that Monica sold the rights to *Troll Magic*. Henry's Jane had helped her find a literary agent and despite the somewhat derivative storyline there had been a minor bidding war.

'The point is we *want* Harry Potter imitators,' the winning publisher had explained to Jimmy at the launch. 'Quite frankly, the closer the better. Just one original hook is all we look for and trolls is fantastic!'

The advance was small but the sales were good and Monica started immediately on the sequel.

'It's year two of their apprenticeship,' she explained excitedly, 'and the three firm friends are in more trouble!'

Despite the family's rapidly improving fortunes, Toby stayed on at Caterham Road. It was his choice. He did not want to leave his friends.

With the tentative lifting of the financial gloom, Jimmy was invited back to Mason Jervis but he declined the offer. His heart was no longer in it.

'It's a mindset,' he explained to Monica. 'To do that job you have to have the right attitude. You have to not care about the consequences. Imagine if you *did*! You're trading years into the future, buying and selling crops that haven't been and may never be grown, using money that doesn't actually exist. If you started trying to work out the possible parameters, variables and consequences of that, where would you start? And not just for you and your firm. For the people involved down the line. The people who grow and make the stuff you're playing with. The people who will one day eat it and wear it and try to heat their homes with it. Who will have to pay for it. Their kids. Their communities. Once you started thinking about it you'd go mad. Well, I've *been* there. I've *done* mad. I'm not going there again.'

Instead Jimmy recalled that the most satisfying job he'd ever had was trying to do up Number 23 Webb Street. He'd actually *enjoyed* doing that. Doing something real and tangible for the good of his family. So he began a joinery course, learning by coincidence under the same brilliant Romanian guy who in a different world had fitted the four locks in the big red door.

They began to see Jodie again from time to time as a family friend. She had married a cricketer, as it happened, although she reluctantly confessed he was an English one. Whenever AC/DC released another album she sent it to Toby.

Who had converted Korfa.

'Oh YES,' he said. 'I LOVE my CLAssic AUSSie ROCK. It is so powerFUL.'

Monica was able to pay back Derek and Nora from her book earnings and to help them eventually exchange their small flat for the cottage they had always dreamed of. She was also able, with the help of the people at the *Big Issue*, to find out Bob's second name. She traced his mother and organized a small memorial service.

In memory of a life that had not been lucky.

And in gratitude for her life and the lives of her family, which had.